SWEET EBONY

by

ROYSTON ELLIS

KICKS BOOKS
NEW YORK, NEW YORK

Books by Royston Ellis published
by Kicks Books for Kindle

GONE MAN SQUARED
Collected beat poems, 1959-1967

BIG TIME
The autobiography of an anonymous pop
star in Britain's Swinging Sixties

THE FLESH GAME
Beach boys in Las Palmas in the 1960s
live by the rules of the flesh game.

THE RUSH AT THE END
A respectable city clerk falls for a young
student in this tale of forbidden gay love
in London suburbs in the 1960s.

SWEET EBONY
Four women in search of romance discover
more than they expect in Kenya in the 1970s

THE SEASON OF THE PEACOCK
An interior designer, a retired actress and
a cohort of pretty boys in this fable set in
Sri Lanka and The Maldives in the 1990s.

THE MALDIVES AVENGER
A swashbuckling historical yarn by a
master storyteller about the Maldivian hero
who saved the islands from Portuguese
colonization in the 16th century.

SWEET EBONY

For Jojolo
Mirany meranyuno
"Don't sing when you're not sung to."
(Masai proverb)

PROLOGUE

Fantasy Tours Inc.,
North Hollywood, California, USA
1979

Meiptayu emala naudo kurum
"A big gourd with a hole in
the bottom cannot be filled."
Masai Proverb

CHAPTER 1

Harrison Muldoon pulled off his blue-tinted spectacles and leaned back in his chair. He closed his eyes tightly, shutting out the gleaming pages of the holiday brochures spread out on his desk in front of him. He was *devastated*! Slowly, he counted five to himself as his analyst had advised him to do when he felt he was getting into a pother. Then he opened his eyes again. It was no good. The woman was still there in his office.

"I'm sorry," she said, frowning at the brochures. "These holidays do seem rather, well, ordinary, Mr. Muldoon."

"Ordinary!" Harrison Muldoon's fingers trembled as he returned the spectacles to his face. "Ordinary they are *not*!" He swallowed to control himself, wondering how he had let the young woman upset him. She was still watching him earnestly.

"My dear young lady!" The aggression in his voice startled both of them. The woman drew back and then smiled apologetically.

"My dear young lady," he tried again on a softer note. "We have just spent the last twenty minutes together. I didn't know you before, did I? Not until you put your head around my door and walked into this office had I seen you. Right?"

The young woman nodded enthusiastically, like a kid. Harrison Muldoon ran his hand through his thick crown of hair in despair. He looked at the note he had written on his pad with her name and address. "Susan. May I call you that?" He ignored her eager nod of consent.

"I have shown you every vacation brochure known to progressive travel counselors and you can believe me when I say I am the most progressive counselor in the whole of California. I am *renowned* for my avant-garde vacations. Film stars go on them; pop stars adore my holidays. The rich and famous let me handle *everything* when they want an exotic break."

Harrison clutched the edge of his desk and almost choked. "But you, you, you sit there with your girly smile and tell me my vacations, my progressive vacations, are *ordinary*!"

He glared across the desk, wondering what else he must say to get the woman out of his hair.

"Susan," he tried again, his voice slow with sarcasm. "Are you really convinced that Fantasy Tours Incorporated is the firm for you? You do understand that I counsel only a Certain-Class-of-Clientele? Liberation isn't enough for the Fantasy Tours Woman, Susan. My clients are, well—," Harrison paused, sweeping his eyes over the young face still watching him keenly; she was apparently unaware that he couldn't wait to get rid of her.

He tried again. "You're a liberated woman, right?" He waved aside her murmur of protest. "Woman's liberation, independence, it's not enough, Susan. My clients are independent *financially*. Perhaps Fantasy Tours are a teeny-weeny bit budget breaking for you, Susan. I don't mind if you say so. I'll understand if you just get up and walk out of my office. You'll save us both a lot of time. But please, don't tell me my vacations, my super *exotic* vacations are ordinary.

Harrison shuddered, closed his eyes and sat back in his chair, clasping his hands together. He was convinced that when he looked again, the woman would be gone. Sometimes one simply had to be brutal.

"I don't know about your rich and famous clients, Mr. Muldoon," the woman said slowly. "I personally would like something more special than these." She gestured at the brochures helplessly.

Harrison blinked open his eyes and gazed at her in disbelief.

"I don't mean to be rude, Mr. Muldoon." The woman picked up a brochure. "Follow the ancient age-old Incas trail and get high, high in the Andes," she read aloud, her voice grating on Harrison's ears. She seemed impervious to the flush of anger spreading across his cheeks.

"You are *murdering* my prose!"

"I'm sorry, but these holidays are for lonely old ladies who want some packaged culture. Now isn't that dull and ordinary? I want something, well ... different."

"The cost -," Harrison began, clutching his throat nervously under his open shirt. He had failed to keep calm. He was going to call his analyst the moment he got rid of her.

"The cost?" The woman gradually snatched the words from him. "I'm budgeting twenty thousand dollars for my vacation, Mr. Muldoon. You see, I do need it and I do want something completely different."

The only sound in the office was the chugging of the air conditioner. The leaves of the plastic rubber plants in the corner shone in the concealed lighting, a thin sheen of dust visible for the first time to Harrison as he stared at the plant. He pulled at his ear, trying to meld his expression of outrage into one of sympathetic concern. He prayed the woman hadn't noticed he was bored with her. His mind was reeling. He took off his spectacles again, wiped the lenses briskly with a tissue and replaced them.

Harrison had always prided himself on being able to tell what his clients wanted before they knew it. This plain, eager young woman bewildered him. He gathered up the brochures on his desk as he studied her again. Even discounting her dreadful clothes, she just did not have the elan of someone with twenty thousand dollars to blow on a vacation. He recovered himself and beamed.

The woman smiled back. Her clothes had misled him. She was wearing beige slacks and an olive green sleeveless top. It was belted around her waist with a frayed, bright green cord. Her auburn hair hung limply behind her ears in two pigtails secured with rubber bands. She looked like she lived in a trailer.

"Susan!" Harrison moved forward, his voice sliding into the smooth drawl of the salesman. "I'm not the usual travel agent. I operate a personal one-to-one holiday counseling service. I need to know a little bit about you before I can suggest the perfect vacation experience."

"My likes and dislikes, you mean?" The woman shrugged her shoulders. "I can understand that."

Harrison moistened his lips. "To be frank, I know nothing about you except your name." He glanced down at his pad again. "Susan Ross," he read doubtfully. "Do you know any of my clients? How did you find me?"

"Yellow pages."

Harrison shuddered again. All his advertisements in *The*

New Yorker and she picked him from the phone book! She was staring at him, the innocent eagerness in her blue eyes making him feel uneasy.

Harrison placed his elbows on his desk and steepled his fingers. He tried to look wise. "Why don't you tell me why you need a *special* holiday so much."

"I was married for nine years, Mr. Muldoon."

Harrison blinked with surprise.

"I'm sorry if that surprises you, Mr. Muldoon. I was married at sixteen to the most conventional, dull, boring husband imaginable. He was a computer executive, Mr. Muldoon, a computer husband. You know what that meant? We only kissed when he left on business trips and the only time we dined together was when we shared a TV supper."

Harrison shrugged his shoulders sympathetically. He was used to hearing the life stories of bored, dull wives. "So you got a divorce?"

The woman nodded.

"And you want to spend the alimony having a damn good time? Of course, Susan, you deserve it."

"I want to see life, Mr. Muldoon. I've been so, well, protected." Harrison watched the woman's eyes mist over. They gave her plain features a soft beauty, like that of a yearning teenager. At last he felt he understood.

"I know, I *know*! You've got your freedom so you want a little *adventure*! A little glamour, a pinch of romance perhaps, nothing serious. Fun, yes, *fun!* You want to *live*."

Harrison permitted himself a small smile of satisfaction and dropped his voice to a confidential whisper. "I believe you want one of my special *fantasy* vacations."

◆ ◆ ◆ ◆ ◆

It had taken Susan weeks to raise the courage to enter Muldoon's office. At first, after the divorce, she moped, blaming herself. She began to doubt the security of her home, the neighborhood, the daily routine. She grew to hate her husband more, now she was divorced, than she did when she was married.

She wanted to get away; from Los Angeles, from California, from the United States. She wanted to see a different world for herself. Somewhere there was a life that wasn't so ordinary, so computerized. She wanted to see, to be with, to touch, real people; to share feelings again. She felt she deserved it.

The tragedy of her wasted years began when she met Kristian. He was different from the boys who dated her at high school but this was a difference that intrigued her. He had the butter-color hair of his Finnish mother and the pale complexion of a serious student about to graduate with honors. Susan's dates had all been dropouts and beach freaks whose sole interest was how soon they could lay her.

Kristian was five years older than Susan and very studious. Everyone said how brilliant he was and no one could understand why Susan with her simple smile and lack of curiosity had captured him. Neither did Susan, but she was flattered by his attention.

One night, Kristian took her for a drive in his old car and parked overlooking the ocean. There, instead of groping under her skirt like her other dates, he gripped the steering wheel and stared out to sea. He began to speak in a low guttural tone that Susan found quite mystifying.

"I'm sorry, what are you saying?" she asked, a tremor of apprehension running through her in case Kristian was having a fit. He banged the steering wheel with his fist - the first sign of any emotion she had witnessed in him - and told her to keep quiet. She glowed and snuggled back in the seat while Kristian muttered his incomprehensible sounds. When he finished, he turned to her with a shy smile.

"Isn't that beautiful?" he said.

"Yes," she breathed, wondering when he would get on with it.

"It's a poem in Finnish that my mother taught me."

Susan nodded. Kristian's mother was a fierce, inspired woman who refused to speak English even after thirty years in California. "What's it about?" Susan put out her hand to encourage him.

"Feelings." Kristian sounded nervous. He ignored her hand. "I've been offered a job, Susan. I'm going to take it when I finish college."

Okay, thought Susan, realizing this would mean the end of her dates with Kristian. Although it was dull, sitting in silence not even holding hands, Susan had grown fond of Kristian and his serious ways.

"It's in computers." Kristian twisted in his seat with excitement. "Very good prospects and a generous pension arrangement. It's exactly what I want."

"That's nice."

"Yes!" Kristian turned his ice-blue eyes on her. "It will be a long time before I can buy a house and so on, but we must be patient. You'll be patient, won't you, Susan?"

"Me?" Her heart quickened when she looked at Kristian's eyes. He was handsome in a cool sort of way. "I'm always patient." She smiled at her lie, wondering when he would kiss her.

"I knew you'd agree. Now that's settled I can concentrate on my career."

"I'm sorry ...?"

It was a few days before she realized that Kristian had proposed to her. It seemed as though her father was talking about someone else when he boasted how she had caught the right guy, an intellectual type who would have a fat pay check every month.

Kristian arranged the wedding with her parents before he told her about it. He was being posted to New York and her parents consented immediately so that she could go with him. Months after the excitement of setting up home in New York had worn off, it dawned on Susan that she had changed from a dull schoolgirl into a dreary housewife.

Kristian expected her to keep the apartment clean and to serve him dinner and breakfast when he wanted. Susan obliged. When Kristian was late from the office, she watched TV. When he came home early, he retreated to his den, and she watched TV.

Before she was married, Susan had vaguely wondered what sex would be like. It would be nice, she had thought, to have a man constantly available. Kristian shattered that expectation on the first night of the honeymoon. He announced that they certainly wouldn't have children until he consolidated his career position. Then he climbed on top of her; thrust a few times, sighed, and rolled off.

Susan spent that night listening to Kristian's snores. Dawn came before sleep soothed her. She was puzzled. She had more pleasure petting and necking with her high school dates than when her husband had entered her. If that was the real thing, then why was she so disappointed? Kristian hadn't even begun to rouse her. Was that what she had saved herself for?

It was only when she read the guidance pages of *She* magazine years later, that she realized Kristian's quick withdrawal was his method of contraception. By then she had begun to think that sex ought to give her some satisfaction too.

Kristian became a whiz kid of computers. They moved from New York to Los Angeles. Kristian began to attend conferences and there were continual demands for his services as a consultant. Every week he flew off somewhere, leaving the apartment early on Monday morning while Susan slept, and returning late on Friday evening after she had taken a sleeping pill and crawled unhappily into bed.

When Susan suggested that she would like to go on some of his trips with Kristian, he was shocked. "It's just boring business," he told her. "None of my associates take their wives. You'd be out of place. Much better for you to stay at home where you belong."

Two years later, without any warning, he asked for a divorce. He explained that he couldn't be a good husband to her because of his work. It was for the best, he told her. He moved out that night. It was all over so quickly.

Susan was sorry. She searched in her mind, back over the years, to see where she had gone wrong. What had she done? He had said it wasn't her fault, but that didn't matter. She was as divorced as suddenly as she was married. Kristian arranged it all smoothly and the alimony was more than ample. It might have helped if Kristian had another woman but she never found out if he did.

She knew she couldn't live with regrets for ever. She had to do something. She had to get away.

◆ ◆ ◆ ◆ ◆

Susan saw Harrison Muldoon smiling at her. It was not a warm smile, it had the lust of a salesman about to make a kill. She felt her hands go clammy as she accepted the envelope Muldoon pushed across the desk toward her.

"One of my Fantasy Tours is what you need, Susan." He paused dramatically to impress her. She stared back at him blankly.

"Yes, a Fulfillment Safari in Africa! The details are here. This is going to be our little secret. I don't advertise this sort of vacation. You have to be a special woman in search of liberty, romance, to enjoy it. It really is about Fulfillment, that's the real F word, my dear. Your wildest desires."

Muldoon leered again and produced a blank contract form. He placed it firmly on the desktop and held out a gold fountain pen. "If you just sign on the dotted line, my dear, I'll take care of *all* the arrangements!"

She drew back. "Safari! Africa! That's so far." For some reason she felt excited. "Will it be safe?"

"Oh, *absolutely*, dear Susan! Not a thing to worry about. Of course it is a long way. A safari is terribly fashionable right now, the in-thing, my dear, the journey of the 1980s. This is perfectly discreet, such *cute* people to look after you. Nobody will ever know, whatever you get up to. You know how they talk in this town. Don't worry. You can do just what you fancy on my Fulfillment Safari!"

"I don't know—"

"Then it's time to find out, isn't it, Susan? Take the plunge!"

"I'll think about it, Mr. Muldoon." She half rose from her chair, intrigued at the idea. It was certainly different.

"Susan!" His tone made her sit down again. "I need your signature. Just sign here. You'll never regret it. You can leave on Saturday?"

"Saturday? I—"

"Good. There are some special arrangements I have to make."

"Well, I suppose so."

"You see, you've made up your mind. Good girl! Use my pen." Muldoon caressed the contract with his finger. "Sign here. This will change your life. I *guarantee* it!"

Her heart was beating so loudly, she was sure Muldoon could hear it. "I'm sorry. This is all so unexpected." She stared at the paper in front of her. Suddenly she knew this was the moment. If she did nothing now, she never would. She seized the pen and signed in a rush. "I do hope everything will be all right."

"Of course it will, dear." Muldoon stood up. "Now you just come in here tomorrow and write me a teeny-weeny check and I'll give you your ticket."

"I've never done anything like this before."

"Few of us have." He winked and she wondered why. "Don't worry, nothing can go wrong. And what fun you'll have! Ten days *and nights*, you understand? Absolute fantasy come true." Muldoon held out his hand.

"Just remember my motto, Susan. Guaranteed is your satisfaction."

"I don't know." She bit her lip and walked out of the office in a daze.

CHAPTER 2

The squeal of a car skidding to a stop broke into Amelia Berger's concentration as she listened with the telephone pressed close to her ear to the breathless voice of Liza Trazel. Amelia frowned at the noise and glanced at her watch. A car door slammed, and a gust of insolent laughter penetrated the well-ordered stillness of her drawing room. Amelia's lips tightened with the reflex action always triggered off by her daughter's late homecomings. She looked at her watch again in surprise; Cora was home early.

Amelia returned her attention to the telephone. "How could you, darling!" she said as soon as Liza Trazel paused for breath. "We all agreed never to buy fur again, except mink, of course."

She warmed to the attack. "How could you buy a leopard skin coat! Leopard's on the protected list. Didn't you think of those poor wild animals murdered just to make you a fur coat?" She heard Liza Trazel's shriek of dismay echoing over the line, and smacked her lips in triumph.

The shrill ringing of the front door bell interrupted her. She was puzzled, wondering why Cora was home so early. She ignored Liza Trazel's retort as the maid padded along the hall to open the door, and then she spoke again.

"Of course it's murder, Liza darling. Animals are living beings, aren't they? I don't care if it was a bargain. It's a shameful thing to do!" She turned to the wall so she wouldn't have to see her daughter pass the open door of the parlor.

"Told you what she thought of you, did she?"

Amelia slapped the phone down, cutting off Liza Trazel in mid-sentence. She swung around angrily. "Cora, you were listening!"

"I couldn't help it, Mama. The whole block can hear you."

Amelia waved her hand to dismiss Cora from her thoughts. "I'm in no mood for a fight tonight. I've got a headache coming on."

Cora grinned and leaned against the doorjamb. "Probably ear-ache, Mama. Was that one of your do-gooder committee pals? You charity ladies really do love tearing each other apart."

"Cora, you know what Liza Trazel did? She went to Africa for a vacation and came back with a leopard skin coat! That poor animal. We're supposed to be preserving the species, not wearing them, even though it only cost her two hundred dollars."

"Sounds as though you're jealous."

"That's enough from you, Cora. What are you standing in the doorway for? Can't you see I'm busy?"

Her daughter shrugged and took a step forward into the room.

"I hope your sandals are clean!"

"Sure they are." Cora flicked her feet so her sandals fell off onto the carpet.

Amelia sighed with exasperation. "I'm having a committee meeting here tonight. Mabeline's been cleaning all day." She paused and frowned. "You're home very early!" It was an accusation.

"Yes, Mama. I want to talk to you."

There was silence. Amelia looked at her daughter and was immediately assailed by a pang of despair. Nature had not been kind to her child. Cora was all limbs and angles, no flesh and none of the winsome beauty that had made Amelia famous as a film star when she was her age. She had no charm, no grace, and no apparent desire to make herself attractive. She had recently cut her hair short in a crewcut. Everything her daughter did seemed to be part of a plan to cause her anguish.

Amelia tried to wave her away again. "Do we have to talk now? Can't it wait until morning?"

"No." Cora shook her head with quiet determination. She was glancing around the room like it was enemy territory.

"Oh, very well then. Will it take long?" She followed Cora's gaze around the parlor, drawing reassurance from the orderliness of the room, where Cora seemed to see a threat.

The chintz covers on the comfortable over-stuffed chairs, the ponderous 1950s furniture, and the photographs from her days as a child star, made her feel proud. They represented security in a rapidly changing world. Although she was no longer a famous star, she was not destitute. She had made her fortune in motion pictures before she got married, and managed to keep it. However, she had lost her husbands. The first drank himself to death; the second was an Italian producer who went off with a stuntman to live in Rome three months after she married him. He left her pregnant with Cora.

To survive the disgrace, Amelia immersed herself in charity work. She found it difficult ever to love Cora and tended to regard her as an embarrassment, her personal cross.

"Mama," Cora was saying. "I want you to meet Scobie."

"Scobie?" Amelia swiveled in her chair. There was a youth in the doorway; she stared at him in horror.

"What -!" She was speechless.

"I told him to wait in the hall, Mama, so I can tell you about him." Cora looked back at the boy shifting his weight nervously from one foot to the other. She smiled to encourage him. "Well, here he is. He wants to go to acting school, Mama. He wants to be a black *kung fu* star."

Amelia swallowed. She stared in dismay at the tall Negro standing on the threshold of her cozy little parlor. Negro! She was of an age when blacks were called Negroes. This one was over six feet in height, his spiky Afro hair almost brushing the paint of the door frame.

He was wearing faded jeans and a sweatshirt with a banana printed on it above the slogan "I had it in Barbados". His face split with a grin so full of zest, he could have been an advertisement for toothpaste. "How do, Miz Berger!"

"Cora! What is this, er, man, doing in my house?" She grasped the arm of her chair and glared at her daughter. She was wondering if any of the neighbors had seen him enter the building. She would have to say he was a friend of Mabeline's if they asked.

"I've brought him to meet you, Mama." Cora reached out and took the youth's hand, leading him across the room to where she was sitting.

She leaped out of the chair in a panic, ignoring his outstretched hand and eager smile. "Cora!" she cried, her voice husky with dismay. "What is the meaning of this?" She took refuge behind the mahjongg table and picked up a piece to keep her hands occupied.

"Scobie and I are going steady, Mama."

Amelia's eyes narrowed as she glanced helplessly at her daughter. "Is this one of your teenage pranks?"

"No, Mama. I'm serious. I've never been more serious about a man in my whole life."

Amelia forced herself to look directly at the youth. He made everything in the room seem tiny and fragile. She forced herself to meet his eyes, although she hastily dismissed the sincerity in them as a ploy.

"My daughter's only fifteen, young man! Did she tell you that? You'd better go now."

"She tell me everything, Miz Berger. I was worried 'bout coming here but Cora said you respect black people and do all your charity work for un'privileged folks like us and that you would be pleased she have a steady guy at last." He shifted his weight uneasily from one foot to another, his eagerness frozen in his broad grin.

"We'd like your permission, Mama, you know, to go steady." Cora put out her hand to touch her arm.

Amelia pulled away. "Cora, you are much too young for steady dates. I can't allow it."

"It's because he's black, isn't it?"

"Cora, how dare you!"

"It's all right to raise money for niggers but when I bring one to your precious house, you don't want that, do you?"

"Cora!" Scobie stepped forward and put his arm around her daughter. "There ain't no need to speak to your mama that way."

"I know her, Scobie. You and the brothers have shown me how hypocritical white people can be. I should have guessed." She pulled Scobie's arm and turned toward the door.

"Cora!" Amelia said, anguish cutting her voice. "I'm sure your friend is a very charming and honorable young man. I know you have enough sense to choose the right friends. However, dear, don't you think you're too young to go steady? Shouldn't you wait a little?"

Cora stared back at her. "I can't stand it when you get so priggish," she said. "When you were my age, you were being screwed from one casting couch to another. It so happens that I'm still a virgin which is more than you were at fifteen!"

Amelia felt her heart churn. "How dare you!" she managed to say, glancing first at Scobie and then at her daughter. She was surprised to see how Cora's face, normally so sullen and ugly, had taken on a glow of excitement that radiated from her eyes and deepened her pale cheeks. Under her grotesque hair and shabby clothes, was it possible, she wondered suddenly, that her daughter could be considered attractive?

She twisted her fingers nervously, determined not to let Cora intimidate her. "I'm sure you didn't mean that, Cora." She smiled apologetically, "Cora's very highly strung, Mr. Scobie. It's because her father doesn't live at home. She has his blood. He's Italian."

Cora giggled, and Amelia jiggled a mahjongg piece to give her time to think. "Whatever Hollywood is like now, in my day it was perfectly respectable," she said. "I am ashamed that you should even think such a thing of your own mother, Cora. And in front of Mr. Scobie, too."

She pulled herself upright. "Now, if you don't mind, Mr. Scobie, perhaps you could leave my daughter and I to talk. It's been quite delightful meeting you."

"If he goes, I go!" Cora clung to Scobie and gazed up at his face.

"No, man, You must do what your mama tells you." Scobie held her away from him.

"I don't care!"

"You must respect your mama, Cora. Don't let her believe the things she is thinking. Why, man, maybe she thinks this black dude's only after a little white pussy."

"How dare you!"

"Okay, Miz Berger. I'm out of here." He turned and walked out of the room, his long strides making the furniture skitter as he swaggered down the corridor. Cora ran out after him.

The muffled sounds of a car chase showing on the maid's television in the kitchen penetrated through to the silence in the parlor. Amelia studied the oil painting of herself hanging on the wall above the fireplace. She must have been Cora's age when it was painted, and she was under contract to the studios in the 1940s. Her blonde hair hung down to her shoulders. He eyes sparkled with mischievous innocence. It was a world if which Cora knew nothing, a world of glamour, of simplicity, of joy.

"My poor child, she said, holding out her arms to embrace Cora when she came back into the room. "Come to Mama."

Cora halted. "I suppose I shouldn't be surprised by your reaction. Scobie says I mustn't blame you for acting with the prejudices of your generation. He says it's to be expected from someone your age."

"He does, does he!" Amelia moved from the mahjongg table to settle down into the comfort of her sofa. "Who does this Scobie think he is to say something like that?"

"I'm not blaming you, Mama. Scobie's made me understand so much."

"Why is it you always rebel against everything?"

"You said you don't want a fight, Mama," Cora shook her head to express her bafflement.

"Damn!"

Cora raised her face and looked at her with a fresh interest.

"You've made me lose my temper. Cora, I said I wouldn't lose my temper with you again. You're just not worth it. I'll get migraine and won't be able to pay attention at the meeting tonight. He can you be so thoughtless?"

"You were the one who was thoughtless by being rude to Scobie."

"You shouldn't have brought that boy into my house. You know nothing about him."

"Yes I do. He's on television every week."

"What?" Amelia was suddenly intrigued. "Which show? Have I seen him?"

"It's called 'Soul Train'. He's one of the dancers.

"Is he? Why didn't you say so! However, you are under age, Cora. You want someone from your own background, someone with a future, someone you can respect, if you want to go steady."

"Mama, you can't tell me what I want. I'm an individual and I am entitled to make my own decisions. I'll be sixteen soon and I could marry then if I've got parental consent."

Amelia sank back into the couch and stared with disbelief at this ungainly runt who was her daughter. "I will certainly never give my consent to you marrying him!" She lowered her voice in despair. "Tell me this is a joke, Cora."

"It's no joke. I know all about Scobie. He's been around, of course. He's got to do certain things to stay alive in this town. Especially being black. I'm going to help him so he can get his act together. He needs me."

Amelia suddenly felt very old. "I'll have to think this over," she said with a sigh.

"Will you speak to Papa?"

"I don't know where he is."

"*Variety* said he is back in Rome. You could call him." Amelia nodded and waved her away. Cora shrugged, turned her back and sauntered out of the room.

Amelia rose from the couch and poured herself a brandy. She drained it while she considered what to do, then she returned to the couch and settled down with the telephone her lap. She pushed the sequence of buttons for Liza Trazel's number.

"Liza, I've got trouble."

"Amelia Berger, after what you said to me this afternoon, I'm not speaking to you." There was a pause. "What trouble?"

"Cora brought some black power dancer from 'Soul Train' to the house. She wants to go steady with him!"

"Is he gay?"

"I don't think so. He looks as macho as King Kong. I thought he was going to burst out of his jeans."

"Honey, then you have got trouble."

"What am I going to do?"

"Nothing. If he's not gay, he might be quite a lay."

"Liza, how could you! He's got to be stopped before it gets serious. Cora's likely to get involved in one of those black radical groups. You know how willful she is." There was silence at the end of the line. She pursed her lips impatiently. "Liza, what are you thinking about?"

"The 'Soul Train' dancer. I wonder if he's the one who wears riding boots. He's cute."

"Liza! What am I going to do?"

"You could send her away."

"How will that help?"

"Amelia, I'm telling you something, so listen. Cora will never live her life the way that you want. She's got to make her own mistakes. If she's got a thing for blacks, then let her see what they are really like."

"I'm not letting her go to Watts!" She shuddered. "Liza, I could have a black grandchild. That's the sort of thing Cora would do just to upset me and show she's liberated."

Liza Trazel's voice took on a satisfied tone. "She wants to shock you, right? Well, shock her yourself. This stud of hers fascinates her because she feels he is from an oppressed minority. It's all the rage. So accept that, and educate her. Send her where I went on my vacation."

"Liza!" She couldn't believe what she was hearing her friend say. "You went to Africa!"

"Kenya. Send Cora there."

Amelia shook the telephone as though trying to throttle it. "Are you on Valium again, Liza? I'm not sending Cora to Africa. She'll fall for some half-baked half-naked savage."

"Exactly! She'll soon change her mind about her oppressed minority dancer being cute, when she is in the minority. They'll be nothing special about a black lay after that."

"Cora's not like that! You're mad." Amelia felt weak.

"So you want a black grandchild?"

She gazed around the parlor. She saw her nice furniture, the painting and the mementos from her film career. The thought that Scobie might have an entrée into her nice home by marrying her daughter was beyond contemplation. And the neighbors, what would they say?

"No!" she sighed.

"Then I'm not mad."

"She's too young to go on vacation to Africa by herself. And I don't have the time to go."

"Don't worry. She has to go by herself, that's part of the cure. The organization I went with is very good, just what she needs. They advertise in the *New Yorker*. Real quality. It's frightfully expensive but very very exclusive."

"Perhaps it would broaden Cora's outlook," Amelia said uncertainly.

"Of course it will! Call Harrison Muldoon." Liza Trazel was almost crowing. "He runs Fantasy Tours. Tell him you want Cora to go on his next Fulfillment Safari. He'll know what you mean. And Cora will never be the same again. I guarantee it!"

CHAPTER 3

The Head of Features glared at Lyn Preston and squeezed his stomach between his pudgy fingers. Lyn saw his nervousness as she paced up and down in front of the big man's desk. She knew excitement upset his ulcer. *You shouldn't be in television if you're weak*, she thought.

"Not Africa, for Chrissake, Lyn!" the man said.

"Why not, Randy?" Lyn paused in front of the Head of Features and hit him with the gaze that made her one of the fastest rising stars on West Coast TV. The gaze bore into the big man's skull, the battery of objections lining up in his mind demolished by her wild, hazel eyes.

"It's a natural, Randy." Lyn resumed her pacing across the floor, her bleached hair straight and shoulder length, flaring behind her like an angry mane. She rarely smiled but when she did her lips curled around gleaming white teeth in a man-eating grin. She turned back to the big man who was watching her unhappily, and smiled her smile. She was sure she looked lethal.

"I've never let you down, have I, Randy? Jesus! You're here because of me. I deliver features that top the ratings and you keep your job. You write the memos taking credit for my ideas and sit on your oversized butt while I do the work."

The Head of Features flapped his hand at Lyn, his small round eyes darting to the closed door of his office. "Keep your voice down, Lyn," he begged. "I may be fat but I'm not deaf."

"Neither is the President." Lyn ran her hand behind her ear and tossed back her hair. "Goldburn's asked me to dinner tonight, Randy. You think I should tell him my idea for this feature? I'm sure our president would be fascinated to hear how you've refused me." She stared threateningly at him.

The fat man gulped. "Did you hear me say No, Lyn. All I said was: Not Africa."

"If it's not Africa, it's not on."

"What's wrong with the Caribbean?" Randy clutched his

stomach again.

"So you do like the idea?" She permitted herself a small gloat of triumph.

Randy groaned. "Maybe I do. I ask myself though, is Africa good for ratings? What about all those atrocities?"

"Randy! Don't forget those close ups of copulating elephants and bare boobs. The Caribbean doesn't have that."

"Elephant boobs?"

"Just give me the nod, Randy." Her voice was soft but she knew it sounded venomous because of its silky tone. "I've done the preliminary research," she added to settle the matter. "You know I don't waste time."

"Lyn, some day you'll find you can't devour everybody who gets in your way." Randy shifted uncomfortably. "I say the Caribbean is better for ratings. Better for budget too."

"Exactly!" The excitement returned to Lyn's eyes as she resumed her pacing of the room. "The Caribbean is boring, predictable. Africa is distant, unknown, thrilling. My theme is what tourism is doing to the continent. Think visually. Naked blacks in grass huts outside luxury hotels where bloated American tourists laze in the sun." She stopped and looked at Randy. "Yeah," she said. "Americans like you! It's the over-privileged I'd be exposing, not the impoverished blacks."

The Head of Features shook his head and his jowls quivered indignantly. His hand slipped under his shirt and he massaged his stomach. He sighed, signaling his consent.

Lyn shrugged. She hated a man who was weak. It made her victory over him seem too easy. "I'll need ten days there, that's all. Then you can send a crew."

"It's worth the expense for ten days without you!"

◆ ◆ ◆ ◆ ◆

Like many dedicated creative people, Lyn Preston was a desperately lonely person. She was forced to admit that to herself as she sat in her small bachelor apartment and wondered why she was not having dinner with Levi Goldburn, the station's president. Of course, the reason was simple: she had lied to Randy. Levi Goldburn had not asked her to dinner, that night or any night.

Lyn reached for the pack of Gauloises on the table by her typewriter, shook out a cigarette and lit it. She drew deeply on the strong tobacco, feeling proud that she no longer choked and wanted to throw up when she inhaled. The smoking of Gauloises, like her other affectations, was adopted to make her noticed, to help push her to the top of the TV garbage heap. Now she found she actually enjoyed the pungent taste of the cigarettes, especially when she was feeling so lonely, like right now.

If that fat slob Randy knows where I am really spending the evening, she thought with a grin at the irony of it all, *he wouldn't believe it.*

Lyn Preston was supposed to be tough. Ms Balls Breaker, a cameraman called her when she was chewing the guts of a trade union boss she was interviewing. The union man, like all her victims, was disarmed by her naivete when the interview began, only to crumple under her ruthless and well-informed interrogation. Lyn enjoyed the slaughter, her teeth baring in a triumphant grin when the interview closed. The name of Ms Balls Breaker stuck.

Lyn knew she owed more for her phenomenal success at the station to that cameraman who had given her the nickname, than to anyone else. The name gave her an image and she lived up to it. However, the president had never dated her, nor was she his mistress, as the whole station seemed to believe.

She had met Levi Goldburn once. He was a happily married family man and his sole interest in life was juggling his investments from the security of his Beverly Hills villa. She had been sent to interview him by *The Herald Examiner* where she was working as a feature writer.

She was doing a story on retirement and Goldburn fitted the pattern of a successful businessman coping happily with old age. The interview went well and she forget all about it until there was a call from personnel at the TV station he owned, offering her a job as Anchor Person at double her salary, She soon learned that the occasional reference at the station to her acquaintance with Goldburn, whom the staff seldom saw, could be used to her advantage.

As she sucked the last drag on her cigarette, she stared coldly at the magazine open on her desk. She had eaten, washed up, chosen her jeans and T-shirt for the next day, checked the TV Guide to see if there was anything she could watch and decided there wasn't, drunk a glass of chilled red wine, and still didn't feel like doing anything at all. The spark wasn't there; she needed a man.

Her sex life was a mess. There had been guys over the years who drifted into her life for a few months, then, apparently with relief, drifted out again. She neither encouraged nor discouraged them. She was herself, it was her life she was living, not their version of it.

Why, she wondered as she clawed at her hair restlessly, *do I feel so lonely tonight?* It was four weeks since had last had a man, and then it was a journalist awash with gin whom she had met when they were both covering the same assignment. Whether it was the gin or Lyn who turned him off she didn't know, but it had been a failure.

"Hell!" she muttered aloud, stubbing out the cigarette and pulling herself up from the chair. "If only I could find a man who'd do his stuff and get out, without any hang ups." She reached for her suede jacket hanging behind the door and wrapped it around her shoulders. A drive, she thought, might clear her head and lift the depression hovering too close.

How she got to Pershing Square, she couldn't remember, and how she got the youth into her car and back to the apartment was an equal mystery. Yet there he was, waiting patiently beside her as she fumbled— yes, Lyn Preston fumbling!— to put her key in the lock.

The man's hand closed over hers. "I'll do it," he said. His voice was young and his breath smelt of spearmint.

The door opened and Lyn marched into the apartment first. "Shut the door!" she ordered quickly as the light from the corridor filled the room. She hid her face. Her jacket collar was turned up and her hair bunched high under her revolutionary-style black beret.

"I can't see," the man said when the door was closed and cut off the shaft of light.

"Don't move," said Lyn. "You'll hit a plant or something."

A soft thud, and the young man's cry of pain showed he had ignored her warning.

"Why don't you put the light on?"

"Wait." She felt her way around the room until she found the tape deck that was set into the bookshelf. She switched it on, and the light from the sound-level display glowed dimly. She snapped a cassette into the deck and turned to look at the man. He was rubbing his head where he had walked into a hanging plant.

"This place is dangerous!" the youth muttered. "I could have lost an eye. I hope you're insured."

"You're not an insurance salesman, are you?" She watched him carefully. In his jeans and sweatshirt he was an attractive and anonymous body. If he had a profession, it would label him; she didn't want to know.

The man laughed. "I don't do anything." He was peering into the darkness, straining to see her. "Is that all the light we're going to have?"

"Yes. Don't you know there's an energy crisis? She pulled off her beret and threw it on the table. Her suede coat followed.

"Huh?"

"Well, you're not a conversationalist, are you? I like that." She moved toward the kitchen. "There's a couch there. Sit down. I'll get you a drink."

"I wouldn't mind something to eat. I haven't eaten all day.

"This isn't a pizza parlor."

"All right! The man found the couch and sat down with a scowl. "You got a cigarette?"

Lyn turned and threw the Gauloises pack at him. "There's a lighter on the table."

"Oh, shit! Is this all you have?"

"Sorry, I don't have Virginia Slims."

"Hey, what's with you?" The young man lit the cigarette cautiously, raising his voice so Lyn could hear him in the kitchen. "I didn't mean to offend you. Sorry I'm alive."

"Aren't we all?" She poured two shots of vodka into each glass and added some V8 juice. She carried the drinks into the sitting room and handed the guy one. Seeing him close up she guessed he was about nineteen. "Your supper. Liquid salad."

"Fine." The youth gulped half the contents of the glass. "Thanks."

"You needn't worry about your manners." She studied his features in the flickering light. His hair was greasy and hung around his shoulders untidily. He had wisps of hair on his upper lip and chin, evidence of a futile attempt to grow a beard. His jeans were baggy at the knees but tight around his thighs and molded firmly to his crotch.

The youth drained his glass and clinked an ice cube into his mouth. He sucked noisily, and sat back on the couch, stretching his legs out in front of him. Lyn moved closer, sipping at her drink.

"I feel nice now," the youth said.

"Why should I care how you feel?"

"Oh, shit!"

"You can't stay all night." She was suddenly worried.

"I don't think I want to."

"I'll call a taxi and give you the fare."

"Already?"

"In a while."

"Oh, shit!" The youth was looking at her face.

She moved quickly out of the glow from the tape deck. Since she had begun to appear regularly on prime time TV, it was difficult to remain anonymous.

"Why are you trying to hide yourself? You shy or something?" The youth opened the zipper of his fly and pulled out his penis. It lay limply across his denim-covered thigh. "I'm not shy." He put his hands behind his head and lay back contentedly.

Lyn gaped at him. "Is that all you?"

"Oh, shit. All you slits are the same. You just go wild about this dong."

She sat on the chair opposite the youth and sniffed scornfully. "It's no use having it if you can't use it."

"What?" The boy lifted his head.

"Come here," she said calmly.

"No, man!" said the youth, clutching his penis in surprise. "I told you I don't do anything."

She sat up and glared. "What does that mean?"

"What I said." The youth shrugged his shoulders. "You've got to get me hard first, baby."

She sighed, slipped off the chair and crawled on her hands and knees across the floor. When she reached the couch, she put her hand on the boy's thigh and slid her fingers over his jeans until she made contact with the soft flesh of his penis. She squeezed.

"You're too rough!" the youth said. Lying back. "Suck it."

The note of command in his voice irritated her but she felt the penis stiffening and filling her fist. She put her lips to the tip and began to mouth it.

"I can't feel you!" The youth thrust at her face.

"Okay, you've asked for it," she breathed. She reached for her glass and filled her mouth with vodka and tomato juice. She opened her lips and closed them over the youth's penis, drawing it inside so that the head was touching the back of her throat.

"Oh, shit!"

She fondled his balls until she felt them tightening, then she lifted her mouth from him and stood up.

"Hey, don't stop now." He looked surprised. "What are you doing?"

She lifted her leg and prepared to straddle the boy.

"No way, man." He wriggled his hips. "I don't do that."

To her annoyance she felt he was going limp in her hand.

"Just blow me," he said. "You can put your finger up my fanny if you like.

♦ ♦ ♦ ♦ ♦

"You look awful, Lyn," Gloria Trotter said cheerfully as she handed Lyn her second cup of coffee for the morning. "You ought to use make up."

Lyn scowled, reached for the cup and sipped at the scalding black coffee. She raised her eyes again when she became aware that Gloria was still standing in front of her desk. "Gloria, what are you doing? Trying to psyche me out, or something? I was up half the night researching so you can't expect me to look like a breakfast commercial."

"Randy's secretary said you were having dinner with god

Goldburn."

Lyn had forgotten that. She grimaced. "You shouldn't be-lieve everything you hear."

"You look bad enough to have *heartburn*, Lyn. You should never go to bed on a full stomach. Especially someone else's."

"Gloria! Leave me alone."

"It's a pleasure."

When her secretary had backed out of the room, Lyn fold-ed her arms and rested her head on the desktop. Thank god no one knew the truth. Ms Balls Breaker herself - the gutsi-est woman with the fastest quip on television - couldn't get screwed properly.

When she lifted her head and looked helplessly at the pile of mail open in front of her, Lyn faltered. What was she going to do? She was a success, she could bully the Head of Features into letting her do whatever program she liked, she had a salary she had never dreamed of as a journalist, she was feared and respected. Yet inside she was just a lonely and sad little girl.

"Oh, shit," she said aloud, remembering the night before. She reached for the mail. She ought to be pleased, she rea-soned, having her feature on Africa to plan. It could even win her an award if she handled it properly. She sifted through the brochures that Gloria had collected form various tour operators in Los Angeles. They seemed to be the usual crap. Blue swimming pools, yellow sands and white hotel build-ings looking like sanitariums amid the palm trees.

Suddenly some phrases leaped off the page of a bro-chure, cutting straight to the root of her mood. "Is some-thing missing in your life? Are you yearning for fulfillment?" the brochure asked. "Are you searching for the experience of a lifetime?"

Lyn frowned. Could there be any value in the trite words of the copywriter?

"Gloria," she called on the intercom. Her intuition soared into high gear as she read further, realizing she was on to something special. "Get me this guy Harrison Mullion on the phone. He runs Fantasy Tours in North Hollywood. It's the outfit I need for my Special." She paused, then thought with a smile: *I guess I need it for me too.*

CHAPTER 4

Margaret Biddle-Macdonald - known as Maggie to her friends, who were legion - stared at the spinach and bacon salad overflowing from its dish on the small, round table at which she always sat when she lunched at the Plaza. Her fingers were shaking as she slipped them around the stem of the champagne glass.

A waiter hovered beside her chair while she raised the glass uncertainly to her mouth. She slipped slowly, pursed her lips and said nothing.

The waiter looked concerned. "Is something wrong, madam?" he asked softly, bowing from his waist so that his lips were close to her ear.

"Wrong? Everything!"

The waiter's eyebrows rose a fraction and he glanced around the restaurant. It was early, just five minutes after noon, so the vast, chandeliered room was not yet crowded. Mrs. Biddle-Macdonald's table was concealed behind a pillar.

"Another bottle, perhaps?" the waiter said soothingly. "Let me replace it."

"No need to do that!" Maggie's voice had the harsh tones of a football coach even when she was trying to speak softly. She twirled the glass in her fingers. "Champagne's fine." She placed the glass on the table and nodded her head for the waiter to fill it.

"Yes, madam." He frowned, his expression reflecting his puzzlement at her mood. He had been a waiter at the Palm Court for twenty years and had known Mrs. Biddle-Macdonald for most of that time. "More butter, madam?"

"Stop fussing, man!" Maggie almost skewered his fluttering hand with her fork. He drew back in confusion, catching his breath. The pride he had in his profession was rudely jarred. His gray brows plunged until they met in a line over his eyes.

Maggie glanced up at him. "Oh, it ain't you!" Her troubled sigh could be heard ten tables away. "I wish I knew what it is. Manhattan blues, I guess." She twirled the raw spinach with her fork.

"Yes, madam." The waiter relaxed. "Perhaps you need a holiday, madam. The winter's not been nice at all." He deftly flicked a non-existent crumb off the tabletop with his starched serving napkin, and straightened his back. "Enjoy your lunch, madam."

When Maggie raised her head, he was already gliding away to the kitchen. She forked spinach into her mouth and munched slowly, her eyes roving around the room. *How the place has changed*, she thought glumly. *Lunch isn't fun here any more.* She pushed aside her salad and sighed again.

The waiter was at her side, emptying the champagne bottle into her glass. "Something else, madam? Strawberries and cream, perhaps?"

"Perhaps not!" She shook her head. She felt she had to get out, do something different, go shopping. "The check," she said in exasperation at her own peevishness.

"Certainly, madam." The waiter hesitated, as though about to speak. Maggie arched her eyebrow which, to her dismay, seemed to encourage him.

"Mrs. Biddle-Macdonald," he said. "I hope you will excuse me for saying this, speaking out of turn, but I have served you for so many years and, well, I look on you as a friend rather than as a customer."

Her heart sank. *He was going to ask for a loan. Was nothing the same any more? Even the Palm Court waiters seem to think they have the right to be familiar with their betters!*

"It's my daughter, Mrs. Biddle-Macdonald, Sophia. Do you remember, you and your late husband lunched here the day she was born seventeen years ago? Your husband gave me ten dollars, such a lot in those days, and told me to celebrate."

Maggie's eyes clouded. If it was seventeen years ago, she must have been married to Arno, her second husband. He had been dead ten years. Raul was next and even he had been dead for two years. *How time flies!*

"Of course I remember," she said cautiously. "How time flies. Is it really seventeen years?"

"Yes, madam." The waiter grinned, his lined face flushing, which made her suspect he may have had a quick drink in the dispensary. "My wife just phoned me, Mrs. Biddle-Macdonald. Sophia, she's my daughter, Sophia's just given birth to a son, my first grandchild."

"How divine!" Maggie wondered what was the current equivalent of ten dollars. It seemed rather a lot to leave as a tip. *Damn Arno,* she thought, *for setting a precedent.*

"So I said to myself," the waiter continued, "why don't I return the compliment you and your husband paid me when Sophia was born? Would you like a drink, madam? To celebrate with me my grandson's birthday, you know."

Maggie had stopped listening. She knew it was a ploy to extract a larger tip than usual. She rose to her feet imperiously, sending the fork clattering to the floor. She opened her purse and scattered some bills over the table, ignoring the waiter.

If he was hurt or surprised, he didn't show it. He scooped up her mink from the spare seat at the table and handed it to her with a small bow. He backed away slowly and Maggie swept through the tables without another glance at him, determined never to come to the Palm Court for lunch again.

Maggie was staying at the Carlyle, as she always did on her occasional visits to Manhattan. She declined the doorman's offer of a taxi and began to walk. Although it was cold, the sun shining down on Fifth Avenue was warm but she had to wrap the mink around her to keep out the wind.

She was looking for the Wordsman Bookstore a few blocks away. She had been meaning to drop in there since Christmas but hadn't had time. On her visits, she always had lawyers and bankers to see, and to sign papers connected with the estates of her three husbands. All of them had been rich, childless, and left most of their wealth to her.

The cold that afternoon was a challenge to Maggie. Living for years in California had spoiled her for the rigors of New York. Yet, she realized as she headed resolutely across Park Lane, oblivious to the traffic straining at the lights, that the cold had a mind-clearing effect. The final problems on the estate of her third husband, Raul, had been settled that morning. Now, to her enormous relief, she had no more lawyers to cosset with their outrageous fees. Unless she decided to take a fourth husband, of course.

She threaded her way through the print stands at the entrance to the bookshop, and pushed open the door to the familiar interior. She was pleased. She had been buying books and antique maps there for years and it seemed as though nothing had changed at all, not like the Palm Court. She was still upset about the waiter being so presumptuous as to step out of his place.

She ignored the assistant walking toward her with a discreet greeting on his lips, and pressed the call button for the elevator. She heard it clang as it descended and she stood ready to enter as the door opened.

"Maps!" she said, without even glancing at the lift boy. She was glad of the warmth and leathery smell of the old elevator; it was reassuring. She decided she would fly back to Los Angles that evening. Everything was finished. She had signed her new will, although she had no intention of dying soon, whatever the doctors said. It was curious, the feeling that shadowed her: a new sense of restlessness, of having no commitment to anybody, and nothing special to do.

The elevator reached the map floor and she left it without a word of thanks to the liftboy. She explained to the gray-haired woman, who had served her many times over the years, that she wanted an antique map to hang in her den.

Instead of arguing as she usually did, she took the woman's advice without hesitation, settling for a fine map dated 1666 showing California as an island. She wrote out a check for five thousand dollars, and arranged for the map to be framed and sent to her home. Buying antique maps and prints always made her feel satisfied, secure; they didn't change.

She pressed the button for the elevator. "You finish already, miss? Mostly, people takes longer than you."

The question startled her. She looked up at the face of the man holding the elevator door open. His eyes glinted and his lips parted in a friendly smile. "You're black!" she blurted out in surprise.

"No, miss. It's the low light."

She ignored the remark and slipped into the elevator with a sigh. Another value lost; a disrespectful youth as an elevator attendant in such an old established bookshop!

She gasped as the door rattled to a close. She was alone with him, and he towered over her.

"You find something good, miss?" The youth's voice was soft, even kind.

She sniffed.

"I hoped you would. You seemed kinda lost when you rode up."

"Were you operating this elevator then?"

"Sure was!" The boy beamed his disarming smile.

"I didn't notice."

The youth chuckled. "I'm not easy to miss, miss."

"You're not!" Maggie found herself warming to his confident smile. He was well over six feet tall. "How do you tolerate being cooped up in this tiny old elevator all day?"

"Ain't easy, miss. Sometimes they let me out to run errands, and sometimes I get to meet nice people like you. That sure helps."

She peered at him out of curiosity. He was long limbed and his clothes fitted him snuggly. His hair was combed, not styled in a wild Afro that was so fashionable. She found his interest in her vaguely touching.

The elevator jerked to a stop. "You ready to get out, miss?" The youth's question took her by surprise. He was watching her intently, his dark eyes unfathomable. He had his hand on the door but did not open it.

She didn't know what to say.

He lowered the handle and the elevator began to rise again. Maggie frowned. *This can't be happening to me*, she thought. *I'm too old!*

She touched her throat, grateful for the protection, fragile though it was, of her mink and winter clothes. There was not much of her exposed, only her face. Even her wig was covered by her mink hat. Unconsciously, she hugged her purse closer. The boy's eyes were appraising her.

"Take me down, immediately!" she commanded, her power of speech returning. She recognized the gleam in the boy's eye and was cross, not with him, but with herself for feeling foolish.

"Of course, miss." The youth grinned pleasantly. "My fault."

Whether she was relieved or disappointed when the elevator reached the main floor and the door creaked open, she wasn't sure. Her heart was thumping and she expected that the youth could hear it.

Was it the champagne, her daily diet of painkillers, or the youth's apparent interest in her that made her light-headed? The doctors had said nothing about mood swings when they gave her the newest prescription. She was inexplicably filled with enthusiasm. "What the hell!" she exclaimed to her own surprise.

"Miss?"

Maggie blinked at the youth; she was still standing in the elevator.

"You're cute." Her voice was husky at her own boldness.

"So are you, miss."

She studied the youth's face to see if he was laughing at her. His eyes reflected what might have been sympathy for a lonely widow, but in his somber gaze there seemed to be the tenderness of concern.

"I'm old enough to be -"

"You're as old as you want to be." The youth's voice was soft. He made no attempt to touch her; one hand was on the door and the other on the elevator control handle. "I finish work at six."

His words seared through her mind like a red-hot branding iron, making her feel weak. She caught sight of the elderly assistant by the entrance, watching her curiously. *This will never do!* She looked long at the youth and then moved away from him.

"I'll be on my way to California at six," she said curtly. The youth's face showed no change of expression. She wondered what his skin felt like to touch. "Where do you come from?"

"From Africa, miss. Kenya."

"Kenya!" Maggie said the word slowly, copying his pronunciation, with its short "e", instead of *Keenya* as the British called it. Then she turned her back on the boy and walked out of the store.

"Kenya!" she said again as she stood on the sidewalk. She had always thrived on impulse, decisions triggered off by chance encounters. It was how she had found Boris, Arno and Raul. The image of the youth's profound eyes still burned into her mind.

"Yes, Kenya," she murmured, stepping over to the taxi that had drawn up to the curb. "I do feel like a holiday. I'll go to Kenya."

"Not in this cab, you won't."

Maggie stared at the cab driver, surprised at him for listening when she was obviously speaking to herself. "The Carlyle!" she snapped.

"That's better," the driver grinned. "I get 'em all!" he said aloud, swinging into the traffic.

BOOK ONE

Mpingo Beach Hotel
Mombasa, Kenya.

Merisio ilkibunjeta le tunjanak
- The fingers of people are not all the same length
(Masai proverb)

CHAPTER 5

"It's all right, Mrs. Biddle-Macdonald," Harrison Muldoon's smile was strained. He kept his voice calm so the pompous old bag would not have the pleasure of knowing she had riled him. "British Airways are very good, such *superb* service." He winked at the man at the check in counter, hoping he would support him.

Mrs. Biddle-Macdonald grunted. "You get *superb* commission, I'm sure."

"We always send our Very Special Guests by British Airways, Mrs. Biddle-Macdonald." Harrison choked back the bile as he emphasized every word. "The British have a way of *pampering* Important People like yourself, don't you think?"

Mrs. Biddle-Macdonald swung away from him and followed the ground stewardess to the First Class lounge. Harrison watched her go with a sense of relief. She had haggled over everything connected with the holiday, making it quite clear that she was expecting royal treatment all the way. He shrugged, and looked at his clipboard before checking his watch.

British Airways Flight 282 was scheduled to take off at 1730 hours. Limousines had been sent to bring each of the Fulfillment Safari clients to the airport for the 1600 hours check-in. Susan Ross had arrived first, as Harrison had expected. She carried only one small suitcase and apologized immediately.

"I just didn't know what to take, Mr Muldoon. I mean with it being so hot there a swimsuit is enough, surely?"

"It might be too much." Harrison winked, only to be rewarded by Susan's startled glance of confusion. She was dressed in the same nondescript outfit she had worn to his office. She certainly did not look like a First Class passenger.

"I'm so nervous, Mr Muldoon," Susan said, dropping her travel documents.

"Whatever for?"

"Such, er, a long flight." She hesitated, taking the travel wallet that he retrieved and pressed into her hand. "And, well, I mean, those Africans and everything..."

"Just relax and enjoy yourself, Susan. You'll come back a changed woman." He tapped his finger against his nose. "Fulfilled!"

She'll be no trouble, he mused as he checked Susan's name on his clipboard. She would probably fall for the room boy and come back starry-eyed, telling her friends how cute and polite Africans were.

The next arrivals were the Bergers, mother and daughter. It was a quiet day at the airport and an alert photographer at the entrance was obviously delighted to have even a former film star to reward him for his long wait for a picture. Harrison rushed over to greet her, unfortunately too late to be included in the photograph. It eventually appeared in several small newspapers with the caption "Star's daughter goes hunting."

For a girl about to experience the thrill of a lifetime, Cora Berger looked remarkably bad tempered. Her harsh features were soured with a peevish expression that her mother's false brightness only emphasized.

"Harrison!" Amelia gushed, aware of the photographer's proximity. "How nice of you to send Cora off on this adventure! Of course, she's traveled absolutely everywhere, but a safari, such an idea! Cora's quite in shock about the whole thing, aren't you, Cora?" She jabbed Cora's side with the edge of her vanity case. "She can't believe it's happening."

The scowl on Cora's face showed more than her mother's words what she really thought. Harrison clucked his tongue, anxious to avoid a scene.

"Oh, she'll love it all, Amelia, darling," he said, waving his hands as though conjuring up a hologram of Africa in the departure lounge. "The endless golden sands, the native warriors, the game drives, the wild animals. Cora will be the envy of all her friends when she gets back."

"I hate fucking animals," Cora said, banging her bag down on the check-in scales. "Almost as much as I hate fucking faggots."

"Cora!" Amelia's voice was sharp. "I don't know what you mean. Harrison, you are such a pet. What can I say?"

Harrison beamed his $20,000-vacation smile and backed away as the ground staff took over. Now he had only one passenger to wait for: Lyn Preston.

Lyn's presence in the group caused him a certain amount of apprehension. Although she assured him she was in search of fulfillment for herself, he did not believe her. A woman like her did not need to fly to Africa to get laid. She could have any stud she wanted here in L.A.

"That's why I am going," Lyn had claimed. "I'm bored when people relate to me because they've seen me on television. I want people to relate to me, as me. Who's going to know me in the ass-hole of Africa?"

"It's Mombasa, not ass-hole," Harrison had gently corrected her.

He gasped when her limousine drew up and Lyn burst out of it in a hurry. He didn't recognize her. Her trademark blonde hair was trapped under her headscarf and her piercing eyes hidden behind her dark glasses. She was enveloped in an enormous Afghan fur coat. The photographer fingered his Rolliflex nervously, uncertain who she was.

Harrison trotted over, shrugged at the photographer and took Lyn's arm. Or tried to. She jerked it away and grinned at him. The smile did nothing for his peace of mind.

"We must keep this quiet," she said from the side of her mouth, leading the way quickly through the concourse. "I don't want anyone to know where I'm going."

"Sure," Harrison said, "It's a vacation. Right?"

"The competition will think I'm on to a scoop!" Lyn laughed and his heart sank.

"Are you coming too?" she demanded.

"I hate flying!" He giggled nervously. "The airline will take care of you all the way. You arrive in London at 1130 hours tomorrow. There's a nine-hour layover. You're booked into day rooms at the Heathrow Hotel. You leave for Mombasa tomorrow night and arrive on Sunday."

"No wonder you hate flying!" Lyn had listened in the manner of someone used to being briefed. "I'll need the sleep in London. What happens in Mombasa?"

"My man there will meet you?"

"Name?"

"Royce. Charles Royce. He's very good."

"He'd better be," said Lyn, grinning with an air of menace. "I'm as horny as hell."

"Don't worry, Lyn. Satisfaction *is* guaranteed." He watched her stride off down the corridor, already engrossed in an animated conversation with the ground stewardess. He swallowed, desperately trying to ignore a horrible feeling of misgiving building up in the back of his mind.

◆ ◆ ◆ ◆ ◆

The man in the commando-green safari jacket and matching slacks stepped clumsily over the pool of sewage oozing into the alley. He swore when excrement spattered his chukka boots. Taking greater care, he edged around a pile of refuse and hurried along the alley to the sunlight.

He breathed with relief when he reached the lane at the end of the alley. It was narrow with projecting upper stories shading the brilliance of the morning sun. Charles Royce liked Mombasa's Old Town with its intricate passageways and blind alleys but it was a damned filthy place. It only survived because a new site was chosen for Mombasa's port in 1931. Now ships berthed at Kalindi, leaving the old port to the dhows from Lamu and Somalia, as it had been for two hundred years.

Although roads had been pushed through the labyrinth in the thirties by determined administrators, a maze of narrow alleys still remained. Charles Royce suspected that the old buildings, even though they were picturesque when shown in tourist brochures, were not solid enough to be as old as they looked. Yet parts of Mombasa's Old Town had been occupied since medieval times and he reckoned that there was enough sewage to prove it.

The Englishman threaded his way carefully through the crowds thronging the lanes, brushing shoulders with women and girls whose heads and dated Western-style dresses were entirely covered with the black *buibui* that Muslim women wear in public. Some of the men wore the full white *kanzu*, an ankle length shirt, with the embroidered skullcap known as a *kofia*.

Royce had lived in the Old Town since his work as a factory manager finished when the British owners, like many other whites at the time, pulled out of Kenya. Unwilling to return to England, he moved to the coast. He was 53 and had a small annuity, which he supplemented as a Tour Guide.

He lived in the Arab-dominated Old Town in defiance of convention, which decreed that expatriates keep a certain standard. It matched his income, too. Not for him the cocktail parties and exclusive heartiness of the Mombasa Club, still very British despite its multi-racial membership. To them, Charles Royce was an outcast.

He greeted the Arab storeowners as he began to make his way up Biashare Street, known as Khanga Lane because of the colorful displays of cloth on each side. Every time he strolled these streets he took in the sights and sounds of the traders, the boys, the coffee sellers walking and clinking their cups together to advertise their sweetly made coffee, and the brash white tourists in their shorts and sun bonnets.

He felt at home. In his safari suit of loose-fitting trousers and many-pocketed jacket without sleeves (a concession to the coastal heat) he felt good. Charles Royce was a boss. Even if his fellow expatriate Britons shunned him, the locals showed him respect.

He became aware of a boy skipping along at his side. The boy reached out and touched the large flapping pocket of his jacket. He brushed his hand away.

"Jambo, bwana!" the boy said, refusing to be ignored

He glanced at him. He was an Arab, naked except for a pair of torn shorts flapping from his waist. His legs showed dark scars where deep cuts had healed and his feet were bare in the dirt of the street. He was grinning, displaying a mouthful of decayed teeth as he gazed up mischievously.

"Jambo," answered Royce cautiously. "I've got no money," he said in Swahili.

The boy's grin broadened. "I come tonight, bwana."

Royce aimed a cuff at his head. The boy laughed and danced away.

"Cheeky monkey!" he muttered, his sour mood lifting. Life, he reflected walking into Digo Street, wasn't too bad. Where else in the world would he get propositioned at ten in the morning?

He started to hum quietly to himself, pushing his hand in his pocket for his key as he approached the post office. The phalanx of mailboxes projected into the street, like bay windows of an English country cottage. He nodded politely to an African he knew by sight and unlocked his mailbox. It was empty. His mood darkened and he stopped humming.

He looked forward to the ritual of clearing his mailbox every day. It was his link with the outside world. He gazed with distaste at the erratic traffic streaming down Digo Road. Tourists he worked with were a link too, but his mail was a link of his own choice, whenever he got any. Nobody seemed to write letters any more. Even when he wrote to his bank in England, it was a computer that replied and a school leaver signed the letter in a silly, girlish hand.

His mood soured as he passed the clothes and shoe stores, the curio shops and the souvenir stalls, and reached the roundabout that is Mombasa's city center. He turned right up Kalindi Road, the main thoroughfare to the port. Picking his way through the pavement peddlers selling pineapples and mangoes, he gained the terrace of the Castle Hotel with a sigh of relief.

The Castle was Mombasa's largest, centrally situated hotel. It was three stories of gray-painted arches, square columns and long verandas, built in 1908 and sharing its fortunes and renovations with the history of Kenya itself. The Veranda Terrace faced onto Kalindi Road.

This morning, as always, it was packed with white visitors of various shades of pink, from the blush of the bare shoulders of a Swedish girl, to the vivid red of a German's bulbous nose. The laughter swirling around the veranda and mingling with the snarl of cars outside, was mostly Germanic. The only black faces on the terrace were those of waiters moving with calculated lethargy, keeping as far away from the crowded tables and braying tourists as possible.

Charles Royce ignored the uproar and sauntered across the terrace and into the hotel. Despite the ravages inflicted on the interior by a succession of European managers and their guests, the Castle retained a genteel, if dated, dignity. The inside was cool, calming to nerves shattered by the clatter of traffic and hearty shouts of the tourists.

He waved his hand in greeting at the young man looking bemused behind the reception desk and walked through the darkly furnished lobby to the rear of the hotel. He turned right down a corridor and entered the tranquility of a patio named the Buibui Bar by an erstwhile management.

A few people were sitting in the bar's canvas chairs grouped around small tables. The wattle roof quivered with the weight of the fans spinning under it. He walked through the room to the courtyard where a fir tree and palm plants created a sparse garden atmosphere. He was pleased to see there were no tourists there. A young man at a table was staring at a sheet of paper torn from a telex machine. Royce sat down beside him.

"Tusker!" he called to the waiter who watched him idly from the bar counter. "Cold."

The waiter blinked in surprise. Royce held out his hand to the youth at the table and took the telex message from him.

"It came this morning," the youth said with a timid smile.

"Anyone see it?"

"The operator. I was there when it came through."

"Good boy." He scanned the message quickly. It lifted his spirits. "We have work to do."

"Yes." The African spoke in clipped English, his accent like Royce's own. "They are coming on Sunday."

"I can read!" Royce seized the bottle of beer the waiter put down in front of him and poured it into his glass. He did not offer the youth a drink.

"What I mean," said the young man, "is that Sunday is when I go home to Kaloleni."

"Your leave's cancelled!"

"Yes, bwana." There was mockery in the youth's voice.

"Now don't sulk with me, Mindelo. You know I need you when I've got these Americans here. How do you expect me to manage without you?" He wiped his moustache with the back of his hand and placed the half-emptied glass back on the table. "Phew! I needed that."

Charles Royce was not a big man. His body was fleshy as though once he had been larger and muscular but, with age and inactivity, had begun to shrink. His hair was a muddy colour, flecked with gray and thinning. When he was riding in the tour Landrover, he wore a slouch green hat to keep off the dust. Today he was bareheaded. A thin line of froth from the beer streaked his graying moustache.

He downed the remains of his Tusker and signaled the waiter to bring another. Sweat oozed on his brow and he mopped it with a grimy handkerchief.

"You want a drink, boy?"

"No, thank you, bwana." Again the mocking tone.

"Bring two," Royce ordered. "One warm, one cold." In Mombasa, they say fight fire with fire. The locals drank beer warm, at room temperature, because of the heat.

"You'll have a beer, boy. We must plan how we're going to keep these tourists happy." Royce glanced at Mindelo's handsome features. They gave no clue about what he was thinking, but Royce knew he was sulking. Mindelo had been looking forward to visiting his village to see his mother and sisters. It was impossible now.

"I'll give you a bonus if this goes well." Royce knew he shouldn't spoil the youth, but he liked him too much to see him miserable.

"Thank you, bwana." Mindelo touched his brow with his finger in the kind of salute he must have seen blacks do in the movies.

Royce waited while the waiter deposited two Tuskers on the table. He took the cold one for himself and pushed the other across to Mindelo. "Snap out of it! You can go home another time."

"My sister is getting married. I should be there."

"Well, you can't go, so that's that."

"Yes, bwana." Mindelo sipped slowly from the bottle.

Royce knew he had won. Mindelo had been with him for six years, since he was thirteen and he had spotted him racing through the long grass of the savannah near his family's compound in the forest around Kaloleni. He had watched fascinated while the boy leaped like a gazelle over the tufts of grass. He was chasing a puppy and was naked, his lithe limbs honey brown and glowing with youthful strength.

His smile, when he beckoned the boy to come to him, was enchanting. It radiated happiness, his almond-shaped eyes crinkling mischievously under long, dark lashes. The boy stood without embarrassment while Royce glanced up and down his nude body. There was not a blemish on him, no festering scars where a panga had sliced into his leg, no unsightly welts from beatings by his uncles.

Mindelo's mother, bare-breasted and polite, listened impassively as she sat in the shade outside her hut. Royce spoke in Swahili, perched on the tiny wooden chair the naked boy had brought for him to sit on.

"School?" The mother had repeated the word with resignation when Royce asked. "The boy doesn't want to go to school."

"That's against the law," Royce had said with relish. "If the authorities find out, there'll be trouble for you as well as the boy." He had patted Mindelo on his bare bottom.

The mother shrugged. She had five children; Mindelo was the middle one. What could she do?

"The school inspector," Royce insisted. "He might come. You'll have to pay a fine."

The mother's eyes rose above her head, not to God but to the coconuts. "With what?" she asked softly. "All we have are the coconuts."

Royce knew what to say. "It isn't good for the boy to miss school. He could learn so much. He could get a job and send you money for your husband and children."

The mother was thoughtful for several minutes, her brow furrowed. Royce waited. Finally she spoke, tossing her head vigorously to show the contempt she felt for his idea. "Job? And where could such a troublesome boy get a job? In Kaloleni? In Mombasa?"

"Yes." Royce smiled agreeably. "In Mombasa."

Both the boy and the mother stared at him. He felt a rush of pleasure knowing he was going to get what he wanted. "Let me take him," he suggested as though he had just thought of it. "I'll take him to my flat in Mombasa. He shall work for me there. I'll send him to school." He paused, then added slowly. "The school inspector won't worry you then."

There was silence, apart from the noise of the bush, while the woman considered his words. The boy nudged his mother excitedly. Royce stood up.

"I'll return tomorrow," he said. "It's your choice. Have

him ready if he is to come. If not," he shrugged his shoulders. "If not, there could be trouble with the authorities. You know what the Mzee says."

He turned on his heels and walked down the track back to the road where he had been driving when he had first seen Mindelo. Whatever Jomo Kenyatta - the Mzee - may have said, it had no bearing on what Royce was thinking.

The next day, Mindelo rode with him in the back of the Landrover, his belongings in a paper bag. Royce didn't allow him to see his mother again for two years, by which time he could read, write and was completely housebroken. He had grown fast and was eager to learn. Now, whenever Mindelo returned to Kaloleni on leave, Royce felt lonely and confused. He dreaded the thought that one day Mindelo might leave him forever.

"All right, Mindelo. I'll tell you what we'll do." He put his hand across the table and patted the youth's arm, hoping to restore him to his usually chirpy spirits, "We'll drive out to Kaloleni for your sister's wedding. We'll leave the tourists on the beach that day."

"It's all right, sir." Mindelo shrugged, smiling brightly.

"Are you sure?"

"Yes." Mindelo raised his bottle of beer in a salute of cheers.

Charles Royce was proud. Mindelo was a credit to him. He had learned that whites liked to see a smiling face, not a sullen one. It reassured them, even if it wasn't sincere.

CHAPTER 6

Through his binoculars, Charles Royce scanned the faces of the passengers disembarking from the Kenya Airways DC9 that they had joined in Nairobi. He had a telex in his pocket with the names of the four wealthy American women arriving from Los Angles. His job was to pamper them, see they met a few likely lads, take them on safari, and then put them safely on the flight back home.

He expected it to be an easy assignment. As in the past, the chemistry of the climate and the good nature of the hotel's willing staff would work its spell.

He lowered his binoculars. The newly built terminal of Mombasa's airport was an airy concrete structure with a long upper gallery open to the elements. It was eleven in the morning and the sun was scorching down on the passengers as they walked eagerly to the arrival hall. A Kenya Airways ground stewardess radiating charm was shepherding four women in front of the others.

"There's the old dears."

Mindelo, his eyes screwed up to temper the sun's brightness, boldly scrutinized each female in the group. "They don't seem so old," he muttered.

Royce frowned and raised the binoculars to peer at them again. He was cross when he saw Mindelo was right. "Run along and meet them, boy. I'll come when you've organized their luggage.

Mindelo nodded and walked briskly across the wide balcony and down the steps to the arrival hall. Charles Royce stroked his moustache and watched. Mindelo was wearing the uniform that was standard on the coast: a short sleeved shirt with pockets worn over trousers of matching color, in his case safari green. He exuded an air of authority as he moved with an easy assurance.

Royce knew that Mindelo, with his obliging smile, would melt away any grouchiness the four women might be feeling after the flight. He strolled to the bar counter, ordered a cold Tusker and spent a leisurely twenty minutes drinking it, and another, before he decided to meet the guests.

His first sight of them shattered his complacency. A large lady with pearls of perspiration glistening on her forehead, and standing with her arms akimbo, was glaring at Mindelo.

"Okay, boy," Royce sighed, wondering what had gone wrong. "I'll take care of this."

The woman swung around to face him. "Who the hell are you?"

He noted her staring eyes reddened with fatigue and her cheeks flushed under a sticky layer of powder. He wondered how long it would be before she collapsed. A waft of mouthwash mingled with stale champagne gusted over him. He smiled weakly.

"I am the Honorable Charles Royce," he said, drawing on the reserve of arrogance bequeathed by his British upbringing. "I have the pleasure of being your host and guide while you are a guest in Kenya. It is my pleasure to welcome you to Mombasa."

He waited while the woman cast her eyes over him, moving slowly from his chukka boots up to his red spotted handkerchief knotted at his throat, and down again. Her nose twitched with disapproval at his green safari uniform, his slouch hat and strained smile. But before she could speak, a blonde woman with outsize sunglasses burst through the door from the arrival hall.

"Blow me, Maggie!" she said with a grin. "You've got one already. Very James Stewart, isn't he?"

Royce blanched. "Charles Royce at your service."

"The *Honorable* Charles Royce," Maggie said in a thick voice, which carried over the expanse of concrete to the Landrover waiting for them.

"I suppose you're the first class touch we've paid extra for?" Lyn gazed around the forecourt where several young Africans were watching them curiously.

"Perhaps he is, but I haven't paid to ride in that!" Maggie pointed to the Landrover. "No way, Honorable! We've been flying for three days. I demand an air-conditioned limousine. Just get me out of this heat. I'm wet all over."

"Why, Maggie? Have you seen someone tasty?" Lyn stared at the youths as though they were waxwork models on display just for her. Some of them shrugged and moved away.

Royce tried to ignore the feeling of foreboding that was creeping up on him. "If we could just wait for the others -" He put his hand out to restrain Lyn when she began to move in the direction of the youths hanging around the Landrover.

"Lyn Preston won't wait for anyone. She's famous," Maggie said. "I'm not, but neither will I." She turned away with an irritable shrug as Cora pushed through the door from the terminal with her suitcase banging her knees.

Mindelo walked over to her quickly. "Let me take that, miss."

"Why should you? I can carry it."

Royce watched with dismay as Cora brushed aside Mindelo's attempt to help her. He blinked at the scene that confronted him: a middle-aged harridan, an earnest teenager, and a restless, leggy blonde. What, he wondered, had he done to deserve this?

"Wow, isn't it hot!" Cora dumped the suitcase by Maggie's foot and flopped down on it.

Maggie sniffed loudly. "The heat is bearable. It's the organization that is at fault. Mr. Muldoon never said anything about traveling in a truck."

Royce smiled. "A Landrover is the customary safari vehicle in Kenya," he said soothingly. "It's more comfortable than it looks."

Maggie's mouth twitched.

"Yeah, Maggie," said Cora. "It looks fun. Just like in the movies."

"*Your* mother was in the movies, Cora. Not I."

A crowd was beginning to gather around the three women, keen to see what they could make out of them. Royce realized he had to get them moving quickly. Already the Preston woman was deep in conversation with one of the rogues who loitered at the airport to prey on unsuspecting tourists like her.

"Mindelo," he said sharply. The boy was hopping from one foot to another beside Cora, gazing at her wide-eyed. "Get a taxi!" he ordered in Swahili.

Yes, bwana!" Mindelo looked sheepish, glanced at Cora who ignored him, and pushed his way into the crowd.

"Mrs. Macdonald -" Royce began, then stopped with his mouth half-open in surprise.

"I'm Mrs. *Biddle*-Macdonald, if you don't mind. One of the Boston Biddles.

"Ah, yes," he sighed. "I should have known. The telex didn't give your full name." He waved the paper weakly. "Well, considering health reasons, after such a long flight, perhaps a taxi could be recommended for you instead of the Landrover. One is coming."

"Health reasons? I'm not sick, my good man." Mrs. Biddle-Macdonald's loud voice cracked. "Not sick, not sick."

Royce snapped his fingers for two boys to pick up the luggage, and then offered the woman his arm. She refused but followed him without protest through the crowd. He led her to a battered Peugeot taxi, which had pulled up behind the Landrover. Mindelo held open the door. Maggie sniffed with disdain before entering the car.

"I want to go in the jeep," Cora called out cheerfully.

Mindelo shut the door on Maggie and followed Cora, trying to take the suitcase from her hand.

"I want that girl with me"!" Maggie's shout through the taxi's open window stopped Royce as he moved away to call Lyn Preston. "I'm not riding in this thing alone." Maggie's eyes narrowed. "The driver, he might -"

"She'll be lucky!" Cora muttered, grinning at Mindelo but not letting him have the suitcase.

Royce frowned. "I don't know what I can do -"

"I'm so sorry to keep you waiting."

He looked up as a young woman moved anxiously through the crowd toward him.

"I thought I'd lost my bag but this gentleman had it.

Royce shook his head with disbelief. The fourth woman seemed to be a hippie. He gave some loose change to the porter who carried her bag and dismissed him quickly.

"Wasn't that kind? Oh, he's gone. I should have thanked him."

"There's no need." Royce dabbed at his forehead with a handkerchief, wondering what else could possible go wrong. He was supposed to have wealthy women with style, not plain Janes like this one. She wore rumpled jeans with a sweater tied loosely around her waist. Her T-shirt hung like a shapeless bag from her narrow shoulders, and her hair was dark and clammy in the heat.

"Come here, Susan!" The voice from the taxi, like the caw of an angry bird, caused the children clustering around the car to fall back in astonishment. "Ride with me, dear, instead of in that awful safari truck."

Susan looked first at Maggie and then at the Landrover where Cora was talking to Mindelo. She turned to Royce. "Oh dear, I don't know what to do. I don't want to be any trouble."

"Please ride in the taxi, miss." Charles Royce was losing his patience. Ten days with these women and he would need a vacation himself.

♦ ♦ ♦ ♦ ♦

From her seat in front of the taxi, Susan stared apprehensively at the hundreds of people hurrying past them. The weary Peugeot was rattling at a walking pace across the planks of the pontoon bridge that linked Mombasa Island with Kenya's North Coast. Smartly dressed children released from school gamboled recklessly in front of the taxi, oblivious to the noise and blue-gray exhaust fumes that shrouded them in the dead heat of noon.

Susan turned back to Mrs. Biddle-Macdonald to express her alarm at the chattering maelstrom of people. Her discomfort increased when she saw how she was sitting with her eyes closed, and an expression of acute pain on her puffy features. Her sour and inflamed face frightened Susan.

Through the rear window she saw a man bent low, his dusty skin dripping sweat as he pulled a loaded cart across the shuddering planks of the bridge. The taxi lurched forward unexpectedly, then came to an abrupt halt. Mrs. Biddle-Macdonald moaned and kept her eyes tightly closed.

Susan was jolted off balance and twisted back so she could see better. The driver, who seemed too big for the small front seat, leaned out of the window and spoke to a man collecting money at the tollgate. He spoke in Swahili, laughed with a flash of sinister teeth, and flung the taxi forward, only just missing the school children rousting in front of the vehicle like unruly goats. They scattered as the car picked up speed.

Susan clutched at the door handle and glanced nervously at the driver. His face was bland but she sensed a roughness in the man. A soft moan came from the back seat, startling her.

"My friend isn't feeling well." Susan gestured with her free hand to the back of the car. "Do you think you could drive a little more carefully?"

The driver swung his head around slowly and gazed at her. His eyes widened so that the whites shone with the intensity of a threat. Without looking at the road, he pressed his foot down on the accelerator and the car careened toward a cyclist. "Say again, miss?"

Susan swallowed. "My friend, she's not well, please go slower."

"Of course I'm well!" The voice from the back sounded like the growl of a wounded animal. Both Susan and the driver turned to look.

"Drive as fast as you like." Mrs. Biddle-Macdonald opened her eyes. "The sooner I get to the hotel the better."

"Be careful!" Susan's shriek echoed the squeal of the taxi's brakes as the driver glanced at the road again in time to avoid a cyclist. "Oh, I never dreamed my vacation would be like this." She clasped both hands in front of her, trying to hold herself in the seat. If all Africans were like this taxi driver, she was sure she was going to have a horrid time.

"It's no worse than the Los Angeles freeways," Mrs. Biddle-Macdonald said with a snort of impatience.

"You're not frightened?" Susan dared not take her eyes off the road. She had the odd feeling that the driver was deliberately trying to upset her. *It isn't fair!* she thought. After the long flight she just wanted to crash into bed, not be in a car crash. *Some people are hateful.*

"What should I be frightened of?" Mrs. Biddle-Macdonald sounded cross.

"These people!" Susan tried to ignore the driver's eyes. "They seem so, I don't know, off-putting."

"What did you expect?"

Susan unclasped her hands and glanced back at Mrs. Biddle-Macdonald. She was relieved to see she looked better now she had her eyes open, even if she did still seem to be in pain. "I don't know really. It's the first time I've ever been *abroad*." She uttered the word with awe.

"Stay close to me, dear. You'll be all right."

"I don't want to be any trouble, Mrs. Biddle-Macdonald."

"Call me Maggie, dear. All my friends do."

"I couldn't."

"Why ever not?"

"I hardly know you."

"Listen, dear, we're in this together. We're going to need each other. I'm Maggie to you, dear. We'll be good company for each other, I know that."

"Yes, er, Maggie." She gripped her seat as the taxi swerved around a corner. The driver grinned. "I'm Susan. Susan Ross."

"I know."

Susan waited for Mrs. Biddle-Macdonald to explain but she didn't. She took her eyes off the road again as her curiosity got the better of her. "How do you know?"

Mrs. Biddle-Macdonald sighed. "By asking Harrison Muldoon, of course. I had to know about the people on this trip before I consented to come."

Susan frowned. "What did he tell you about me?"

"Only your name and a little background, dear. I thought then how nice it would be to get to know you. I'm not disappointed at all. I'm sure we'll be great friends."

Susan paled. She had imagined a more glamorous traveling companion for her vacation.

The taxi swung off the main road, throwing her against the driver. The big man ignored her as she pulled herself away from him. She became aware of his heavy body odor, a musky smell that made her senses tingle. In confusion, she looked out of the window at the cluster of crudely built wooden huts where crowds of near-naked men squatted at the side of the road. She was horrified by the poverty. She longed to ask Maggie about it but thought it might offend the driver. She wished she wasn't so naïve about everything.

"Nyali," the driver said suddenly, taking his hand off the steering wheel and sweeping it across the windscreen to indicate the view. His other hand rested on the window and Susan held her breath until he gripped the steering wheel again.

"What's Nyali?" She tried to keep the nervousness out of her voice.

"Best class dwelling. Boss people."

She gazed out of the window, noticing the change in the scenery. The shanties of the native quarter had given way to wide avenues and clipped hedgerows. Villas stood back from the road and sprinklers spun in the sun, showering their lush green lawns. The only Africans she could see were weeding the flowerbeds or brushing up leaves. There were white-painted wrought iron grilles on the windows and verandas of the houses. She began to feel better even though it was so hot.

"Nyali Beach," the driver muttered, waving out of the window at a dazzling strip of sand beyond two villas and a thicket of coconut palms. "Best beach near Mombasa," he added. "Plenty hotels."

"If we want a guided tour, we'll tell you." Maggie's harsh voice interrupted the driver. He ignored her.

"Nyali Beach Hotel." He waved both hands at the roofs of the whitewashed buildings visible through coconut palms and bougainvillea. "Built nineteen-forty-six. Very posh."

"Looks like a fortress," Maggie snapped. "See those security guards. Spoils the fun."

Susan wondered what Maggie meant but couldn't ask because she was too worried about the driver's hands. One brushed accidentally against her thigh when he reached for the gear lever. She tried to shrink away from him. She was aware of a tingling sensation and she could feel her heart beating against her breast. She fixed her eyes out of the window and stared at a long flat-roofed building of balconies and outside galleries, its stucco a brilliant white in the sun.

"Mombasa Beach Hotel," the driver said, his hand brushing Susan's leg again. He changed gear and turned to face her with a huge grin. "The Mzee open it nineteen-seventy.

Not bad."

There was growl of disapproval from Maggie. The driver ignored her as he turned off the main road in the direction of the thatched roofs of a third hotel. The car entered a shaded wood and Susan was relieved to be out of the unrelenting glare of the sun.

Peacocks posed in the glades that she glimpsed through the plethora of eucalyptus, conocarpus, palms and casuarina trees. She wondered if they were intruding in someone's private paradise.

"It's lovely," she breathed. The driver's hand rested on her knee. She twisted her leg away, yet the touch of the man's firm fingers lingered. She quivered inside then, to her relief, the taxi rounded a clump of flowers and jerked to a stop in front of an archway of coral entwined with bougainvillea. Two uniformed youths jumped to the taxi, opening doors and bowing low.

"Jambo!" they said with broad smiles. "Karibu! Hello and welcome to the Mpingo Beach Hotel."

Mrs. Biddle-Macdonald was staring over their heads. "I hope all those damn flowers won't give me hay fever.

CHAPTER 7

Susan followed the bellboy carrying her small traveling case out of the hotel's main reception building into the lushness of the gardens. She narrowed her eyes at the brilliance of the sun and the vivid colors of the flowers blooming around the path. The dazzling blue of a swimming pool glimmered through the bushes; the lazy laughter of tourists splashing in its water reassured her.

She was tired and felt vaguely faint. She was still shaken by the antics of the odious taxi driver and her nervousness had made her reluctant to leave the company of the others. Mrs. Biddle-Macdonald's fruity voice booming her complaints to Mr. Royce had been oddly reassuring, giving her a chance to bring her emotions under control.

She found Mr. Royce sweet and patient in dealing with the different demands of the four of them. She did not want to cause any trouble and so didn't tell him what the taxi driver had tried to do. Her knee still burned where his fingers had pressed her. She hoped none of the others had noticed she was trembling. She had accepted her cottage key and followed the bellboy meekly. She needed time to analyze why she felt so upset.

She peered anxiously at the bellboy leading her through the bright gardens past the guest cottages nestling in the foliage. In his gold-colored uniform of shirt jacket and matching pants, he looked unexceptional. Perhaps it was the warmth from the sun, or simply the relief that she was near the end of her journey, which made her feel so shaky. She studied the young man's back

His hair was neatly trimmed and combed. His shoulders swung easily as he walked along the path and his whole body seemed lithe and athletic, as though he bristled with muscles under the gold of his clothes. That she should think of such a thing shook her. She clutched her British Airways shoulder bag close to her breast.

The bellboy must have sensed her appraisal. He slowed down, turned, and grinned impudently. His skin shone in the sun with the mysterious hue of a moonlit night. His dark eyes, lost in the shadows of his countenance, were searching for hers. His wide mouth stretched open across his gleaming white teeth in a grin. It startled her. She drew the bag tighter to her body and lowered her eyes.

The youth's grin broadened. "First time here, bibi?"

His words, spoken softly and with apparent friendliness, puzzled her. It took a while to decipher what he was saying from the garbled cadence of his speech. He had paused in the path and she could feel him eyeing her, although she dared not look at him directly. She found herself focusing on the tight whorls of hair curling where his shirt was unbuttoned at his throat. She wondered if the hair was coarse or soft to touch.

"Oh!" she said, glancing up nervously when his hand reached out to her.

"We are at your cottage, bibi. Let me take your bag."

"No." She clasped the bag closer. She felt her chest tightening. The youth dropped his hand.

"Very well." The youth grinned again. "Kenya sweet country, bibi. Lovely hotel." He gestured at the flowers and nodded in the direction of a screen of bougainvillea. "Your cottage behind here, bibi. Very private."

Her legs felt so weak as she followed the youth toward the guest cottage set in a glade of bushes and tropical blossoms. She knew it was beautiful yet she was too worried about the bellboy to appreciate it. He made her feel shy, timid. He was only a few inches taller than she was but he seemed massive. His strength was exaggerated by the lightness of her luggage, which he carried with nonchalant ease.

He mounted the steps to the porch at the front of the cottage and reached out a huge hand to push the door open. He stood at the side and turned to her. A welcoming smile spread across his face but she wondered if there was a hidden meaning in it. "Please to enter, miss."

Susan stood on the path and looked up at the porch. The interior of the cottage was in darkness and she could not see beyond the doorway where the youth was waiting. She hoped it would be cool inside. There would be a bed where she could lie down and feel safe.

She tried to climb the steps but her legs refused to move.

The weariness accumulated during the long journey swept through her in a heavy wave. She reached out to grasp the porch rail for support. She slipped.

The arms that caught her and swung her up through the air were strong. She felt tempted to relax completely and trust herself to them. She felt so weak. The youth was carrying her in his arms out of the sun as though she were a child. The wash of cool air on her skin from the air-conditioning was refreshing after the clinging, dusty heat of the drive from the airport.

Someone murmured with pleasure. She was surprised to realize it was herself. She was floating through the air and being laid down gently on a cloud. She knew when the arms of the giant who held her were withdrawn, and she was sorry. His was a warm, reassuring touch. There was silence.

She opened her eyes. She was alone. The bellboy had gone. Or had he been a dream? The telephone was ringing incessantly. For a moment she wondered where she was. She reached out in the darkness of the room and connected with the phone. She lifted it, and yawned.

"Susan, dear? Are you there?"

She tried to place the voice. Shaking her head to clear it of sleep, she answered slowly, "Who's calling?"

"This is Maggie, dear. Are you all right?"

"I fell asleep, I think."

"A bit of jet lag, that's all," said Maggie.

Susan suddenly remembered. "Oh dear, I must have fainted." She found the switch of the bedside lamp and gazed around the suddenly brightened room. "The bellboy must have carried me into the room as well as my bag," she said, feeling embarrassed.

There was a chuckle at the other end of the line. "Some people have all the luck!"

"It's true!" She caught her breath with shame. "The bellboy! Oh dear, what must he think of me?"

"Come and see me, dear. You'll be all right after a drink."

Susan put down the phone. An overwhelming sadness, of helplessness, of loneliness, throbbed through her. She began to cry, sorry for being such a nuisance.

Carefree shouts and the sound of a tennis ball hitting the hard surface of a court bounced over the chain of shrubs blocking Maggie's view. She walked cautiously beside the hibiscus hedge, keeping her eyes alert for snakes.

At the end of the shrubbery she raised her head and peered through the wire fence surrounding the tennis court. A woman in a starched white tennis costume was concentrating on the man serving her. Maggie dismissed the woman instantly as not being worthy of her attention. She turned her head to inspect the man.

He looked absurdly young. He was wearing bleached tennis shorts that shone against his dark body. His legs glistened, his youthful muscles rippling as he skipped across the court. He was naked from his waist up with only a white sweatband at his wrist. He looked clean and wholesome, reminding Maggie of the boy in the elevator who had set this pilgrimage in motion.

If he was aware of her presence, he gave no indication of it. Even when she entered the court and stood in the shade of the overhanging trees at the side, he didn't glance at her. He was concentrating on his service, occasionally calling words of advice to the blonde tourist, whom Maggie decided must be Swedish. She grew impatient for their game to finish.

She successfully distracted the Swedish woman by clapping when she hit the ball and laughing when she missed. The game faltered. The woman glared at her, muttered something in Swedish and ran off the court. The youth shrugged his shoulders and strolled toward Maggie.

She studied him eagerly as he approached. He was medium height, and compact. His skin was moist and glistening after the game. His shoulders were broad, tapering to a narrow, hard waist. She swallowed nervously.

"Why did you do that?"

"Oh, you startled me." She lifted her eyes from the man's crotch to his face. It was like a mask, serious and unyielding. His eyes, set deeply under a high forehead, were curious but showed his annoyance.

"I ask you why you do that." His voice was firm.

Maggie's interest turned to umbrage. "Do what?" she demanded indignantly, fiddling with her beads. She was not used to being questioned by the staff.

"Why you make my client, that lady, feel foolish?" The youth's eyes swept over her with barely concealed contempt. "Do you wish to play tennis? I am booked for the rest of the day." He turned away brusquely and walked toward the kiosk where the balls and rackets were stored.

Maggie stared at him open-mouthed. Her outrage was about to bubble over into a cutting remark when she realized the youth, with his magnificent physique, was moving out of her potential grasp. "Are you the pro?" she called out after him.

The youth stopped but did not turn. His shoulders were hunched warily as he waited for her next remark.

"I want you!" she said, without hesitation.

"To teach you to play tennis?" The youth turned and smiled. It was a slight opening of the mouth, which would have passed for a smile in Los Angeles. In Kenya, however, where people were generous with their smiles, it was weak and wanting. "You can arrange it at the front desk, madam."

"I prefer to arrange it with you!" Maggie felt she needed a stronger hold on the conversation before it was too late. The youth was reaching for a towel. He wrapped it around his neck and faced her, his dark eyes expressionless.

"I'm from California," Maggie said. "It's my first time in *Keenya*. I don't want to play tennis. I'm sure you could show me some other sports?" She parted her lips, hoping she looked enticing.

"We call our country *Kenya* now, madam. We are independent."

"I'm sure you are. Independence needs financing. I think you understand? Mine's the first cottage along that path." She gestured into the bougainvillea. "Come for a drink when you've finished your lessons."

The youth slapped his face with the towel. He looked so strong and virile. "Alas," he said politely. "It is not permitted to socialize with the guests."

"What nonsense! My travel counselor said the staff here is trained to be obliging. It's what I've come for."

The youth's eyes flickered with distress. "The security guards will not permit me to enter your cottage," he said. "I have no business there."

"I'll make it your business, theirs too, if you like." Maggie tried to smile but she was puzzled at not getting her own way.

"I must go now," the youth said. "I have to prepare for my next lesson."

Maggie was irked by his defiance, yet she found his arrogance stimulating, a challenge. He was wiping under his arms with his towel, deliberately ignoring her.

"Harrison Muldoon told me everything was guaranteed" she protested lamely as he began to walk away to the gate. "I shall speak to the manager!"

◆ ◆ ◆ ◆ ◆

Susan emerged from her cottage and blinked. According to her watch, it was late afternoon but her body and mind were still several hours behind Mombasa time. She decided a plunge in the warm waters of the Indian Ocean might help revive her.

She left the porch and walked through the flower bushes in the direction of the shimmering sea. She wanted to soak herself in that sea and wash away the embarrassment of fainting in the bellboy's arms.

Someone stepped out of the bushes and gripped her arm. She shrieked.

"Susan!" a voice hissed.

Susan gasped and looked up to see it was Maggie Biddle-Macdonald who was holding her. Her eyes were blazing behind her shades and her lips were parted in an intense half-smile. She was clutching her arm with a fervor that showed no sign of easing. Susan smiled with relief as her own fear subsided.   "I'm sorry, you startled me. I was thinking."

"Were you, dear?" Maggie's tone suggested she thought she was incapable of such a thing. She clung to her, urging her along the path. "Whatever could a nice girl like you have on her mind?"

"It's nothing, really." She felt herself blushing.

"Nothing?" Maggie's voice swooped through two octaves. "Have you seen something you fancy already, Susan? You've turned redder than the Palm Court's strawberries."

"I'm sorry, Mrs. Biddle-Macdonald. I'm so mixed up."

"Now, you know my name's Maggie, dear. I may not be quite as young as you are but when it comes to matters of the heart, I do understand. We don't forget *lust* as we get older, dear. And I have had three husbands." She sounded wistful. "Who have you seen?"

Susan gazed longingly at the beach. It was vast. There were lots of tourists sitting on it, while a few Africans moved among them. The sea seemed lazy and inviting. "It's all such a new experience for me, Maggie," she said, trying to remove her arm from Maggie's grasp. "These people..."

"The Africans? They are absolutely gorgeous, dear. They seem so strong!" Maggie's voice trilled. "Let's sit down here," she said, pulling Susan's arm and leading her off the path to a bench in the shade of a magnificent flowering tree. They could see the beach from where they sat; it made Susan wonder how she could escape Maggie and run out on to the sand.

Maggie was swathed in an ankle-length garment of red cotton that matched the brilliance of the hibiscus flowers. Her head was swaddled in a bright scarf without a wisp of hair showing. The total effect, against the puffy aristocracy of her features, was intimidating. Susan stifled a giggle when she realized that Maggie seemed determined not to be outshone by anything a tropical garden could produce.

Maggie pulled her closer and leaned over sending her peppermint-scented breath wafting in front of her nose. "Do tell me, Susan, do you think this hotel is what it is supposed to be?"

Susan shifted uncomfortably. Below, on the beach, a girl was sitting topless at the edge of the sea. Her fair skin had tanned a deep rose and she faced the sun as though worshipping it. A youth sauntered past her, stopped, and gazed back meaningfully.

"I'm not sure what you mean," Susan said.

"Come now." Maggie squeezed her arm. "You don't have to be coy with me. I know what a blush signifies. Perhaps you've had an experience already?"

The youth turned gracefully and walked back along the sand, stopping behind the topless girl. He stared for a moment then knelt down beside her and whispered into her ear. The tinkling of laughter drifted up to them.

"Experience?" Susan's heart sank as she realized what Maggie meant. "Oh, no! I'm not looking for an *experience*. I fainted, that's all. The heat, jet lag -."

"You can tell me the truth." Maggie's lips parted in a smile of conspiracy.

"I wanted to get away from Los Angeles. After my divorce, I wanted a change. Some freedom. I'm sorry, I don't think this holiday was a good idea now I'm here."

"Then we must make it a good idea!" Maggie gestured at the girl on the beach who had leaned back on her hands and was gazing into the youth's eyes. "Like that."

"Oh, no!" Susan put her hand to her mouth.

"Well, a pretty girl like you could get any man she wants without having to do all that. Not like me, alas." Maggie shook with a dry, painful cough.

"What's the matter?" Susan pulled her arm free. "Are you all right?" she asked anxiously.

"Don't go, dear. Don't leave me."

"Shall I take you back to your cottage."

Maggie looked alarmed. "Not there. I need action."

"I'm sorry?" She was puzzled by what she had said.

Maggie looked keenly at her. "My dear, you sound as though you would like to help me."

"Well, if I could." She wondered what was coming next.

Maggie turned her eyes back to the beach. She pointed, "Look at that!"

The girl was touching the youth's leg. Susan gasped when she saw the girl's hand, vivid against the youth's skin, creep gradually up his thigh.

Maggie pulled her caftan around her. "I've heard it said, dear, that they have rather large equipment."

The youth shifted his stance so that the girl's hand

brushed against his crotch. He laughed, leaping away form her and plunging backward into the sea, showering the girl with spray.

"Do you play tennis, dear?"

Susan swallowed nervously. She was intrigued, envying the blonde girl's freedom and lack of inhibitions. She wondered if she could ever lose her inhibitions and be like that.

"I asked if you play tennis, dear."

"I'm sorry, I didn't hear." The warm feeling surging through her, chilled at the despair in Maggie's voice. "A little," she said sharply.

"You could learn to improve, dear. Why don't you let me pay for your lessons?"

"Whatever for?"

"I do like to give, dear, especially to someone as nice as yourself. I wouldn't want to see you wasting your time on the beach, cheapening yourself like that silly girl. Tennis would be fun, don't you think?"

"I'm not really keen on it."

"The tennis is pro is quite young, dear. He's very nice, actually. I could come and watch him teach you. Then we'd take a little champagne together after your lesson. You, me, and the tennis pro."

Susan stood up, surprising herself at her boldness. She shook her head. She gazed at Maggie, seeing how pathetic she was, trying to buy her company.

"Please don't think I'm being rude, Maggie," she said, keeping her voice steady. "It is very kind of you to offer to pay for tennis lessons but I can afford it myself if I want. I'm sorry, I didn't come here to play tennis, I'm on holiday."

Maggie quivered as though she had been slapped. Her mouth formed a moue of disappointment. "I thought you were my friend."

"I'm sorry, I'm sorry." She moved away, wondering why she was apologizing. She walked as fast as she could in the direction of the girl and the handsome beach boy at the water's edge.

CHAPTER 8

Lyn sat in a wicker chair on the patio of her cottage and watched people ambling up from the beach. A girl with a towel draped around her shoulders was walking toward her. She picked up the Bloody Mary she had mixed for herself from the contents of the cottage's mini-bar fridge, and sipped it thoughtfully. The shadows chasing away the brilliance of the day as the sun was setting made her feel somber rather than happy.

"Hi!"

Lyn raised her eyes warily. The girl stood on the patio in front of her. Lyn waited for the words that would come next. *Haven't I seen you somewhere before?* Lyn longed to forget she was a television face and people wouldn't feel she was someone they had actually met and whom they couldn't quite remember.

"Just arrived?"

She stared at the girl. "Why, yes," she answered in astonishment. The girl seemed to have no idea who she was.

"I thought so. From England?"

Lyn chuckled. "Oh, no! From California."

"You're American?" It was the girl's turn to laugh.

"What's funny about that?"

"Such a long way to come."

"So why is it so funny?" Lyn persisted.

"It isn't really, I suppose." The girl paused and her eyes seemed to be studying Lyn with renewed interest, "I'm from Sweden." Her towel hung loosely over her shoulders, revealing her bare breasts. She had a statuesque body glowing with emphatic good health.

Lyn was suddenly aware that her own figure, matured on a diet of alcohol, Gauloises, and hamburgers, was not as trim as it could be. "Would you like a drink?" she said, waving her Bloody Mary at the girl.

"Do you have a plain tomato juice, nothing in it?"

Lyn snorted. "Are all Swedes so healthy?" She rose from her chair, indicated the spare seat for the girl to sit, and went into the parlor to find another tomato juice. She filled a glass and glanced at the mirror.

Compared with the Swedish girl, she looked dreadful. The pallor of her face, which made her intense and interesting on television, now looked sickly. Her jeans, which she wore with pride in Los Angeles as a neutral uniform, were hot and baggy.

She shrugged, picked up a cigarette pack and strolled back to the patio. The girl's trim, firm figure and shining smile made her prickle with envy.

"Here." Lyn thrust the glass of tomato juice at the girl and threw herself into a chair. She lit a cigarette, wafting a cloud of smoke over the patio.

"Why do Americans smoke so much?" the girl asked, almost accusingly.

"Insecurity. Oral fixation. And because it feels good." Lyn glowered. "Why do Swedish girls look so young. Don't they ever grow old?"

"Oh, yes." The girl grinned over the rim of her glass. "And alcoholic too."

"You won't."

"Who knows?" The girl smiled simply. "In Sweden, our life is very difficult. We work hard, many hours a day. The climate, it is not nice. Very cold. So when we leave Sweden for a holiday, many Swedes do silly things. Some drink too much."

"Others sun bathe too much?" Lyn's eyes flashed.

"Perhaps."

"Too much sun can cause cancer," said Lyn, waving her cigarette.

The Swedish girl gurgled with laughter. "Americans say anything."

Lyn sipped her drink and, watching her, she decided she would prefer to risk cancer trying to look beautiful. She stuffed out her cigarette. "Have you been here long?"

"Two months. I stay more one month."

"Two months!" Lyn was amazed. "How can you stand it here all that time?"

"I told you. Sweden is cold. I work hard, saved my money. Now I'm soaking up the sun, " she waved her hand at the shrubbery surrounding the cottage, "the scenery, and just enjoying myself."

"How? Have you got a boyfriend?"

The girl gave an elaborate shrug.

"What do you do for sex?"

The girl's tanned face took on a deeper color, her blue eyes widening. Then her expression softened and she laughed. "Is that all American women think of?"

"Isn't it what attractive girls in their teens think of?"

"I'm twenty-four." The girl giggled.

Her answer was like a blow to the gut for Lyn. She reached for the Gauloises pack, fumbled to extract a cigarette and then gave up. *The girl is twenty-four,* she thought. *Only six years younger then me. How could I ever get laid here with competition like her!*

"What's your name?" she demanded, angrily throwing the cigarette pack aside.

"Eva."

"Eva, you're six years younger than I am, and you look fucking fantastic. I don't know if you work in films or a factory, but you're spending three months, that's ninety nights, in Africa. It's an obvious question, isn't it? I'm a woman too. Now, tell me, what do you do for sex?"

"You are serious?"

"Listen, honey. I *need* to know." She tried to make the question sound professional but she couldn't keep the passion out of her voice.

Eva seemed baffled, but not embarrassed. "It's not a problem." She shook her head lightly.

"Perhaps not to you, honey." Lyn grinned ruefully. "It might be to me."

"I'm not that fond of men." Eva paused and looked expectantly at Lyn.

"Why not?"

"Such strange questions." Eva shifted uncomfortably in her seat. "Does it matter?"

"Not to me, honey." She drained her drink. "I'm just curious."

"Ah!" Eva sat back and watched her.

"Now, listen, Eva." She leaned forward, forgetting she

was not on camera. "How do you pick up a black stud here?"

Eva's face puckered with disapproval. "An African is a person, not a 'black stud' to be picked up because you want sex!" Her eyes flickered angrily.

"Nice old fashioned values you have in Sweden."

Eva kept quiet.

"Aren't Swedish girls like the rest of us, Eva? It doesn't matter if a guy's black or white, if you want him."

"It does matter," Eva said. "An African deserves respect. Just because he is not white does not mean he has no culture or dignity. What right have you got to abuse him?

"Eva, honey, I don't want to abuse anyone. I only want to know what a girl does in this town when she wants to get laid."

Eva stood up, pulling the towel around her. "I must go," she said. "It's turning chilly."

"Being Swedish, you should be used to the cold."

"I am, but not to you. You make me feel..." Eva searched for a word. "Repellent."

"That's all I need to end a perfect day."

"You came here just for sex, didn't you?" Eva was shaking.

"Sure!" Lyn stood up and reached out to touch Eva's shoulder. "Come on, you can trust me. I want to score too"

The girl twisted away from her grasp. "I think you're revolting!" she said. "You Americans bully everyone to get your own way. But the Africans aren't slaves that you can whip and beat to do what you want."

Lyn reached over calmly and pulled at Eva's towel. Her breasts were proud and rounded, tanned evenly. "Is that the way, Eva?" Lyn said. "I must go topless. Like that. Where's *your* dignity and respect, Eva?"

The girl stared at Lyn in dismay, and then she covered her bare breasts with her hands and fled from the patio.

◆ ◆ ◆ ◆ ◆

Cora was too excited to sleep. She had dozed throughout the flight, refusing the champagne and ignoring the other women in the group. She had been bored and irritable, angry with her mother for packing her off on this idiotic trip. She had sulked during the wait at Nairobi airport for the onward flight, but when the plane landed at Mombasa, she began to take an interest. She suddenly realized that she was now part of a minority: a white girl in a black land.

The guy who had escorted her out of the airport tried to put her at ease. He spoke politely with a singsong accent that made her laugh. He was cute. He had an air of subdued self-confidence that was a contrast to the brashness of the brothers she met with Scobie. Her boyfriend, Scobie, was real smooth, yet at times it seemed to be an act. Not so with this African cat. He was really cool.

She was intrigued to find herself thinking of him. She paced around the room. There was no reason why she should try to sleep when the sun was blazing down outside. Jet lag was for those old cows like Maggie and Lyn who had spent the entire time on the plane getting smashed. She walked across the bedroom floor to the glass door. She slid it open, unlatched the mosquito screen and slid that back too.

She had expected not to be impressed, but the sight of the sea glistening beyond the exotic red and yellow blooms of the bushes surrounding her cottage, was irresistible. She turned back into the room and rummaged through her case until she found her cut-off Levi's. She changed hurriedly, adding a bikini top. She studied herself in the mirror. Boy, was she white! It was time to work on her tan.

She strolled out of the room onto the patio. The sun struck her body like a slap; it's effect exaggerated by the air-conditioned coolness of the room she had just left. She flopped into the plastic chaise longue and stared upward, blinking at the sun shining through the fronds of the coconut palms.

"Isn't it just too much!"

Cora sat up in surprise. All she could see after gazing at the sun was a star-filled blackness. She blinked. Lyn Preston, standing on the patio of the neighboring cottage, was watching her.

"Isn't it glorious?" Lyn said. "Of course, I don't know what this sun will do to my complexion. Show my age, I suppose. But it makes one so relaxed, don't you think?"

Cora looked at Lyn Preston without answering. She wasn't very impressed by her; she always seemed to be trying too hard. It was the sort of thing people did when they were old and wanted to suck up to kids. Who cared if she was famous.

"I'm so relaxed, Cora, I could fall into bed with a dude right now, and let him do everything! Yes, everything."

Cora frowned, wondering what was coming next. The woman was clearly still smashed.

"Don't look so sulky, kid. You know what I mean. It's natural to feel this way. The sun's hot, I'm hot. That's what we're here for, isn't it?"

This puzzled Cora; she tensed as she stared at Lyn. "What do you mean?"

"Interested in what I'm saying now, are you?" Lyn chuckled. "You see I know a thing or two. Isn't that why your Mama sent you on this trip? Been too much trouble at home, screwing around, have you? So Mama's sent you here to get well and truly laid."

Cora was shocked. What was wrong with Lyn?

Lyn seemed to have no idea about the effect of what she had said. She was lighting up another cigarette, blowing the smoke out at the sun. "Can you imagine what it's like being on television every day, Cora?" She seemed about to launch into a reverie.

"It plays hell with your sex life. How can I have a proper relationship with a man who's watched me on TV explaining the issues of the day to millions of viewers. I'm a trophy for him, not a woman." She puffed reflectively on her cigarette.

"So that's why I'm here, kid, to get laid by men who don't know me." Lyn smiled ruefully. "And by men who can do it good, but good!" She blew more smoke in the air and then turned to Cora again. "Now tell me about you. What are you really here for?"

"I don't know."

"Kid, where have you been? Do they still have love in your generation?"

"Yes!" Cora flushed, stirred to a response. "I'm going steady. I don't have your hang-ups. I've got a guy who wants me because of what I am, not because I represent something to him. And he's black."

"Aha!" Lyn ground out her cigarette firmly in the ashtray on the patio table and grinned. "So you're his trophy, too. Is he a good fuck?"

"I ... I don't know. We've never..."

Lyn sniffed with contempt. "Well, when you do get down to it, you'll have the dudes on this trip to compare him with, won't you."

"Is that what you really came to Kenya for?"

"To get laid on safari? Yes." Lyn slapped her hand against her hip in apparent enthusiasm.

"The others?" Cora spoke in a hushed voice, unable to believe it. "Susan and that awful Biddle-Mac woman? Is that what they came for too?"

"Right, kid. This is billed as a Fulfillment Safari, so that's what we're all here for. The F word."

"No!" Cora felt the blood rushing to her face.

"Like I said, the sun's hot here, Cora." Lyn had a mocking glint in her eye. "You must be careful not to have too much, and burn your lovely white skin."

"Why should you think that's why I came on this vacation? You don't know me. Even if you are right about what the others are here for, you are wrong about me. I'm not the same as you!"

She jumped out of the seat, the plastic strips leaving stripes across the bare skin of her back. She was angry with herself for allowing Lyn Preston to goad her into losing her cool. She should have known it would happen because that's what she was famous for doing on television.

Lyn looked smug. "Suit yourself. The only problem is that I have been here three hours now, and haven't been laid yet. Hey what about him?"

Cora looked at where she was pointing; at a tall bellhop lolloping down the path from a guest cottage. "That's gross!" She turned her back on Lyn, disturbed by the ideas she had planted in her head. Surely that was not why her mother had sent on this tour? There had been some mistake.

She stepped off the patio and moved away from the cottages, not hearing what Lyn was shouting at her. She had to walk on the grass verge of the path so that her bare feet didn't burn on the sun-hot concrete slabs. Lyn's words buzzed in her brain with cruel persistence. In despair, she pushed her way through the flower bushes and ran out on to the beach.

The sand scorched her toes. She grimaced and raced for the water's edge. The sea was lapping its way up the sand lethargically, too lazy to move faster in the heat. She splashed into it and collapsed in the shallows so that the waves rolled gently over her back. She rolled over and closed her eyes, feeling the sun's rays probing her face. The sea lifted her from the beach and sucked her out, then rolled her slowly back in again.

◆ ◆ ◆ ◆ ◆

A shadow lengthened on the sand at the water's edge. Its dark shape drew closer as Cora lay spread-eagled in the surf, letting the warm water trickle between her legs. The shadow paused, then swelled until it fell across her face like a clenched fist in front of the setting sun.

She opened her eyes with a start. The light that outlined the shape looming above her was dazzling. When she turned to sit up, the sea held her, so she fell backward into the water with a splash. She glanced along the beach, relieved when she saw she was not alone.

Tourists were splashing in the surf near her, while others were lazing under the thatched roofs of the safari-style sun shelters. A heavy-set woman squeezed into a shocking pink swimming costume was jogging with determination along the beach toward her.

"You frightened me." She sat up again and shook her head, splashing the sea out of her hair.

"I'm sorry." The man's voice was soft and melodious. Although his face was hidden as he had his back to the sun, she could see he was wearing the uniform of the tourist trade: a safari suit. He was smiling. She moved out of the sun's glare so she could see him clearly.

"It's you!"

"You sound pleased."

"Yes, I am. I didn't think I'd see you again."

"I work for Mr. Royce. It's my job to see that you are enjoying yourself, that everything is all right."

Cora looked at him carefully. Her head was level with his thighs. She swallowed and raised her eyes. "What's your name?"

"Mindelo."

"I'll try to remember that." She held up her hand and the youth grasped it, helping her to her feet. When she was standing beside him, he released her slowly. She felt shy, almost trembling. "Do you get a lot of visitors, I mean, does Mr. Royce -?"

Before he could answer, the large woman who had been pounding resolutely along the sea's edge, splashed up to them. She stopped and, with her wide chest heaving and her whole body shaking with rolls of fat, glared suspiciously from Mindelo to Cora and back again.

Cora was angered by the interruption. There were vibrations between herself and Mindelo that had been lost because of the woman's arrival. She turned her head to avoid her gaze.

"Ya!" the fat woman said emphatically. "Zey haf guards, ya? Call ze guards." She waved her hand in the direction of the palm grove at the entrance to the hotel's gardens.

Cora looked and saw two men in gray uniforms watching them. "Why the hell should I call the guards?"

"Ze black boys," said the woman with a withering glance at Mindelo. "Zey rape."

"Mind your own fucking business," Cora said angrily, reaching for Mindelo's hand and clasping it to her chest.

"I tell you!" The woman waved her finger in her face and resumed her ponderous jogging along the beach. Cora stared after her in disgust.

"Now you've upset her," Mindelo said, gently withdrawing his hand.

"She deserves it. What business of hers is it, what I do?"

"She was being kind. She wanted to warn you about what could happen here."

"Is it true what she said then?" She remembered what Lyn had been saying. Mindelo merely shrugged.

She studied him. His skin was the soft complexion of honey, with opaque eyes that hinted at unfulfilled promise. His hair was cut short and cleanly shaped, his nose was small above fine, sensitive lips. He ignored her question and began to walk up the sand. She followed him.

"Mr. Royce sent me," he said briskly. "To ask if you've taken your prophylactics."

"What?" She stared at him in astonishment.

He laughed. "Against malaria. There are tablets in your bathroom. Please remember to take one every day."

"Oh, yeah." She stopped walking and sighed. She was wondering if this cat was always charming or was he just putting it on for her. A sun-tanned woman in a bikini waved to him. He bowed to her and smiled.

"Is there anything else you have to tell me?" she asked, starting up the slope toward the shade of the trees. She wondered who the woman was and what was the relationship, if any, that Mindelo had with her.

"Yes, Miss Berger." His face was serious with concern. "The sun here is very strong, especially for someone with a fair complexion, like you. Until you are accustomed to it, you should keep your body protected. Take only a little sun each day, increasing the amount gradually."

"You sound like a guide book, Mindelo."

"It is necessary."

They entered the shade of the trees, Mindelo standing aside to let her walk in front of him. A middle-aged couple approached them on the path. The man beamed at Mindelo and Cora watched the eyes of his wife. They brightened as Mindelo smiled at her and wished her good afternoon. Again, she felt a stab of apprehension.

"You're a sexy cat, Mindelo," she blurted out when the couple had passed, "All the women here get hot just looking at you."

"Miss Berger!" He lowered his eyes.

"It's Cora. Call me Cora. Try it."

"It wouldn't be proper. You're a guest."

"Why the hell not?"

"Mr. Royce -."

"Stuff Mr. Royce! I'm telling you to call me Cora. If your boss complains, tell him I said so."

"Yes, Miss."

"Shoot! I'm Cora, not Miss."

"Yes, Cora." Mindelo looked away unhappily.

"Why are you so formal?"

"It's our custom to be polite, Miss Cora."

"In the States it is the custom to call one's friends by their first name. I'd like you to think of me as a friend, Mindelo." She could swear he blushed. "You're something else!"

"Excuse me, er, Cora?"

"It doesn't matter." She halted and reached over and twisted the top button of his open neck safari shirt. His skin was smooth and hairless under the cotton fabric. She extended her finger and touched him lightly on his cheek.

"You ain't wasting your time, kid!"

She dropped her hand and swung around in the direction of the mocking voice. Lyn Preston parted the branches of the hibiscus bushes and stepped onto the path beside her. She stood with her hands on her hips and her hard eyes gloating. "I see there are no holds barred in this game!"

Cora flushed deeply. Mindelo bowed his head, mumbled something, and scuttled off down the path. Cora turned away so Lyn couldn't see her face. She felt she would cry. With her head down, she ran behind the bougainvillaea bushes to her cottage.

CHAPTER 9

Charles Royce sat at the desk assigned to tour operators in the reception hall. He was leafing through a pile of papers with one hand and holding a cold Tusker in the other. He put down the papers, raised the bottle to his lips and drank deeply.

Mindelo stood in front of him, waiting until Royce nodded his head for him to speak. "I've checked on all of them," he said, when he saw Royce was ready. "The room service boy says he's taken two bottles of champagne to the cottage of Mrs. Biddle-Macdonald. She made him open one and gave him twenty-five cents."

Royce heaved a sigh of bitterness. "That's the type I loathe. A rich lush who's mean. What's she doing here anyway?"

Mindelo shrugged. "The blonde is prowling around as randy as a lion in heat. The other one, Susan Ross, keeps apologizing to everyone she meets and seems bewildered at being here."

Royce gazed mournfully at the empty Tusker bottle in his hand. "It's bad," he said, thinking aloud. "They should be sleeping. What happened to jet lag?" He shook his head. "I've got an awful feeling these four bitches are going to give me more trouble than they're worth." He raised his head and looked at Mindelo.

"What about the girl? She's Amelia Berger's daughter. Doesn't have her looks. I remember seeing her mother in films years ago. Thought she was dead."

"Not dead, sir. She was on the beach."

Royce scowled. "The daughter?"

"Yes, sir. Cora."

Royce's eyes narrowed and he gazed sharply at Mindelo's face. "Cora, is it? Not 'Miss Cora?'"

Mindelo avoided Royce's glance and stared across the reception hall to where Myna, one of the receptionists, was checking the guest register. She smiled at him behind Royce's back.

"Mindelo!" Royce's shout was edged with anger. "Don't

forget my rule, boy. I'll have your guts for garters if you do. Leave the Fulfillment Safari guests alone. *That's* not your work."

Mindelo's mouth twitched. "Not interfere, sir!" he said hastily, annoyed with himself for letting Royce get the better of him. "She by herself. You say she special, I take special care."

"You bloody well better had, boy!" Royce pounded his clenched fist on top of the desk. Mindelo hadn't seen him so angry since the time he had forgotten to put bitters in his pink gin.

"I'm warning you! Just because she's young and with this group, doesn't mean she's like the others who come here. Her mother didn't send her here to get shagged by you! You understand?" Royce leaned across the desk and waved the empty Tusker bottle at Mindelo's crotch.

"You keep that pecker buttoned up, or I'll chop it off, you hear?"

Mindelo stepped back awkwardly. Royce's outburst had surprised him. He glanced over at the reception desk and was relieved that Myna had gone and didn't hear what he had said. She was always telling him not to let Royce bully him. That wasn't easy when he had to let the white man think he owned him, even though it was really he who controlled Royce.

The urgent ringing of the phone broke the tension. "Answer that!"

Mindelo kept his defiance buried behind his bland expression. He reached for the phone. It seemed to erupt in his hand. He listened for a few seconds then covered the mouthpiece. "It's Miss Lyn Preston."

"Deal with her."

"Not me." His eyes glinted as he saw a way of riling Royce. "You said *that's* not my work."

Royce glared at him and snatched the phone from his hand. "Royce here," he drawled, disguising his fury. "Can I be of service?"

"You bet you can, Royce. I want a man." Lyn's voice squawked angrily out of the telephone and Royce put his hand over the receiver and looked helplessly at Mindelo.

Mindelo avoided his look, pleased at his discomfort.

"I beg your pardon, Miss Preston." Royce tried to sound soothing.

"I've been in this hotel for four hours, Royce, and there's been no action. The bellboy took off like he'd shit his pants when I suggested a little fun. I've walked the length of the beach and there's nothing with more than a cocktail sausage in his bath pants. Muldoon promised me satisfaction. I think I've been conned."

"Miss Preston, Lyn, rest assured I personally will do everything to see that you are satisfied."

"I don't want you, Royce. I want a well-hung stud on room service. What the hell do you think I've paid for?"

"Yes, yes, Lyn. Everything will be arranged. We must keep our guests happy, what!" Royce mopped his brow. "May I suggest you try the beach after sundown, if you want a little, uh, adventure. The barracks is nearby and the soldiers are, uh, very amenable."

"Look, Royce, I'm not looking for a military gang bang. Just send a tasty buck to my room, and fast." The telephone clicked as she slammed down the receiver.

Royce stared at the instrument in his hand and replaced it unhappily. Mindelo was watching his anguish with interest. "You hear that?"

"Yes, sir."

"Bloody Americans. They think money buys everything. I hope she's just suffering from jet lag and won't be so randy all the time." He drummed his fingers on the desktop. "Well, what are you waiting for?"

"Me, sir?"

"Get your bloody arse out of here and fix her up."

He gulped. "Me, sir"

"Not you, boy!" Royce's face reddened and he seemed to be gasping for breath. He slapped the desk. "My god! Where's your brain, boy? Try to help me, Mindelo, please." His voice was thick with sarcasm.

"You can round up someone to shag her, can't you? What about Njonjo? Yes!" Royce smirked. "When he gets his antenna up our spoilt little TV star, she'll not give me any trouble again. Go for Njonjo."

Mindelo smiled with pleasure. "Can I take the bike, sir?"
Royce nodded, waving his hand to dismiss him.

With a cheery wave at Myna, now back behind the reception desk, he stepped out of the lobby. His spirits soared. Now he knew how to get his revenge on Charles Royce for cancelling his leave.

♦ ♦ ♦ ♦ ♦

Mindelo pushed his bicycle along the narrow trail. He was hot but the thought of what he was about to do absorbed him. He had ridden the four miles from the Mpingo Beach Hotel to the small village of Utange as fast as he could.

He rang the bell on his bicycle to let Njonjo know he was coming. The trail through the scrub curved around a huge baobab tree and entered a clearing. There were three huts ahead of him. Mindelo smiled and leaned his bicycle against a coconut tree.

Small children, their naked bodies caked with dust and brown like the soil under their feet, scampered around him, their grimy fingers tugging at his pants and shirt-jacket. Mindelo bent down and hugged each one, laughing happily.

He could see Njonjo lying on his bed in the shade outside his mud-walled hut. The bed, made of wood and cord, seemed too fragile to support the enormous bulk of the man. A woman squatting on the ground shelling coffee beans, rose as Mindelo approached. She walked around the hut to the back.

Njonjo opened one eye. He gazed up serenely and then opened the other eye. He sat up lazily and greeted Mindelo in Swahili.

Mindelo smiled politely and enquired about the health of Njonjo's wives and children. While he was speaking, a child brought out a small wooden chair from the hut for him to sit on.

When the ritual of greeting had been completed, silence descended on the two men.

Mindelo studied Njonjo carefully, waiting the moment to begin. Njonjo himself was in no hurry. He was a big man who moved slowly with perfect grace. His only clothing was a faded *kikoi*, a long piece of material fastened around his waist. The extended bulge under his *kikoi* drew Mindelo's glance.

"Hah!" Njonjo said with a chuckle. "When you disturb a man who is hunting in his dreams, he needs time to lower his spear."

"A man who hunts should not dream. He might fire his spear at a spirit."

"Hah! Mindelo, you are wise." Njonjo nodded his head with approval. "Do not worry about Njonjo. His weapon is always ready." He reached under the fold of his *kikoi* with his long fingers. "Even now."

Mindelo did not know Njonjo's age. His big body was untouched by years, his skin shiny and his muscles hard. In contrast to his great strength, his face was softly featured. His cap of thick hair crowned small ears, a handsome brow, languorous eyes and full, ardent lips. Njonjo had never left the Kilifi district where he was born, yet he was known far beyond Africa for his ability to satisfy women.

"You have come a long way to see Njonjo," the big man said. "I was expecting you."

Mindelo was surprised. "How?"

"My brother who drives a taxi, you know. Another group of your women from America has arrived?"

"Yes, that's why..." He lapsed into silence and let Njonjo talk.

"Those women are so foolish. Sometimes they make me careless with my work. They are so easily spent, not like my Digo wives." He gestured with his massive hand around the compound. "Those white women, they do not live well in their homelands." He held up his huge fist. "My finger alone can satisfy them."

Mindelo joined in Njonjo's laughter. "You have worked hard to earn your reputation, Njonjo," he said.

"You are right, Mindelo, I have. I like a challenge. I hope your new group of females will be suitable for my talent."

"I hope so too, Njonjo. That's why I am here."

"You have something special?" Njonjo lazily shifted his body.

"No, nothing."

"What do you mean?"

Mindelo watched Njonjo's eyes slowly darken. He swallowed nervously to keep the truth blurting out from his lips unaided. "There is nothing," he repeated, glancing away.

"Nothing? No white women?"

There was a pause and he felt Njonjo's eyes probing him.

"I am sure my brother said four *wanawake*, white women, arrived at the hotel this morning."

Mindelo's heart was thumping. "It is true, Njonjo. I cannot lie to you." He fiddled nervously with the collar of his shirt. "When I say nothing, I mean nothing that deserves your mastery."

The word was well chosen for it pleased Njonjo. He repeated it, rolling it slowly over his tongue. "Mastery, hah, *mastery!*"

"Mr. Royce himself sent me to you," Mindelo continued, the palms of his hands clammy with nervousness at his lie. "He presents his compliments to the great Njonjo and says your services will not be required this time. Next time, yes, but not now."

"My services?" Njonjo sniffed with suspicion. "Why not?" His voice deepened. "Did he say why not?"

"Yes. I'm sure you know already. You have your eyes everywhere. Did they not see the *wanawake* for themselves? One is a child of fifteen years who resembles a boy, another is an old woman whose only desire is a bottle, the third is a shy lady who is scared of the dark, and the fourth a female eunuch."

"Hah." Njonjo fell silent.

Mindelo waited uneasily while the big man considered what he had said. Whether he believed the story or not, Mindelo had to convince him to keep away from the hotel. "Mr. Royce..." he began again.

Njonjo raised his head and waited for him to continue.

"Mr. Royce was very disturbed about asking me to bring you this news. He felt you might be offended. I told him that Njonjo would not be offended. I said that Njonjo is a proud man who cannot be asked to waste himself on such women. I told Mr. Royce it was his duty to inform you about these inferior women sent to us."

He paused and gazed anxiously at the big man perched like a gorilla on the edge of his bed. He was perturbed when he realized that Njonjo was scowling with disbelief.

Suddenly he had an idea. There was a hundred shillings in his shirt pocket, which Lyn Preston had given him as a tip at the airport. He had planned to save it for his sister's wedding. He took out the note and folded it across his thigh. Njonjo's scowl vanished.

"Mr. Royce asked me to give you this, Njonjo. I said you would not accept it."

"Why not?" Njonjo withdrew the hand he had stretched out to take the money.

"I told him you are an honorable man and did not beg for money. I said you would not take the money without rendering some service in return."

"Hah," said Njonjo, nodding his head at Mindelo's wisdom. "You are right."

"However, there is the matter of compensation."

"Compensation?" Njonjo scratched his chin in doubt.

"Yes. I told Mr. Royce that you should receive compensation for not being able to perform your usual services."

"Hah, of course." Njonjo held out his hand, a broad grin spreading across his face.

Mindelo smiled too and handed over the money. "You do not have to come to the Mpingo Beach Hotel for ten days, Njonjo. You are being compensated because there is nothing for you."

"Right, Mindelo. I admire your concern. Wisdom is not always gray-haired."

Mindelo smiled happily at the compliment. He took his leave with proper ceremony from Njonjo and the dusty children. He mounted his bicycle with a light heart. He was sure he had put Charles Royce in big trouble. It was fine revenge for cancelling his leave.

CHAPTER 10

The knocking on the door was drowned by the sound of the shower. Lyn only heard it when she stepped from the bathroom wrapped in a towel and padded back to the bedroom. The tap was so timid; she stopped to see if she had heard it properly. Someone was on the patio, knocking softly on the glass door.

"Yes?" she said, catching her breath hopefully.

"I heard you in there," said a voice, a female voice. "I hope I'm not troubling you."

Lyn sighed. "Oh, no." She scowled as she switched on a lamp. The room was a mess, but what the hell. She walked to the door and rolled it open.

"I was just wondering..."

Lyn's anticipation faded at the sight of Susan Ross standing nervously on the patio. "Come to borrow a cup of sugar?"

Susan looked blank. "I'm sorry to disturb you." She was wearing a simple dress, which Lyn thought she must have made herself. Her legs were bare and she wore sandals. Her hair was neatly combed and straight, damp from swimming. Her face was plain, no make up. Her eyes glimmered anxiously.

Lyn relented. "Come in, Sue. Have a drink?" She beckoned Susan to follow her across the bedroom into the parlor. "There's plenty here. Fix yourself something. I'm on vodka." She moved back into the bedroom to get dressed.

"I don't drink, thank you."

"Oh, god! It's one of those days." Lyn slapped her forehead. "Well, could I trouble you to fix me one?" She turned from the doorway. "I'm going to put my glad rags on, not that it makes any difference, I'm sure."

She pulled out a Bill Blue gown from the closet and studied it. It had traveled well. White always made her look good, even though she felt dishonest wearing it. She dressed carefully. She didn't want to look as frumpish as the Ross girl. She admired herself in the mirror. "Back to battle," she said, trying her smile. "I can't find my cigarettes," she called to Susan. "Are they in there?"

"I saw them outside. I'll get them." Susan brought the pack and handed it to her.

She gazed at Susan in silence for a few seconds, then accepted the cigarettes and lit one. She sat on the couch. "Are you for real?"

"I beg your pardon?" Susan blushed and handed the vodka to Lyn.

"Oh, forget it!" She sipped at the vodka then pulled heavily on the cigarette "Of course you're for real. Some people are made nice." She looked rueful.

"In my line, you tend to overlook that." There was a pause while she waited for Susan to speak. The silence made her restless, so she broke it herself. "I guess I miss the TV studio. This place is too damn quiet."

"I think it's heavenly." Susan's plain face came to life. "I've never known anything like this. It's exciting, and frightening too, if you see what I mean."

"I don't." She drained her glass, determined not to let Susan depress her with her silly parochialism. "Why did you come to see me?"

The fire in Susan's eyes died and she frowned. "I'm sorry to trouble you, only I don't know what to do, or who to ask. I'm looking for Mrs. Biddle-Macdonald. I wondered if you've seen her?"

Lyn shook her head.

"I went to her cottage," she continued in a voice fraught with concern. "She's not there. I hope she's all right."

"Why shouldn't she be?"

"Well, we had a row, you see. She seemed so upset, I wanted to apologize."

"What for? It's probably the best thing you could have done, standing up to the old bitch. Don't worry about her. You're here to have fun, aren't you? That's probably what Maggie is doing."

"Having fun? I don't think so."

"Sure she is. She's got more guts than the rest of us. She's probably giving head to some stud on the beach right now."

Susan stiffened. "Why, why are you being so rude about her? She's got her funny ways but I think underneath she is just a lonely old lady."

"So what. Can't a lonely old lady blow an African dude if she wants?"

Susan blanched and fingered her throat nervously.

"Don't tell me you're prejudiced, Sue. A sweet thing like you!"

"I think you're just trying to shock me. You're making fun of me, aren't you?"

Lyn shrugged. "I seem to be saying all the wrong things this afternoon. Must be the vodka. Don't worry about Maggie. She's survived until now without you."

Susan glanced at her reproachfully.

"Oh, god!" Lyn stubbed out her cigarette on the ice cubes in the glass. "You give me horrors looking at me like that," she said thickly. "So what do you think when you see Lyn Preston, the tough television star, dissolving into depressing reality in front of your eyes, eh? I'm not super woman because I'm on prime time TV, Sue. I'm as lonely and as fucked up as Maggie or you, honey."

"I'm sorry."

"For me? What the hell!"

"Not for you. I shouldn't have bothered you. I'll go and look for Maggie."

"Sure, kid." She sprawled across the couch. "Try the beach. If you see something worthwhile, send him up for me."

Susan got up to go. She hesitated. "There's a notice on the beach."

"A notice!" Lyn laughed, a bitter sound. "What does it say?"

Susan peered across the room, uncertain if she was being mocked. She had memorized the sign word for word. "It says," she recited slowly, "the management wishes to remind guests not to walk on the beach in the evening after 6pm, for their own security."

"My god!" Lyn scrambled up from the couch.

"It's after six now," said Susan.

"I know!" She headed across the room.

"Where, where are you going?"

"Where the hell do you think I'm going? To the beach?"

"To look for Maggie?"

"To look for me. That really must be where the action is."

◆ ◆ ◆ ◆ ◆

Mindelo dismounted from his bicycle and wheeled it across the forecourt to the hotel. He grinned at the security guard who waved at him grudgingly. The guard's reaction was the kind he often encountered in is dealings with small-minded people in official positions. His status depended solely on his relationship with Mr. Royce and Mindelo resented that, even as he encouraged it.

His resentment warmed him as he leaned the bicycle against the trunk of a tree. He was pleased with the evening's work. He had informed every beach boy and gigolo he knew that there were no Americans for them for 10 days. He told them that Royce had instructed the security guards to run them off the beach. They believed him.

Sometimes Mindelo wondered why white women came to Kenya for their men. Did they not have men in their own country? Nobody, not even Charles Royce, had explained to him the reason for a wealthy white lady wanting to lie with a fool like Njonjo. Njonjo was rough and unused to white ways. He, Mindelo, knew about white women, but none of them ever wanted him. Was that because they believed he belonged to Royce?

"Boy!" The cry startled Mindelo. He raised his head. Charles Royce was bearing down on him, his face red with anger. "Boy, you've really done it this time! Two hours I've been waiting for you."

Royce stood in front of him with his hands bunched into fists. Mindelo was unimpressed. He knew Royce would never strike him. He needed him too much. It was his power over the Englishman. He played his role, but it was he who owned Royce, not the other way round.

"I was busy, bwana," he answered contritely. "Not my fault, sir."

"Who the hell's fault is it, then? Mine?"

Mindelo saw that Royce had not been lonely. His vivid cheeks and foul breath showed he had spent his time in the company of a whisky bottle. He tried to edge Royce off the path so the guests wouldn't see him.

"Mr. Royce, sir." He lowered his voice. "Something terrible has happened."

"Uh? What's that?"

Mindelo looked across the path to see if anyone was watching. The thatched beach bar was opposite them. The happy hour drinkers were perched on stools gazing out blearily at the blackness above the beach. Mindelo nodded toward them as a warning to Royce.

"What the hell's the matter with you, boy?" Royce sniffed suspiciously. "I ought to beat the living daylights out of you. There's work to do. I've got the manager's cocktail party to attend in a few minutes."

"Sir!" Mindelo spoke in a whisper.

"Speak up, boy!"

"I would have come sooner, sir, but I was busy. You told me to arrange a buck."

"Yes?" Royce looked around quickly; none of the American women were in sight. He dropped his voice too. "Well?"

"No, sir, not well. Njonjo's sick. He's got the clap. No good for three weeks, sir."

"Damn the bugger! There's others though."

"That's what delayed me, sir. I searched for everyone I knew."

"Everyone?"

"Yes, sir. One's gone to Nairobi, another is preparing for his marriage, another's got religion, one of them's on safari and the only other man who's any good is booked by a Marchioness and her husband at the Beach Club."

"Don't bother me with details. You're late!"

Mindelo bowed his head. "I've failed, sir. I can't find a buck to satisfy your Americans."

"They're not my Americans!"

"No, sir." Mindelo smiled to himself. Royce was rattled. "There's nothing more I can do," he added. "May I go home?"

"No!"

"I should prepare your supper, sir."

"Blast the supper!" Royce laid his hand on Mindelo's

shoulder to steady himself. "Why is it when I want those buggers I can't get them? Any other time and they would be begging me to have them for a shilling." He weaved uncertainly.

Mindelo flinched and pulled away. "What shall I do, sir?" He tried to keep his feeling of triumph out of his voice. Now he had Royce in a stew!

"Wait in the Landrover until I am ready to go."

"Okay, boss!" He swaggered down the path and glanced back briefly to see the effect of his lies. It was super! Royce was shuffling toward the bar with his shoulders hunched in despair. He felt a brief spasm of conscience and then began to fell lightheaded at how easy it had been.

Perhaps, he thought, *the Americans would get angry and leave*. Then he could go to Kaloleni for his sister's wedding. He clapped his hands together with delight.

"Something's turned you on."

Mindelo spun around. He was dismayed that his instincts had let him down and not warned him that someone was watching. His victory over Royce had made him grow careless. "Good evening, miss," he said politely, hiding his surprise.

"Not 'Miss'. It's Cora." The joyful warbling of the insects and lizards in the gardens filled the night air. Cora patted the bench beside her. "Come and sit here. I want to talk to you."

"I'm sorry, miss. It's not permitted."

"Cora."

"It's not permitted, Miss Cora."

"I said Cora, goddamit! Why are you so damned respectful? You're just as good as I am, We're equals, you know."

He peered at the girl and frowned. Why did foreigners like to break traditions as though they were barriers, instead of accepting them as pathways guiding behavior? "I'm sorry, Cora. It's our way. I didn't mean to offend."

The girl stood up and came close to him. "All this scraping and bowing makes me sick. Do you enjoy sucking ass all the time?"

"It's my job to be courteous, as well as my upbringing and good nature." He licked his lips nervously.

"Well, be courteous and good natured and talk to me. I'm feeling homesick."

He stepped backward in alarm. There was a gleam in the girl's eye that confused him. "Th...there is a cocktail party," he stammered. "For the hotel guests."

"I know that." Cora scowled again. "That's no fun. No one my age there, only some gross WASPS. What do you do in the evenings?"

"Me?" He was unused to eyes as intense as hers. He felt weak and looked away. "I don't do anything."

"Of course you do. You'd go out of your mind otherwise. What about movies, or a disco? Where do you take your girl?"

He was shocked. "I don't have a girl." He wanted to run from this forceful American. Something about her made him feel threatened. "Excuse me, miss. I must go."

She caught his wrist and squeezed it. "I'm not letting you go until you call me Cora."

"Cora, Cora, Cora!" He pulled his wrist free and stared at her. She was making him angry. Suddenly she laughed.

"Now you're acting like a man."

"Am I?" He felt like turning around and walking away from the girl.

"You didn't answer my question."

He considered, trying to remember what she had asked. Her energy unsettled him. "There's a disco here at the hotel, and another at the Beach Club. You'll meet young people there."

"That's for tourists!" The girl looked scornful. "Where do you go, Mindelo? Somewhere ethnic."

"Ethnic?" He was puzzled by the word. "I stay at home when I'm not working. Mr. Royce doesn't like me to go out."

Cora's brow furrowed with surprise. "You *live* with that faggot?"

"Excuse me?" He frowned again at another strange word. The girl was criticizing him and he wasn't sure why.

"You don't know anything, do you?" Cora grinned. "That's what makes you so cute. Not like Scobie, he's my man back home in LA. Mama hates him. I wonder what she'd make of you?"

"Me?" Mindelo twisted his hands together nervously.

"You're not gay, are you? I couldn't stand that."

He swallowed, wondering what he was supposed to say. The girl was speaking words he had never heard before. With her spiky hair and fierce expression, she resembled a young Masai *moran*, a warrior. She seemed to be at war with something, or somebody.

Suddenly he felt a new emotion, a tension that seemed to be bringing them together. Something was stirring within him, hard and demanding. The girl recognized it too. She reached up and gripped his shoulders. He tried to move away but she came closer, raising her face to his. He caught his breath, unable to move. Her hands slipped around his waist and pulled him to her. She placed her lips gently on his.

He was startled, wanting to respond. Instead, he twisted his head and wriggled out of her embrace.

"You're not gay!" Cora giggled triumphantly. She turned and ran down the path, leaving an echo of laughter hovering on the night air.

He rubbed his lips and stared after her. He guessed that she had kissed him as a kind of bravado, and that she was just using him for her own fun. Yet she had captivated him. Her lips were soft and tasted sweeter than a Lamu mango. Her searching eyes haunted him.

One day, he vowed, *I will have that girl. One day, soon, she will be mine.*

CHAPTER 11

The manager's cocktail party was a weekly event at the Mpingo Beach Hotel. It encouraged new guests to meet each other and provided entertainment on an otherwise dull evening. Mrs. Biddle-Macdonald who, during her three marriages, had stayed in most of the world's grand hotels, was appalled by the idea.

It was quite unlikely, she thought, that anyone above the status of Food & Beverage manager would be there, and she certainly did not want to meet other guests.

After the initial impact of the luxury of the beach cottage and the handsome stewards had worn off, Maggie realized that the Mpingo Beach Hotel was a sham. It was not a hotel like the Carlton in Cannes, or even the Cloisters at Sea Island; it was a processing plant.

"Pax" (short for passengers; they weren't even afforded the dignity of being called guests) were shuttled to the plant from the flying tubes that brought them from their northern countries. Ten of fifteen days later, bloated, tanned and euphoric, they were packed back in those tubes and returned to the slaughterhouse of their humdrum existence.

It was the same routine at beach resorts throughout the world. Maggie felt she had been duped. Mpingo Beach Hotel was not what she expected: a place where her whims would be indulged and her fantasies come true, according to Muldoon's brochure.

It was no more than a vacation-package factory where "pax" were obliged to follow the rules if they wanted to enjoy themselves. Not Maggie! She made the rules.

She began to perspire, even in the air-conditioned atmosphere of the cottage, when she considered the ignominy that she, Mrs. Margaret Biddle-Macdonald of Bel Air and Boston, should be staying in such a place. It defied her principles.

What weakness had led her willingly to Muldoon? Such a strange whimsy, and now she was paying for it, not just with money, which she could easily afford, but also with time, which she could not.

The persistent tapping on her cottage door and the timid cry of "Maggie" increased her distress. She recognized the voice of that nonentity, Susan Ross. She cursed under her breath and retreated to her bedroom where she couldn't hear. The girl had refused to help her snare the tennis pro, so why should she have anything more to do with her?

She surveyed the interior of her cottage. The bedroom had a king-size bed, lots of closet space, and a bathroom of ample proportions. The parlor was furnished in a baroque hunter's lodge style, with over-stuffed chairs, fur rugs, and animal skins hanging on the walls. The cocktail refrigerator was stocked for the thirstiest hunter. In general, the accommodation was tolerable. Providing she could find a suitable attendant, she could make herself comfortable.

Her eye fell again on the invitation to the manager's party. It would be too humiliating to go, Maggie knew, but she wanted to see the limey who was Muldoon's representative. So she dawdled in her dressing, sipping a large gin while she considered her tactics. When her wig was in place and the ravages of age toned down by make-up, she called the front desk.

"Send a boy to escort me to the manager's party," she demanded.

"I'm sorry, miss, we can't do that."

"Nonsense. Of course you can. What about the tennis pro? He can't be playing tennis at night. I want him."

"He's on the court, miss. It's floodlit."

"Well, send someone else then."

"We don't have staff for that, Mrs. Biddle-Macdonald."

Maggie paused when she heard the receptionist saying her name. That was a good sign. "Let me speak to the manager," she said.

"The manager is at the cocktail party. You could speak to him there."

She sighed and hung up. She drained her drink, let herself out of the cottage and set off with determination along the garden path. To her annoyance the manager had left the party by the time she found her way there. She snatched a drink from a passing waiter and posed irritably at the entrance until Charles Royce noticed her and hurried over.

"Did you have a good rest, Mrs. Biddle-Macdonald?"

The care in the way he addressed her was not lost on Maggie. She gazed at him archly over the pool of gin in her glass and waited for him to grovel.

"The tempo of life here is ideal for relaxation, especially after the pace of Los Angeles, don't you find?"

She studied him slowly. He was wearing a buff-colored shirt jacket with embroidered pockets. A red handkerchief with white dots was knotted around his neck.

"I'm not here to relax, Royce!" she said, pitching her voice to a stage whisper that could be heard by the circle of guests standing nearby. "I'm here for more than that!" She nudged her elbow into Royce's waist, making him splutter.

"We do go on a balloon safari...," Royce began.

"Balloon?" She drained her gin in astonishment. "What do you mean, *balloon*?"

"It's a superb way to see the game, actually."

"Listen, Royce." Her voice took on a hard edge. "The only game for me should be in my bedroom, not in a balloon! Arrange it, Royce, arrange it."

She drew away from him with a haughty glare. She was sweating and could feel the wetness forming on the wispy hairs of her upper lip. She dabbed at her face with a lace handkerchief, dislodging her wig slightly and adding to her strained appearance.

Unaware of this, she barged into a group of guests, which split apart at her approach so she sailed right through them. There was only one person in her way, staring around at the others as though she were lost.

"Susan, dear," Maggie cried, filling her voice with warmth and forgiveness. She was determined not to be left alone now she had put Royce in his place. She would settle her score with Susan another time. She opened her arms to embrace her. "How lovely to see you."

Susan pulled away. "I was looking for you."

"To apologize, I suppose. How right you are. All is forgiven, dear. Is there anything of interest here?"

Susan flushed with discomfort. "Are you all right? I went to your cottage but you weren't there."

Maggie ignored Susan's question and fastened her fingers on her arm for support. She gazed around the poolside patio where the guests were gathered, then switched her attention to the waiters weaving their way through them. She sighed with despair and turned back to Susan. "That's a pretty dress, dear," she said tartly.

"Do you think so? I made it myself."

"I thought perhaps you did. They do have a boutique here, dear. You could buy yourself something nice for the evenings." She pulled Susan's arm before she had the opportunity to digest the insult. "Come, dear child, let's liven up this dreadful party."

Maggie bellowed over the heads of the guests for a waiter. When one came sheepishly to her side, she pressed a drink from his tray into Susan's hand and took two for herself. "It's awful stuff, dear. Drink up and take courage. Now where shall we find some men worth meeting?"

"I don't want to meet anyone."

"Nonsense, dear. You must, you must. That's what you're here for, isn't it?"

"I don't know why I'm here." Susan sounded distressed. "Please, Maggie, people are staring. There's something I must tell you."

"Is there?" She glared at Susan with distaste.

"It is important."

Maggie's cry of exasperation could be heard above the babble of cocktail chatter. "Go ahead, dear," she said wearily. "I'm all ears."

"It's about Lyn Preston."

Maggie's face went rigid. "I don't want to hear about that woman."

"She's disappeared."

"At last, some good news."

"She went off to the beach by herself. I think she was...," Susan paused. "Drunk."

"Good for her!" Maggie was annoyed. This Susan Ross really was a dreadful pain. "Have some more gin, dear."

"No, thank you. I must tell someone about Lyn. She might need help."

Maggie's eyes glinted. "Of course she needs help. We all

need help." She squeezed Susan's hand and blundered off into the crowd to see if she could waylay one of the waiters who had caught her eye.

◆ ◆ ◆ ◆ ◆

Lawi was a fisherman. He was 38 years old, with a pock-marked face laced with an imperfect beard. His eyes, long accustomed to searching out his prey in the dark, were reddened with fatigue. He was naked, fishing with his net close to the reef, when his ears picked up an extra sound above the splashing of the sea.

He peered through the darkness, his senses tingling. When he saw the woman strolling along the illuminated section of the beach, he hastily gathered up his net. It was empty. He wound it into a sling in his hand, and crept out of the sea. He withdrew into the darkness and sank to the ground, waiting for her to come to him.

There had been no fish for four nights. Lawi's children were hungry; his woman wanted money. He knew what to do. He had heard his friends talking about these rich tourists as they shared a calabash of *pombe* together. His friends laughed at him because he went fishing every night. They told him that tourists would be better fish for his net. He touched the net cautiously, testing his swing.

The woman left the arc of light embracing the hotel's area of the beach, and walked into the darkness. Lawi rose silently and tracked her across the sand so stealthily that not even an animal would have heard him. He tensed, cast the net from his shoulder and let it fly into the air. There was a clunk as the lead weights in the net hit the woman behind her ear. She fell, tumbling backward into the sand.

Lawi crouched and waited. He expected the woman to thrash about in the net and cry out. She didn't move. He crept to her side and crouched on his haunches. The woman's eyes were closed. The weights had knocked her unconscious.

Growing bolder, he lifted the woman's head and removed his net. He coiled it beside her body and looked around for her purse. He was puzzled. This was not the way his friends had told him it should be. This *wanawake* had nothing with her.

Lawi contemplated the body in front of him. The women's face was turned upward to the stars. Her fair, silky hair was snagged with sand. Her skirt had ridden up to her thighs, showing long, slender legs; too thin for a Bajuni woman, he thought. His throat was tightening. He muttered to himself with anger, wondering where this woman kept her money.

He leaned over and squeezed her breasts to see if she had money hidden there. Her dress was sheer and fitted like a skin. Lawi was surprised when the woman's bare nipples responded to his touch. He moved his hand down to her waist. No pockets, no money; not even the key to her room.

He slid his hand up her thigh to see if she had money concealed in her underwear. He stopped. She was naked under her dress and his fingers had come into contact with moist flesh.

He was filled with rage. He had done this deed for nothing. Now he would have to return to the sea in the hope of catching some fish so his children could eat. He rose up, muttering to himself.

Then, as he stood over her, he became aware of the straining in his crotch. He tapped himself sharply with his finger but the heat in his loins was overpowering. He looked down at the woman's body stretched out in front of him, her white dress rucked up to her waist.

With a cry of anguish, he fell on her. He lunged and twisted, grinding himself into her with the fury of frustration. He avenged his woman, his children, and his people for their misery. Each thrust was a spear driven against the spirit that condemned him to luckless poverty. He heaved and thrashed until he could bear it no longer. He tore to the root of the woman, bursting with seed inside her.

When he raised his head, his lower lip was bleeding where he had bitten it in rage. His eyes were glazed as he glanced south along the beach to the distant lights of the hotel and, far away in the sky, the glow of Mombasa. All was quiet.

He pulled out of the woman and shook himself. He scooped up his net and cradled it in his arms, walking slowly back into the sea.

◆ ◆ ◆ ◆ ◆

"I'm sure Miss Preston's all right, Susan." Charles Royce drawled, straightening his cravat. He sipped at his whisky. "There's no need for you to be alarmed."

"She hasn't come to the party," Susan said, gazing around the room for the hundredth time that evening. "She isn't in her cottage. Something is wrong."

"I don't think so, Susan. Believe me, I'm an old hand in this business. We don't restrict our guests. Each of you is free to do what she wants." Royce's speech sounded slurred. "Why don't you relax? You're here for the time of your life, so enjoy it."

Susan gaped at him. How could he be so heartless? "I'm sorry," she said. "I'm sorry if I've caused you any trouble."

"No trouble. Do excuse me. I must make the rounds."

She watched the Englishman edge away, clearly anxious to escape from her She closed her eyes in despair.

"You look about as bad as I feel."

She opened her eyes quickly and saw Cora standing in front of her. "Oh, Cora," she sighed with relief. "I'm worried about Lyn. She went off to the beach and there's a notice that says you shouldn't. She hasn't come back!"

"Really?" Cora sounded bored. "Show business types are peculiar, Susan. I know from my mother. You needn't concern yourself."

"That's what everyone keeps telling me."

The sound of drumming erupted from beside the pool. There was the patter of hands slapping rapidly against skins stretched taut over hollow logs. It was a raw, passionate beat that made Cora's eyes blaze.

Susan was startled. "Whatever is that?"

"Show time. Isn't it fun?" Cora pushed through the circle of tourists gathered around the drummers. Susan followed her, reluctant to be left alone.

A man wearing a gaily-patterned cloth around his waist, and nothing else, stood behind a large drum that had four legs to support it, like a coffee table. The man was massive with a mat of short curly hair covering his chest. He quivered when he leaned forward to pound the skin of his drum. His face shone in the spotlight and his eyes danced wildly. Sweat oozed over his body.

"My god!" breathed Cora. "Look at that! It can't be true. He's colossal." Cora's eyes were fastened on the man's crotch, which bulged provocatively under the tightly wrapped *kikoi*.

Susan shuddered and averted her gaze. A younger man was playing a smaller drum, crouching low and clasping it between his thighs. He beat it energetically while another musician shook a flat instrument from side to side.

"That's a *kayamba*," said Cora with a giggle of pride.

"How do you know that?"

"I was talking to that cat before the band started to play. He said it's made of dried reeds with loose seeds inside to make the rattling noise."

The youth with the *kayamba* began to sing plaintively. At the front of the crowd surrounding the band, Susan saw Mrs. Biddle-Macdonald watching the huge drummer with an expression of ecstasy on her face.

"I see Maggie's flipped." Cora grinned.

"I do wish Lyn was here," Susan said anxiously. "I'm sure she'd want to see this."

"She's all right, Sue. Don't worry. She's probably getting screwed at last."

"How can you say that?"

"You're not shocked, are you? Lyn told me herself that's what she's come for."

Susan's mouth tightened. "She may be in trouble, Cora. Please help me search for her."

"Okay." Cora nodded her head. "I'm getting bored with that environmental gleam in Maggie's eye. She's seen a native she wants to preserve. God help the poor bastard."

The rhythmic pounding of the drums and the melancholy chant of the singer drifted across the hotel gardens as Susan and Cora walked down the path to the beach. They peered to the edge of the circle of light radiating from the spotlights fixed high in the coconut trees.

"I wonder why it's not safe on the beach after six?" Cora asked when she saw the notice board.

"Perhaps the tide comes up quickly." Susan pointed at the low waves rushing in with whirls of foam glistening in the spotlights.

Cora laughed. "Mombasa muggers is my guess."

"Oh!" Susan's hand trembled as she reached for Cora. "Do you think we'll be safe?"

"No idea." Cora moved away from her side.

Susan observed Cora's reaction and bit her lip, peering unhappily into the darkness beyond the sphere of light.

Cora followed her gaze and trudged up the beach. "Come on, Sue. You call her. You're the one with this crazy idea."

"Lyn! Lyn!" she shouted. The words were whipped away from her mouth by the breeze. "Lyn! Lyn?"

◆ ◆ ◆ ◆ ◆

Lawi moved silently through the waves following a parallel course with the two women on the beach. They were walking out of the halo of light. He bared his teeth in a smile of inevitability, his grip tightening around the knife clasped in his fingers.

He tracked the two women with the stealth and patience he had learned as a child when he hunted fish with his brothers. He was a Bajuni. From early times his tribe had lived near water, working as sailors, fishermen, ocean merchants and other occupations connected with the sea.

The Bajuni were a hardy group of people able to adapt to changing ways. In ancient times, the Bajuni were more numerous, but the Galla who moved down from the north had pushed them out of their land.

Lawi knew about suffering, about hungry children crying to be fed, about his woman carrying yet another child, about medicines and food and even water from the pump that all cost money to buy. He cared nothing for white women who wore no underwear and carried no money. He listened to the strange cries the two women were making.

"Lyn... Lyn."

What did it mean? Soon, he realized, they might stumble on the woman he had left unconscious on the beach, unless the tide had taken her. He knew he must attack before the two women became alarmed.

He moved rapidly to the shore, using the gentle rushing of the waves to conceal the noise of his approach.

"Lyn, Lyn," one of the women called again.

"This is stupid," the other said. "I'm going back."

"No, don't leave me, Cora."

"Why keep on looking? Lyn isn't here."

"Hush!" said one as the other bumped into her.

"What is it?"

"I'm sure I heard something."

"You're dreaming!"

The waves lapped the sand, scooping up loose pebbles and shells at the edge of the water and sucking them back noisily. Lawi remained motionless, breathing in time to the surge of the sea.

"I did hear something! Look." She pointed into the depths of the darkness. A shape rose out of the water in front of them. They screamed.

"What the hell!" a voice grumbled.

"Lyn? Thank god! What happened? You're soaking wet."

"What do you expect? You can't bathe without getting wet."

"You went bathing with your dress on?"

"I must have done. Oh, my head!"

"Did something happen? I was so worried that's why I asked Cora to come with me to look for you."

"I'm not sure what happened, Sue. I must have passed out. Like something hit me. Too much vodka, I guess."

"So that's what a television superstar does in Kenya. Falls flat on her fanny and loses her memory."

Lawi frowned when he heard the women speaking. Such ugly tones. He listened, distinguishing each voice. There were three of them. He knew what to do. He would creep up and seize one from behind and tell the others to hand over their money.

The women were moving slowly away from where he was crouched in the waves. In a few moments they would be embraced by the light and in sight of the security guards. He knew he must strike now.

He leaped up from the water and, keeping low in the

waves, ran after them.

"Who's there?" Susan shrieked when a shape suddenly materialized in front of her.

"Thank god, Mindelo, it's you." Cora cried nervously. "What are you doing here?"

"I've come for you all, of course," he announced sternly. "Don't you know it's not safe on the beach after sunset?"

Lawi sank back into the sea. There would be no dinner for his hungry children tonight, and no breakfast for them tomorrow. He cursed, slung his net over his shoulder and trudged wearily through the surf in the direction of his home.

CHAPTER 12

The waiter in his mock safari suit of powdered blue deposited a plate on the table and stood back. Susan eyed the contents of the plate then raised her head enquiringly at Lyn. They were sharing a table at dinner on their second evening at the hotel.

Maggie wasn't in the open air restaurant and Cora had already eaten her meal and left them. Susan waited for Lyn to say something.

Lyn looked from the plate to the waiter. "What's this?"

"Kenya cheese," the waiter said timidly.

Susan sensed the man would rather be somewhere else, perhaps on the savannah hunting antelope. "It looks nice," she said.

"What do you call it?" Lyn's notebook lay open on the table beside her plate. She picked up her pen.

"Bibi?"

Lyn raised her voice. "Tell me the name of the cheese."

"I get the headwaiter, miss."

"No!" Lyn was emphatic. "You know what you call the cheese, don't you?"

"I believe so, miss."

"Then tell me!"

The waiter gazed around uncomfortably.

Susan realized she was wrong. The man would be more comfortable sipping *pombe* through a straw than chasing antelope. "I don't know the names of cheeses at home that I like," she said, feeling sorry for him. "This one looks like a blue cheese." She smiled encouragingly at the waiter.

He responded. "Yes, miss. That blue cheese. From the Highlands."

Susan cut off a piece. "It tastes good."

"That white Highland, miss." The waiter leaned forward and stabbed his finger at the second piece on her plate.

"Okay, okay," said Lyn, waving him into silence. "Now we know."

The waiter's smile vanished. He bowed his head and backed away from the table.

"What are you trying to do, Sue? Show me my job?"

She stared at Lyn in dismay. "No. Why do you say that?"

"The way you questioned the waiter."

"He was nervous, poor thing. He's probably not used to so many questions."

"He's a person, Sue, even though he's a waiter. He didn't need to be babied."

"I'm sorry." Sue was puzzled. "I didn't mean to be condescending but you frightened him. He's a native. I mean he hasn't had experience of someone like you. He's not a union leader or corporate president."

"For Chrissake, Sue! I only asked him what the cheese is called."

"You demanded, not asked." Susan was surprised at herself. She sipped her coffee to cover her embarrassment at speaking so boldly. What right had she got to criticize a woman she watched regularly on television. Lyn would probably hate her now.

"Demanded?" Lyn uttered the word to herself, swallowing hard. Her eyes clouded over. "Yeah, you're right, Sue."

"Oh dear, I hope I haven't upset you."

"No, Sue, don't worry your head about that. I'm thick skinned. Too thick skinned perhaps. Maybe you know something I don't."

"I don't know anything, Lyn." She put down her coffee cup. She was feeling tired although she had spent the whole day lazing on the beach and swimming in the pool with Cora. Lyn had been in bed, nursing what she called a massive hangover.

"To tell you the truth, Lyn," she said, leaning forward so none of the guests seated around them could hear. "These people scare me. I'm intrigued, you know, but they really frighten me."

"Why?" Lyn pushed the cheese aside. "They're male, aren't they? You wouldn't be on this vacation if that didn't interest you."

Susan toyed with her coffee cup to hide her confusion. It was all a dreadful mistake. She wanted to discuss it with someone. She glanced at Lyn. On television the woman seemed so alert and intelligent. Tonight, her face was drawn and rueful. Her blonde hair was bunched under a silk scarf and she wore a formless caftan that softened her usual aggressive appearance.

"I don't know why I came here, Lyn," she began. "It's not for what you think. I mean, I wanted to distance myself from my marriage and the divorce. I wanted to do something different. I wanted to *live*! But this is just a tourist resort with native waiters..." She stopped.

"Go on," Lyn said gently.

"It's the way they look at me. As though they want, well, you know..."

"You're luckier than I am! Relax, try it." Lyn's eyes blazed with an evangelistic passion. "What do we mean when we say 'making love'? We mean fucking, right?"

Susan felt her cheeks redden. She gripped the side of her chair to control herself. "Yes..." she said, her voice throbbing with emotion. "I suppose so."

"Well if you want to 'make love', you look for a guy. It's simple. It doesn't matter if you know him or what color he is. But I tell you, the more tropical he is, the hotter it will be."

She stared wide-eyed at Lyn. "That's behaving like an animal. There must be feeling."

"Feeling? Who has time for feeling? It hasn't got you anywhere, has it?"

◆ ◆ ◆ ◆ ◆

The morning light seeped through the heavy curtains. Birds sang with persistence, calling Susan to breakfast on the patio where they could swoop down to raid the sugar bowl and peck at the toast. On her door, Susan had hung the *Do Not Disturb* sign, a photograph with two lions asleep and a slogan printed across it in Swahili. Obviously birds don't read Swahili, she thought, as she gazed around the room in the gray light of the day's beginning.

Today, she hoped, she would start to enjoy the vacation. She smiled to herself as she remembered Harrison Muldoon trying to get her out of his office. It was really only because of his supercilious attitude that she had decided to come. She had no objections to a vacation affair but it would have to be romantic. Lyn Preston was wrong!

She was sorry for Lyn and she didn't know why. Lyn was everything she envied. She was attractive, assertive and successful; yet she seemed so lonely. Well, she was lonely herself too, although not with the vengeance that drove Lyn.

She lost herself in her thoughts and prepared for the day. The steward brought her breakfast and a large hibiscus blossom that he pressed into her hand. She accepted it nervously, wondering what threat lay behind the man's enchanting smile.

She ate on the patio and watched the early sun-worshippers rolling out their towels and facing the sun with religious dedication. The clean sound of a tennis ball bounced over the bougainvillea. It stirred her. She finished her breakfast and abandoned her tray to the restless birds.

By the time she reached the tennis court, it was empty. She had changed into her white shorts and a T-shirt, with her hair secured with a rubber band in a ponytail so it wouldn't fall into her eyes and distract her.

She was disappointed by the empty court and was about to leave when she noticed a movement in the kiosk. She walked to it through the bushes. A young man dressed in neatly pressed white shorts and a clean tennis shirt was writing something in a book on the counter.

"Excuse me," she said softly. "I wanted the professional, you know, the tennis professional?"

The youth continued to write in his book while an audible sigh escaped from his lips. "I'm the pro," he said without looking up. "Appointments should be made at Reception."

"I'm sorry, I didn't know." She backed away, wondering what she had done to upset him.

The youth raised his eyes from the book, alerted by the plaintive note in her voice. "Hey, wait!" he said quickly. "Don't go." He leaped over the counter and ran up to her. "I didn't see you. I thought you were one of those old bags coming to ... Well that doesn't matter. What can I do for you?"

"I'd like to play tennis, but if it's not convenient."

"When? Now?"

"Well, yes, but..."

"Right, let's go. I don't have a lesson now. This is when I have breakfast."

"Oh, I...I couldn't," she stammered.

"Yes, you could. Here, take this racket."

When Susan overcame her initial shock at the pro's age, his good looks and his charm, she settled down to enjoy the game. The youth was good and several times offered her advice.

He told her his surname was Katana but she forgot that while concentrating on her service. She was drenched in perspiration, her hair was damp and her T-shirt wet and clinging to her body. She played enthusiastically, ignoring the fatigue creeping into her legs and arms. It was exhilarating.

Katana ran up to the net after thirty minutes, grinning broadly. "Time's up, Susan. It's the heat. Don't overdo it on your first day."

"Phew! That was terrific." She felt buoyant, like a teenager.

"You keep in shape."

"Not really. I play twice a week at home. It gets me out of the apartment."

"I hope you'll come back?" The youth walked beside her to the booth.

"Sure." She was panting. "You play so well. I'm exhausted." She sank down on the bench outside the kiosk and wiped her face with the towel he handed her.

"So am I." He laughed, a clean, warm sound.

"You're not serious."

"Yes, I am. Most of my clients are old *manamouki* who can't play tennis at all. They just want me to flatter them for an hour."

"How awful."

"That's how it is when you're poor."

She glanced at him in surprise, then noticed the twinkle in his eye. She grinned. "Where did you learn to play?" She passed the towel back to him and he wiped his neck with it. His skin glowed.

"At the Nyali Club. Very prestigious place. I used to work for a white man who liked me. He sponsored my lessons.

He's dead now but he had shares in this hotel. That's why I'm here."

"I did think you were rather young to be the pro."

"That's the way the old women like it."

"You sound sad." She was aware of his deep eyes searching her face. He looked so dashing on the tennis court but sitting beside her he appeared slight and vulnerable. She realized he had grasped her hand and was squeezing it. She pulled away gently.

"What do I owe you?" she asked.

"For what?" His eyes held hers.

She blushed. "The lesson."

"That was my pleasure; your free sample."

"You must let me pay. I can afford it." She bit her lip, regretting what she had just said so thoughtlessly. The youth stood up and carried the rackets over to the booth.

"The hotel gets the fees, not me." His voice had gone cold.

"I didn't mean to offend you."

"I'm not offended."

"It's difficult for me. I haven't been to Africa before. In America we have to pay for everything. I don't look rich, well, I'm not rich but I am paying for this vacation myself."

"Are you?" He busied himself with his appointments book. "You can arrange your next lesson with Reception. Early morning or late afternoon is best, when it's not so hot."

"I'm sorry."

He looked up. "What for? You've done nothing." He grinned, his eyes steady on her face.

She felt her legs go week as she stood up. "I'll come tomorrow."

"Wait!" He smiled. "I have to go for my breakfast now. I'll walk with you." He stacked the rackets behind the counter, locked the balls and his diary in a drawer and joined Susan on the path.

"My cottage is over there."

"One of the expensive ones?" He frowned.

"It's very nice." She was puzzled by the change in his mood. She glanced at him curiously. His face was in profile, his soft flat nose outlined against the sun. He was good looking in an African sort of way.

"Is something wrong?" she asked when he didn't say anything.

He shrugged, his face clouding with concern.

"Please, Katana," she said, remembering his name at last. "Tell me what it is." She watched his tiny Adam's apple bob up and down when he swallowed.

"Which group did you come with, Susan" His eyes narrowed into slits of suspicion. "Charles Royce's?"

"Yes. Do you know him?" She was pleased he was taking such an interest in her.

"Not you!" He sounded disgusted. "I'd never have guessed."

"Guessed what?"

"It just shows you can't tell what white people are really like."

"I don't understand." She felt anxious. "Why are you looking at me like that?"

"You're just like the other women who come here from Los Angeles. You just want to drag me into bed with you."

"Oh dear, no!" She blushed. "That's too silly for words. Why should I want to do that?"

Katana stopped walking. "You're with Royce's group?"

"Yes, I am." Her lip trembled and she felt like she wanted to cry. "That doesn't make me the same as the others."

He stiffened, and resumed his way along the path. "Which is your cottage? The one with the hibiscus outside it?"

She nodded, too scared to speak now. He seemed to have come to a decision. Perhaps Lyn was right. He was nice, pleasant; she felt she knew him. But well enough for *that*? Somewhere deep within her she was troubled. She wondered if he could hear her heart pounding.

He pursed his lips. "My Christian name is Paul."

She said it softly. "Paul."

"You don't mind me calling you Susan, do you?"

"I love it."

"Some of these old crones won't even tell me their first names. 'Come at six, boy,' they say. 'Turn the light out, boy.' Why are you with such women, Susan?"

"It's for convenience, that's all." She felt ashamed.

"Paul?"

There was silence. He gazed at her, his eyes mellow and his tongue, a flash of pink darting between his deep colored lips.

She put her hand out to touch him, her fingers like a white butterfly on the mahogany of his arm. "Paul? I'm not used to this."

"Neither am I. Come on. I have to be back at the court in fifteen minutes." He turned to walk in the direction of her cottage.

The magic snapped. Susan dropped her hand and frowned. "I'm sorry, I didn't mean to delay you." She was embarrassed in case he knew what she had been thinking. It was no good.

"There's time. Here's your cottage. Give me your key." He held out his hand.

"No, Paul." She shook her head sadly. "I'm really not like the others."

"Aren't I good enough for you?"

"Paul! Don't even think like that. I think you're sweet. I'd like to know you better, I really would. When you have the time."

"I'll come tonight."

Her heart lurched. "I don't know..."

She looked around to see if anyone was watching and was dismayed to see Maggie at the edge of her patio, staring at her. She was wearing a pink bathrobe that engulfed her from neck to toes. Her head was swathed in a white bandanna. She looked formidable, and frosty. In her hand she held a bottle of champagne.

"Katana!" Maggie called, ignoring her. "Come here!"

Paul leaned close to Susan, taking her hand and squeezing it. "Tonight," he whispered, stepping away from her and turning to go to Maggie.

She gazed after him. "Yes," she breathed softly, so Maggie wouldn't hear. "Tonight."

"I can't get this bottle open!" Maggie bawled at him as though it were his fault. "Damn thing!" She thrust the bottle at Paul and leered triumphantly at Susan.

"I'll try, miss," Susan heard him say. He held the neck of

the bottle and pressed his thumb against the cork. It flew out with a sudden pop and champagne showered Maggie's face.

"Damn," she said, holding out her glass blindly. He filled it. "Have some."

"No, thank you, madam." He placed the bottle down on the table and stood back. "I have an appointment. I must go.

Maggie snorted with disgust. "Cancel it!"

Paul's nostrils flared angrily. "I'm not your personal trainer, madam," he said, keeping his voice steady.

"I'll pay you well."

Susan saw Paul hesitate. He looked across the flowers at her, and then at his watch. He shrugged his shoulders and turned back to Maggie. "How well?"

Maggie's eyes gleamed. "Let's go inside," she said, holding open the curtains.

He slipped through, leaving Susan gazing in disbelief at Maggie's empty patio.

CHAPTER 13

Lyn lay in bed and listened to her ears ringing and to the calling of birds, and people, passing her patio. She reviewed the memory flashes that flickered through her brain like the newsroom ticket tape.

She still ached from what had happened two nights before. *What had happened?* She hadn't told the others everything. She herself didn't know everything. She squirmed in the bed and sighed, putting it behind her.

Lucky it happened to her and not to Susan Ross. That girl would have died! She was surely going to have a rude awakening on this vacation. Her way of life was such a waste of time. A woman must know what she wants and then strive to get it. 'Making love' was what Sue called sex. It was a high school euphemism based on inexperience.

Making love! She chuckled to herself. By the shores of the Indian Ocean would she find time for 'making love' herself? Harrison Muldoon had promised as much, even if Charles Royce had yet to deliver.

She leaned across the bed for the telephone. She dialed the operator. "Put me through to Mr. Royce, please."

"I'm sorry, Miss Preston," the man's voice said. "Mr. Royce does not have a telephone."

"Impossible! I want to speak to him."

"I can arrange for you, miss. His boy is in the hotel."

"His boy?"

"Mindelo, Miss Preston." The operator sounded friendly and efficient. "I ask him to phone you?"

"I really want Mr. Royce."

"Anything wrong, Miss Preston?"

She paused, taken aback by the concern shown by this unseen man. It seemed genuine. "It's all right."

"If there is anything I can do, Miss Preston, please call me."

She was intrigued. "Maybe there is. What's your name?"

"Mathias, Miss Preston."

"Well, Mathias, when do you finish work?"

"At three, Miss Preston."

"I'd like to see you, Mathias."

"The operator's room is next to the reception desk." The disembodied voice at the other end of the line sounded amused.

"Well, I'll come there some time. You're most helpful."

"It's nothing, Miss Preston."

Lyn replaced the receiver on the phone and laid her head back on the pillow. She had a feeling that today would be better than yesterday, which she had spent in bed nursing her hangover and wondering what had happened. She had wanted to speak to that fatuous faggot, Royce.

She needed answers to satisfy her own curiosity as well as to get background for her TV special. Yes, her special feature. She needed visuals supporting her theme of tourist decadence and ingenuous penury. She wanted to show real Africans, not the servile, hotel-bred parasites she had met already. She needed to find genuine tribesmen, from the bush.

Her pain lessened as her ideas took over. She visualized shots of herself interviewing a half-naked tribesman daubed with paint and sheltering in the shade, then cut to a male tourist smeared with lotion and willingly basting himself in the sun. What a contrast!

She planned a devastating indictment of exploitation, not of the tourists but of locals by the tourists. It would be sensational television.

The telephone rang. She reached for it by habit with the quick reflex action of a journalist. "Preston here."

"Miss Preston, this is Mathias."

Her brain reacted slowly. She was still in the studio planning her program. "Mathias...?"

"The operator." His cheerful tone intrigued her. "I've found Mindelo. He'll be coming to your room shortly."

She hung up. She showered quickly and donned the two piece bathing suit her assistant had persuaded her to bring. "You'll need to sit on the beach to see what it's like from the tourist's angle," Gloria Trotter had said when she protested.

She studied herself in the full-length mirror. She was resolutely pale since she avoided the Californian tan that was the trademark of West Coast television stars. If she was going to parade on the beach, she must remember to keep her tummy in.

With a sigh, she opened the curtains and the sliding door, blinking at the sun's brilliance. She settled herself in a reclining chair on the patio and lit a Gauloise. It was a blissful feeling, inhaling the raw, rich taste of her cigarette while lying indolently in the sun. Maybe tourists weren't so stupid after all, she thought, closing her eyes.

She had finished the cigarette when a shadow fell across her body. She stared at the shape and sat up. It was Mindelo, standing politely at the patio's edge. She wriggled her hips provocatively and laughed at him. He stiffened.

"Mathias said you asked for Mr. Royce?"

She let her gaze wonder over him; he was too young and innocent. Suddenly she became aware of her out of shape condition. She reached for another cigarette. "Where's Royce? Why isn't he here?"

"He is making arrangements for tomorrow's safari, Miss Preston."

"He should be here to look after us. This is a very expensive vacation. We're entitled to his personal attention."

"Mr. Royce will come at once, if he is needed." Mindelo mouthed the platitude he had been told to say. "Is there anything I can do?"

She studied him again. "I doubt it." She gestured to a chair and waited while Mindelo perched on the edge of it with obvious reluctance. "Is this vacation a con?"

"Miss Preston?"

"Don't pretend you don't understand. You're too smart for that."

"Thank you, Miss Preston. Please explain what you mean." Mindelo was twisting his hands together anxiously.

"Listen, man." She leaned forward and tapped his knee. "I haven't come ten thousand miles for sun and games, Mindelo, I've come for-."

"For sex!"

They both looked up in surprise. Standing at the corner of the next-door patio, a leer on her face, was Cora. Lyn was intrigued by Mindelo's reaction. He jumped up from the chair, his features clouding with embarrassment.

Lyn beamed. "How right you are, kid," she said sarcastically.

"Don't listen to her bullshit, Mindelo. She's only trying to get you into bed. It's obscene. She's almost old enough to be your mother." Cora's eyes blazed with anger.

"Really?" Lyn belched out smoke at her. "Well, what are you trying to do with him, kid? Play doctors and nurses?"

The blood drained from Cora's already pale face. "You can't piss on me, Lyn Preston. I know what you were doing on the beach that night, even if you lied to Mindelo and that kook Susan."

"Jealous?"

Mindelo backed away, frowning. "May I go, Miss Preston? I will tell Mr. Royce you want to see him."

"Sit down!"

"I'll come with you, Mindelo," said Cora.

Lyn looked at her worried face and burst out laughing. "So that's the way it is. You're scared I'll steal this little plaything from you?"

"You're hateful!" Cora's eyes flickered with pain.

"You're a spoilt brat."

"At least I don't look like mutton undressed and pretending to be lamb," Cora retorted with the uncanny instinct of the young to wound where it hurts most.

Lyn stabbed out her cigarette and was surprised to see she was trembling. She ached, and longed to lie down with a stiff drink. "You can have him," she said sadly. "I like my men to be out of diapers." It wasn't a very satisfactory retort, but she felt drained.

Mindelo made a half-bow, remembering his manners despite his obvious confusion. She waved him away and watched him follow Cora, with her ridiculously slim young body, hurrying along the path to the beach.

♦ ♦ ♦ ♦ ♦

"She's a bitch," Cora said. "You ought to keep away from her."

Mindelo sat down beside Cora on a bench overlooking the sea. He waved cheerily to the security guard, who scowled and turned away. Charles Royce had used the same words to him the night before, but about Cora.

"You ought to keep away from Cora Berger," he had said as Mindelo helped him remove his trousers. "Those kind of women aren't for you."

Mindelo had wondered to himself what kind of women were for him. Instead of speaking, he had pulled off Royce's trousers, folded them, and placed them neatly on a hanger while Royce droned on in his drunken monotone.

"Keep away from Cora, Mindelo. Keep away from all women. They won't do you any good."

Mindelo half listened, tugging off Royce's socks and wrinkling his nose at the smell. He placed the socks in the wash basket and prepared to leave the bedroom.

"Where are you going, boy?" Royce demanded, the odor of whisky floating across the room. Mindelo frowned unhappily.

"Don't turn sulky with me, boy. I won't have it! I know what's right. Women are no good. Come here, boy. Sleep with me tonight."

Mindelo stopped at the door and sighed. *Would it never end?* "Sir, I have my work to do. The chores-."

Royce swayed in a wave of drunkenness as he sat on the bed. He lunged at the mosquito net and grabbed it. It fell around his head and he floundered helplessly on the bed, cursing.

Mindelo took his time disentangling him. Royce was tired by the effort to free himself and fell back on the pillow with his eyes closed. His mouth dropped open and he was soon snoring.

Mindelo spent much of the night cleaning the apartment. He ironed clothes he had laundered the day before. He swept out the room they used for an office and sorted through the papers on Royce's desk, placing the safari file on the top.

When he was sure he had finished everything, he stripped down to the swimming trunks he wore as underwear, and knelt down beside the couch. Although he was tired and sleep was addling his brain, he prayed dutifully for the health of his mother, father, and family members.

Finally he had prayed that all would go well for his sister's wedding in Kaloleni and that one day he, too, would get married.

"Why are you so quiet? I rescued you from that woman, didn't I?"

Mindelo opened his eyes and gazed around him in surprise.

"You were half asleep, day dreaming!" Cora said. "I was talking to you."

"I was thinking."

"What about?"

He turned to face Cora. She was beautiful with her probing eyes and tough smile. Her body was lithe and exciting. He wondered if she would put on weight when she was older, like the Digo women of his tribe.

Cora laughed. "What's wrong? You look so serious. Tell me what you're thinking."

He shrugged.

"It's about us, isn't it?"

"Yes."

"I thought so. You can't understand why white women behave in such a silly manner, can you?"

He smiled at Cora's wrong conclusion.

She took his grin for agreement and continued, "I can't understand it myself. Scobie, my boy friend, says that we have become over-civilized in the States and we need to get back to places like Africa to rediscover ourselves. Don't you think that's cute?"

"You have a boy friend?" He hoped not.

"Yes. He's black too."

"Tell me about him." He didn't want to hear, but it would be good for him to know. It was wrong to think of this girl as being more than one of Mr. Royce's clients. He saw her tense.

"There's nothing much to tell, really. Right now, he doesn't seem so great, you know, as I'm here with you."

He grinned ruefully. "Enjoy yourself here, Cora," he said, standing up. "Take care."

"Where are you going?"

"I have work to do."

"When will I see you again?"

He was puzzled. "You want to see me again?"

"Of course I do."

"But you said you have a boy friend"

"So what?" she passed her hand across her brow, irritated by his question.

Mindelo felt desire swelling in him. He turned away from her. "I'll see you later, " he said, his voice catching in his throat. "When I've done my work.

"Good," said Cora. "I'll wait."

CHAPTER 14

The Mpingo Beach Hotel, in common with most luxury resorts in Kenya, served a sumptuous buffet luncheon. Tables
were set up in the center of the open-air restaurant under a
canopy of thatch to provide shade.

A waiter hovered at Susan's side as she gazed on the
spread and proudly named the various delicacies. These included shell fish from the Indian Ocean lapping the beach
fifty yards from the buffet tables, cold meats, salads, and an
African stew.

"I've never seen so much food in my life," Susan said to
Cora who was admiring the buffet with her. "I couldn't pos-
sibly eat more than a little salad."

"Take as much as you can." Cora grabbed a plate off the
table. "I am. We don't know what we'll get tomorrow."

"Tomorrow?" Susan followed Cora's lead and took a plate
from the stack. "Why do you say that?"

"The safari begins tomorrow. We'll be living in the jungle,
won't we?"

"I've read that the game lodges are very nice."

Cora forked large prawns on to her plate. "That will please
your friend."

"My friend?" Susan paused as she served herself a slice
of ham and some lettuce.

"Maggie, of course."

"She's not my friend."

Cora paused in her attack on the prawns and eyed Susan quizzically. "You sound jumpy, Sue. What happened between you and Maggie? I thought you felt sorry for the old
bitch."

Susan could feel herself turning red as she tried to control her feelings. "I think Maggie is, well, shameless!" She
spooned more salad from the bowl, hoping Cora would
change the subject.

"Why's that?"

She shrugged. "I just do, that's all. I've got enough to
eat," she said. "I'm going to sit down."

Cora followed her to a table placed under a thatched sunshade. A waiter held Susan's chair, but left Cora to fend for herself. Another waiter filled their glasses with iced water, serving Susan first and giving her a broad smile. A third waiter, wearing the powdered blue uniform of his confreres, hurried over and asked if everything was all right.

Cora watched, bemused. "You've made quite a hit in this hotel," she said, sounding envious.

Susan opened her eyes in wonder. "Do you think so?" She was wearing her bikini under an old shirt. Her hair was straggly, hanging at the side of her face, damp from splashing around in the shallows of the clear, blue sea.

She followed Cora's eyes to the waiters. "It's nothing to be envious about. Those waiters are trained to be nice to guests."

However, she knew what Cora meant. On the beach that morning, several young men had stopped where she was sitting in her deck chair. They were all carrying something: carvings, jade, or models of the narrow wooden fishing boat with its outrigger floats that is typical of Mombasa. None of them tried to sell to her; they just wanted to talk.

"It's you," said Cora. "Lyn and Maggie don't get treated so warmly. These dudes have taste."

"Thank you." Coming from Cora, the compliment was especially surprising.

"It's true. They can see you're not like the others who just want to get inside their pants. You're a kook, Sue, but you're kind of cool, especially with the locals."

Susan frowned over her ham. "I wish I was. I don't know anything about them. They terrify me."

"I don't believe you." Cora was speaking with prawns protruding from her lips. "I admire your style. It turns them on. I know a few guys like them in LA. You know, dancers and dealers. Blacks."

Susan laid her fork down and pushed her plate away. "These men are different, Cora. They're so...well, African."

"You don't say!" Cora grinned. "A few more days and you'll have forgotten the culture shock and be dying to get into bed with one of them."

"I won't!" Her protest, she realized, was a little too loud. She took a sip of water. "Cora, I hope we're going to be friends."

Cora eyed her sharply. "What do you mean?"

"My life has been so sheltered, Cora. I couldn't run after a man, not like Lyn and Maggie. I need you as an ally." She watched Cora nervously, wondering how she would react to her plea for friendship.

Cora was still grinning, her shorn hair resembling a swimming cap. "You are old fashioned, Sue. If you don't get some action, you might finish up like my Mama."

Susan was puzzled. She had seen Amelia Berger in old movies on television. She couldn't see any resemblance to Amelia in Cora, nor could she see how she could ever be like the former child star herself.

Cora swallowed the last of the prawns and reached for the ice cream. "Do you know," she said, her eyes gleaming, "Mama is president of a Cock Club."

Susan went rigid. "Whatever is that?" she asked hesitantly.

"It's like a Hen Club. All the women meet to swap stories about the biggest cocks they've heard about."

Susan felt herself blushing. "You're making it up."

"I'm not. I've listened to them. They have a file on all the new guys in town. They even keep measurements."

"It's awful."

"It's the only fun they get. Isn't it a laugh? That's what I mean, Sue. If you don't get some action for yourself, you might end up like that. Just wishing..."

She plunged a spoonful of ice cream into her mouth. "You should try it," she spluttered. "It's delicious."

Susan shook her head and gazed beyond Cora to the beach. Eva, the Swedish girl, was sitting at the very edge of the sea so it eddied around her. She was topless as usual and contemplating the deep green of the ocean beyond the reef.

Two pairs of German tourists, all wearing white sun hats, the women topless and the men with sun reddened paunches hanging over their scanty swimming briefs, paddled past in the shallow water.

She took in the beach scene and marveled at it. There was a tranquility she enjoyed; no crowds, no hassling, no one was uptight about anything. Even the beach boys, who made her so apprehensive, were complacent and peaceful.

She was enchanted. Kenya was a delightful country, and its people were proud of it. The beach boys, who had never seen a lion except in movies, actually boasted about the game parks, the wild life, and the natural beauty of their country.

The pride of these simple people made her see the intentions of Lyn and Maggie as shameful and repulsive. She shuddered, wondering how she had got involved with a famous television personality hot for a man, any man, and a selfish woman whose wealth was exceeded only by her rudeness to others.

The thought of what Lyn and Maggie wanted to do to the polite Africans, horrified her. She shivered again.

"You sick or something?" Cora gave her no chance to reply. "Hey, look what Maggie's landed," she said, pointing beyond Susan's head.

She turned warily. Maggie was moving in their direction like a royal visit. She was preceded by the restaurant captain who clasped the plastic-bound menu to his breast with pompous grace.

Maggie wore a voluminous gown, an elaborate turban, and a choker of pearls at her throat. She held herself regally, not deigning to glance at the youth on whose arm she clung. Behind her, waiters scurried like courtiers with ice bucket, champagne, and a plate of fresh Indian Ocean oysters.

The procession halted at their table. A waiter materialized with a chair, there was much bowing and smiling, and Maggie eased herself down. She waved her hand and the waiters dropped back. The champagne was opened, poured and tasted.

Glasses were provided for Susan and Cora. Susan gazed up at the youth standing behind Maggie, and her heart raced.

Paul Katana avoided her eyes. His tennis clothes, she noticed, were creased. He looked tired, embarrassed and anxious. "I must go," he said, sounding chastened. "I didn't have breakfast..."

"Indeed, you must," said Maggie, rewarding him with a sickly smile. "Thank you so much for escorting me here."

She dismissed him with a wave.

Susan saw the hatred flare in his eyes. She wanted to stand up and seize him and hug him. He trotted out of the restaurant and up the path to the tennis court without looking at her.

Maggie leaned forward, gushing. "Won't you girls join me in a toast?" She raised her glass. "To Fulfillment."

"Well," said Cora after she sipped the champagne. "You know how to do things in style. Walking in here with the tennis pro! He's a bit young, though, isn't he? Any good?"

"Yes," said Susan, unable to bear it. "I played tennis with him this morning. He is good."

"I'm not talking about tennis."

"Do you hear that, Susan? I believe she wants him too." Maggie turned to Cora. "Well, he's anybody's for a few shillings."

Susan gritted her teeth, startled by the despair welling up inside her. Cora was glaring at Maggie.

"Come, Susan," Maggie said. "You haven't drunk your champagne. You're not jealous, are you, dear? I did see you were standing rather close to the boy this morning."

Susan didn't trust herself to speak as the tears welled up in her eyes.

Cora finished her second helping of ice cream and let the spoon clatter to the plate. "I must ask that cat what he thought of you," she said sarcastically. "After all, you're anybody's for a few inches, aren't you?"

One of the hovering waiters refilled their glasses with champagne. Susan glanced uneasily at Maggie. She saw her bloodshot eyes, already puffy, appeared to swell with indignation at Cora's remark.

Maggie titled up her chin defiantly and spoke in a tone brittle with sarcasm. "I can't make up my mind about you, Cora. Are you a girl inside that boy's body of yours, or perhaps a boy inside a girl? Has your dear mother had you examined by experts?"

There was silence. Cora's sullen face was flushed with fury. Susan wondered why she didn't leave. Instead, Cora reached for her champagne glass and raised it to her lips.

"If you must know," said Maggie, almost purring with

malice, "his feet smell. I'm sure he would be perfect for you."

Cora spat out a stream of spittle and champagne into Maggie's face and scrambled to her feet. Her eyes were glistening with tears. Susan put out her hand to comfort her, but the hunch of her shoulders deterred her. Her face was ugly with anger.

Maggie seemed unperturbed. She dabbed the mucus off her cheek with a table napkin, and gazed disdainfully at Cora who turned away and ran from the restaurant.

From her large purse, Maggie produced a compact, snapped it open and applied powder judiciously. She looked at Susan with the air of a martyr.

"I am not," she said, her voice husky with arrogance, "going to leave this restaurant because of a teenager's tantrum."

She fluttered her hand in the direction of a waiter. "Another bottle of Dom Perignon," she called. "And some clean glasses. Clear away this mess at once."

"You provoked her," Susan said accusingly.

"Did I, dear? Show business children are so tiresome. No breeding."

The waiter pressed a fresh glass in front of Susan and began to fill it. "No, thank you." She raised her hand and the waiter stopped pouring.

"Nonsense! Have what's good for you, dear." Maggie pointed at Susan's glass and addressed the waiter in a tone that couldn't be refused. "Fill it up!"

"I really don't want it, Maggie. The sun."

Maggie raised her eyebrows. "Please don't defy me, Susan. Just a little drink. You wouldn't want me to sit here alone, would you?"

Susan sighed, cross with herself for letting Maggie fool her with that piece of emotional blackmail. She picked up her glass and sipped at it, to contain her anger not to please Maggie.

"I wonder if you can imagine how lonely it is to be an old widow, dear?" Maggie sighed. Susan opened her mouth but didn't get a chance to speak.

"It isn't the same loneliness as being divorced or married to an uncaring man. An old widow is near the end of her life, dear. All her husbands are dead; perhaps she will follow them soon. And all the time she is alone with no man around to do things. No little courtesies and attentions, no surprise presents, no escort to dine with, no one to take her to the theatre."

Maggie gazed at her empty glass. "And no one to love. Did that ever occur to you, dear? The need for love doesn't fade with age."

"It doesn't?"

"You're young, dear. You have everything ahead of you. For all my money I can never regain my youth, however hard I try. It was foolish of me to think I could." Maggie coughed, snapped her fingers for the waiter to fill her glass, and smiled archly. "Are you going on that ridiculous balloon safari tomorrow?"

Susan nodded her head, too confused by Maggie's words to know what to say. She could only think of Paul Katana and what he must have been doing in Maggie's bedroom.

"You are?" Maggie looked disappointed. "I rather hoped you would stay here with me. We could have such fun together."

◆ ◆ ◆ ◆ ◆

Lyn began her research at the hotel's reception desk. The Mpingo Beach Hotel was a sprawling complex with ten luxury beachfront cottages and one hundred rooms in a white-washed block set back from the beach.

The block had been built in a garden of tropical splendor landscaped with skill to soften the harshness of its functional design. It was ideal for tourists who came in packages every weekend from Europe and Scandinavia. All the vacationers, according to Myna, the girl at reception, looked alike.

Myna smiled with such charm when she spoke that Lyn scrutinized her carefully. She was short and slender with large eyes that monopolized her small, delicate face. Her skin was soft, almost a translucent honey in color, and her smile had the smooth quality of self-assurance.

Lyn, whose natural instinct was to distrust her informants, warmed toward the girl. "Have you worked here long?" she asked.

"A few months." The girl's eyes assessed her swiftly. "What is your room number, please?"

"I've no idea," said Lyn. "A cottage."

A flicker of doubt entered the girl's eyes. "You are on a Fulfillment Safari?"

The remark rankled Lyn; it was almost as though the girl had said: *We know all about you.*

"Yes," she said, daring her to comment. "Do you get many of Harrison Muldoon's clients here?"

"Occasionally." The girl's eyes dropped. "The cottages are reserved for Fantasy Tours and for guests on long vacations. You are Mrs. Susan Ross?"

"No, thank god." Lyn gritted her teeth. "I'm Lyn Preston." She found it was strange to say her name and to find no stared at her.

"Yes, I see your name here."

Lyn realized that the girl had checked her name on the registration cards under the counter top in such an efficient manner that she was not aware of it. The girl was very good. The badge on her yellow uniform dress gave her name.

Lyn leaned across the counter and lowered her voice. "Listen, Myna, I'm not the usual Fulfillment Safari tourist. I'm a journalist. I'm writing an article on tourist facilities in Kenya."

Myna's smile strengthened. "Then you must see our general manager, Miss Preston. He is out now. Come back later and I am sure he will tell you all you want to know about this hotel."

"So could you, Myna." She noticed the girl's enormous eyes waiver and follow the progress of someone moving through the reception lobby.

She turned in time to see Mindelo rounding a corner. She persevered. "What do you think of the tourists who come here, Myna? Do you like them?"

"Some of them are very nice."

"And some of them not so nice, right?"

"I can't really say, Miss Preston."

"Have you got a boy friend, Myna?" She noticed the girl falter.

"No, miss."

"Perhaps there is someone you'd like as your boyfriend?"

"Beg pardon?" Myna no longer smiled so confidently.

"Mindelo, Royce's boy. You like him, right?"

Myna gaped, her eyes swiveling to the corner of the lobby. Mindelo was out of sight. "Has he said anything to you?" she asked nervously.

"I guessed. So tell me, Myna," Lyn leaned closer, "how do you feel when Mindelo sleeps with tourists?"

The girl's eyes narrowed, their innocence giving way to the rabid glare of jealousy. Her features hardened and her smile vanished. "What Mindelo does is his own affair, Miss Preston. However, he doesn't sleep with hotel guests, so you don't have a chance."

It was Lyn's turn to be shocked. "You don't think I...!" She was appalled at the idea and stepped back from the counter in surprise. The girl had turned the tables on her so neatly. "You're a smart ass," she said in astonishment.

"Miss?" Myna's smile was back in place. "Do you require other information?"

"Yes." Lyn paused pointedly, wondering what the girl was thinking behind that synthetic grin. "Where's the telephone operator? I want to book an overseas call."

She listened to Myna's instructions and walked away, conscious of Myna's eyes watching her. She was the only female she had seen in the hotel's staff. The cashier was a man, there was not a woman serving in any of the restaurants and men cleaned the rooms. She smiled at the thought of another controversial angle she could put in her program.

She studied the hotel's notice board. There was the usual information about taxi fares, church services and water sports. Notices in Swedish and German named each package group's local representative, and gave their visiting hours and home phone numbers. Charles Royce was not listed.

She was moving away when something caught her eye. It was a photocopy of a public letter. She glanced at it and then tore it off the board to study it in detail. Headed NUD-

IST IN PUBLIC BEACHES, it was addressed to all hotel managers and tourist operators. She read it in amazement.

"At a recent discussion between myself and hotel managers, the above subject was the subject of important discussion. It is now reported that many cases of RAPE have been reported in public beaches and we all agree that this is caused by constant walking or lying nude on the beach."

Who's we? She wondered. The letter was from a government official.

"We must resist any behavior which could seem to corrupt the young generation, one of them is a display of women who walk in the nude and top-less in public places. It is more important at the coast which is predominantly Muslim area, the women tourist would be advised that it is against any form of customary behavior for the women to go top-less or nude in areas of public interest."

She was puzzled. This was Africa! Half a mile from the hotel was a village where the customary dress for women was a *kanga* around the waist and nothing on top. But the letter went on to say:

"All incoming visitors are expected to adhere to the many code of local customs and one of them is that women should not be allowed to display themselves top-less on public beaches."

Perhaps anticipating the tourists' perplexity as to why she couldn't go topless when all around her African women were topless, the letter justified itself by explaining:

"This would decrease the problems and particular when tourist women are walking in quiet places which have been confirmed to be the source of constant RAPE cases."

"Are you in trouble, miss?"

Lyn folded the letter quickly and stuffed it into her pocket. She brushed a strand of loose hair from her face and glanced at the young man hurrying along the corridor toward her.

He was wearing brown trousers with a loose-fitting brown shirt jacket in the same uniform design as the other hotel staff. His face was round and challenging.

"No trouble, thank you. What do you do here?" She had learned from her newspaper days that it was a useful ploy to ask a question when caught doing something suspicious. Even better if the question was a flattering one. "Are you the manager?"

"Oh my goodness, no." The young man gurgled with delight.

"I know that laugh," she said.

"Yes, Miss Preston. I'm Mathias."

"I was coming to see you."

"I know."

"You've got a damn good spy network in this hotel." She watched him closely. "Or are you just nosy?"

"We care for our guests' welfare, Miss Preston, but don't pry." His young face, fresh and lively, contrasted with his elderly, mannered speech. "Would you like to see where I work?"

He opened a side door off the lobby and waited for her to enter. The telephone switchboard was made of wood and stood in the middle of the tiny room. It seemed to be a revered object, like an antique upright piano. A light began to flash on the operating panel.

"Excuse me, miss..."

Mathias eased past her and their bodies touched. Her hopes flared as she contemplated him with interest while he plugged in a jack, listened, plugged in another cord, and spoke into his headset. A second light flashed. Mathias turned to her and grinned apologetically.

"Now I am back, they all want me." He put more jacks into different holes, speaking to each caller with elaborate politeness and playing the switchboard with the skill of a master.

"You love your work," Lyn observed wryly.

"It's my job. It is my duty to do it well."

She was suspicious. "That doesn't sound for real. How long have you worked here?"

"Eight years."

"You don't look old enough!"

He flushed. "I'm twenty-eight."

For the second time that afternoon, Lyn was shocked. This boy was only two years younger than she was. She couldn't help resorting to sarcasm. "I suppose you have a wife and three children at home?"

"One wife, five children."

Lyn shook her head but refrained from expressing her feelings about that. Mathias pulled a cord and spoke rapidly into this headset. She listened for a moment. "Your voice, it's so educated."

"Maybe my voice is," Mathias replied with a shrug. "But I am not." He unplugged all the cords and spun around in his swivel seat to face her. "Anglican missionary school until I was sixteen. Four years wasted, praying for employment. Then, by the grace of God, I was taken on here."

Lyn grimaced. "Anglican? The colonial pattern. Does religion still have influence here?"

"Oh, yes!" Mathias was shocked. "God is in everything we do."

"Christians and Muslims live here on the coast, right?" She acknowledged Mathias' nod.

"A Muslim woman is supposed to be completely covered when she goes out of doors, right?" Lyn quoted what she recalled from the fact sheet prepared for her by Gloria Trotter.

"What do you call that large black mantle that Muslim women wear?"

"A *buibui*."

"And what does your mother wear?"

Mathias laughed. "A *kanga* of course. She's not a Muslim."

"Does she cover her breasts when she's wearing it?"

"No." Mathias looked puzzled.

"Right. That's cleared up that point. She tapped the letter in her pocket and smiled with satisfaction. She intended to film an interview with the tourism official who had written it, cutting from shots of bare-breasted African women to topless Swedes. It would show the absurdities of the tourist office edict.

"I'm trying to understand your country," she said to sooth the perplexed Mathias. "Does religion play a big part in your life?"

"Without the help of the Lord I'd be a wretch at home in my village."

"What's your tribe?"

"Giriama."

She studied Mathias and wondered about him. He had a tribe, an ethnic identity, a faith; things many people in the States never had. "I know this is mostly a Muslim area," she said speculatively. "So the Muslim influence is probably stronger than the Christian one. Tell me, Mathias, are there Africans here with an African religion."

"I don't understand."

"Islam and Christianity came with the colonizers. What about an African religion, one that began in Kenya? Are there any Africans who haven't been tainted by foreign ideology?"

"Miss Preston!" Mathias spread his hands. "I'm a hotel telephone operator."

"You're Kenyan! I want to know about the real people of your country, not just about copycat versions of Europeans and Arabs. I want to know unadulterated Kenyans."

Mathias swung back in his chair, reached with apparent relief for a cord and plugged it in. He fitted his headset around his ears and listened carefully. When he completed the connection, he turned to Lyn, the whites of his eyes like quarter moons in the night of his face.

"There is a Kenya tribe, the Masai. They drink the blood of their cattle. They are picturesque, mysterious and live by their own codes."

"Great! That's it. I want a Masai!"

"You *want* a Masai?"

"For my program," she explained hastily, ideas beginning to tumble over each other in her mind.

Mathias was silent, his eyes gazing at her as she stood framed in the doorway. "You are a journalist, I believe?"

"Television."

Mathias frowned slightly. "Kenya is a beautiful country, Miss Preston. The people are warm-hearted. However, Kenya is not a zoo and we are not animals. Imagine, Miss Preston, if I were a television reporter from Nairobi and staying at your Beverly Wilshire Hotel. Would it not be ludicrous for me to discuss with a telephone operator there about my wanting a Red Indian squaw?"

He held up his hand to stall her interruption. "No, Miss

Preston. We have respect for Americans. You are a brash and soulless people to us, but not quaint animals in a reserve to be photographed and teased."

"You don't understand!" Lyn couldn't contain her excitement.

"I hope I don't. Excuse me, you see my board is demanding my attention." He swung away from her.

She took the rebuff philosophically, staring at his slender neck and straight back, at his cheap digital watch strapped around his slim wrist, and at his regulation hotel uniform. She listened to his carefully modulated replies, his serious concern and his polite little laugh.

Yes, she had wanted him at first. He was accessible and could speak intelligently. Then, as she listened to the man's soft tones and saw his sensible brown leather shoes, she recoiled. She wanted a hot-blooded savage in her bed; not an Anglican missionary's puppet.

She wanted one of those Masai.

CHAPTER 15

Charles Royce drew himself up to his full height and pulled back his shoulders. He focused on Lyn, his right eyebrow arching haughtily. "I beg your pardon?" he drawled.

Lyn saw that Royce was making an effort to control his temper, so she decided to goad him some more. "Royce," she said, her voice soft and deceptively soothing, "I want a Masai."

All four members of the Fantasy Tours group were in the hotel's private lounge for a briefing about the safari the following day. Mindelo had telephoned each one of them before dinner, and served them drinks when they arrived for the meeting.

Charles Royce had outlined the departure time and general information before Lyn had spoken. Maggie, sitting alone on a couch was swirling her drink thoughtfully. Susan sat in the chair furthest from Maggie, while Cora stood at the door near Mindelo. There was no one else in the room.

"The Masai are very peculiar people, Miss Preston," Royce said carefully. "They smell rather a lot and have quite repulsive habits like smearing themselves with cow dung and sucking their animals' blood through a straw."

Susan caught her breath with a start; Maggie fanned herself knowingly.

"When you see them, and see them you will, Miss Preston, you will be inclined to move away as rapidly as possible. They are neither pleasant to observe, nor - how shall I put it delicately? - nice to be with."

"Put it as delicately as you like, Royce. You've been a let down so far, haven't you? Harrison Muldoon promised Fulfillment with a capital F, and we're not getting it."

Royce raised his head and peered down his nose at Lyn as though he hoped to silence her with British disdain. "Americans, Miss Preston, have a reputation for being an enterprising race, even if of mixed ancestry. Rather like mongrels really. The opportunities for the Fulfilment you require are indeed here at Mpingo Beach. I cannot, uh," he hesitated, "force a horse to drink."

"Or a dog to mount a bitch in heat, you mean." Lyn's upper lip curled in scorn. "I haven't seen a dog worthy of the name yet. A teenage tennis pro, a missionary telephone operator and your own acolyte, Mindelo. Is that what you're offering four horny ladies in search of Fulfillment?"

"Lyn, you're not on camera now." Cora's voice cut across the silence of embarrassment. "Don't count me as one of your horny ladies. I'm only fifteen, remember?" She pushed open the door. "I don't want no stinking Masai near me."

"Is the meeting over?" Susan had paled and her voice shook.

Lyn realized she had lost the support of the others. "Cora," she called, "stay to hear what Royce has to tell us. Don't you want to know if Mindelo is going with us tomorrow?"

"I'm going, Miss Preston," Mindelo said, keeping his head lowered and his eyes averted from Royce.

"Okay." Lyn put her hand on her hip and tossed her main of hair. "Junior's all right. Now what about us consenting adults, eh, Royce?"

"Miss Preston!" Royce cleared his throat, making his distaste for her obvious. "Perhaps an analyst would be more help to you than a tour guide? You're in Kenya, guests of a beautiful and friendly people. Any kind of human relationship is possible, given the will and the, uh, ability."

He waved his hand at the window overlooking the patio dance floor. The rhythmic throb of African drums from the band playing in the shadows by the swimming pool, drifted through to them above the whir of the air-conditioner.

"You have here a paradise. You have your own luxury beach villa cottage in a tropical flower-filled haven. The most handsome Africans are your personal hotel staff to care for you. There is a vast stretch of coral sand, and sea and pool for you to enjoy under the hot sun. The ingredients are here for magic, but it is for you to cast your spell, not I."

"That's beautiful," said Susan with a sigh.

Lyn clapped mockingly. "Baloney! We're not here for that tourist brochure bullshit, and you know it. Am I going to get my Masai or not?"

"Tomorrow, Miss Preston, at Fisi Lodge, you will see lions, elephants, zebras, giraffes; wild animals by the hundreds. And, yes, you will see Masai. However, you will no more want one than you will want to handle a hyena." He glanced at his clipboard.

"Please carry only one bag with you. Your clothes will be perfectly safe here in your villas. Of course, valuables should be deposited in the hotel safe. Mindelo will pick up your bags at eight."

Maggie scoffed loudly. "I ain't going, Royce."

He turned to her with a pained expression. "Don't say that, Mrs. Biddle-Macdonald. We fly in a private plane to the lodge, it's very comfortable, and the balloon trip from there is the highlight of the safari. There is champagne breakfast afterward."

"In the middle of a wild animal reserve? No, Royce, I'm staying here. Susan, too."

"I couldn't stay, Maggie. I'm sorry. I really do want to see those animals and fly in a balloon. I'm not sure about the Masai, though."

"They'll suck your blood, dear. You'll be better off here with me."

Susan turned her head so she did not see the pleading expression in Maggie's bloodshot eyes.

Lyn grinned. "That's my girl, Sue. Not afraid of a little adventure after all."

The sound of drumming through the half-opened door grew frenetic. Cora could no longer restrain herself and she began to shake to the beat. "Oh, boy! That does something. Come with me, Mindelo."

Mindelo bit his lip and glanced at Mr. Royce.

"It is not permitted," Royce snapped.

"Okay." Cora shrugged and slipped out, banging the door behind her.

"Charming," Lyn murmured. Royce ignored her and walked to his desk in a corner of the room and sat at it, shuffling papers.

Mindelo stepped forward. "Can I get you another drink, Miss?"

"He's got you well trained, hasn't he?" Lyn raised her voice so that Royce could hear what she was saying. "Don't you ever want to tell that pompous limey to kiss your ass."

Mindelo paled, his eyes pleading with her not to say anything more.

"You're really shocked!" She was puzzled. "I misjudged you. I thought you don't care a shit, but you do." She paused thoughtfully. "I know, it's the missionaries, isn't it. Did missionaries raise you, like Mathias?"

"Mr. Royce did," he said softly, his eyes hard.

"Indeed? Cunning bastard. Got you shackled to him by gratitude. Moral blackmail. Slavery in another guise."

Royce raised his head from the papers spread out in front of him. He gazed coldly across the room at Lyn. There was silence while she gloated, sensing that she had finally irked him into losing his temper.

He opened his mouth to speak, then closed it. He raised his arm with his elbow resting on the desk and beckoned Mindelo with his forefinger. "Whisky!"

"Yes, bwana." Mindelo slipped quietly from the room, heading for the bar. Susan gazed after him to avoid having to face Maggie's reproachful stare.

Royce stroked his sandy moustache and seemed to be considering Lyn's taunts. "In Kenya," he said carefully, "one is allowed to live the life one chooses, providing one doesn't offend the authorities. It's a good life and I have tried to share what little I have with others, such as Mindelo, who otherwise would not have been so fortunate.

"To survive myself, I have had to become an escort to rather boorish visitors who are remarkable only for their selfishness, prejudices and ignorance. The more I meet of my fellow westerners, Miss Preston," Royce paused, placing his open palms up on the desk top, "the more I value the friendship and loyalty of the Kenyans of my acquaintance."

Lyn's eyes glinted. "Are you saying I'm prejudiced, Royce?"

"How typical of your kind that you should choose to misunderstand me. Royce shook his head sadly. "Please excuse me, ladies. I have work to do."

"Sure!" Lyn flounced angrily toward the door, hoping her action would somehow convey a threat. "Get on with your work, Royce. Just don't forget my Masai!"

✦ ✦ ✦ ✦

In the security of her cottage, Susan wondered why Lyn was being so hateful. The Masai sounded repulsive and she was sure what Mr. Royce said was right. He was a nice English gentleman and it was wrong for Lyn to be so mean to him.

She had pleaded a headache when Lyn asked her to join her for dinner after the meeting. She wanted to get away from Lyn and Maggie for a while. She was glad Maggie wasn't going on the safari. There were bad vibrations around her, even though she was basically just a lonely old lady.

She sat on the couch and put her legs up. Her skin was tingling with the effects of her day in the sun and she felt a warm glow all over. She was tired, and the distant throbbing of the drums accompanying the folkloric dancers at the poolside, lulled her into drowsiness. Soon, she told herself, she would go to bed.

The gentle tap on the door penetrated her mind slowly. At first, it seemed to be part of the drumming, until it became more insistent. When she heard her name being called she sat up in alarm.

"Who's there?" she called. At the bottom of her heart she knew, and she was surprised after what had happened in the morning. She licked her dry lips nervously.

"Katana," a voice whispered urgently. "Open the door."

"Wait a minute." She crossed the floor to the bathroom and peered in the mirror. She patted down her hair, wondering if she really wanted this to happen. She wore a simple dress in yellow with a zodiac pattern, and sandals. She was okay. She pattered over to the door and opened it quickly. She stared at the youth outside, uncertain what to say.

"I said I'd come." Paul Katana stepped inside the cottage without waiting for her to ask him in. He shut the door behind him. "You didn't think I would."

She twisted her fingers together and shrugged.

"Let's sit down?" Paul put his hand on her elbow and guided her to the couch. She felt so weak.

"I've been longing for this evening to come, Susan," he said. "I mean it. I want to explain what happened this morning."

She reacted to his pressure on her arm and sat down. Paul was gazing at her with a smile of understanding. "Do you have any beer?" he asked.

She had expected him to say something else, perhaps something romantic. The feelings stirring within her were alarming. "In the mini-bar." Her voice quavered.

Paul got his beer and returned to sit down on the couch beside her. Its over-stuffed cushions engulfed him. He raised the bottle to his lips. "You don't want anything?" he asked, remembering his manners.

She shook her head, not trusting herself to speak. Paul looked so strong and confident, older than when she had played tennis with him that morning. As though sensing her apprehension, he put his arm along the back of the couch and moved closer. She hung her head.

"What's wrong, Susan?" He placed the beer bottle on the mahogany coffee table and turned to face her. "I thought you liked me, just a little bit?"

"You went with Maggie!" The accusation fell from her lips before she could stop herself.

"That's right." He caught her fingers in his hands and gazed at them. "Such beautiful hands, Susan," he said, squeezing them in his own.

She withdrew her fingers slowly. Her flesh was tingling and an ache had sprung up inside her, which she hoped to ignore. She shifted nervously. "Why, Paul? How could you do such a thing?"

"It's not what you think." He looked crestfallen and put his arm at the back of the couch again. "She's very domineering, that friend of yours."

"She's not my friend. I only met her on this vacation."

"That pleases me. I could not understand your relationship."

She relaxed. Paul's face was cute, full of concern and with a short, flat nose she wanted to rub against her own. "Why did you go with her?" she asked again.

"I said it's not what you think. You do believe me, don't you?" He rubbed his hand gently against her shoulders but she held herself still, not giving in.

"She made me cancel my tennis lessons for the morning

and told me to put all the fees I was missing on her bill. I tried to get away, but I couldn't."

"She kept a strong man like you hostage?" Susan giggled. "You fibber." She moved slightly so she was closer to him. She was still apprehensive but the sincerity in Paul's smile reassured her.

"It's true! You must know how she is. Besides, she said she would pay me and, Susan, I need money."

She pulled away in alarm. "You took money from her?"

"She gave me a hundred dollars."

Susan bit her lip. She felt awful.

"A hundred dollars for nothing!" Paul laughed and reached out, pulling her to him. He tightened his grip around her shoulders. "The old biddy was just lonely. I had to shift some suitcases for her, and open a bottle of champagne. Most of the time she spoke about her husbands and not having anyone around any more. She got drunk and passed out."

Susan was still not convinced, but she relaxed as Paul hugged her. "She passed out on the couch, not the bed. I read a magazine and waited till she woke up. She hadn't paid me in advance, you see, so I couldn't go."

She pulled away from him so she could look at his eyes. They were dark, and vibrant with an emotion that made her shiver. She breathed softly, hardly daring to move. He was drawing closer and his eyes seemed to bewitch her. She opened her mouth, and his lips closed on hers.

Gently he lay her down on the couch. His breath tingled her cheeks, causing her to quiver with pleasure. He lay on the couch with her and ran his firm hands down her sides. She struggled to resist the ecstasy of feelings he was stirring within her. She wasn't relaxed; she was teetering on the edge of an abyss and sensed that one push from Paul and she would leap into it. Willingly.

"You have a present for me?"

"What?" She opened her eyes and saw his face so close to hers, grinning eagerly. She wriggled out of his embrace and sat up.

"Cash is best."

She tried to clear her head, to understand what was happening. Deep inside her there was knot. It was almost untied, but now it was tightening again. Paul should have untied it. "I think you'd better go."

He sat up. "If you like."

He left the couch without another word and she watched him uneasily as he moved around the room. "What are you doing?"

"Your purse," he said, "where is it?" He winked at her. "It's all right, you needn't get up." His eye fell on her handbag on the floor beside the couch. He leaned over her and lifted it up.

"Leave that alone," she said, surprised at the strength on her voice. The knot tightened, choking her. She struggled for breath.

"It's all right, Susan." He winked again. "A little present for me before I go?" He held up some notes. "That's enough." He snapped the purse shut and put it on the coffee table. "I'll come and see you another time, when you're ready. It's all right. I understand."

He stepped over to the door, opened it, looked out, and then turned back to her. *"Asante!"*

He waved and was gone.

CHAPTER 16

Maggie smiled hungrily at the room service waiter. The thick drapes drawn across the patio doors masked the harsh brilliance of the mid-morning sunlight. She saw the man who hovered beside her bed as a darker shadow in the gloom of the room. He laid the tray with her fresh Kenya coffee on the bedside table. The aroma aroused her.

"What do you want, boy?" She sounded more intimidating than she meant. The waiter took a step backward.

"The curtains, Missus..."

"Leave them!"

There was silence. "Is there anything else, Missus - "

She cut him off in mid-sentence. "Depends what you have in mind." She sank deeper into the depths of the bed. In dim profile, the waiter was athletic and attractive.

"Champagne, Missus?"

"Know my habits already, do you?" Maggie wriggled her shoulders in the array of pillows behind her head. Before telephoning room service to send coffee, she had brightened her face, and put on her wig. Now she sighed. The others, Susan, Lyn and Cora, would have gone off on their damn safari. She was alone. "Maybe later," she said, waving the waiter away.

"Thank you, ma'am." He slipped out of the bedroom and out of the cottage.

Maggie eased herself to a sitting position and poured coffee from the pot, letting the warm, charred fragrance waft over her. She inhaled it, smiling wistfully. *Would the waiter have climbed into bed with me if I had told him to?* she wondered. The idea was stimulating.

She slid her hand under the sheet, trying to see herself as the waiter would have done. Her hand explored her body. Her breasts, well they had gone. Only the skill of her dressmaker could give her the curves of a figure now. Her fingers sank into the soft flesh of her stomach and she groaned. She hadn't always been so fat.

Before she had eloped from Boston in 1939 with her first husband, Boris, she had been admired for her wild beauty.

She used her looks to make men weak. In marriage, she was faithful; she cared well for all her husbands and loved them dearly. With her happiness came indulgence. The sylph-like Margaret of her youth ballooned over forty years into the formidable Maggie of her widowhood.

Now she was bitter. At an age when she needed a strong man to take care of her, she had none. Her wealth meant nothing. What satisfaction would there be in having the room-service waiter in her bed? In her mind there was desire, but it was overwhelmed by a furious sorrow for the lost days when men had hungered for her and she had the pick of the best of them. She began to cry softly.

Margaret Biddle-Macdonald, she thought to herself as she raised the coffee cup to her lips, *what is happening to you?* The coffee jolted her and she sipped it easily. Now she felt rational enough to wonder where the yearning that had seized her in that Manhattan elevator had come from.

Was it chemical, a reaction to the pills her doctor had prescribed? Or was it a desperate urge for a final fling? Whatever the reason for the overwhelming feeling of lust that was bedeviling her, she knew that eventually she would have to exorcise it.

She dozed. It was late in the morning, but there was no need for her to get up. She lay staring at the ceiling, only gradually becoming aware of a new sound in the room. She raised her head and listened. The noise was repeated, a gentle tapping, and then it stopped, only to start again a few seconds later.

"Damn! It's the maid," she said aloud, struggling out of bed and wrapping her robe around her. She swept into the parlor. There was no one there. She paused. There was a tap, more loudly this time, on the front door.

"Who is it?" The tapping stopped as soon as she spoke. "I said who's there?"

"Mrs. Biddle-Macdonald?" a rough voice demanded.

"Yes." She remembered men, not maids, cleaned the cottages. "Can you come back later to clean. I am resting now."

The deep voice spoke more politely. "Not your room steward."

"What do you want?"

"I send by Mr. Royce."

"Oh, very well." She opened the door and peered out. When she saw the tall African standing on the porch, she hesitated. Slowly it occurred to her that he wasn't one of the hotel staff because he wore a ripped T-shirt and jeans, instead of a safari suit uniform.

She tried to close the door but the man lowered his head and stepped into the room. He shut the door with a push from his massive hand, and glanced around.

"You alone?"

"What do you want?" She stepped backward. There was a telephone on the bureau. "What are you doing here?" She wondered if she could reach the telephone without him becoming alarmed... or violent.

"Hah, alone!" The realization seemed to give the huge man satisfaction. He beamed.

"My husband is coming!" she said sternly.

The man shook his head. "No husband." His voice was calm and confident.

Sounds filled the room as they stood staring at each other. There was the giggling of tourists returning from the beach, the clatter of a room steward at work in the next door cottage, the wheeze of the air-conditioner, the caw of curious birds, and the gentle rush of the ocean on the shore.

She gazed up at the man's face. His eyes were dark and unfathomable and his features heavy. His broad body seemed to burst out of his T-shirt, and his jeans were so tight she found her eyes drawn to them. She flushed, and clasped her robe around her when she realized the man was appraising her too.

He smacked his lips together and flung himself down on the couch. It skittered under his bulk. He lay back with his head on a cushion and put his bare feet up on the other end. They were caked with dried mud. He seemed quite at home.

"I walk plenty to get here," he said. "You have beer?"

"Who the hell are you?" Maggie had overcome her surprise. She reached for the telephone. "I am going to call security and have you removed."

The man grinned, making no attempt to move. His appearance changed with his smile, it gave him a distinct and not unattractive allure. "Go ahead," he said, a twinkle in his eye. His hand, which had been resting on the back of the couch, fell casually on his crotch.

He was still grinning when Maggie withdrew her hand from the phone.

"Who told you to come here?"

"No one. What about that beer, bibi?"

"Get it yourself!"

"Hah!" The man's sigh of pleasure signaled a subtle change in the atmosphere between them. He knew he had been accepted and this indicated too that he was not a threat to her. He stretched, flinging his arms out behind his head and extending his legs over the side of the couch. Maggie swallowed appreciatively. He arched his hips, revealing the contours of his massive body.

She opened the refrigerator and took out a beer. She tossed it to him. It fell on his crotch. The man picked it up without flinching and smiled at her. She felt coquettish under his gaze.

"I usually have champagne," she giggled nervously. "Not beer."

The man shrugged, opened the beer and poured it into his mouth, draining the bottle in one gulp.

"What do you want?" she asked coyly, toying with the belt of her robe.

"I look for Mr. Royce."

She sat down and pouted. "You won't find him here. He's gone on safari." She waved her hand sadly at the closed curtains. "They've all gone."

The man took time to digest this information. Maggie surveyed him again from where she sat. He was in superb shape. With a bath and good clothes, perhaps white pants and a Gucci shirt with a gold chain around his neck, he would be devastating.

The man saw her watching him. "Mindelo say don't come," he announced, swinging his legs off the couch and preparing to stand up. "He right!"

"No!" Her misgivings returned, but for a different reason. There was something about this creature when he smiled that softened the brute-like quality of his appearance, and made him seem vulnerable. She was intrigued.

"Don't go," she said softly, walking to the couch and standing in front of him.

The man faltered. A line of concern streaked across his fine, wide brow. "You want me stay?" He sounded surprised, but not offended.

"Why not?" She opened the refrigerator and pulled out a bottle of Dom Perignon. She put it in his hand. "Open this, will you. There are glasses behind you."

She moved toward the bedroom. "I'm just going to fix myself up." She smiled at him. "What's your name?"

"Njonjo," he said, frowning at the bottle.

He was still regarding it with curiosity when she returned. She had straightened her wig, powdered herself and changed her robe to something less revealing. Even in the soft glow of the parlor with the curtains closed and only the sunlight filtering through the fabric, she didn't want him to see too much. Not yet.

"Darling!" she said, raising her hands in mock amazement. "Why haven't you poured my drink?"

"What beer this? It have wire instead of cap."

"Of course it has. Oh dear, I suppose you've never had champagne before." He shook his head as though it didn't matter to him at all.

"You'll love it. Just remove the wire and ease out the cork with your fingers. Be careful now, it will fizz out if you shake it too much." She giggled as his huge hand enveloped the bottle.

There was a loud pop and the cork shot out and bounced off the ceiling. The man stared at the bottle in astonishment.

Maggie held out her glass and nodded to him to pour. The champagne frothed into it. "Slower, darling," she said. "My, you have such a lot to learn."

"First time this beer." He smiled simply. Maggie warmed to him.

"What's your name again?"

"Njonjo."

She giggled. "I can't say that. I'll call you Joe." She raised her glass and held it out to him. He stared at it. "Put your glass against mine, it's a toast."

Njonjo shook his head in bewilderment but he did what she showed him. "Let's drink to us," she said, clinking her glass against his. He watched her without moving while she sipped.

"Why aren't you drinking."

"To us? Us?" he frowned.

"Why not? Fate has been generous and thrown us together. Let's accept that." She could hardly believe what she was saying, far less what was happening. She felt wanton and quite wicked.

There was a pause as Joe tasted the champagne. He swallowed it with pleasure and quickly filled his glass from the bottle.

"I'd like some more too." Maggie held out her glass, excited by the man's lack of sophistication. "What do you do, Joe?" she asked when he had filled it. She settled down in the chair opposite him. She had drenched herself with her most expensive perfume and hoped he could smell it.

Njonjo shrugged his broad shoulders and grinned again. "Mindelo no tell you about Njonjo?"

She leaned forward. "Are you famous for something? Let me guess. Are you a limbo dancer? No, with a body like that you'd never get under the bar. I give up. What should Mindelo have told me?"

Njonjo put down his glass and placed his hands on his knees. He looked crestfallen.

Maggie was touched. She walked over to the couch and sat beside him, putting her arm around his neck. It was as broad as an ox's. "I don't mean to pry," she said. "My! Joe! You have the most magnificent physique."

His face brightened.

"I've never met a man so well developed." She gulped. "Why don't you take off that old T-shirt and let me see your body?"

He responded immediately. She was pleased. He was obviously used to obeying such orders. It made things easier. She gasped with surprise when he stood up and began to flex his muscles. He was truly enormous. But even she didn't expect what happened next.

He suddenly snapped open the fastener at his waist and

peeled down his jeans. He kicked them off so they fell in a heap by the door. He stood in front of her in his yellow swimming trunks and posed like a bodybuilder.

"My god!" Maggie breathed. "You're beautiful."

"Yes, I am." Njonjo grinned with childish pleasure.

She swallowed her champagne, unable to take her eyes off him. "Come here," she whispered.

He moved toward her without hesitation. She put out her hand to touch his stomach. It was rigid with muscle. "Now I know what you're famous for," she giggled, running her fingers over the tight, hard muscles. He stepped out of her reach.

"Come back," she said, making a grab for him. He beamed. She wondered if he understood the game they were beginning. He was obviously rather simple and probably had never been in a hotel room before. The condition of his clothes showed his poverty, and he seemed to have no education. Despite his superb physique, he was like a child.

"Joe," she said, feeling weak at what it could lead to. "After your long walk here, why don't you take a shower? After that, let's...talk."

"You like my body?" he asked, his voice deep.

"I'll like it much more when you've had a shower."

He hesitated, seemed about to say something, and then shrugged his shoulders.

"Shower, Joe!" Maggie's voice rose to a command. He turned in the direction she was pointing and padded across the bedroom to the bathroom. She followed him, and sat on the bed sipping champagne, waiting.

When he emerged, he was holding his wet swimming trunks in one hand and clutching a skimpy towel wrapped around his waist with the other.

"I've prayed for a man like you," she said, feasting her eyes on him. "Someone strong who'll do as he's told."

He looked at her blankly.

"You will do what I tell you, won't you, Joe."

He shrugged his massive shoulders and glanced around the room. He threw his trunks onto the chair beside the bed.

"Come here."

He moved closer. She reached out and pulled the towel

away from his waist.

"Hah! Njonjo good?"

"Oh, I hope so," she said. "I do hope so.

BOOK TWO

Safari

Miim nkoitoi are; mikibela ilomorin
Never take two paths; the pelvis will collapse
(Masai proverb)

CHAPTER 17

The long grass was pale in the fierce sun. It quivered listlessly in the wake of the minibus bouncing along the track from the airstrip. Thick dust swirled through the shaking vehicle, settling like a brown veil on its occupants. The savanna stretched into the haze of the horizon, a few straggly trees being the only break in the pallid landscape.

"This is lion country," a voice drawled from the back of the minibus. "Prides of up to thirty lions aren't uncommon." Charles Royce's monologue broke into Susan's contemplation of the endless plain. He was sitting in the back because Lyn had bagged the best seat, in the front next to the driver.

Susan squinted through her sunglasses. She had expected scenery more lush and interesting than this dry blanket of grass. The promise of prides of lions seemed an unlikely one. The rough road, the dust and her desperate need for a toilet dimmed the thrill for her of being in the heart of Kenya's game country.

Together with Lyn and Cora, she had flown the 800 kilometers from the coast in a state of sheer apprehension. It was her first flight in an aircraft smaller than a jumbo jet and she had felt duty bound to pray throughout the flight to keep the plane in the air. The spectacular views of Mount Kilimanjaro increased her nervousness when she pictured the plane slamming into it.

Her feeling of discomfort continued as she clung to her seat in the minibus. Royce was droning on about the animals to be seen in the park, but her thoughts were on Paul Katana. The misery of this journey was a penance for what had happened. He had completely fooled her. She never wanted to see him or any other African again.

Lyn had been just as quiet on the trip and only Cora, who had insisted on sitting in the back with Mindelo, seemed to be enjoying herself. Susan heard her gasp with delight at the sight of gazelles leaping deep into grass. She glanced around and saw that Cora's eyes were shining with excitement. And something else: radiance. Susan sighed with envy.

"We'll soon be there, Miss Ross," Mindelo whispered.

"The Masai Mara Game Reserve," Royce was reciting, "is Kenya's leading wildlife reserve. It has eighteen thousand square kilometers of rolling grasslands and an unrivalled abundance of wild life. It's an extension of the Serengeti."

"Imagine!" Susan murmured, to be polite. Three tribesmen swathed in clay-red cloth were standing ahead of them beside the trail.

"Masai!" shouted Lyn, suddenly coming to life and raising her camera. She leaned out of the window as the minibus slowed down. The driver, a burly man with a khaki bush shirt, put out his hand and tapped her vigorously on her shoulder. She glared at him.

"Don't photograph the Masai. They throw stones and break the bus. Photograph that!" The driver pointed to the other side of the trail where zebra were gazing.

"Stuff your fucking animals," Lyn said, smarting at the rebuke. "The people are what I'm here for."

"Please do what he says," Susan said anxiously. "I can't take much more of this, not if you provoke the Masai to attack us."

"Would they do that?" Lyn turned in her seat and glared at Royce.

He hesitated, then found the words he wanted. "The Masai used to be a terror throughout Kenya. They're subdued now but occasionally one meets a bad egg."

The minibus slowed to a crawl and Susan peered out anxiously. The three men standing at the side of the road had their heads shaved and plastic-covered wires hanging from their ears. They wore blankets from their shoulders to their ankles. They watched the minibus impassively as it passed.

"It's all right, Miss Ross." Mindelo leaned forward and smiled to reassure her. "The Masai women won't throw stones."

"They are women?" She gasped. "Oh dear, I thought they were men. Why are their heads shaved?"

"The Masai have their customs, Miss Ross. I really don't know."

Susan glanced around her as the minibus came to a halt under an arch of stone rising in isolation in the middle of the savanna. A wooden sign, which hung from the arch, was carved with the name: Fisi Lodge.

"This lodge is built on the site professional hunters used as a base, in the days of the big game safaris."

She ignored Royce and gazed out of the window. The driver was talking to one of the lodge guards. Through the arch was a compound of modern, native-style huts. She wondered if they housed tame Masai. Ahead, its deep-eaved roof duplicating the curves of the arch, was Fisi Lodge. A bevy of minibuses was parked in front of it. Well-mown lawns emphasized the difference wrought on the savanna by the property developers who had replaced the great white hunters of old.

There was a commotion at the front of the minibus. Unnoticed by the others, Lyn had attracted the attention of one of the colorfully clad tribesmen who had been squatting in the shade of the archway. She had persuaded him to raise himself off his haunches. He now stood a meter from the minibus, regarding Lyn curiously.

He was enveloped in a blanket and carried a spear. Under his blanket, Susan saw the clay-red of another robe. His legs were gnarled and sinewy in contrast to the youth of his face. His hair was woven into fine plaits like strings of tiny beads. In each ear he wore a small red bauble suspended on a blue wire, and a choker of brightly colored plastic around his neck.

She was fascinated by his opaque eyes, which were contemplating Lyn from the depths of his dark face. She sensed the effort the Masai was making to bridge the gap between his culture and Lyn's. He showed no emotion, only a stare of mild interest. His eyes flickered briefly over Susan and she felt disturbed. Cora must have felt the same because she heard her gasp.

"What does that ugly brute want?"

"Quiet!" Lyn hushed Cora into a reluctant silence.

The Masai returned his attention to Lyn. His lips, large and fleshy, parted slowly. He did not speak but raised his thumb to his open mouth and put it between his lips. He closed his mouth around it without a sound, then opened it again and withdrew his thumb. An expectant look entered his eyes as he repeated the gesture. There was silence in the minibus.

"Does he mean what I think he means?" Lyn said softly.

"You've met your match now"! Cora snorted with contempt. "Didn't your mother ever tell you not to speak to strange men? He wants you to go down on him."

Susan was deeply shocked. "How can you say such a thing. He looks so proud and noble, a little terrifying though."

Cora giggled. "I'm sure he's perfectly charming too."

Lyn pointed to herself and patted her breast with her open hand. "Me?" she asked, her eyes glinting.

"It's not you he wants," Royce said wearily. "He's asking for a cigarette. All these buggers are scroungers dressed up for tourists."

The driver revved up the minibus and lurched through the archway, leaving the Masai standing solemnly beside the road, staring into space, his spear grasped in his hand.

◆ ◆ ◆ ◆ ◆

It was what Charles Royce called *Sundowner Time,* but he wasn't there. Susan gratefully joined Lyn and Cora at the low table on the veranda of the Lodge's cocktail bar. A steward hovered, took her order, and back away. She glanced at the faces of her two companions.

Cora's eyes were bright and she was watching the lawn by the swimming pool where a group of monkeys were gamboling. Lyn seemed exhausted and had a distant look in her eyes.

They had all spent a grueling afternoon and shared a turmoil of experiences that left Susan dazed. After their arrival they had checked into their cabins and had a traditional Kenya buffet lunch. There had been little chance to rest before the three of them were herded back to the minibus and bounced for hours across the savanna on a game drive.

They had seen game, enough to last Susan for a lifetime. Giraffe, gazelle, topi, elephant, hyena, jackal, zebra, wildebeest, lion, goats, sheep, and cows. The driver had worked hard, intuitively swinging the bus through the grass to find more animals to impress them, But he kept them away from the Masai.

"Look, a zebra," Cora said suddenly, pointing into the spreading gloom of the night descending over the Lodge grounds.

"Not another fucking animal," groaned Lyn. "The only animal I haven't seen swinging his balls today is a human one."

The steward strolled over to them. Lyn reached for her vodka and started to drink without waiting for the others. Susan took her juice and sipped it slowly. Cora gazed around the hotel grounds, where safari buses were disgorging their occupants: middle-aged men festooned with cameras and bulky ladies clutching bags.

"You won't see Mindelo there, Cora," Lyn said, finishing her vodka. "He's in the compound where the staff sleep. It's off limits to guests."

"Leave me alone," Cora said sulkily.

"I'm sure you must miss companions of your own age," Susan said, to stop the row that was brewing.

"I don't know about Cora, but I do." Lyn reached for a cigarette and lit it quickly. "What do you think of those Masai, Sue?"

She was startled. "I don't know..."

"For heaven's sake, Sue! You can do better than that. "What's got into you? You've been moody all day."

"I'm sorry," she stammered. "The Masai do seem strange, sort of remote."

"Don't they intrigue you?"

"Not really."

Lyn drew heavily on her cigarette, her eyes searching her face as though she expected to find more there than she could see. Susan bit her lip nervously.

"Let me tell you about the Masai, Sue." Lyn pulled a tourist leaflet from her pocket and waved it at her.

"It says here that the Masai are settling down and beginning to ranch. That means they were wild animals and now they're becoming domesticated. Imagine a proud lion turning into a Siamese cat. That's what so-called civilization means in Africa."

"Does it?" Susan swirled the melting ice around in her

glass. She was flattered that Lyn was trying out some ideas on her that might eventually appear in her TV program. Yet she had her doubts.

"Lyn, I hope you don't mind," she said cautiously. "Isn't civilization of any kind better for these people than the dreadful existence they have in this wilderness?"

"You do have a brain. I knew it!" Lyn's eyes stirred. "The Masai aren't fools, Sue, I'm sure. It says here that they are keeping many of their traditions intact, including their red ochre dress and bead work decoration -"

"Those beads are plastic!" Cora was scornful. "I've seen those necklaces on sale in the gift shop here."

"That's civilization!" said Lyn triumphantly. "Listen to this. Other traditions remaining are their diet of cow's blood and milk, and their *moran* system where the youth of the tribe is segregated and brought up under a rigid code of discipline and self-denial, *sex excepted!*" Lyn threw down the leaflet on the table. "Now, what do you make of that?"

"I knew sex would come into it somehow," said Cora.

"Mr. Royce said the Masai share each other's wives. They even circumcise their women." Susan was trying to be helpful. "Are you going to do a TV program on the Masai?"

Lyn's face clouded. She shook her head as she stubbed out her cigarette. "They intrigue me, that's all. I wonder if they wear anything under those robes?"

"You're sure to be the one to find out." Cora twisted restlessly in her seat. "I'm going for a walk."

"Isn't that dangerous?" Susan looked worried. "There's a notice on the path which says that the Lodge accepts no responsibility for personal injury whether fatal or otherwise by wild animals."

"You love notices, don't you." Lyn sneered. "Your mind is over-conditioned to authority."

"That notice is just to fool us into believing we're living dangerously," Cora said. "Those elephants and monkeys by the pool are tame really. It's a show for us paying guests."

This upset Susan. "Those animals are *wild*! That's why they have security guards posted behind our cabins. When you go to your cabin after dark, a guard has to go with you in case an animal attacks."

"Really?" Lyn leaned forward, her tired eyes showing interest.

"Only to the cabin door, Lyn, not inside!" Cora stood up. "I'm not having dinner tonight. I'm going to bed."

"I think I'll go too," said Susan. "It's been a long day. Please excuse me." She rose from her seat and followed Cora.

The men drinking Tuskers at the bar watched her appreciatively as she crossed the lounge.

When Susan reached the lobby she saw a man alighting from a Range Rover in front of the Lodge entrance. She couldn't help staring at him. He was classically handsome with strong features and a skin glistening like oiled ebony.

He was dressed in a tailored safari suit with the jacket belted tightly at his waist. He wore expensive-looking, polished leather boots, which she noticed as he placed his feet firmly on the gravel drive and flexed his knees, as though testing the ground.

Apparently satisfied, he reached his hand inside the vehicle. A svelte young woman, her hair long and lustrous around her shining face, stepped down beside him. The man raised his head and looked into the lobby.

He exuded such a strong presence, everyone in the lobby seemed aware of his arrival. Stewards were rushing forward to greet him. The receptionists looked alert.

Susan stared and for a moment the man's eyes met hers. She saw how beguiling and passionate they were.

A hand touched her arm respectfully. "You wish to go to your cabin, miss?" A guard was standing at her elbow with a flashlight.

"Yes," she answered meekly.

She was in a daze as she followed the guard out of the lobby and along a floodlit path to her cabin. She realized vaguely that the guard was telling her something about the elephant standing in the middle of the lawn. She listened without hearing. Her mind was full of the image of the tall stranger so elegantly dressed and self-assured, and of the probing glance he had given her.

It was a glance that, even though it lasted only a few seconds, made her forget the doubts in her heart.

CHAPTER 18

Susan blinked away the dream that had enthralled her. The polished cedar paneling of the cabin walls enhanced her feeling of contentment. The cabin was small, she could have been on a luxury yacht, and she felt secure. In the night when she had been woken by a noise, she felt no sense of alarm. Peering out of the window onto the moonlit lawn, she had seen a zebra staring back at her. It seemed natural and quite safe.

Now there was a repeat of the tapping on the door and this had roused her. She was warm and comfortable. The essence of her dream lingered. She tried to recall the reason for this extraordinary pleasantness but it slipped back into her subconscious.

"Mrs. Ross?" There was a heavier rapping of knuckles on the door. "It's Mindelo." She yawned. "Time to get up."

She glanced at the small traveling clock on the table beside her bed. "It's only six-thirty!"

"That's right." Mindelo sounded cool and efficient through the wall of the cabin. "The balloon takes off at seven."

She cradled her pillow close to her cheek and rubbed her nose in it, smiling happily. She felt good. She wondered if her marvelous feeling would evaporate when she left the warmth of the bed and the security of the cabin. She was nearly 2,000 meters above sea level, in the middle of an African game reserve, and she was happier than she had been for months. It was incredible.

Reluctantly, she released the pillow and rolled over. She closed her eyes, casting inward to locate the source of her wellbeing. The image of the broad-shouldered, well-dressed stranger leaped into her mind.

The gentle, almost mocking smile, which played on his lips when his eyes caught her glance of amazement, still thrilled her. Yet her heart was troubled when she thought of the young woman, stunningly beautiful, who clung to his arm with fierce affection.

She threw back the covers and got out of bed. Her mood

darkened and she prepared herself for the day, quickly and crossly. It was absurd, she thought as she brushed her hair severely, one minute she was soaring without even being in a balloon, the next minute she felt downhearted.

She let her mind conjure up the vision of the man again; his graceful movement as he descended from his vehicle and the supremely confident way his eyes had swept the lobby, until they latched onto hers. Did she dream it, or had the man's delicately fine eyebrow curved up in a query, as if to say: *who are you?*

"Mrs. Ross!" The tap on the door was emphatic. "Time to go."

She sighed and turned away from the mirror. "I'm coming, Mindelo."

When she opened the door he was still there, waiting. His face lit up. "You look very nice this morning."

The compliment flustered her. She concentrated on closing the door, which was divided into two sections, top and bottom. She was wearing her usual outfit of T-shirt and jeans but Mindelo, with a strange perception, had noticed a difference in her appearance. She did feel different, but she didn't know it showed.

"Well, I'm looking forward to this balloon ride," she explained. "Where are the others?"

"Cora is waiting in the lobby. Miss Preston says she isn't coming."

"Why not?" She followed Mindelo along the path. The air was cool and she was grateful for the knitted woolen jacket she wore around her shoulders. "Perhaps she went to sleep late last night."

"I don't know, miss."

"I went to bed early."

"Yes, miss." Mindelo's tone showed that he was not surprised at her sober behavior.

"There was a man checking in when I went to my cabin last night. An African, well dressed. He was tall and looked pretty impressive." She felt silly. "Everyone seemed to know him," she added to explain her curiosity. "I was wondering who he is."

Mindelo's soft smile suggested that he understood a

deeper reason for her interest. "I'll find out for you."

"It's not that important." She lapsed into silence, wondering how the stranger had spent his evening. Probably dining on the terrace with his girl friend, then drinking at the bar with the hearty men gathered there like buffalo around a watering hole. He was probably asleep in one of these cabins, she thought as she glanced around. He was surely not alone.

Mindelo led her beyond a row of luxury cabins into an open paddock. There were two blocks of rooms enclosing the paddock on one side and a steel framed tower supporting a water tank. The manicured lawn of the paddock rolled up to the long grass of the savanna, which stretched into a clump of straggly trees on the horizon. The sky was gray, dawning leisurely as the brilliance of sunrise overtook it.

In the middle of the paddock stood Charles Royce. His hands were on his hips and he was contemplating an expanse of nylon, striped yellow and orange, which was lying on the grass in front of him. A large wicker basket lay on its side and five men wearing orange overalls and black rubber boots, stood beside it. They seemed to be waiting for someone.

"Good morning, Mr. Royce." She regarded the scene with surprise. "Where's the balloon?"

"There." Royce pointed at the nylon laid out on the grass.

"I bet you've never been up in this thing!" said Cora as she advanced on them. Her thin face was pinched by the morning chill. Her eyes shifted from Royce to Mindelo. She grinned at him.

"Of course I have, Cora." Royce sounded agitated. "So has Jacqueline Kennedy Onasis and three thousand others."

Cora sniffed. "That's not many."

"Then you'll be among a small elite."

"Screw that!" Cora scowled. "Why have we got to start so early?"

"Two reasons," Royce drawled. "One is because that's when the game is around, but secondly and most important, is that the air is cooler at this hour. A calm African morning makes conditions perfect for ballooning."

The men lounging around the basket began to move with an air of purpose. Susan saw the reason was a fair-haired man in white shorts who was striding across the grass. One of the men kneeled beside the basket and started a small motor. It growled noisily as it powered a large fan that swirled air into the striped nylon that was spread over the lawn. This was the bag of the balloon. As air wafted into it, it bellowed open.

"He's your pilot," Royce nodded at the fair-haired man. He was checking the apparatus inside the basket.

When the balloon was inflated, the pilot stepped inside the bag while the crew held the mouth open for him. He checked ropes inside it. He hadn't acknowledged the presence of Charles Royce and his group.

Susan felt small. She wondered about the wisdom of what they were about to do. She would have been happier if Lyn was with them. She glanced at Cora for encouragement but she was chatting animatedly with Mindelo.

The balloon expanded, twisting like an awakening snake, its colors enlivening the dull green of the shaved grass. The blast of propane gas startled her. The pilot was crouched in the framework of his basket, intently watching the balloon as he fiddled with dials and sent a squall of flame into the bag.

She shouted at Royce above the noise. "Won't it catch fire?"

Royce shook his head. "The flame is warming the air that's trapped inside the bag. The balloon's lift comes from the hot air." He turned away and frowned meaningfully at Mindelo.

The balloon rose proudly into the air, straining at the ropes holding it down. Susan felt a rush of excitement. The crew ran forward and pulled the basket to an upright position. The pilot climbed inside and adjusted the gas burners above his head. The balloon's nylon bag swelled into the sky. It was magnificent.

"It stands as high as a ten story building," Royce was saying, but Susan was too intoxicated by the balloon's shape and splendor to listen properly. "This is the largest operational balloon in the world. At sea level, it could lift a ton."

All five of the orange-clad men who formed the crew were leaning on the gondola to hold it down. The pilot extinguished the flame and signaled to Royce.

"Off you go, Susan," Royce cried, placing his hand in the small of her back when she hesitated.

"Aren't you coming too?"

"Actually, I'm not."

She glanced over at Cora and Mindelo. Cora was approaching the gondola with apprehension while Mindelo stayed behind.

"This way, please," the pilot called. "Just sit on the basket's edge and lift yourself over. My men will help."

"You go first." Cora prodded Susan from behind. She scrambled into the basket and stood in a corner, gripping the rim nervously.

"Can Mindelo come with us?" Cora asked Royce.

"What ever for?" Royce turned away crossly.

The pilot grinned. "Let him come, Royce. There's space."

Mindelo was startled and began to protest.

"Shut up and get in," Cora said impatiently. "You're not scared of a new experience, are you? You're taking Lyn's place. She's paid for it so why not?"

She climbed into the gondola and gestured to Mindelo to stand beside her. Royce was grinding his teeth and eyeing Mindelo under brows heavy with disapproval.

The pilot briefed them briskly, assuming a high degree of intelligence and comprehension from them. "Don't touch this lever or you'll cut off the gas; don't hang on this rope or you'll let the air out of the top. If we have to land suddenly, crouch down, hold the safety handles and bend your knees. And don't worry!"

He gave a signal to the ground crew and the gondola was released. It jerked erratically across the lawn; there was a full, long blast from the burner directly above Susan's head, and the balloon rose skyward.

Cora looked sick and hung on to Mindelo's arm; Susan clutched the basket's edge. It was too late to change her mind. She stared down anxiously at the Lodge. The balloon's shadow was trailing across the lawns. It was an eerie feeling, dangling precariously in a basket under a candy-striped bubble of hot air.

Suddenly, her heart leapt. A man was standing on the lawn, his hand shielding his eyes as he gazed at the rising balloon. She knew from his stance that he was the man she had seen in the lobby the night before.

"Mindelo," she said quickly. "Him, that's him." She pointed down at the ground but Mindelo refused to look.

"What do you mean *That's him?*" Cora asked suspiciously.

The balloon soared away from Fisi Lodge and floated over the plain. The man was nowhere to be seen when eventually she persuaded Mindelo to look down at the ground.

When the burner was off, all was silent except for the whisper of wind that carried the balloon swiftly in the early morning air. The pilot was scanning the plains below. Susan watched the balloon's shadow drifting below them.

"We're not going very fast," Cora said.

The pilot shrugged. "Balloons don't fly in winds greater than fifteen miles an hour. This kind of gentle breeze is just right for us."

"How do you control which direction we're floating in?" Susan was wondering how they would get back to Fisi Lodge. Would her mystery man still be there?

The pilot smiled. "Balloons have to go where the wind takes them. Winds at different heights often blow in different directions. We can fly higher by opening the burner to heat the balloon. That means I can change direction by changing height."

"Oh dear, it sounds very complicated." She gripped the edge of the basket while the pilot turned his back on her and raised his hand to the burner. The flame shrieked into the air enveloped in the balloon. Perhaps the pilot sensed her misgivings for he turned and grinned to reassure her.

"The envelope is made of rip-stop nylon. We replace it every year. It's the same size as Double Eagle II, the balloon that the Americans used to cross the Atlantic last year, nineteen-seventy-eight."

She relaxed at his calm assurance and open smile and began to enjoy the sensation of drifting, apparently aimlessly, under the sky above Africa. Cora was gazing in excitement below, her hand firmly grasping Mindelo's arm. Even he, as the flight progressed, managed to lose some of his tension.

"Look there!" The pilot pointed to the grass three hundred feet below them, in front of a clump of trees.

"It's a lion!" Cora exclaimed happily.

The balloon began to descend toward the lion. Mindelo was anxiously watching the pilot, but he showed no sign of alarm. Susan felt differently. "If we go much lower, we'll land on it!" she shouted.

The pilot ignored her, letting the balloon swoop downward. She gasped. The pilot opened the burner and the noise disturbed the lion so it ran leisurely toward the trees. The balloon continued to fall until the tall trees scraped the bottom of the gondola and the hot air lifted it skyward again. They zoomed safely over the treetops to be confronted by a file of elephants ambling across a track.

It was an exhilarating hour. Every minute unfolded new wonders: buffalo stampeding through the grass, a rhino lumbering anxiously, giraffe archly superior and an ostrich waddling willy-nilly. This magical time had its effect on all of them. Cora glowed, her coarse behavior mellowed. She pointed out each animal to Mindelo as though she was personally responsible for discovering it.

The pilot opened the burner and Susan watched the view of the ground broadening as the balloon soared upward. Darker lines of trees marked the banks of riverines meandering through the landscape. A larger river cut across the panorama below.

"There's the border with Tanganyika," the pilot said. "That's Serengeti. The wildebeest migrate from there every year."

She was in a state of euphoria. Cora and Mindelo seemed to feel it too. They had lapsed into silence, overawed by this flying at ease, like a graceful bird, across the sky. She thought with sorrow about Lyn and Maggie, each locked in their personal torment, who were missing this liberating experience.

And the man at Fisi Lodge? His strong features intruded into her thoughts with a strange persistence. She wondered if she would ever see him again. Desperately, she wanted to.

Whatever it was about him, no man - white or black - had ever affected her the same way. She wanted to know why.

Suddenly the balloon began to fall rapidly. "My God!" she shrieked, gripping the edge of the basket in fright. Her stomach rose to her mouth.

The pilot raised his hand to the burner, looked at his gas cylinders and then scanned the ground below them. The balloon gathered speed as it hurtled down.

"What's wrong?"

"Nothing." The pilot's voice was crisp. "Remember what to do when we touch down. Crouch below the rim of the basket and hold tight!"

The ground rushed up toward them as the balloon lost altitude. Susan glanced around her. They were coming down in an open plain. There was not a building or a road in sight. She wondered about the elephants and lions they had been flying over. Were they waiting for them in the long grass? She looked at the pilot again. He wasn't even carrying a gun.

An article she had read in an adventure magazine flashed through her mind. "Balloon accidents on the rise," it had said. At the time she had thought nothing of it, never expecting that she would one day fly in a balloon herself. She remembered the statistics, over a hundred injured in ballooning accidents in the USA in the past decade.

"Get ready!" The pilot shouted the warning as the gondola plunged to earth, its burner dead. It skimmed over the tops of raddled trees and plummeted to the grass below. Susan screamed as a lion, at the edge of the glade, lifted its head and roared angrily.

CHAPTER 19

Lyn eased her long legs into the driving seat of the Volkswagen and reached out to close the door. It would not move. A hand was holding it firmly. When she bent her head out of the car to see what was wrong, she found herself gazing into a pair of somber eyes set deeply into a serious face.

The man was dressed like a Hollywood version of a big game hunter, with polished leather boots, neatly pressed khaki pants and a safari hat perched rakishly on the side of his head.

"Thank you," she said, expecting the man to close the door. "I think I'm ready to leave now."

"You're not supposed to go without a scout." The man's deep voice concealed a chuckle. "It's dangerous out there."

"Are you offering your services?"

The man ignored the question. "I'll be in my Range Rover." He nodded his head at the maroon, four-wheel drive vehicle parked next to her small rented Beetle. "We might meet."

"Who knows?" She turned the ignition and felt the VW shudder into life. She raised her eyebrow at the man. He chuckled as though at some private joke and firmly closed the door.

She knocked the car into gear and scorched away, scattering gravel and sand over him. *Good!* His patronizing, macho attitude had annoyed her.

She glanced into the rearview mirror. The man had not moved and stood gazing after her. Even with distance between them she could feel the impact of his stare.

Whoever that cat is, she thought with a shiver, *he knows what he's worth.* She swore angrily to herself and swung into the gas station under the Lodge archway.

"Fill it," she ordered. The attendant rolled his eyes and she fumed while he filled the gas tank at his own leisurely pace.

Africans! she thought glibly, still rankled by the man's attitude. *They are either too smart or too stupid.* She paid the boy and drove off before he too told her not to go into the bush alone.

She followed the rough dirt track beyond the airstrip and headed for what her guide book described as "the vast rolling plains and rounded sea green hills, intermittent groves of acacia woodlands and dense thickets of scrub."

Thank god, Mindelo's gone on the balloon, she thought. He was so damn smart, if he had seen her hiring the car he would have told Royce and the Englishman would have tried to prevent her going. She glanced in the driving mirror. Fisi Lodge was out of view. Now she was free.

The track was nearly engulfed by the long grass on both sides. On her right, she saw the proud necks of giraffes protruding from the scrub where they munched small trees thoughtfully. She ignored the other animals pounding through the grass, but had to brake in a hurry when a file of elephants crashed across the trail. Far above them she saw the flamboyant colors of the balloon soaring toward Serengeti.

She picked up speed. She was searching for a Masai village where she could stroll through the huts and speak to the tribesmen. She had brought her camera so she could take some shots to convince Randy at the studio of the superb locations.

She was planning the program in her mind, until she noticed the lions blocking the trail. She skidded to a stop, cut off the engine, and wondered what to do.

There were two of them. The female was rolling in the loose dry mud of the track while the male watched. Neither of them was concerned by the car and its impatient occupant.

Lyn quietly rolled up the windows. The male lion raised its head and eyed her. He was a mangy beast; his mane sparse and his body thin and scarred. He turned away from the car with a snort and padded over to the female. He nipped her affectionately and climbed on to her.

"I don't believe it!" Lyn cried aloud in exasperation. "That's all I need."

Oh yes! the lion seemed to growl, thrusting himself at the female as he languidly mounted her.

"Just like a man," she muttered to herself when the lion uttered a final yelp and clambered off. He sauntered into the grass while the female rose to her feet, shaking herself as though she had a headache.

"Don't knock it, sister," Lyn said, starting the engine. "You don't know how lucky you are."

There was a thicket of trees and mounds in the distance. As she drove nearer, the mounds became wattle and mud huts. Pleased, she halted the car and got out, forgetting the warning she had been given when she hired the vehicle that she should not leave it, whatever happened.

The sun was searing down. She parted her hair, drenched in sweat and sticking to her cheeks, away from her face. She picked up her camera and tramped through the tall grass to the huddle of huts.

They were crudely made dwellings, resembling heaps of dung in the withered landscape. A solitary tree with fruits like long, gray sausages stood at the entrance to the compound. She paused. There was a stillness that was unnerving.

She had once talked her way on board an airliner that had been hijacked by an armed maniac; she had faced rioting mobs in Watts; she had done many dangerous, foolish things but never had she felt so apprehensive. It wasn't fear; it was a sense of foreboding.

She shook her head, scoffed at her fertile imagination, and stepped backward. Something touched her shoulder.

She raised her arm to protect herself and spun around. She stared at the open scrub land. There was no one in sight. One of the long, sausage-shaped fruits on the tree was spinning where she had bumped into it. She groaned with relief.

"What the hell's happening to me?" she muttered to herself. "There's no one here."

She raised her camera for a picture of the fruit and the wine-colored flower blooming limply beside it. She photographed the deserted huts baking in the sun, then hurried back to the car.

The back tire was flat.

She swore, puzzled by her growing sense of unease. She looked down the trail, hoping to see another vehicle so she could get help to change the wheel; there was none to be seen. She cursed and crouched down to inspect the tire. It was then she noticed that the front one was flat too.

The feeling of foreboding was overwhelming. She glanced at it again and gasped in horror. Beside it, a foot was planted firmly in the red earth of the trail.

She raised her eyes slowly, seeing the foot becoming a leg, then a bare thigh, a hip, and a chest, wrapped with a vivid clay-red robe. Above was the scarred and scowling face of the ugliest man she had ever seen.

She pulled herself up, leaning against the back of the car for protection. "Who are the fuck are you?"

The man regarded her through heavily hooded eyes, no more than slits in an evil countenance. His skin was stretch tautly over his high cheekbones and flat, broad nose. The lobes of his ears had been bored and stretched until they were huge holes, with plastic bead work woven around the outside of the holes.

His fierce appearance was accentuated by yellow paint daubed on his nose and under his eyebrows. His hair, matted in small tufts, was coated with a thick, blood-colored paste.

Above the red sheet that he wore like a toga exposing the naked left side of his body, a pattern of welts crawled across his chest up to his shoulder. The welts were in pairs, each the size of a coffee bean.

In his left hand he held a spear. His mouth hung open showing teeth filed to points, yellowed and broken. He wore a band of red, blue and white plastic beads tied tightly around his neck. The effect added to his menace instead of alleviating it.

There was nothing proud and noble in this savage. "Who are you?" she demanded again, her courage faltering. "What do you want?"

The man's lips parted over his teeth and he gurgled a response that made her shudder. It was a signal that brought forth Masai who materialized from the long grass and stood at the other side of the car. The only sounds were their snorts and grunts, and the clink of metallic bracelets jangling on their arms and chafing against the blades of their spears.

She hoped that the Masai practice of puncturing holes in

the necks of their cattle and siphoning the blood to drink, was confined to cows. She tried to slide along the side of the car, wondering if she could lock herself in it until help arrived.

The slap of the Masai's spear against the car, only an inch from her hand, dashed that hope. His half-closed eyes seemed to mock her. She withdrew her hand and pulled herself to her full height.

"I'm an American citizen," she said. "You can't do this." She remembered Royce's words about the occasional bad egg among the Masai. She had found enough to make an omelet.

There were three of them behind her clanking their bracelets and spears. All were dressed in variations of their leader with a similar animalistic gleam in their eyes.

Whatever they were on, it must be pretty potent, she thought. She decided to concentrate on just one of them, instead of losing her wits trying to convince all four to let her go.

The leader scowled then jabbed his spear in front of her, so that it quivered in the mud between her feet.

"All right, all right!" she said, sensing that somehow she had offended him. She was more outraged than scared now. After all, she thought, what could happen to her?

The leader stabbed the air in front of her face. One of his gang pulled the camera from her hand and held it out to him.

"Hey, that's mine! What are you doing?"

The leader looked at the camera with disapproval, shaking it vigorously. When nothing happened, he began to finger the moving parts on it, touching and testing each one in turn.

"Give me that." She tried to snatch it from him but the Masai just brushed her away with his spear.

He opened the camera and shook it until the film fell to the ground. One of the others tapped the film along the track with the stick he carried, flicking it up into the air. Another Masai caught it and stuffed it under his toga.

"Why did you do that? I'll have nothing to show..."

The tall Masai tossed her camera to one of the others. She

turned to see what was happening but a hand snaked around each of her wrists and gripped her tightly. She screamed.

The Masai bent his head so it was close to hers. He seemed to be studying her, cocking his head, first on one side and then on the other. She had seen people in art galleries studying incomprehensible sculpture with the same perplexed manner. She wriggled.

"Take your filthy hands off me!"

She could see the pore marks on his skin, caked with dust and paint. She was afraid to breathe. The odor of the man was bestial. Her heart pounded against her chest; she was frightened now, but curious too. An uncanny feeling of destiny wafted over her with the stink of cattle. She saw the man's protruding lips, which drank blood from the necks of live animals, moving closer to hers.

CHAPTER 20

The balloon bumped twice before coming to rest. When Susan opened her eyes and peered over the edge of the gondola, she saw the pilot running away from the balloon. He had a rope in his hand, which hung down from the top of the balloon. He glanced back and when he saw her standing up, shouted urgently: "Stay in the basket!"

She reached for Cora's hand and tried to hold it. "Wasn't that frightening? I thought we were going to crash."

Cora pulled her hand away. "That's a normal landing for a balloon. It's no worse than jumping off a three-feet ledge."

"You've been in one before! Why didn't you say?"

Cora shrugged her shoulders. "No point. I went up with some of the guys in Napa Valley last summer." She was watching Mindelo. "I'm sure you've gone pale."

Mindelo grinned sheepishly. "That was quite an experience. Thank you!"

"How do we get back now?"

"It's all right, Sue." Cora turned at the sound of a vehicle. "Here comes the cavalry."

A jeep and one of the ubiquitous safari minibuses rattled through the grass toward them. Two of the ground crew leaped out of the jeep and ran to help the pilot, taking the rope from his hands.

"It's okay," the pilot called to Susan. "You can climb out now."

She surveyed the landscape anxiously, wondering where the lion was hiding. Perhaps the clatter of the vehicles had frightened it away. The crew was swarming around the gondola. In the distance, she saw an ostrich galloping for the thicket of trees that lined the horizon.

"We're okay here," the pilot said when he joined her. "We haven't lost a passenger yet."

He helped her descend while Cora leaned on Mindelo, laughing happily and squeezing his hand. When they were out of the basket, the ground crew worked like a competition team. The balloon was pulled down to the ground, deflated and folded. The basket was lifted onto the back of the jeep. Two crewmen unpacked the picnic hamper.

Soon a red and white checkered tablecloth was laid out on the grass, and the three blue gas cylinders from the balloon placed around it as seats. There were two bottles of champagne in an ice bucket, and a tray of chicken legs, sandwiches and hard boiled eggs.

"A champagne picnic is traditional after a balloon flight," the pilot said, beckoning the three of them to sit.

Cora sat at one end of the cylinders and pulled Mindelo down beside her. Susan sat opposite them. The pilot handed her a plastic cup. He opened the bottle of champagne with a flourish and the cork soared into the air with a loud pop.

Susan giggled. "They'll charge you for hunting with a loaded champagne bottle." The pilot grinned and filled her cup to the brim. "I really don't drink," she protested.

"Forget your silly inhibitions, Sue! You should enjoy yourself." Cora shifted on the gas cylinder so that her thigh was pressing against Mindelo's.

Susan sipped the champagne, wrinkling her nose at the bubbles. "Maggie should be here."

"Shoot! Leave that old bitch out of this." Cora waved her plastic cup and winked at Mindelo. "Let's not spoil this moment."

"Did you enjoy the flight?" the pilot asked, breaking the uneasy silence.

"It was..." Susan was lost for words. "Just... wonderful!"

"It's the only way to see the game," he said. "When the wildebeest migrate from the Serengeti plains, it's unbelievable."

"I'm sure it is," she smiled, relaxing for the first time since leaving Fisi Lodge. "Do you need a lot of training to be a balloon pilot?" She toyed with a sandwich.

"I've had extensive professional training. In England. Is that what you mean?"

"You must get a lot of old bats wanting to *fly* with you?" Cora grinned to emphasize the double meaning behind her question.

The pilot, Susan decided, was either very cool or a fanatic for his work. Cora didn't faze him at all.

"It's a self-screening process of elimination. A lot of people want to go, but not all have the courage. Women," he said carefully, "see balloon travel as something romantic. They think it's beautiful floating around the sky suspended below an enormous balloon." He gestured in the air and smiled, looking at Mindelo.

"Men on the other hand regard it technically and worry, wondering how it will stay up, how it steers, etc."

"How fast were we flying?" Mindelo asked, encouraged by the pilot's acceptance of him.

"About fifteen miles an hour."

"Passengers mostly Americans?"

"Mostly Americans. The price..." The pilot smiled and spread his hands. "About sixty percent of our passengers are from the USA. Thirty percent are European and ten percent other nationalities. We've had forty-eight nationalities in total."

"Including Kenyan?" Mindelo watched the pilot carefully.

"Of course," he said without hesitation.

The champagne, combined with the flight, was a heady experience for Susan. She was quivering with anticipation when the pilot, driving the minibus, finally deposited them at Fisi Lodge. She looked eagerly at the parked cars, searching for the maroon vehicle that her mystery man had been driving when he arrived the night before. Her high spirits evaporated as she realized it wasn't there.

"Come and join us for coffee," the pilot urged her.

She sat at the veranda table with the others and tried to be polite. Cora and Mindelo were talking softly until Charles Royce strode over to the table. He jerked his thumb at Mindelo who got up quickly and hurried away.

The pilot was writing out certificates. He handed one to her. It read: *This is to certify that Susan Ross has flown over Africa in a hot air balloon. Flight time: one hour.*

"Where's Mindelo?" he asked. "I have his certificate here."

"He doesn't need one." Royce sounded angry.

"He flew on the balloon with us," said Cora. "Of course he must have a certificate too."

Royce scowled. "You don't understand how we do things

here, Cora. Mindelo is staff. It's a mistake to treat him in the same manner as a guest."

The pilot's lips tightened but he said nothing. He completed Mindelo's certificate and handed it to Cora without a word. She took it, smiling her thanks.

"Perhaps you don't know what I mean," Royce said grumpily, since everyone was ignoring him.

"I know what you mean!" Cora's eyes flashed and her skinny face colored. "You come from another century, don't you? Tell Mindelo to come back here, Royce. I want to give him this."

"He's busy now."

Susan was gazing around the lobby, still hoping to see the man from the night before. "Oh, he's not," she said without realizing the ruckus it could cause. "I can see him in the lobby."

Cora grinned triumphantly while Royce pushed back his chair and stood up, glaring at her. "You can give me that certificate." He held out his hand. "I'll see he gets it."

"I'll take it to him myself!" Cora rose to her feet and sauntered out to the lobby, leaving Royce gazing after her in speechless fury.

◆ ◆ ◆ ◆ ◆

Lyn was pinioned against the car. The stench of the tribesman leering close to her face was overpowering. She closed her eyes and held her breath, waiting for his decayed teeth to sink into her flesh. Her arms were stretched above her head and held down by one of the Masai over the roof of the car. The shaft of the spear cut into her thighs.

Her captor uttered a short cry and Lyn wretched at the smell of his breath. Her arms were released and the spear withdrawn.

She opened her eyes and rubbed her wrists as she looked around in surprise. Another Masai had joined the group. He was speaking in sharp tones to which her captor answered sulkily, pointing at her camera and at the compound.

She wondered if this newcomer was going to be an ally or was their comrade who wanted first strike at her. At least he looked an improvement on the others. He was wearing a loose red cloth fastened around his chest just below his nipples. The cloth was open down one side of his body, revealing a thigh as muscular as a stallion's. He wore neither beads nor earrings and his hair was close cropped.

His face gave no clue as to whether he was a friend or a foe, and his eyes were impenetrable under heavy lids. The simplicity of his appearance served to make him more threatening than the exaggerated dress of the other Masai. To judge by their nervous and meek attitude, the others held the newcomer in high esteem.

He had a naked boy, probably ten years old, with him. He barked something at him and the boy took to his heels, haring up the track as though terrified.

Her captor gestured angrily at her, but his protest was cut short by a curt grunt from the newcomer. They exchanged more garbled sounds. She got the impression that she was being haggled over, and that the new arrival was winning the argument.

"Let me go, at once!" she said, giving way to outrage at what was happening.

The newcomer raised his eyebrow and looked at her, as though for the first time.

"Don't touch me!" she shouted. "I'm an American. From Fisi Lodge. A tourist...!"

The new Masai ignored her and continued to utter his incomprehensible sounds.

The other Masai responded when he paused, and then he spoke again.

She gradually realized that the sounds were part of a ritual exchange of words, like a chant, uttered first by one and then the other. It seemed they were making a deal.

"Can't you speak English?" She felt so helpless. She gazed around, wondering if she could escape while they were talking. They were bound to out run her, and anyway they had spears.

The newcomer was looking at her again and this time she thought she saw a glint of amusement in his eyes. He had an intelligent face and now that his authority over the others had been accepted, his eyes sparkled. His complexion was smooth and his shoulders and chest were free of the decorative welts sported by the others. His face, when the harshness had faded from it, was handsome and powerful.

"You do speak English, right?" she challenged.

There was another flicker of humor in the man's dark eyes.

"I knew it! You can't keep me here, you know. Look, I'm sorry if I upset any Masai traditions by photographing the huts." She pointed to the camera still dangling in the hand of one of the Masai. "I'm a television journalist. A camera is like...it's like a spear to me. I can't go anywhere without it."

The tall man watched her quietly as though digesting her remarks. After a few seconds silence, he addressed all the other Masai. Their expressions lightened and they began chattering. Slowly, the one with the camera stepped forward and handed it back to her, touching his spear as he did so. The message had got across.

There was a roar of a vehicle hurtling along the track toward them. "Thank god," she breathed with relief. "Someone's coming at last."

The Masai flashed a row of perfect teeth. "Thank not your god."

She was dumbfounded. That man's accent! His voice was deep and his English well modulated. She looked at him closely. He was obviously naked under his red robe. His spear was polished and the hand that gripped it was tough. There was something about his bearing that marked him apart from the others. He was refined, a quality that, in the States, would have been associated with a good family background.

"What the hell's that?" She shielded her eyes with her hand as a cloud of dust rolled noisily toward them. She wondered why the Masai didn't run since they surely knew she would report them to whoever was coming to her rescue. She peered through her fingers as the dust settled.

It was the naked boy in front of her, astride a motorcycle.

"Thank my Suzuki!" The Masai grinned proudly. "More help right now than your god." He took the bike from the boy and threw his long leg over the saddle. She reared back in surprise when he indicated that she should ride pillion.

"What about my car?"

"Lock it."

She opened the door and rolled up the windows, locking it securely. She stepped back to the bike. "Where are we going?"

The Masai didn't answer. She looked around for the others. They were walking, proud and indifferent, away from the abandoned car, the naked boy gamboling along beside them.

The motorcycle roared into life. She scrambled on and clutched the man's waist to avoid falling off as it bucked forward. She felt the firmness of his stomach, and the tight muscles under the thin fold of his robe. The wind rushed to meet her, tugging at her hair. She clung on, smiling grimly to herself.

CHAPTER 21

The Masai drove the bike at speed along the track, weaving to avoid the dips and bumps.

Lyn leaned forward and shouted in his ear: "You drive this thing well."

The man grunted and accelerated some more.

She dug her fingers into the solid wall of muscle of his body. She waited for a reaction and when there was none, she moved her hand down slowly toward his crotch.

His massive shoulders, like rough onyx against the fine alabaster of her cheek, jerked angrily and he opened the throttle wider.

"Okay, okay," she yelled. "So I'm sorry. You know how to drive a motorbike, right? I'm getting shaken to bits. I must hang on to something!"

The man didn't answer. The speed and the bumps made her lose interest in his crotch; she just clung on frantically to stop being pitched off.

She put her mouth to his ear and shouted again. "So you're the strong, silent type. Where the hell are you taking me?"

He ignored her.

"Come on! I know you speak English. Am I being rescued or sold into white slavery?"

The man throttled down, slowing the bike.

She squinted ahead and was relieved to see the Fisi Lodge sign swinging across the road in the distance. "Now I know."

The Masai's smooth shoulders heaved. He sighed and said: *"Minum enkashe olekipa."*

"I beg you pardon?" She was pleased that she had stirred some reaction from him. "What does *that* mean?"

He turned his head so she was gazing at his profile. His skin had a sheen of dust on it giving him the appearance of a clay god. His finely shaped lips quivered with apparent amusement. As he spoke, his words were whipped away in the wind. "In English it means *Don't pinch the heifer's vagina.* It's a Masai proverb. Never argue with a new bride."

She was stunned. "Is that what happened back there. I'm your bride?"

He drove the bike up to the gas station where a few hours before she had filled the tank of her car. He stopped the engine and supported the bike with his legs, nodding for her to get off.

She climbed down gratefully, holding on to the camera swinging from its strap around her neck.

He said something in Swahili to the attendant who turned to her.

"We'll send for the car, miss."

"Great. What about -?" The revving of the motorbike cut her off. "Hey, wait, you can't go like that!"

The man looked back at her, a mocking smile on his lips.

"I want to talk to you. I have to thank you. What was all that about anyway?"

The man exchanged a glance of resignation with the attendant, switched off the engine, dismounted from the bike and handed it to him. He pursed his lips and glanced through the gates of Fisi Lodge to the neat lawns and cabins inside the compound walls.

"You can come to my cabin," she said, praying that he would. "We can talk there."

He pointed to the shade of the compound wall. He walked over to it and slipped down on his haunches, waiting for her. She sat beside him but before she could comment on this odd place to talk, he began to speak.

"In the past, Masai never kept domestic slaves. Men captured in wars were absorbed into existing Masai families. Women were taken as wives for their captors."

"You're my captor, right?" She laughed cynically.

"Yes. Alas, however, Masai men do not marry a woman unless she has been circumcised." He turned his eyes on her with an expression of interest. "Is there any chance that you have been circumcised?"

"Don't give me that bullshit."

He nodded his head as though agreeing. "A Masai hardly speaks ten sentences without using at least one proverb. I tell you now: *ore pee einosa olidia inkik mme ololiki etala*. That means: *the reason the dog ate its own shit is not because it lacked an adviser."*

Lyn was speechless. She stared at the Masai. Even squatting down in his robe he had a dignity. His head was cocked aristocratically and his eyes glinted with amusement. Then she saw his expression grow serious.

"I apologize for my brothers who waylaid you. Unfortunately, every nation has its criminals. Rinko and some of his age-group have lost faith. They see white visitors as an easy source of wealth and fun."

"I suppose I provoked them, using my camera."

His eyebrows lifted and he looked at her closely. "You are not angry? You are not going to complain to your ambassador? Rinko could have done some very unpleasant things to you."

"It was my fault."

He held his eyes on hers, studying her calmly.

She returned his gaze without flinching, marveling at the smoothness of his complexion, his strong features and the powerful wisdom of his eyes. He wore his maturity lightly. She guessed he was about her age.

"Where did you learn English?" she asked, breaking the spell of silence. "You speak it so well..."

"For an ignorant Masai savage? Why are you Americans always so patronizing?"

"We Americans are curious, and perhaps a little foolish sometimes."

"You learn quickly. That's good."

"So tell me?" She edged closer, putting her hand out so it grazed the man's bare thigh.

"There was an intermediate school in Narok, the town near my village, and that's where I came across English."

"You make it sound quite unimportant." She shifted her position against the wall, brushing against him again. She sensed that he found her attractive. If only she could get him to her room! She felt herself getting wet just at the thought of it. *A Masai! And a good looking one at that!*

"Tell me more," she said slowly, smiling to encourage him.

His eyes flickered with amusement again. "I discovered English in Narok, but I perfected my knowledge of the language at the London School of Economics where I took my degree."

She moved away in surprise. "You have a degree?"

He grinned. "Are you disappointed?"

"I'm surprised." Her heart thumped. She had the feeling of being saved at the last moment from the jaws of a lion. This cat was educated, not the simple stud she had assumed. "Your dress..." She spread her hands in an effort to explain herself.

"You mean the lack of it!" He laughed. "Now I understand. You thought I was like Rinko? No, I'm not your picture book Masai, the noble savage. I hope I haven't shattered your romantic image of us?"

"Of course not. It's unexpected, that's all."

He laughed again. "You Americans are so naïve. You believe you have the monopoly on sophistication. It's true that there are not many graduates in Masailand. I am here because I feel it is my duty to teach my people what I have learned. If I break away from the Masai because I have a degree, I would be losing faith, just as Rinko has done."

"You live here?" She waved weakly at the scrubland. "In those huts where you found me?"

"I don't. That's why I have my Suzuki. For when I visit. I come here as often as I can."

"What do you do?"

"Educate my people. See they are not denied their rights. Rescue damsels in distress."

She swore silently to herself. "What do you do for money? Don't you have a job?"

"How very American you are. Straight to the root." He spread his hands open and gazed at the sky. "We Masai say: *imintodol oekeny ilala*, which means *Never show your teeth to a monkey*. In other words, don't tell others your secrets."

Lyn was exasperated. Despite his insufferable arrogance, she found him appealing. What lay under his thin toga intrigued her too, even if he wasn't the simple, corruptible savage she had assumed. "Look," she said, facing him squarely, "come to my cabin. We can't speak properly here."

"I'm sorry. I forgot you might not be comfortable sitting on the ground."

"I don't think you are either. I think you're a weekend Masai. Is your name a secret to be kept from monkeys too?"

He laughed quickly, and then leapt to his feet, extending his hand to pull her up. She ignored it and scrambled to her feet without his help.

"I'm Tony Kintai," he said, pulling his red robe around him with a flourish. "And you?

She looked at him trying to work out his angle. Was there a note of interest in his voice? She sniffed. "One of our group told me not to speak to strange men."

He nodded. "The Masai say: *how fortunate is the mouth that speaks.* Do you know why? Because it can tell others what it needs." His eyes glinted triumphantly.

"You're impossible! How can you stroll about this barren savanna dressed as a savage and be so proud of yourself?"

A pickup truck pulled out of the gas station. The driver shouted something to Tony Kintai who waved back in acknowledgement. "They're going for your car." He raised his eyebrow. "Do you intend to continue your solo safari when you get it back?"

"Yes. Your cronies in drag haven't put me off." She was satisfied to see him flinch at the insult. "By the way, my name is Lyn Preston."

He smiled wearily. "Believe me, Lyn Preston, those men are dangerous. They were serious. You have no idea what they would have done to you. Rinko and his age-group are outcasts; the live beyond the law." He strode away angrily and mounted the motorbike, kicking it to life.

He couldn't hear her shout above the roar of the engine, so she ran over and put her hand on his shoulder to restrain him.

He raised his eyes and looked deeply into hers. She was shaking in time to the juddering of the bike. She squeezed his shoulder.

"What is it?" he asked.

"I don't know." She paused, feeling herself grow limp after all that had happened. "I'd like to see you again."

A maroon Range Rover swung in off the trail and passed under the Fisi Lodge sign. It sent a shower of dust over them, breaking the hold of their eyes on each other. The vehicle roared up to the reception area.

"If you are driving that car to Nairobi," he said suddenly, his eyes gleaming persuasively, "you can give me a lift."

That surprised her. "Nairobi! I'm supposed to be flying back to Mombasa in a couple of days."

"Very well. I'll manage." He opened the throttle, hit the gear change and tensed his legs to move off.

"Wait. I'll take you to Nairobi if you want. It's important, right?"

"It is the eyes that trouble."

"Masai proverb?"

"Right. And it would be helpful if you were to make the journey as soon as they fix the car."

She sensed his need and wondered what had happened to make him suddenly worried. "I have a friend, Susan," she said. "I'd like her to come to Nairobi too."

"As you wish." He lifted his legs from the ground and jerked the bike away, pulling himself out of her grasp. She watched him hammer onto the dust track, his red robe billowing as the wind cuffed his bare chest.

She sighed, waiting until he had disappeared into the scrubland before walking to the Lodge entrance. She was disconcerted by the encounter, which had stirred emotions she had forgotten about. Tony Kintai was physically appealing, but it was more than that. He had an aura of destiny. That intrigued her.

The maroon Range Rover was pulling away from the Lodge as she walked up the drive. It was moving fast and she glanced at the windscreen to see who were the occupants. In a flash she realized that she was standing in the path of the vehicle and it was racing toward her.

"Hey!" she called in alarm, but it was too late.

She hurled herself off the gravel driveway onto the lawn. As she fell, she glimpsed the driver. It was the same suave looking dude who had spoken to her that morning. His face was contorted with anger and he had his arm across the chest of a girl in the seat beside him. She was struggling, trying to get out of the vehicle. The man's eyes were on the girl and he didn't see Lyn, nor hear her shout.

"Lyn, are you all right?"

She shook her head to clear it as a cloud of dust descended on her. The sun was blazing down and the air was stifling. She raised her eyes until they were level with a notice board on the lawn. Orange blossoms hung over it and the printed letters danced before her eyes. *105 miles south of the Equator* swung into focus. She felt very, very thirsty.

"Stand up, Lyn. You're not hurt, are you?"

"Sue? I'm all right, but I need a drink. Did you see that mad man? He nearly ran me down."

"Yes." Susan's voice was flat. She helped her to her feet. "I'm sure he didn't see you."

"The macho bastard! You're right. He wasn't watching the road at all. I wonder what that girl did to him?"

"She's very pretty."

Lyn noticed the anguish in Susan's voice, but ignored it and for once she didn't pry. She needed to concentrate on her own dreams.

CHAPTER 22

Susan waited in the lobby and studied the carved silhouettes of animals on the wooden board hanging behind the reception desk. Beside each silhouette were numbers showing the amount of animals viewed at the Lodge the previous day.

Fisi Lodge was in the eastern portion of the Masai reserve, where great herds thrived. Every animal imaginable seemed to have been sighted within its vicinity. Now, she thought wickedly, Lyn had spotted a Masai and seemed to regard him as a rare species of wild animal too.

She pondered Lyn's description of her Masai. She had made him seem like an African Superman with his flying robe and motorcycle. She was amused because it had taken only one day in the bush for Lyn to lose her careful cynicism. This man should be worth meeting!

She tapped her fingers on the reception counter as she waited for Lyn to complete arrangements with Royce for their departure to Nairobi.

There was a commotion in the lobby and someone bumped into her, causing her to stumble against the counter. A strong hand reached out and held her steady. "I'm awfully sorry," said a voice deep with concern.

She raised her eyes. A herd of package tourists were stampeding through the lobby to their safari minibuses.

The man who had barged into her gesticulated apologetically. "They just swept me right into you," he said. "I hope you are all right?"

She nodded without speaking, removing her arm from the man's long-fingered grip. He was dressed in a dark business suit with a white shirt and a striped tie. His face showed his concern as he searched her eyes enquiringly.

"I'm glad you're not hurt," he said with a wry grin. "Believe me, it was an accident."

"It's all right." She was shaken but the man had taken the impact from the shoving crowd and his body had actually protected her.

"Tourists get so excited. They can't help bringing their

competitive instincts on holiday with them."

She smiled politely.

The man beamed. "That's better. I thought I had permanently damaged Kenya-US relations."

"Do you work here?" The man's appearance puzzled her but he was friendly and spoke excellent English. She was bored waiting for Lyn so didn't mind talking a bit.

"Not here at the Lodge," the man answered evasively.

"In the game reserve then?" Before he could reply Lyn strode into the lobby, followed by an anxious Charles Royce. "Excuse me," Susan said and turned her back on the stranger. "Is everything ready?"

"Yes, Sue. Royce seems reluctant to lose us. He says we should take Mindelo as our guide."

"Do we need a guide?" Now Susan was worried.

"It's not really necessary," said Royce, wiping the sweat off his face onto his moustache. "It's most irregular for someone to leave the tour. Everything is prepaid, you see. You won't get a refund." He gloated as though the remark would make Lyn change her mind.

"You know what you can do with your refund, Royce." Lyn smirked. "Anyway, we'll be back in Mombasa in a couple of days."

"I would be happier if you take Mindelo with you. He knows his way around. Are you leaving Cora here?"

"Let Mindelo look after her," said Susan. "She needs him more than we do."

Royce spluttered, his Pink Gin face turning an ugly puce.

Lyn pulled her away. "Naughty, naughty, Susan," she said softly. "You're stirring it. Now where's my Masai, he's supposed to be here." She cast her eye around the lobby, ignoring the African standing behind Susan.

"I'm here." The African stepped forward. "Perhaps you didn't observe me in the gloom."

Lyn stared at him in dismay.

"Oh dear," said Susan with a gasp. "Is he your Masai?" She wanted to laugh but Lyn seemed so crestfallen

"I am Masai," the tall African said. "However, I do not belong to Lyn Preston." He reached for Lyn's bag. "Allow me. The car?"

Lyn's hand tightened around the handle of her bag and she frowned irritably.

"You don't look the way that Lyn described you," Susan said amiably. "I suppose you're wearing your Clark Kent costume now?"

"Shut up!"

Lyn's anger shocked her. She flushed, feeling more embarrassed when she saw the man's face darken with discomfort.

"Is something wrong?" he asked in a pained voice.

"Nothing's wrong!" Lyn strode out of the lobby to the car, pulled open the front door and flung her bag in. Susan and the African followed. Lyn was glaring at them. "Well, who's going in the back seat?"

"I will." Susan stepped forward. "You and he must have a lot to talk about."

Lyn pouted. "I didn't know you could be so bitchy, Susan."

"I'm not!" She recoiled, depression stirring in her. "I didn't expect a Masai to look like him."

"Neither did I." Lyn threw up her hands in despair.

Susan saw the man's brow crease with concern.

He seemed quite agitated. "I really do have to get to Nairobi. Are we leaving now?"

"Sure. Get in." Lyn turned the ignition key. "Why I let you talk me into this, I don't know. And what happened to your robe. Are you wearing it under that awful suit?" She gripped the steering wheel.

"It's here."

"In your brief case?" Lyn laughed. "That's ironical, isn't it. I said you were a weekend Masai, now you look like a full-time civil servant."

"I'm still Tony Kintai." He settled into the seat, adjusting his long legs to the confines of the car.

"I'm surprised you don't have a proverb for this situation."

Susan studied the man with more interest. He could be regarded as good looking, she thought, but with a collar and tie he didn't look like someone who would appeal to Lyn. No wonder she was cross.

"Just what do you do for a living, Mr. Kintai?" Lyn's voice was thick with sarcasm. She pressed down the accelerator and the car leaped forward, showering gravel over Royce who was standing behind it.

"Tony to you, Lyn. Only the president calls me by my title."

"So you're a pal of the president?" Lyn's nose twitched.

"I am."

"Tell me more." Lyn calmed down as she steered the car under the Fisi Lodge arch and along the track that was signposted for the Olemelepo Gate.

Susan was relieved to see the angry hunch of her shoulders had eased. She wondered whether it was her professional curiosity or another emotion that had cooled Lyn's anger.

"There's nothing to tell," Tony said, relaxing now they were underway.

"I asked, right?"

He chuckled, his teeth flashing. "I thought you asked out of politeness. We are not going to drive two hundred kilometers without speaking of something."

"Perhaps we should! This morning you accused me of being patronizing. Now what about you?"

"Lyn! I'm sure Mr. Kintai didn't mean to be offensive."

"Shut up, Sue. You don't know anything about him. You didn't see him the way I did."

"And what do you know about me, Lyn?" He paused. "Are you usually so aggressive? You're not in Los Angeles now. You are on vacation in my country, so why don't you relax."

"Don't tell me what to do!"

Tony raised an eyebrow in surprise, which made Susan feel sorry for him. She was used to Lyn's brashness and felt uneasy for this stranger being lashed by the rough side of her nature.

"Lyn's in television," she said, hoping this would explain her behavior.

Tony turned and smiled at her in a manner that showed he understood everything. She sensed an aura of strength then, and realized he certainly did not need her help in dealing with Lyn Preston.

"The Masai say a zebra does not despise its own stripes," he said. "That means one should not abuse his, or her, traditions." He glanced at Lyn. "We are from two different cultures. Yet she and I are two people with a common passion."

Susan stared at him in astonishment. She didn't know Lyn had already gone that far. Tony smiled at her again.

"That passion is a profound interest in people, isn't that right, Lyn?" He turned back and watched Lyn as she negotiated the bumps in the track.

"You're very free with your snap character assessment." She was silent for a moment. "I suppose you are right."

Tony sat back and grinned.

"Is this where you live?" Susan saw the cluster of mud huts in a grove off the track. "Lyn told me about your village."

"No. I live in Nairobi although I was born near Narok that's the nearest town. We pass it on the way."

"I hope your cronies aren't waiting to stone the car."

"You sound bitter, Lyn." Tony laughed easily. "I suppose you should be. They've moved on. They won't molest you again."

"They won't have a chance. I'm not coming back here in a hurry."

"Why not? I thought you were interested in Masai lore?"

"You ask me why not!" Lyn's voice grated with scorn. "Look at you, that's why not. How can I believe the Masai I'm interviewing isn't going to turn into a civil servant?"

"Now I understand." He grinned. "I'm relieved to know the cause of your anger, or anguish, which is it? Does everything have to have a name tag and conform to an accepted pattern? A savage is a savage is a savage."

"Yes, dammit," said Lyn. "And a zebra is a zebra is a zebra, right? Masai proverb."

"Touché. Man is always beaten by his own stick."

"The way you two argue, you'd think you'd known each other for years." Susan put her head forward between the two of them. "Isn't anyone interested in the animals, the scenery?"

"You watch the animals, Sue. It's bad enough concentrating on this track and this person beside me without -." She braked quickly as an elephant forged across the road twenty yards ahead. "What did I tell you?"

"Just like downtown Burbank."

"What do you know about downtown Burbank?" Lyn demanded, turning to face Tony before she slipped the car back into gear.

"Nothing," he said lightly, in a manner that made Susan, listening in the back, believe he knew a lot more about everything than he admitted.

It was dusty and hot inside the car and as they drove on in silence, Susan began to feel drowsy. Several times she caught herself drifting off to sleep, jerked herself awake, and then slipped back into sleep again. She didn't wake up properly until the car bumped to a halt and she heard voices around them.

They had arrived in Narok, a sprawling township where Masai in traditional garb mingled with Africans dressed in the pants and shirts of western civilization. She sensed a new atmosphere in the car.

Lyn and Tony had been talking softly while she slept and seemed to have reached an understanding that was beyond her. Lyn's face was flushed and Tony had an expression of excitement in his eyes.

They were parked next to a large truck loaded with Tusker beer, outside a one-story building with a chimney poking out of its flat roof. Bare headed Masai in a variety of robes were gathered around its entrance. The building's white walls were stained brown with dust. A sign on the roof proclaimed it was the Uhuru Hotel.

"Iced drinks or warm ones?" asked Tony.

"Warm?" Lyn's usually harsh voice was tempered with a softness Susan had not noticed before.

"Fight fire with fire."

"Not another Masai proverb?"

"A British one actually. They drink hot tea to cool down. It works."

"I'd like a cold coke," said Susan, interrupting them.

"I'm glad you're awake. Is our scenery so boring?"

She blushed. "I must have had too much to eat."

"It's a compliment to my driving." Lyn smiled benevolently at her, which she found more disturbing than Lyn's sarcastic grin.

"It doesn't say much for our conversation."

"Are you going to get those drinks, or aren't you?"

"Wait!" Tony suddenly threw himself across Lyn and pulled her head toward him. He pressed his lips over her mouth, gripping the back of her neck with his hand. She bunched her fists and beat them on his back, her eyes blazing.

Susan was embarrassed. "What's going on? Shall I go for the drinks?"

Tony raised his mouth slightly from Lyn's and spoke in an urgent tone. "Please keep your head down. Hide. Lyn pretend you're kissing me."

"No pretense..." she murmured as Tony chewed off her words.

Susan reacted slowly to Tony's request and as she lowered her head to hide herself, she glimpsed a vehicle pulling out of the parking space a few yards away. It had been hidden from view by the Tusker beer truck parked next to them.

She gasped. It was the maroon Range Rover that had been at Fisi Lodge.

CHAPTER 23

"Tony Kintai! Is that Masai hospitality?" Lyn's face was flushed and her hair ruffled by his rough handling. Her heart was beating loudly and her blouse was soaked with sweat. Her eyes shone, she knew. She held him at arm's length, pressing her fingers into his shoulders.

"That's expediency, Lyn. Sorry I had to take advantage of you like that." Tony turned to the back seat. "Susan, you can get up now."

"Who's the man in that Range Rover?" Susan's question brought a glimmer of surprise to his eyes.

Lyn was scornful. "What are you talking about?"

"Ask Tony. A Range Rover was parked behind that truck. I think Tony didn't want the driver to see us, that's why he did that." Susan sounded breathless. "It's the same Range Rover that was at Fisi Lodge. You know, the one that nearly knocked you down."

"You are right." Tony sounded cautious.

"Are you in trouble? Why are you hiding from that person?"

"I'm not hiding, Lyn. Let's go, shall we? I'd like to get to Nairobi as soon as possible."

Lyn was pensive as she drove out of Narok. It was a frontier town with untidy stores and clusters of dejected people idling outside them. Masai women with their heads shaved and jewelry clattering around their necks, picked their way along the road. A herd of cows crossed lethargically. The Masai herdsmen watched the car with studied indifference, but there were some shouts of recognition when they saw Tony. Lyn glanced at him as she drove.

He was poised in thought. She had to admit that even in his city clothes, he exuded an aura of immense personal attraction. It was almost a spiritual quality that the drab suit could not suppress. She saw it as an inner animal-like strength that complemented his soulful eyes. In thought, he seemed as vibrant as when he was speaking, and his eyes shone with passion.

A rush of emotion soared through her, released by his

proximity to, and then stanched by, the impassable block between them.

She knew that his unexpected kiss and furious embrace was a calculated move to protect him, not to impress her. Yet she was stirred by it. He was animal, his body rough and hard under his formal clothes. She wondered if she meant anything to him at all, or was she being used solely for safe passage to Nairobi?

"Okay!" she said forcefully, stepping on the accelerator to pass an overloaded bus. "I've waited long enough for an explanation, Kintai. You kissed me so that dude in the Range Rover wouldn't see you, right? Why?"

He smiled weakly. "I'd rather not say, Lyn. You enjoyed it, didn't you? I did."

"Hear the man!" She pressed her foot down, speeding up in front of the bus. "Women have a struggle in this country if yours is a typical male ego."

"Excuse me," Susan leaned forward, interrupting her. "Could you tell me the name of the man who drives that vehicle."

He frowned. "Why do you want to know?"

"She's got some crush on him." Lyn was sarcastic because she was angry with herself for being roused by his embrace.

Tony seemed alarmed by what she said. He turned to Susan, his voice grave. "Have nothing to do with that man, I beg you."

"Why not?"

"I can't say."

Susan sank back in her seat, considering his warning.

Lyn's curiosity was roused. "Come on, Kintai, who is he?" She overtook a truck and waited for his reply.

The traffic had increased since they left Narok. The road was crossing the valley floor, surrounded on both sides by scrub, while in the distance were the mountains of the interior. The only animals to be seen now were occasional giraffes and small herds of cattle.

"His name is Samson Odongo," Tony said softly. "He's an entrepreneur." He fluttered his hands to show his contempt.

"So why shouldn't Sue fancy him?" She grinned in the

driving mirror at Susan who was leaning forward to hear his answer.

Tony was weighing each word carefully as he spoke. "He is a predator, Lyn, like the hyena. He preys on white women. He chooses them carefully, those who are lonely or unhappy or guileless. Perhaps they are too eager and don't see how he is using them.

"Women have left their husbands to lie with him. Only then does a woman find out the truth. When he has done with her, he sends her away. She can't go back where she came from; she is broken and dirtied."

"What a great guy!"

"He's evil!"

"I'd love to meet him."

"Why?" Susan sounded worried.

"To kick him in the balls, of course."

Tony masked his surprise. "You're very outspoken."

"And you're bloody pompous. What right have you got to warn Sue to have nothing to do with him? You are using me to get to Nairobi. You're going to drop me when you get where you want to go. It's the same thing. Just like a man!"

Susan broke in quickly before Tony took Lyn's bait and started an argument. "If you feel so bad about Mr. Odongo, why are we chasing him?"

"There you go again," snapped Lyn. "Always straight to the point. That's your middle class upbringing for you."

"Sorry." Susan sat back. "You did ask Tony why we're doing this."

"Don't be sorry, Sue. I don't know what's got into me." Lyn bluffed her way through an apology but in her heart she knew what had unsettled her. Tony Kintai himself. It galled her that he had managed to breach the barriers she erected around her emotions. He excited a reaction she found difficult to quell.

"It's not Odongo I am chasing," Tony said, ignoring Lyn's outburst. "It's the girl with him."

"What!" Lyn's eyes blazed. "I'm chasing a girl for you! Who is she?"

"Yes, who is she?" echoed Susan as though she too was afraid to hear the answer.

"His sister."

There was silence in the car. Lyn drove purposefully, following the straight, flat road with more attention than was necessary. They were passing the satellite receiving station plopped in the middle of the wildness of the Rift Valley as a reminder of progress of the 1970s.

She glanced at Susan through the rear-view mirror, trying to read her thoughts. Susan had probably expected to hear that the girl was the man's mistress. She herself felt pissed off.

"What the hell am I doing chasing this man's sister for you. Are you in love with her?"

Tony's eyes opened wide and he seemed about to deny it. "Why do you ask that?"

"Oh, come on!" She snorted with scorn. Was she at Fisi Lodge to meet you and her brother found out? He doesn't dig you, right?"

"Something like that." Tony settled back in his seat, his eyes staring at the road ahead. "I don't think one needs to look too closely into another's private life, do you?"

"Don't the Masai have a proverb for that?" She spoke sarcastically to get over the dark mood descending on her. She understood now that Tony had no interest in her at all, and the embrace really was just play-acting. She was a fool to let fantasy override her common sense.

She turned to speak to Susan. "Do you want to meet this evil dude? Maybe he's not as bad as Kintai says. Since he fancies his sister."

"Samuel Odongo is rotten, believe me."

"Maybe you're rotten too. How do we know?"

"You've forgotten how I rescued you?"

"I am merely getting interested in this man you don't want us to meet. It's a journalist thing. I'd like to meet him."

"You don't know what you're saying." Tony scowled. "Odongo has no sensitivity. He's not human. He's ruthless. He possesses people, he destroys people."

"That bad, huh?"

"Yes."

"His sister, she's not like him?"

"She's the sweetest, kindest girl in Kenya."

"Bravo!" She thumped the steering wheel and laughed mockingly. "You get the picture now, Sue?"

Susan was puzzled. "I'm not sure that I do."

"Kintai here is in love, good, old fashioned romantic love! He is pursuing his sweetheart, courtesy of me, the sucker, to rescue her from the clutches of her cruel brother."

"Why are you laughing at me?" The wisdom had slipped out of Tony's voice and for a moment he sounded like a petulant teenager.

"It's her way," Susan said. "Don't mind it."

"What I have I done to upset you?"

"You really don't know?" She concentrated on the road again as it zigzagged up the escarpment through thickening vegetation.

"You fooled me, Kintai, with that kiss. If that's what you're like when you are pretending, my god, I can't wait for you to get serious." She took refuge in her sarcasm, and was rewarded by Tony's look of bafflement.

"What will you do when we reach Nairobi?" she asked.

"I've no idea."

"Yes, you have. Catch up with Odongo's sister. Any thoughts about me?"

"You?" The self-assurance had returned to his voice and he gazed at her without emotion. "You don't need me. Nairobi's a city, not the Masai savanna."

The road was wider now and its bends were painted with yellow lines. "Is this the home stretch?" she asked, conscious of the irony of her remark.

"The end of our journey together? I think so." He stroked his smooth chin. "It's been a stimulating encounter."

"I'm sure! I was almost your bride and now I'm your chauffeur."

"I've always found American women fascinatingly complex."

"You've known many? What would Odongo's sister say about that?"

"Are you trying to insult me?" He looked pained.

"Not really. Just to knock some of that stuffing out of your fatuous ass."

"*Miro -*"

"Don't give me any more of your Masai bullshit."

He stared at her in bewilderment.

Lyn, glancing at him quickly before negotiating a tight corner, was thrilled. She gripped the knob of the gear lever and twisted the palm of her hand around it. His eyes, she saw, had registered what she was trying to tell him.

"You will stay at the New Stanley Hotel," he said, his voice hardening with a sudden decision. "I will arrange it. We shall meet there after dinner, at the Thorn Tree Café Terrace."

Lyn was silent, relishing the emotions triggered off by his change to a domineering tone. It ran against her nature to let him take charge, but she was turned on by it. At least she would see him again, when this chase of some silly African broad was out of his gorgeous head.

The road was becoming a highway. On both sides were vendors, their territory marked with wattle fences flagged with white sheepskins. Arrayed on the grass were colorful mats, baskets and baubles in beadwork. Kikuyu boys danced up and down by the roadside, holding out boxes of fruit and using suicidal antics to entice cars to stop.

The three of them sat in silence as the traffic increased and the car swept across the steep hills. The sight of tin-roofed and thatched dwellings in the dull mud depressed Lyn. The slopes around the road were covered with trees, grassland or shambas riddled with banana plants. There were plots of maize and roadside mills which ground the maize into the *posho* staple of the people. Tracks of white-flowered pyrethrum enlivened the untidy vista. She was relieved when they reached a Kentucky Fried Chicken parlor heralding the outskirts of the capital. She followed Tony's instructions without question.

When she caught sight of Susan's face in the driving mirror, it was a picture of astonishment at her submission. She smiled to herself. She was enjoying the feeling of being ordered around. It was only temporary, just until she got Tony Kintai under her control.

They reached the New Stanley Hotel. A chain blocked the entrance road running parallel to Kimathi Street. She braked and waited while a flunky in a chocolate brown frock-coat ambled over. When he saw Tony he lowered the chain immediately and allowed the car to pass.

"Stop!" Tony ordered, opening the door and jumping out. "We must hurry," he said. "Unload the bags."

Lyn began to protest but Tony disappeared into the hotel. She removed their bags, heavily begrimed with dust, from the front of the Volkswagen. A bellhop in dark green collected them from the curb without a word.

"What do we do now?" Susan was gazing nervously at the busy street.

"You've forgotten your street smarts?" Lyn scowled. "What's he up to?" She hurried into the lobby but Tony appeared and blocked her way. The doorman was gesticulating at the car.

"Give me the key," Tony ordered. Lyn handed it over in a daze. "I've got you a room. See you later!" He dashed past her and got quickly into the car.

As he drove off and eased the car into the traffic, a maroon Range Rover drew up in its place at the curb. A girl opened the door, stepped down and walked over to a table on the Thorn Tree Terrace. The Range Rover drove off.

CHAPTER 24

The New Stanley Hotel was an institution in Africa and its illustrious reputation made Lyn suspect public relations overkill. With Susan at her heels, she strode into the lobby in an aggressive mood. She was disconcerted to find that everything seemed familiar. She had never been to the hotel before, but the atmosphere made her feel at home.

No heads turned in astonishment at their bedraggled appearance as they walked to the reception desk. The clerk was middle-aged and European in manner; he beamed a warm welcome. There was not a flicker of disdain at the dust on their clothes and their windswept hair.

A bellboy hurried forward with a smile, carrying their bags, as Lyn accepted the room key. She surveyed the small lobby again, trying to identify the secret of its intimacy.

She decided the friendly atmosphere must have evolved out of years of fulfilling the demands of discerning guests. She sensed that in this hotel traditions, which were ignored in the modern guest factories where she usually stayed, were meticulously maintained.

The elevator was exactly where she expected it to be. She could have found her room without the bellboy. There was no walk in despair down long corridors past anonymous doors. The room was a short step from the elevator. The door was open as though the room was waiting for them.

The suite amazed her. It was furnished in the manner of an upcountry hunting lodge. Skins covered the floors and couches, and the furniture was dark, polished mahogany. Both the bedroom and the parlor were decorated in sub-dued, masculine tones that gave the room a warm, homely atmosphere.

"Wow, this place makes me horny!" She threw herself face down on the bed with an exaggerated shriek. "I'll leap on the waiter if you call room service."

Susan blushed. "It's marvelous," she said, standing by the bedroom door and gazing around with awe. "Just like a movie."

"Not like a movie I've ever seen. Everything is genuine

here. You can sense the calm in this place. Even Maggie would approve."

"I feel guilty when you mention Maggie. Do you think we should phone her?"

"Why? The old bitch is probably half way through the kitchen staff by now."

A glimmer of shock entered Susan's eyes. She busied herself unpacking her bag. There was an uncomfortable silence between them. Lyn broke it suddenly.

"Let's go down and see her."

Susan looked up sharply. "Maggie?"

"Not Maggie, Kintai's girl. He doesn't know that she is sitting downstairs in the café."

"You go. I must take a shower and clean up."

"Okay. Meet me downstairs when you're ready." She brushed her hair quickly, feeling comfortable that her disheveled appearance wouldn't attract much attention.

At the entrance to the Thorn Tree Terrace Café she stood surveying the crowded tables. It was difficult to make out the girl in the crowd of faces on the terrace, so she walked to the only vacant table and sat down.

The café bustled with excitement and laughter, strangers and regulars were caught up in the sensation of being at the center of the action in Nairobi and, thus, in the whole of Kenya. There were forty round tables on the open terrace, which was separated from Kimathi Street by a low wall and plants in pots. The famous thorn tree, which gave the place its name, towered up to the hotel's eighth floor.

She soaked up the lively atmosphere, feeling a part of it. There were safari-suited tourists, immaculately dressed Africans drinking seriously, and partying aircrews. It was a tropical Paris sidewalk café, but less parochial. The customers had the elan of rugged sophistication and each of them surely had a fascinating life story to tell.

A waiter stepped in front of her and snapped a brown cloth over the table, securing it with elastic at the sides. "The breeze," he explained with a gesture.

He placed a candle with a red glass shade on the cloth and, with a flourish, lit it. Waiters were performing a similar ritual on the other tables, and the café was transformed from an afternoon gossip center to a pre-romance rendez-vous.

She looked at her watch. It was six o'clock. "Vodka and tonic," she ordered crisply, taking her cigarettes out and lighting up. She inhaled with satisfaction. She was pleased with the table. The wall of the hotel lobby was behind her and she had a view of the street panorama, together with the café's changing scene.

The tourists were going, leaving tables of middle-aged men with faded bush jackets, highly tanned faces, gray hair and white moustaches, drinking Tusker beers and speaking Swahili to the waiters. Charles Royce, she realized, came from the same breed.

When the waiter brought her drink and she was sipping it contentedly, she noticed the girl.

She had emerged form the snack bar at the back of the café and stood nervously, like a gazelle, peering around for an empty table. Several Africans hailed her. She waved back without stopping and advanced on a table by the street.

She sat down with the grace of a dancer. Lyn was intrigued. She watched the girl pat her lacquered hair and then, under fluttering eyelashes, glance around the café to see who was watching her. She was attractive and obviously aware of it.

Susan arrived and pulled out the chair beside Lyn and sat down. She smelled freshly scrubbed.

"You were quick."

"I didn't want to miss anything." A waiter rushed over. "A coke, please."

"What about another vodka tonic?"

The waiter frowned at Lyn and dashed away.

"There's Kintai's true love, Sue. The one drinking a beer. She looks like a hooker to me."

Susan colored with confusion. "She can't be!"

"Watch her." Lyn was excited. "See how her eyes follow all the men who come in. She's not the only one. See that girl three tables to the left of her. She's on the same scene."

"How do you know?"

The waiter placed the drinks in front of them, and smiled at Susan. "Do you wish to see the menu?"

Susan took the menu and studied it. "I've no idea what these dishes are." She passed the menu to Lyn.

She grinned and glanced at the menu, pointing to an item. "For two."

The waiter nodded and hurried away.

The girl they were watching was smiling boldly at a white man who was sitting at a nearby table. She raised her beer glass to her lips and ran her tongue, startlingly pink, around the rim. It seemed to be a private joke.

"That's that," said Lyn, delighted she could prove to Susan that what she suspected was true. "She's found a trick."

"You really think she is offering herself to that man?"

"Irio with stew," the waiter said, putting two plates down in front of them.

Susan squirmed.

"Culture shock?" Lyn tasted the food. "It's potatoes mashed with sweet corn and spinach with stew poured on top. "You'll like it."

Susan looked unconvinced as she prodded the mess with her fork.

"You know what," said Lyn thoughtfully between mouthfuls. "My guess is that Odongo is nothing more than a glorified pimp. I doubt if that girl is really his sister. Kintai probably wants her to live with him in his Masai village but Odongo won't give her up."

"A pimp?" Susan gasped with despair and put down her fork.

"I've asked you before if you're for real, Sue. Haven't you ever heard of a pimp?"

"Of course I have." She looked cross. "How can you be sure? You're always making snap judgments about people. Does it occur to you that you could be wrong?"

Lyn finished her stew and looked at Susan shrewdly. "We'll see. Let's ask the girl to join us."

Susan shook her head.

"Why not? Kintai's supposed to come here to meet us. Let's ask her what this is all about."

"I'm going to the room."

"You don't want to be at the same table with a whore?"

"It's so silly."

Lyn sat back in her chair, stretching her long legs. Her jeans were tight and accentuated the roundness of her hips. She tossed her head so that her hair cascaded around her shoulders. She was no match for the svelte beauty of the girl but she reckoned she could hold her own.

"If you want to speak to her, why don't you ask the waiter to invite her over?"

"I thought you were going to the room?"

Susan pouted. She was silent for a moment and then beckoned one of the waiters. "You see that lady sitting by herself with the beer?" She nodded in the girl's direction.

"Miss Odongo?"

"Why, yes!" Susan's eyes gleamed triumphantly, as that indicated the girl was Odongo's sister. "Ask her if she would like to join us. My friend here wants to interview her."

The waiter smiled broadly and moved away.

"Sue!" Lyn rocked her chair upright and glared across the table. "She is his sister? You've spoilt my fun." She pursed her lips. "Odongo could still pimp for his sister, though, couldn't he?"

The waiter led the girl over to their table. She was tall and slender and moved with the grace of grass swaying in the wind. Her complexion was the translucent hue of a ripe blush. She was stunningly beautiful. Susan smiled and stood up.

"You wish to speak to me?" The girl spoke English with a convent accent.

"Sit down." Lyn indicated the empty chair and stuck her legs out aggressively.

Susan slipped back into her own chair and said politely, "We saw you today, at Fisi Lodge."

"Yes, I know."

"You were with your brother?"

"That's right."

Susan sat back, satisfied. The girl smiled expectantly. Lyn signaled to the waiter to bring more drinks.

"Lyn's a television reporter," Susan said, hoping to explain the reason for her own questions.

"Yes, my brother told me."

"Did he now?" Lyn felt her interest stirring. "Does he

know me?"

"Those he doesn't know, my brother invariably knows of, Miss Preston."

"He must be a very accomplished man." Susan sounded impressed.

"I think he is."

"Do you, uh, work for him?" Lyn rolled her eyes as she glanced around the café, intending to convey what she really meant.

"Work? Yes, I do."

"Here?" Lyn leaned forward, nodding her head sympathetically, the way she did on screen. "In this café?"

The girl laughed, a small happy sound like the tinkling of chimes. "Sometimes, when I have contacts to make. My work takes me everywhere."

The drinks arrived and Lyn waited while the waiter sorted them out. But it was Susan who jumped in and asked the crucial question. "Just what work do you do, Miss Odongo?"

"I help my brother."

There was silence while the three tasted their drinks. Lyn decided to play her trump card. "We brought Tony Kintai to town." Anyone else would have missed it, but she noticed the slight flicker of the girl's eye as she momentarily lost her poise.

"Indeed?"

"You know him?"

"Tony Kintai, Miss Preston, is one of Kenya's most ambitious and talented young patriots. Most people have heard of him."

"And you know him personally?"

"Yes." The girl sounded indifferent.

"He spoke very highly of you," Susan said, ever eager to please.

"And not very highly of your brother." Lyn spoke between clenched teeth to conceal her dismay at Susan butting in. She was the one doing the interview.

"It is to be expected."

A European with a natural tan and an athletic build came over to the table and stood behind the girl's chair. He put her hand on her shoulders and said something in Swahili.

She looked up, her eyes dancing with pleasure.

Lyn stared hard at the man and then looked across the café to where he had been sitting. This was the man the girl had been trying to pick up.

"Let me introduce my fiancé, Miss Preston," the girl said with a shy smile. "Larry Leacock."

CHAPTER 25

Cora emerged from the swimming pool and stood at its edge, letting water trickle from her torn off Levi's down her legs. The pool was located at the top of a bluff. The lodge cabins were behind her while in front, at the other side of the pool, the face of the bluff fell to the plains. At last, Cora let herself soak in the magnificence of the view. For most of the afternoon, after Lyn and Susan had left for Nairobi, she had sulked in the cabin.

It had been Royce's treatment of Mindelo that upset her. Royce had offered to arrange an evening game drive for her but when she asked if Mindelo could go with her, he had refused. He said 'his boy' had work to do.

"Dammit, Royce!" she had shouted. "I'm not going to steal him. I want company, that's all, someone close to my own age." Then she had flounced off to her room and slammed the door.

Mindelo had knocked on the door a little later. It didn't take him long to persuade her to bathe in the pool while he watched for animals. He was sitting behind her like a security guard.

She swung away from the view and stared at him. "What the hell are you doing, then, Mindelo? Get your clothes off!"

He shifted uncomfortably in his seat.

"Come on," she said, walking over to his chair and tugging at his shirt. "Come in the pool with me."

"No, Cora!" He laughed, standing up to fend her off.

She moved quickly, pulling open the top of his shirt.

"No!" he said, glancing around, his face stiffening. She slipped her hand under his shirt and tickled him.

"Stop it!" he cried, stepping backward and seizing her wrists. He forced her arms gently up to her breasts. He gave her a push and released her. She stumbled back to the edge of the pool.

"You bastard!" she said happily as she toppled into the water.

She twisted, letting her plunge carry her to the bottom of the pool. Her wet Levi's hugged her skinny frame. She wondered if Mindelo was watching her through the water. She held her breath and swam along the bottom of the pool to the deep end. Her chest was bursting, but she wanted to stay under as long as she could, to see what he would do.

She waited and then broke the surface of the water, gasping for air. Her ears hurt and her eyes were sore. She expected to see him watching for her but he wasn't. She was annoyed as she pulled herself out of the pool and saw he was still sitting comfortably in his chair.

"What kind of security are you?" She ran over to him. "I could have drowned. You don't care!" She shook her head, showering water on him.

"I can't swim," he said with a chuckle. "You wouldn't drown, but you might get chased by a baboon."

She flung herself down on a chair beside his. "I'd let it catch me." She stretched out so that the lingering afternoon sun would dry her. She knew she wasn't much to look at with her boyish body and wet jeans and T-shirt, but being with Mindelo, it didn't seem important.

"Don't say that, Cora."

His seriousness puzzled her. "Why not?"

"You're in a game park. The animals here are wild. Any of them could attack you."

"Lions, you mean? I wouldn't give them a chance."

"Good. There are some ferocious animals here. They might seem cute from a distance, but they are not. Do you know what 'Fisi Lodge' means?"

She shook her head. She didn't care.

"Hyena. This lodge is named after the hyenas around here. There are hundreds. They are predators, Cora. Their jaws are so strong, they can bite through bone. They pick a weak animal, chase it and tear at its hind legs, eating it alive."

She put her hand out to touch him. "It sounds just like life back home."

She tried to squeeze his hand but he withdrew it and moved his chair a few inches away from her. She grinned and moved hers closer. "Is this some kind of game?"

Mindelo shook his head. "People might not understand."

"To hell with people. I like you, Mindelo."

"Thank you. I like you too."

"I don't just mean that." She was thoughtful. "You're sort of reliable, dependable... even wise? I've never met someone like you."

"Isn't that how a man should be?"

She shivered slightly; it was cooler there than on the beach. "Perhaps." She was silent, feeling his presence so close without actually touching him. He was a great guy!

"Hey," she asked, turning to see his expression, "what makes a man anyway?"

He smiled, replying without hesitation. "When he has his own house."

"His own house!" She was astonished and her reaction made him sit up.

"Did I say something odd?"

She read the concern in his face. Perhaps he made sense. "In the States, I guess a boy would say it's the number of girls he has screwed that makes him a man."

Mindelo nodded his head like a tribal elder. "Your world is odd. A man's women mean nothing if he does not have his own house to give them shelter. Only then is he a man."

"Will you have your own house?"

He was thoughtful. Cora tried to imagine what was passing through his mind. His face was so innocent; it reflected emotions that her friends, the brothers, would never let anyone see.

His mouth tightened, and he put his head on one side as though considering a new idea. "Yes," he said, "soon. I will be a man soon."

"Great!" She placed her hand over Mindelo's where it rested on his knee. He shifted it sharply. She leaned forward. "Why don't you want me to touch you?"

"You startled me."

She sighed. "Sometimes I like to touch people, especially people I like."

"It's difficult here..."

She didn't hear him. "Words often lead to misunderstandings. A touch says so much more."

"In your country, perhaps. The message is different here." He glanced behind at the tourists drinking in the bar. None of them seemed to be watching them.

"Your boss isn't there," she said with a wry smile. "I am glad you don't think that screwing a girl would make you a man, Mindelo. Royce thinks that's what you want from me."

Again, Mindelo tensed. Cora tried to guess from his change of expression what had upset him. Then he surprised her. He put out his hand and laid it gently on her arm. His eyes sought hers and he smiled. "I touch you," he said. "Is that what you want?"

She noticed how his voice had deepened. She laughed. "How brave you are, touching me in public."

He withdrew his hand and bunched it into a fist, slapping it into the open palm of his other hand, "One day I'll have my own house, with a porch." He rolled his eyes. "Then I can sit on my porch and talk, and touch, and no one could say anything. Not like here."

"Are you afraid of Royce?"

"He is my boss. I must do what he says."

"That's no reason to be afraid."

"Afraid?" Mindelo sighed. "Sometimes there are no reasons for fear." He leaned forward and squeezed her hand. "I am not afraid of him. Why should I be? Without me, he is nothing."

She was touched by his faith in himself. It made her feel almost motherly toward him. She wanted to fling her arms around his neck and kiss him.

"Take me to the cabin, Mindelo. Royce won't mind that, will he? Think of those monkeys and hyenas you warned me about."

The sun had almost set and, true enough, there was a troop of monkeys gamboling at the crest of the bluff. He strode along beside her without saying a word. They reached the garden in front of her cabin and she stole a glance at him. He turned to face her. His eyes stared into hers as though he could see her thoughts.

Her head spun and again she wanted to cling to him, to feel his hands holding her firmly. "Mindelo...?"

He took her hand in his and walked her across the last few feet of lawn to her cabin. At the door, he paused and drew her close to him. She could feel his breath was hot on her cheek. She trembled; it was the sudden chill of the sun going down. She tore her eyes away from his and sighed.

"No, Mindelo!" she said, cooling the bond she could feel warming between them. "You must go."

He raised his hand to stroke her cheek. "I thought..."

"So did I," she said sadly, turning to the cabin door and slipping the key into the lock. "Just not now."

He looked so crestfallen she felt a bit guilty but then he stepped away from the porch and gave her a cheery grin of farewell

♦ ♦ ♦ ♦ ♦

Dinner that night was awful. Cora longed to escape back to her cabin. The dining room was packed with chattering Europeans on safari tours from Nairobi. She tried to sit by herself but was paired with an enthusiastic German lady who insisted on describing in detail all the animals she had seen that day. The service was worse than on the plane, with plates of portion-controlled food dumped in front of her.

The only bright point was that Royce stayed in the bar drinking with his cronies and didn't bother her until she was leaving.

"Cora," he called as she crossed the bar to go to the lobby. He waved his whisky glass and lurched over to her. "Enjoying yourself?" He caught her by her arm.

"No!" She pulled away from him.

"All these animals here. It's an experience of a lifetime, what."

"Where's Mindelo?"

Royce stopped swaying. He focused his eyes on her suspiciously. "Want something?"

"Yes. Why do you keep that guy under your thumb so much? I know he works for you but he has to have some time for himself. He's not a slave, is he?"

"You don't know about what you're talking." Royce slurred drunkenly. "Run along to bed now. We have an early flight back to Mombasa tomorrow. You'll be able to see Kilimanjaro close up."

"Stuff Kilimanjaro! I asked you where Mindelo is. Can't

you let him come and talk to me? How do you think I fell be-ing the only one left on this crappy tour?" She really want-ed to see Mindelo to apologize for her behavior earlier. She hadn't meant to lead him on.

"Mindelo's gone to bed." Royce emptied his drink and looked uncomfortable, as though he needed another one. "Trot along. See you in the morning."

"Where?"

"In the lobby."

"I mean where's he sleeping?"

Royce ran his finger under the scarf knotted at his neck. "Staff quarters. Look, I'm sorry Lyn and Susan have left you."

"I bet you are!"

"I mean, if there is anything you want, a book or some-thing, just pick up the phone. The desk will call me. All right?"

Cora scowled. "Okay," she said with sigh.

"Fine!" He snapped his fingers and a uniformed guard with a long flashlight in his hand like a policeman's night-stick, stepped over. "Take this young lady to her cabin."

"Yessah!" The guard raised his hand to his cap.

"Good boy!" Royce spun around and headed in the direc-tion of the bar.

Cora told the guard the number of her cabin and stepped out onto the gravel path behind him. She was miserable. She had upset Mindelo and yet she was the one who could help him. He needed her, she knew that now. He had to es-cape from Royce's hold on him, otherwise he would never be the man he wanted to become.

"Where do the staff sleep?" she asked the guard.

"Beg pardon, miss."

She repeated the question and the guard seemed to be evaluating it as though giving an answer would be revealing classified information. "In the staff quarters," he said with great effort.

"Okay," said Cora, swallowing her impatience. "Next question: where are the staff quarters?"

The guard, who was a tall, middle-aged man with a thick waist, stopped walking and pushed back his cap. He peered down at her suspiciously. He was about to speak, then thought better of it. He waved his flashlight in the direction of the bush.

"Over there?" asked Cora staring at the blackness of the night. "I can't see anything." She remembered the modern, native-style stone huts she had seen surrounding the boundary wall of the lodge compound.

The guard resumed walking. "It is dangerous to go out at night."

"Is it?" She was felling rebellious. "What would you do if an animal attacked us now?"

"I chase it off."

"How?"

"With this." He waved the flashlight.

They reached the cabin and she bid him goodnight, entering the room and bolting the door noisily. She listened at the door to the guard's deep breathing. He was waiting outside, as though aware of the plan that was forming in her mind.

He can't be there all night, she thought. She reached in her bag for her flashlight, a small pocket-sized one, and changed rapidly from her dress to a pair of jeans. She switched out the light and lay on top of her bed, waiting for the guard to go.

After fifteen minutes, she crept to the window and peered out. The guard had gone. On the lawn a few meters from her door were two zebras, standing motionless in the moonlight. She held her flashlight in her hand, softly unbolted the cabin door and stepped out. The zebras regarded her without surprise. She slipped out of the light illuminating the path and moved behind the cabin into the darkness.

Someone coughed in the silence. Cora froze. There was a security post behind her cabin and the cough of the guard sitting outside warned her to skirt it.

She crept stealthily around it and across the grass to the boundary wall. She had no idea where she would find Mindelo, nor why she was looking for him. She gripped the flashlight firmly. Perhaps she would help him escape, she thought. They could hire a minibus and drive to Nairobi. Somewhere Royce wouldn't find them.

She worked her way cautiously along the boundary wall. The moon hung high and bright in the sky and its pallor was enough for her to distinguish the trees and other obstructions. There was a wooden gate in the wall, which she guessed was the staff entrance. She pulled it open and sneaked through.

The grass at the other side of the wall reached up to her knees. There was a path trodden through it but she didn't want to take that in case she met someone. About a hundred meters ahead there was a glow of light. She thought that must be where the staff slept. She decided to go to the edge of the compound and look for someone who would take a message to Mindelo.

She pushed her way cautiously through the grass. Around her she could hear the babble of night noises. A growl of some animal echoed over the savanna in the breeze. She ignored it.

In the darkness only the shadowy outlines of trees were visible, but she didn't want to use her flashlight in case she was seen. She wasn't frightened. The lights of the compound were near and she could see people there.

She paused as a tree loomed in front of her. She bit her lip, wondering which way to go. The grass was almost waist high and she had lost sight of the path. She moved to her left. Another tree stood in her way. She turned back to the right and stared. The first tree that blocked her way had gone.

Saliva drained from her throat and her heart thumped. She cupped the flashlight in her hand to shield the light and pressed the switch. In the beam was a bundle of dark red cloth hanging on a bush. She sighed with relief, laughing at herself for her fright.

The cloth moved and a shining black head stared at her, sharpened fangs grinning in place of teeth. She opened her mouth to scream but a hand slipped over her face and an arm pinioned her from behind to a hot, vile-smelling body.

She kicked back with her foot, her soft sandal making contact with her attacker's leg. The flashlight fell into the grass and a shape scooped it up and switched it off.

She felt herself falling as her assailant flung her forward.

Her knee banged against a stone and she yelped with pain. Someone felt for her face, found it, and clapped fingers over her lips, forcing them against her teeth.

She twisted her head and snapped at the fingers, catching one in her mouth. She bit as hard as she could and felt the blood trickling down her chin. There was a grunt from the person holding her.

Someone was at her feet, pulling off her sandals. A hand clawed up her leg. She arched her body and kicked out, her foot jamming into the man's crotch, knocking him away. Another hand seized her wrist and felt her watch being torn off.

She was choking, almost stifled by a foul smell as if she was being rolled in steaming cow dung. Her face was pushed down into the ground and her arms held behind her back. Rough hands patted her body, fondling her breasts and hips. She opened her mouth to scream but a hand filled it with dusty soil. She spat it out and lay still on the grass.

She didn't believe they had gone. Although no one was holding her, she was sure the men were crouched in the dark, waiting for her to move. She opened her eyes and looked up. The only shapes were the slender outlines of the thorn trees against the moon. The grass scratched against her face and she sat up.

She sniffed. The smell had gone. She listened. The only sound was a rustling of grass and the chilling, melancholy howl of a hyena. She shivered and tried to stand. It was agony. Her knee was badly bruised and she found it difficult to walk. She tried, gritting her teeth with determination.

The wall of the lodge compound was not far away. If she could make it by herself and get back to her cabin, no one, not even Mindelo, would know what had happened.

She winced again as she tried to stand. The pain was excruciating so she began to crawl, painfully making her way through the grass toward the wall. An odd chuckle sounded near her ear. She stopped, sinking down to the ground with fright. If she screamed, the men would know where she was.

She dragged herself carefully a few more inches. There was a wild cackle that made her blood curl. She felt a dash of wind on her cheek, as though someone was breathing on her.

Suddenly there was another chuckle close to her side, and the sound of someone rushing at her. She felt a sharp pain at her ankle. She reached down and touched the spot; it was moist with blood.

There was another lunge through the grass. She screamed and stood up, trying to run. Something hurtled at her chest and knocked her down. The sound of greedy laughter filled the night air.

"Help!" she shrieked, her voice high pitched with terror.

The starving hyenas, crazed by the scent of blood, closed in, one by one.

CHAPTER 26

Tony Kintai did not return to the Thorn Tree Café that night as he promised.

Lyn waited for him after Rena Odongo and her fiancé had left and Susan had trotted off to bed. She waited out of pique for finding out she had been wrong in her quick assessment of Rena, and because she was angry at being stood up by Tony.

She drank heavily and alone; no one spoke to her. It was midnight when she pushed back her chair and weaved with slow deliberation across the lobby and into the elevator.

She was woken next morning by the jangling of the telephone. "Good morning, Lyn." The voice was sunny and bright.

"Who the hell is this?" The roof of her mouth was parched. The bed next to hers was empty and the noise of water running in the shower sounded like a thunderstorm. She groped on the bedside table with her free hand for her cigarettes.

"Who the hell do you think it is?" the voice chuckled.

She lit a cigarette, drew on it deeply, and sighed as the smoke billowed around her. "Tony Kintai, you're a bastard!"

"About last night. I was busy. I know you were okay though."

"I wasn't okay at all.

"I've turned the car in."

"Mr. Hertz will be pleased! What time is it?"

"Ten. I'm in the lobby. I'm coming up."

"And I'm in bed...waiting! Bring coffee." She slammed down the phone, ground out the cigarette and groaned. "Fucking man!"

"Oh, excuse me." Susan hesitated at the bathroom door. "I tried not to wake you."

"The whole damn evening I'm sitting like a Nairobi whore waiting for that man and the only time I get him is now."

Susan sat on the bed toweling her hair. "I liked Rena. I wonder if her brother is like her.

"You can tell Kintai that. He's on his way up."

"Here?" Susan rose from the bed in panic, clutching the large bath towel around her.

Lyn gave her a withering look. "Don't worry, kid. It's me he's coming to see, not you."

"I'm not dressed!"

"What the hell difference does that make!" She paused when she saw Susan's lower lip tremble. "Gee, kid, I didn't mean it that way. You're too sensitive. Kintai won't mind how you look. He's a Masai, remember."

"Couldn't you entertain him in the parlor while I stay here in the bedroom?"

"Hell, no. Bedroom's the place. Let him get the idea from the start. I've wasted enough time already. *You* stay in the parlor."

There was a knock on the door. They looked at each other with startled eyes. "It's him!" Lyn struggled out of the bed. "I look a fright." She headed for the bathroom. "Let him in."

"I can't open the door; not like this!"

"You'll remind him of his Masai women. I've got to piss before I wet myself."

The knocking continued. "Who is it? Susan called warily.

"Room service."

Susan shrugged and padded over the animal skins laid out on the polished wooden floor of the parlor. She paused at the door and secured the bath towel above her breasts with a knot. She had a smaller towel around her head. She unlatched the door and opened it.

"Jambo!"

"Tony!" She tried to close the door on him but he stepped

smartly into the room. His hand closed around her faltering fingers and he shut the door himself. He was dressed in a coffee-colored blazer, brown boots, tan slacks, a beige shirt and a matching tie.

She moved uncertainly across the room and turned to consider him. "You startled me."

"Where's Lyn?"

"She'll be out in a minute. Susan sat down on the hide-covered couch, clasping her towel.

"Is something wrong?"

"I'm not used to so much energy early in the morning. Or at any time, really."

He grinned. "I've had two meetings already. I've got half an hour to spare."

"Lyn's expecting you to stay longer than that." She rose from the couch, held the top of her towel to make sure it didn't slip down, and walked carefully across the room. He was conscious of Tony watching her with interest. She opened the door to the bedroom and slipped in quickly.

Lyn was standing naked in the center of the room. She had brushed up her long blonde hair and it was gathered in an untidy chignon. She made no move to cover herself. "Not bad, considering I'm thirty, huh?"

"Hurry up!" Susan was flustered. "He's in there." She gestured frantically at the parlor door.

"So send him in."

"But you're naked."

"Exactly. This cat's a Masai. When in Rome, honey..."

Susan put her hands to her eyes. She was close to tears. "I don't know what to do."

"I told you, send him in."

"All right, I will! Don't blame me if it doesn't work out the way you think." She wiped her eyes and flung open the door to the parlor. "Mr. Kintai!" Tony raised his head sharply. "Miss Preston will see you now. There!"

She padded across the parlor to the window. The drapes were closed. She peeked through them and gazed down on Kimathi Street below. Tony walked across to the bedroom. At the door he stopped.

"Come in, Tony! I'm just getting dressed."

Lyn felt him studying her. She held in her stomach and sauntered toward him holding out her hand. She was moistening at the glint in his eye.

"Surely you're not bashful?" She grasped his hand and led him to the bed. She stopped and spun around to face him, raising her hand and tweaking his tie.

"You're very formal, Kintai. Not like yesterday." She loosened the tie while she spoke. "I'm the Masai now."

"Stop that!" Tony's hands gripped her wrists and he pulled her close to him.

She saw the pore marks on the skin of his soft nose. She closed her eyes and rubbed her breasts against the gold buttons of his blazer. "Kiss me!" She raised her mouth expectantly.

"Not now!" He released her wrists, turned away from her, and began to pace the room. "I don't have much time. Rena will be here in a few minutes."

"Rena!" Lyn's desire faltered. "What the hell's she coming here for? A threesome?"

"I asked her to meet me here. We don't get much chance to be together, Lyn. Her brother -"

"I thought you came here to see me!"

"I did." He stalked around the room in agitation.

"You make me feel like a piece of shit. And for god's sake, stop moving around like that." She scooped up a pillow and flung it at his head.

He caught it and, with a grunt, threw it back on the bed. His expression changed.

"Don't say that. I didn't expect to find you like this..." His fists opened and shut as he searched for the words he wanted to say. He crossed the floor to her and reached for her waist. He faced her directly, his eyes probing. A rush of happiness swept through her.

"We don't have to hurry this. I'll come back later." He let go of her waist and frowned. "I've never met anyone quite like you before."

"Yeah?" She sank on the bed and covered herself with a sheet. "I've let myself be fooled by you three times now, Tony. It won't happen again."

"Fooled?" He seemed puzzled.

"The first time was you kissed me in Narok, the second time was last night and you didn't show up, and now here you are rejecting me. Later's like tomorrow, it never comes, Kintai. Jesus, how do you think I feel!"

"I feel something too, Lyn. I'm not a stud from the Mombasa beach."

She tossed her head, dismissing his remark. "So what's a girl to do? I fancy you, Kintai. I want you inside me."

There was a knock on the parlor door.

Tony seemed relieved at the sound of other voices. "We must talk, Lyn." He put his hand on the bedroom door handle, his eyes showing concern.

Or was it pity? She glared at him then pulled the sheet over her head, burying herself in the bed.

She was waiting for him to rip away the covers and seize her, begging forgiveness for his callous behavior. Nothing happened. She lowered the sheet slowly. The room was empty and the bedroom door closed.

"Damn! Damn! Damn!" She pummeled the pillow frantically with her fists.

◆ ◆ ◆ ◆ ◆

In the parlor, Susan was pink with embarrassment. She was facing Rena Odongo and Larry Leacock, clutching her towel around her body and wondering what to say. Tony bounded into the room and hugged Rena affectionately. Susan hurried to the bedroom door.

"Wait, Susan." Tony's stern voice stopped her. "Lyn's angry with me. " He winked over Rena's shoulder. "Tell her that I will explain everything. Are you going to Mombasa today?"

She shrugged, not sure what she was doing. "It's up to Lyn."

"I can arrange it if you like. Tell Lyn that. Larry here will contact you later."

She fidgeted nervously, conscious of how she must look standing in the towel in front of the three of them, people she had met only the day before.

"We're going Susan," Tony said, as though understanding how she felt. "Don't worry." He led Rena and Larry out of the room and Susan closed the door firmly behind them. She rushed into the bedroom.

"Kintai?" Lyn pulled the sheet from her head and gazed out hopefully. "What the hell are you doing, Sue? Where's Kintai?"

"Gone, I hope. I have never felt so ashamed in my whole life. Standing in front of the three of them like this. I'm not even wearing my underwear! It was so demeaning."

"What about me? My head's splitting, my stomach's boiling and my cunt's aching! Some vacation, this is."

"Tony said Larry will arrange for us to get back to Mombasa today."

"Back to LA would be better. What's that?"

They listened to the sound of discreet knocking on the outer door.

"I'm not going to the door again like this!" She was emphatic.

"Get dressed then, for God's sake." Lyn tugged the sheet off the bed, wrapped it around herself and sauntered out to the parlor. She opened the door slowly. A formidable room service steward stood in the corridor beaming behind a trolley bearing an ice bucket, two glasses and a bottle of champagne.

"Mrs. Ross?"

"No, but come in." Lyn simpered at the steward as he wheeled the trolley past her.

Susan came out of the bedroom and stared dumbly at the champagne. "Who sent that?"

"With the compliments of Mr. Odongo, miss." There was a note of awe in the waiter's voice. He poured champagne into each glass and then added orange juice. He offered a glass to Susan. She took it reluctantly.

"From Mr. Odongo? For us?"

"Yes, for Mrs. Ross."

"Was there any message?" Susan clasped the glass without drinking.

"No, miss." The steward slipped out of the room while Susan was staring thoughtfully at the champagne in her hand.

"Drink up, Sue. It won't kill you." Lyn drained her glass then put it down as she lit a cigarette. She saw that Susan was wearing a yellow dress with pleats. Her hair fell around her shoulders instead of being confined to the rubber band she usually wore.

"You're dressed for action, honey!" Lyn filled her glass from the bottle.

Susan shrugged and tasted the champagne. She grimaced.

"You bug me sometimes, Sue. Aren't you curious why the notorious Samson Odongo should send us champagne?"

"Us? I thought the steward said it was for me."

"There were two glasses, honey, unless Mr. Odongo himself plans to make an appearance to share it with you."

Susan sipped again from the glass and smiled. She felt a zest she didn't expect just from two sips of champagne. She put the glass down on the table. "I don't really believe what Tony Kintai says about Mr. Odongo."

"Of course, you don't. One glance of him in Fisi Lodge and you were ready to throw up your legs for nothing. You should have sent this back."

"I never thought of that."

"Quite right. We'll send back the empty bottle and tell him we flushed his bubbly down the john." She poured herself another glass and sat down. The sheet fell open and she made no attempt to close it around her.

"This certainly does something for a hangover. What are you doing by the window?"

"Just looking?"

"For a maroon Range Rover? Hey, Sue, you look marvelous in that dress, against the light. I don't know how you do it."

"I gave it to the room steward to press last night."

"I didn't mean that."

"What do you mean?"

There was a new tension in the room. Lyn stood up, letting the sheet slip from her shoulders to the floor. She walked unsteadily toward Susan. "You're a wholesome, pure young woman, right?" She raised her eyebrows. "Right now you look kinda sexy to me!"

"Really?" Her mind was far away. She gasped and turned in surprise when she realized Lyn was standing close to he, pressing her naked body against her back.

"Have a sip of this, honey." Lyn passed her glass in front of her, rubbing her arm against her breasts. She raised the glass to Susan's lips.

"What are you doing?" Susan eased herself out of Lyn's clumsy embrace. "Be careful! You'll spill that on my dress."

"Damn your dress!" Lyn raised the glass and looked as though she was about to splash it over her. Susan stared, unable to move.

Lyn sighed. "You're right. What am I doing!" She held the glass to her lips and tilted her head back until she drained it. "Why waste the stuff." She lowered the glass and cupped the bowl of it over her mound of ginger pubic hair.

"Sue, honey, I'm so fucking horny!" She shook herself in despair and headed back to the bedroom, lifting the champagne bottle from the bucket and carrying it with her.

Susan shuddered with disgust and gazed out of the window to the traffic in Kimathi Street. She looked for her glass, drained it and tried to dismiss Lyn from her mind. She abandoned herself to the rising feeling that what Tony had said about Samson Odongo and his relentless pursuit of a woman he wanted, might be coming true.

CHAPTER 27

Larry Leacock drove with caution through the city's late afternoon traffic. Susan and Lyn had spent the day with him driving around the sights of Nairobi. They had lunched at the New Stanley buffet table, visited the Bombas of Kenya for the native dancing and model villages, and taken tea on the Lord Delamere Terrace at the Norfolk Hotel.

Susan found Larry polite and precise, preserving his distance. She wondered if he was shy, because he seemed nervous and hardly spoke.

"You've been so kind, Larry," she said as he edged the Range Rover up to the sidewalk outside the Nairobi railway station.

There was so much she wanted to ask but his reticence deterred her. Lyn, who normally handled such situations with panache, had spent the entire day grumpily nursing her hangover.

"Where the hell's this?" Lyn asked, glaring out of the window from the back seat.

"We're going to take the train here." Susan tried to keep her voice even, but she was losing patience with Lyn's broodiness. "To Mombasa. We're going First Class. Larry's organized it all."

Lyn's brow clouded. "Sue, has it occurred to you to ask why?"

"Yes, but I didn't think that was polite."

Larry's prim face relaxed for the first time that day. "Let's go and have some tea," he said, swinging out of the Range Rover and sliding his seat forward for Lyn to get out too. The boy who had traveled with them in the back of the vehicle jumped out without a word and carried their bags into the Upper Class Restaurant.

A waiter in a starched cotton jacket with crested silver buttons and wearing tennis shoes, took their order. There was a stained white cloth on the table and fresh flowers. Framed photographs of His Excellency Mzee Jomo Kenyatta and of His Excellency Daniel T Arap Moi, President of the Republic of Kenya, stared at them from a wall.

Ice, for Larry's coke, was presented in a big silver bowl. Lyn swayed in her seat and fastened her eyes on Larry.

Susan leaned forward expectantly. She sensed it was question time again. She had been surprised when Larry had collected them from the hotel in Samson Odongo's Range Rover. He explained that Rena had arranged it.

Larry smiled confidently, as though he knew all about Lyn and wasn't fazed by her. "Before you ask me anything, Miss Preston, I must tell you that Mr. Odongo has forbidden me to answer any questions about him."

"Forbidden?" Lyn rapped the silver teaspoon on her saucer. "So let's talk about you."

"There's nothing to tell about me. I work for Mr. Odongo. I'm his token white."

"You don't sound ashamed."

"Why should I be? It's an honor. He is a great man."

"You're not supposed to tell us anything about him, remember?"

Larry's blue eyes didn't falter.

"Are you really engaged to his sister, Rena?" She lit a cigarette and blew smoke across the table, trying to intimidate him.

"Officially, yes."

"You're not going to marry her though, are you?"

Larry set his glass firmly on the table and stared at Lyn. His eyes were hard and even Susan could see that she had gone too far.

"You're gay." Lyn smiled dauntingly.

Susan was appalled. "Lyn, how can you say such a thing! You're not on TV now. I'm so sorry," she said, worrying that Larry would think that she was somehow responsible for Lyn's outrageous behavior.

Larry shrugged, then nodded his head slightly, indicating agreement. He reached for another ice cube and dropped in his glass, twirling it around with his finger. He astonished Susan by how unconcerned he seemed at what Lyn had suggested.

"Rena is your front, right? She's crazy about Tony Kintai but the great Mr. Odongo doesn't approve." Lyn barely waited for Larry to nod his head again.

"So why is Mr. Odongo laying on this treatment for Sue and myself when we are friends of Tony Kintai?"

"I have no idea." He sounded indifferent and not as disturbed by Lyn's questions as Susan thought he would be.

He pushed back his chair and stood up. "My job was to bring you here. The train for Mombasa leaves in thirty minutes." He bowed to Susan, bid them goodnight curtly and strode out of the restaurant.

"You upset him!"

"How did you guess?"

"Why did you tell him those things? He's been so kind to us, driving us around. You made it all up, didn't you?"

"I guessed. I like my men to have balls."

"Like Tony Kintai?"

Lyn grimaced. "I don't think I'll see Kintai again. I shouldn't have tried to rape him. I must have been mad."

The train for Mombasa was waiting at the platform. There were fifteen carriages behind a diesel engine. The platform was thronged with people scrambling to board. The seats in the new Swedish-built Third Class compartments were already filled with placid Africans.

As she followed Lyn out of the restaurant, Susan shied at the chaos. "We'll never find where we are supposed to go. Larry would have stayed to help us if you hadn't been so rude."

Lyn grunted, and elbowed her way into the crowd.

A hand touched Susan's arm. She shrieked, thinking it was a pickpocket. A boy stood beside her grinning broadly. She sighed with relief as she recognized him as the one from the Range Rover.

"Lyn," she called. "Larry's boy is here. He'll show us where to go."

Lyn was intrigued. "So we've still got our minder even if bwana's gone for a sulk."

The boy showed them to their compartment. It was better than Susan had expected, with its green leatherette upholstered bench seat and upper bunk, and a washbasin in a corner. She was thrilled by the sounds of people shouting farewells, the functionaries busily walking up and down the corridor, and the engines exercising on the adjoining track.

Lyn seemed to feel the excitement too for she stopped frowning and went into the corridor to lean out of the window and watch the performance of departure.

The boy pointed to the ledge over the door where he had stowed their bags. Susan thanked him and sat down. The boy stood uncertainly, looking at Lyn in the corridor and then at Susan.

"Oh dear," she said, opening her purse. "I really should give you something, but I can't understand the money. Perhaps Lyn -."

The boy shook his head vigorously and put his finger to his lips.

Susan was bewildered. "What do you mean? Don't you speak English? I have a Swahili phrase book somewhere." She rummaged in her purse.

With another glance at Lyn to make sure she was not watching, the boy put his hand deep into the pocket of his shorts and produced a small trinket box. He thrust it at Susan, a pleading look in his eyes. She took it nervously.

"What's this? Not your tame spider, I hope."

The boy looked relieved. He rolled his eyes, and darted into the corridor, jumping off the train as it was preparing to leave.

"How strange," Susan murmured to herself. She placed the box on the washbasin and peered out of the window. The train gave a warning lurch and there were whoops and shouts from the people on the platform. Doors banged and more functionaries scuttled along the train's corridor.

"We're off!" Lyn cried. She leaned out of the window and stared along the platform as the train began to pull out.

Susan joined her. "Isn't this fun?"

Lyn didn't answer. She was watching a man chasing after the train, scrambling to jump on board before it slipped away. She clutched Susan's arm. "Look at that man! It's Kintai, I'm sure."

Susan followed her gaze to where a man stood on the platform, watching the train pull away from him. "Wishful thinking, Lyn. It doesn't look like him at all."

"It was him, I tell you!"

"All right. Doesn't matter now since he missed the train

anyway." She returned to the compartment and Lyn flopped down on the seat beside her.

Susan gazed out of the window at the outskirts of Nairobi slipping by in the gathering gloom. She was worried about Lyn. Her disapproval of her had been growing since the car ride from Fisi Lodge. It increased with Lyn's odd behavior that morning. Lyn was aggressive and insensitive; she scared off people with her callous approach. She was sure Lyn would never see Tony Kintai again. She was just too demanding for someone like him.

"You think I'm a fool, don't you?" Lyn's challenge broke into her thoughts.

"No. I was just thinking about the scenery."

Lyn was undeterred. "I really liked that man." She sighed. "He's got charisma. It's not just the sex. If you'd seen him in his Masai robe, so simple yet absolutely dynamic, you'd feel the same way about him. It's not often you meet a man with his kind of presence. Such a strong aura!"

"You'll soon forget him, Lyn. When we get back to the hotel, you'll tell Royce to fix you up with one of his beach boys."

"That doesn't sound like you!"

Susan shrugged. "Well, I'm fed up with you, and Maggie, and this endless hunt for men as though they are chocolates you can buy and can nibble to your heart's content. Oh!" she said as though realizing what she was saying. "I'm sorry."

"Don't be. My hunger is too much for you, isn't it? I'm a success in a profession dominated by men. I've had to become like a man to compete, to protect myself. The way I regard men is the way they regard us women. Sue, we're just pieces of meat for them to enjoy.

"Chocolates? That's nice. Sure, I look on men as chocolates. I like the ones with hard centers. I wish I had one at home to share my life with, that's all. Someone like Tony Kintai."

"You're serious about him? You'd live with him?" She stared at Lyn in disbelief.

"It's a thought. He'd be a sensation in the States. I could get him a job with the station. He could be the African expert. Africa's a big thing these days. He could live in my apartment..." Lyn was open-mouthed as the possibilities of her idea raced through her mind.

Susan shook her head, amazed at this new side of Lyn. "You don't even know him. Anyway, if you took a man like him from Africa to LA, you'd emasculate him."

"He had that affect on you too, did he?" Lyn took her hand and squeezed it. "You've made me see I am right. You're a sensible, level headed, mediocre-minded woman. Yet you sensed the essence of that man; his vitality, his latent power.

"He doesn't have to lose that in Los Angeles. The station would package him properly. We could do a program together. I can see it now: 'The Preston-Kintai Report.' It's got a ring to it, it really has. And wouldn't we look great on screen together!"

Susan withdrew her hand politely. The train began to pick up speed. "Why don't you sleep on it. Shouldn't you get to know him better first?"

"Shit! When I get an idea, I don't do feasibility studies before I act. If I did, I'd never get off my ass. As soon as we get to Mombasa, I'm going to find out everything there is to know about Tony Kintai. I'll offer him a part on the program I'm going to do on Kenya. He'll be a natural as a co-host. Everything will develop from there."

Susan sank into her own reverie. Although she was beginning to dislike Lyn, she was impressed by her determination. She wanted Tony so much, she would probably get him, even though it would be a one-night stand, whatever dreams she had for him.

Susan was more sorry for herself. She didn't know what she wanted. She had divorced her dull husband but she was beginning to think she was the dull one. Here she was, racing through Africa by train, sharing confidences with the famous Lyn Preston, and what did she feel? Nothing! No excitement.

Well there was something. A sense of emptiness, a void aching to be filled. She felt she was asleep, waiting to be woken the way Lyn was awake, the way even Cora and Maggie were awake. Perhaps that was why she had come on this vacation, to rouse and discover herself, not Africa.

A face beamed at the door of the compartment. A hand

stretched out and handed Lyn two tickets. "For dinner," the steward said and then shuffled away down the corridor.

Another face appeared offering sheets and blankets. Lyn accepted, paid the required fee, and shut the door. She looked around the compartment.

"What's that?" she said, startling Susan. "In that box. Is it yours?"

"Yes, Larry's boy gave it to me."

Lyn picked up the box from the washbasin, "What's in it?"

"I haven't looked."

"For heaven's sake, Sue! Aren't you curious?" Open it." She handed it to her.

"I expect it's some childish memento. He ran off before I could thank him."

"It might be drugs. He might have planted something on you. You wouldn't accept that from a youth in California without being suspicious."

Susan laughed. "To tell the truth, I am suspicious. It might be the boy's collection of poisonous spiders."

"Oh hell!" Lyn reached for the box but Susan held it out of her grasp. The train lurched, hitting points at speed, and Susan fell against the open window. The box slipped out of her hand. It dropped to the floor, breaking open.

Lyn bent down and snatched up something.

"What is it?"

"Now you're curious, huh?"

"He gave it to me!"

Lyn opened her hand slowly. A green gem stone in a setting of yellow gold lay in her palm.

"A brooch! Isn't it lovely." She took it from Lyn's hand and pinned it on her yellow dress. She turned to admire it in the window above the washbasin.

"Jade. Expensive," Lyn said with authority. She was reading the card in the box. "Until we meet, Samson Odongo."

"I don't understand," said Susan. "Why should he give me a present?"

"That's his method, part of his campaign. He's obviously decided to add you to his harem. And you're an easy sucker considering how you've been mooning about him ever since you set eyes on him."

Susan's heart skipped a beat. "I'll send it back." She touched the brooch warily.

"You didn't send back the champagne, or the guided tour of Nairobi. Come to think of it, who paid for this compartment? Did you? I didn't."

"I thought it was Tony. Perhaps it was Mr. Odongo."

"Right, so there's no point in returning a measly jade and gold brooch, is there?"

"Are you sure it's all right?"

"No. But go for it, Sue, go for it."

Susan sat back in the corner of the bench seat and watched the darkening view from the window. The industrial sprawl of the Nairobi outskirts was giving way to flat scrubland. She wondered when she would meet Samson Odongo and what would happen.

Was he the reason, at last revealing itself, why she had come on this journey?

CHAPTER 28

The journey to Mombasa took the whole night. When Susan returned to the compartment with Lyn after dinner, they found it had been transformed with two narrow bunks made up with the blankets and sheets they had paid for earlier.

Susan offered Lyn her choice of bunks. Lyn didn't answer but left the compartment with a shrug of petulance. Susan chose the top and soon fell asleep, despite worrying about Lyn's new animosity toward her. Two hours later she was woken by Lyn returning, staggering drunkenly with the roll of the train.

"Been drinking with the boys," she mumbled and lay down fully clothed on top of her bunk. Susan waited, tense and worried, until Lyn's snores showed she was asleep. She slept fitfully after that, waking when the train jerked into motion after its many stops.

She listened anxiously to Lyn thrashing in the bunk below. She wondered why she had chosen to hate her. It made her own distaste for her seem superfluous. She was beginning to feel sorry for her, just like she did for Maggie.

They shared the breakfast table in silence. Both stared out of the open window at the palm trees and sandy scrubland as the train snaked slowly to its destination. Susan was excessively polite to the stewards, trying to compensate for Lyn's moroseness. She smiled gratefully at the head steward when he bowed them out of the restaurant.

"Why are you sucking up to him?" Lyn turned on her with a tight sneer. "I tried to get him to fuck last night and he wouldn't."

She followed Lyn to the cabin and sat speechless on the seat until the train began to joggle slowly into Mombasa station.

Lyn glowered in the opposite corner, occasionally wiping the sweat from her brow. She made no attempt to fix her hair. Her blouse and jeans were creased and she looked crumpled and defeated. The heat was suffocating.

Susan wanted to cry.

The train creaked to a halt. People were leaping off, and

soon the empty platform was filled with jostling crowds. Susan sighed and stood up. "We're here, Lyn," she said with an effort at politeness. "I wonder how we'll get to the hotel?"

Lyn rolled her eyes upward without answering. She stood up and angrily yanked her bag off the ledge. At that moment the door was flung open and a burly man blocked out the light. "Hello," he said, his face split with a wide grin. "I help you."

"Get the hell out of here. We don't want any more of Odongo's heavies around."

"What do you mean. Lyn?" Susan was appalled. "My friend's got a headache," she explained to the man who was still smiling cheerfully.

"I don't have a headache! I'm just pissed off. Everywhere I move, there's one of Odongo's goons watching me. Last night, the same thing happened in the restaurant car. Two men watched us the whole time. They made me nervous."

"I never noticed."

The man took Susan's bag and put out his hand for Lyn's. She held on to it.

"Go your own fucking way, Sue. I'm not getting involved."

"I don't know what you mean." Susan glanced at the man standing patiently in the corridor. He was still smiling.

"We have car outside, Miss Ross. Miss Preston, please to give me your bag. I take care it good."

Lyn handed the bag over with a scowl.

"I don't understand, Lyn. Last night you seemed to think I should accept Mr Odongo's hospitality. Now you've changed your mind?"

"If I were you, I would accept. But I'm not you, that's the galling part."

They descended from the train and followed the massive shape of the man as he cleared a way through the crowd. Conversation was impossible and Susan wondered what Lyn meant. *Was she jealous?*

It was laughable. How could someone with Lyn's talent be jealous of her? She dismissed the idea, amazed at her conceit for thinking of it.

They emerged from the station and stood side by side while the crowd milled around them. Susan looked for a maroon Range Rover in the cars gathered in the yard. There wasn't one.

"Look, he's over there," said Lyn, nodding with her head to the right of the parking lot. Susan saw the man beckoning them over the heads of the crowd. "Leave that one to me," said Lyn quickly. "You've got the boss, let me have the lackey."

Susan felt ashamed. Lyn's sarcasm hurt and puzzled her. She trailed behind her to the car, her eyes downcast. As she got close to the vehicle, she released someone was sitting in the back seat. She stopped and stared.

"Maggie! What are you doing here?"

"My dear, I simply had to sacrifice my beauty sleep to find out what you've been up to in Nairobi." She patted the seat beside her and Susan got in and sat down.

The man who had carried their bags turned out to be Maggie's driver and he held the door open for Lyn to sit in the front seat. "I'm warning you, Lyn!" Maggie said immediately. "Keep your hands off Joe. He's mine, all mine."

"I don't understand." Susan settled back in the car. "I thought that Mr. Odongo sent this man to meet us."

"Mr. Bongo? This is my treat, dear. You've no idea how devastated I was when you didn't come back from that bloody balloon trip with Cora. She was in such a state, poor thing. If Joe hadn't taken care of me, I swear I would have gone berserk."

"Is he really taking care of you, Maggie?" Lyn asked archly.

"Of course! And I've booked him day and night for our entire stay. Cora says you've gone gaga over some naked Masai?"

Maggie kept up a constant prattle about Cora while the car moved through the busy streets of Mombasa. She told them how the guards had saved Cora from the attack before the hyenas did any harm.

"She's all right now, Maggie said. "The doctor's given her all sorts of shots. She was only grazed really. Mindelo sits with her all day, so she loves it."

"It must have been horrible," said Susan.

"Serves her right!"

Lyn's humor seemed to be restored. They were soon clattering over the Nyali Bridge and driving through the garden suburbs to the Mpingo Beach Hotel.

Susan was puzzled by the change in Maggie. She seemed so much brighter and nicer than she had been when they left.

"What have you been doing while we've been away? I hope you haven't been bored?"

Maggie gloated. "Oh no, dear. This colossus has been taking me on outings. As soon as I discovered he could drive, I hired the car. You must come out for a drive with us."

She drew away politely. "I wouldn't want to impose on you."

"Come this afternoon, dear. Joe is going to take me to his village. To meet his mother."

"It must be romance!" Lyn laughed, glancing sideways with interest at the driver.

"Romance with this hunk?" Maggie's vehemence surprised Susan until she caught the glint of happiness in her eye. "None of that. He's a worthless, mindless giant, aren't you, Joe?"

"Yes, Mrs. Biddle-Mac," the big man answered grimly.

"Maggie!" Lyn was incredulous. "How did you train him so fast? You could shit on him and he'd be happy!"

"I never thought of that..."

"It's awful!" Susan paled. "I've had to endure Lyn's tasteless remarks for three days. Not yours as well!"

Maggie glanced at her warily. "I've not heard you be so critical before, dear. Has something happened between you and Lyn?" Her mouth parted in an attempt at a beguiling smile. Susan was overwhelmed.

"There's a macho Kenyan playboy chasing her, Maggie. Our Susan's got airs now."

"No, I haven't." She nearly lost her temper. "You're making too much out of this! I would never feel that I am better than you or Maggie. It's not my nature." She was close to tears.

"I don't mind coming for a drive with you, Maggie," Lyn said with another glance at Joe. "I'd like to visit your driver's village. You never know..."

"I know, Lyn, I know. Hey, Joe, any more at home like you?" Maggie asked loudly. "Not so gross as you, something cute and sweet for my friend Lyn?"

"Sure, Mrs. Biddle-Mac."

Susan concentrated her eyes on the broad back of the chauffeur to take her mind off the way she was feeling. She guessed that he didn't fully understand what Maggie was saying. Perhaps that was why Maggie had mellowed, because she had found a man who agreed with everything she said.

The car stopped and Susan stepped out when the bellhop opened the door. She avoided his eyes. Lyn stalked off in the direction of her cottage without speaking.

Charles Royce bustled over. "Good trip, was it? Everything all right?" He wiped the sweat from his moustache, his blue eyes studying her with a new curiosity.

"Oh, yes. Thank you, Mr. Royce."

"Probably feeling a bit tired, are you?"

"Yes," she said, touched by his consideration. "I didn't sleep that well on the train." She patted her hair and tried to brighten up her spirits. "It was so kind of Mrs. Biddle-Macdonald to meet us at the station."

"Kindness isn't one of my virtues, dear. This thing here suggested it." Maggie nodded at Joe. It occurred to Susan that if the driver had a tail he would have wagged it; he seemed totally devoted to Maggie.

"What are you planning to do today, Mrs. Ross. If you don't mind my asking." Royce was unusually polite.

Maggie glared at him. "You've got a lot of cheek for a limey. Are you going to check on me too? I'm taking Joe to my cottage and he's going to teach me all about the Kikuyu male circumcision ceremony."

Susan blushed, but Royce came to her rescue. "I'm sure Mrs. Ross has no plans to equal yours."

Maggie gave him a withering look and stomped off through the lobby. Joe went to park the car.

"I hope they'll be very happy," Royce muttered. "Njonjo dotes on old ladies, especially rich ones. I don't know what they see in him."

"Excuse me, Mr Royce. I do feel I should go to my cottage." Susan watched the bellboy carrying her bag down the path. She felt drained.

"Of course. Will you be here all day?"

"I think so." She was puzzled. "Why do you ask?"

"No reason," he said airily. "Well, I'd like to send you a basket of fruit."

"That's very kind."

"If there's anything you need, please ask me," he said, the concern in his voice sounding genuine. She wondered why he was showing so much interest in her after his disapproving attitude when she first arrived.

"Please come straight to me with any problems." He seemed nervous. "Don't tell anyone else, please. Let me fix things immediately."

"Why, yes, I will." She backed away. "I really must be going."

"Of course, how stupid of me." Royce walked with her to the pathway. "As you Americans say, have a good day."

She puzzled over Royce's curious manner as she hurried along the path to her cottage. Everybody was behaving strangely toward her and she had no idea why.

She was relieved when she saw Mindelo at the door and not the bellboy. He greeted her brightly and unlocked the door, holding it open while she stepped inside.

"Oh, dear!" she said, her hands flying to her cheeks in surprise. "What's happened to my room?"

"Isn't it lovely, miss?" Mindelo rolled his eyes with pleasure.

The parlor was filled with flowers, some in vases, and others trailing from pots suspended from the ceiling in macramé holders. The room had been transformed. The curtains were opened onto the glass doors of the patio and she saw there were more flowers outside.

She gazed about her with delight and astonishment. When she inhaled deeply her senses tingled with the perfume of all the blossoms. She felt very feminine and wanted.

She reached for Mindelo's hand and squeezed it. "It's such a beautiful surprise." Releasing Mindelo self-consciously, she sank to her knees in the center of the room, falling back to a sitting position, and gazing around her in wonder.

"Here, miss." Mindelo picked up a thick white envelope off the table and handed it to her. She hesitated.

"Is there anything wrong, miss?" His features were wreathed with concern. He lowered himself to his knees beside her.

"No, Mindelo." She touched his hand. "I'm just a little scared."

"Why?"

"These flowers..."

"People don't get scared of flowers." Mindelo spread his hands and laughed. "Only Mrs. Biddle-Macdonald could hate something so beautiful."

His innocence made her laugh too. "You're sweet," she said. "I guess I'm tired after that trip." She patted his hand and opened the envelope. It contained a small, ivory white card. On it was written in black ink: *Welcome home, Samson Odongo.*

Mindelo took the card from her shaking fingers and laid it on the coffee table.

"Mindelo, you must send all of them back!"

"Oh, no, miss."

"Yes, you must. I don't even know Mr. Odongo."

"That doesn't matter, miss. It would be wrong to refuse them. Mr. Odongo would be very insulted."

"Is he a bad man, Mindelo?"

"I don't think so."

"Do you know him?"

"I've seen him when he comes here."

"He comes to this hotel?" She felt weak.

"Of course, miss. He owns it."

The shrill ring of the telephone shattered the silence. She looked aghast at Mindelo.

He returned her gaze with unruffled brown eyes. "The telephone, miss," he said quietly.

She frowned at the flowers. She was tired, she wanted a shower, she wanted time to think.

Mindelo answered the phone. "It's for you, Miss Susan. A man." He smiled impishly, keeping his hand over the mouthpiece.

The sun was shining with an intensity that made the white walls of the patio seem to blister. There was a vapor of heat in the air and the shrubs outside bobbed bravely in a burst of breeze that wafted across the vista. A bird, pretty with its bright yellow markings, fluttered idly from one glorious bloom to another.

"What shall I tell him, Miss Susan?" Mindelo's polite voice brought her back to reality.

"Tell him I am resting and can't be disturbed."

Mindelo raised his eyebrow and repeated the message, seeming fearful of the consequences. He put the receiver down gently. She smiled her thanks. She had made her gesture of defiance.

"Don't you want to know who was calling?" Mindelo's eyes flashed with excitement.

"It was Mr. Odongo, wasn't it?"

Mindelo was scornful. "Mr. Odongo wouldn't phone you. He'd get his assistant, Mr. Leacock, to do that."

Susan was deflated. Her legs were aching and she pulled herself up from the floor and sank onto the couch. "I give up, Mindelo," she said wearily. "Who was it?"

"Tony Kintai!" Mindelo voice was filled with awe. "Tony Kintai himself is here. In the hotel!"

BOOK THREE

Sweet Ebony

Tenenjuei olderoni nelo enkaji enjotonye
When the big rat smells bad,
it goes to its mother's house
(Masai proverb.)

CHAPTER 29

Lyn was in a sour mood; the heat, the overnight train ride, her lack of control over developments, and her raw need: all troubled her unreasonably. When she opened the door of her cottage and saw the crest of an ebony head at the back of her couch, she erupted with a cascade of curses to vent her feelings.

The man resting his head there leaped to his feet like a jungle cat and spun around, his wily eyes clashing with hers.

Her bitterness and anger dissolved instantly into surprise and eagerness. The drapes were joined across the patio window and the room was bathed in soft warmth. She entered quickly and shut the door behind her, swaying in the dimness. She felt she was melting.

"Tony!" she whispered. "How...?"

"Early plane." He lolled against the back of the couch, making no attempt to move.

"Rena?"

"In Nairobi." He shrugged.

"Oh, Tony...!" His name escaped from her lips in a moan of desire. She dropped her bag on the floor and ran to him.

He moved from the couch to the center of the room and stood erect and tall, his legs apart. She raised her lips to meet his, but he held her off.

"Relax!" He reached over to the side table and lifted the telephone receiver off its cradle. "Now we won't be disturbed." He opened his arms to her and she fell into his embrace, rubbing her face against his chest.

"I've got a great idea for you, Tony!" She felt powerless to stop the words spilling out. "Something to make you money, give you prestige and..." She raised her eyes and looked into his face. What she saw stilled her tongue and set her heart pounding.

Tony lowered his head, the hard glint of lust flashing in his eyes.

Her mouth gaped open as his lips drew near. She gasped, and his tongue drove deep inside her mouth. She submit-

ROYSTON ELLIS

ted, limp and yielding, to the forceful embrace of his strong arms. She was flowing to him even before she was ready.

"Hush!" he cautioned, his lips as soft as velvet, caressing her cheek. He placed his hand under her legs and lifted her from the floor so that she was cradled in his arms.

"You can't lift me!" She was worried, knowing that her appearance made her look lighter than she was. "I'm heavy boned."

He smiled, said nothing, and carried her to the bedroom. He laid her gently on the bed and studied her. He shook his head.

"What's wrong?" She was terrified that even at this stage he could walk out and leave her. She'd had disappointments before; too many too often. He placed his long lean finger on her lips and ordered silence with his eyes. She obeyed.

His fingers traced a chain encircling her breasts and fettering her stomach. He tugged open her jeans and rolled them down her thighs, losing patience when they caught her ankles. Passion was building in him, ready to explode, and his tenderness gave way to a rage of adoration. He fondled her savagely and his loving became brutal, like a punishment.

She trembled beneath him, feeling small and wanted. She dared not breathe in case he stopped. She was being vanquished and her heart, even her soul, soared with ecstasy and longing.

He penetrated her harshly, driving himself as though a whip was lashing his backside. She struggled to meet the fury of his strokes, wrapping her legs around his waist to hold him.

He paused then, his eyes twinkling with amusement, while she thrashed and writhed below him, reaching for her climax.

He bit her ear, sending a shiver of pain through her as he withdrew. She moaned, tumbling over the brink like a waterfall.

Then his hands were clenching her waist and rolling her over. His fingers plunged between her thighs, probing and rubbing until his hand firmly entered her.

She shuddered, bucking her hips against him as he lay

wrapped around her. His other hand slipped between her buttocks, opening her smoothly.

She fought, twisting against the hand inside her and trying to draw away from him. The more she moved, the more she succumbed to the relentless passion dashing though her.

He pressed closer to her until, with a rip of bliss, he drove into her. She gasped.

He was gnawing at her neck, stroking her with his slender fingers as he grew inside her.

She almost fainted. It began as a tiny ripple stirred by his finger and his limbs merging with hers. It swelled to a wave that swept through her with a rush; a feeling she had never known before. It flowed on and on. She couldn't breathe. She was being smothered by it.

Did she faint? She never knew. She screamed, she shouted, she cursed, and she sighed. She wept. She clutched at Tony with fear in her heart. This man must never leave her! She loved him, yes she knew it; she loved him. She would be his slave! She would do anything, anything for him.

He withdrew abruptly, unwound himself from her limbs, and rolled off the bed.

She gasped and heaved until the heat subsided. She stared up at him in alarm. He wasn't even naked. His trousers were gathered around his ankles. He pulled them up and fastened his belt efficiently. He smoothed down his shirt and tucked it into his pants.

She reached for her pack of cigarettes. She lit one quietly and lay back on the pillow to smoke it. Her body still throbbed but now she felt only the shadow of his presence in her. She wanted to say *I love you!* But it seemed unwise.

He had grunted while he was in her, but uttered no words of endearment. He was sitting opposite the bed on a straight-backed chair. She inhaled on her cigarette. Despite his lack of any show of affection, or because of it, she felt exhilarated.

"You must come to Los Angeles, Tony. You'd like to come, right? I can get you a fantastic job at the TV station. You'd be great..." She prattled on, knowing most of what she said was a lie, but she had to keep him.

He just stared at her.

She ground her cigarette out in the ashtray. Her hand was trembling. She gritted her teeth and swung off the bed. She walked across the room and stood beside him, happy and naked. "What do you think, Tony?"

He was silent.

She put her hand on his shoulder, touching him gently. "I asked you what do you think? Will you come to the States?"

"Sure, sure."

"You mean it?" Her voice rose with excitement.

He removed her hand from his shoulder and squeezed it.

She was fascinated to see her fingers gobbled up by his hand, so much larger than her own.

He released her, shrugging his shoulders and sighing. "Lyn, you're not thinking clearly. Get dressed, relax, I'll be back later."

"Where are you going?" She faltered now that the shared mellowness of after-sex was about to be shattered.

"Why should that be of importance to you?"

Her heart lurched. She didn't want to lose him so soon. She groped her way to the bed, barely seeing him in her despair.

"Tony, I just gave myself to you," she said softly, a current of shame running through her. "I'm part of you, now. Is it wrong to want to know where you are going when your imprint is still on my body?"

His teeth flashed. "There are many questions a woman must not ask a man."

"Nonsense! I am not a Masai."

"Exactly. I am."

"Tony, how can you be so insensitive? I simply asked where you're going."

"In my own country, Lyn? In Los Angeles would you always want to know my whereabouts? Would you want to control what I do, whom I see? You want me as your tame savage, don't you? Me Tarzan, you Jane?"

"No!" she shouted too loudly. She glared at him desperately, seeking his eyes with hers. "No, Tony," she said again, searching her mind for an argument to convince him. Yet she realized that his native shrewdness had revealed to her the very reason she wanted him.

"Believe me, Tony," she began, her voice dropping to a whisper, in awe of her own words. "I want you, I want you... as my husband, Tony."

"Hah!" His smirk was rich and condescending. "A full commitment. How very American. Shouldn't you do a feasibility study on me first before you ask me to make an honest woman of you?" He walked toward the door.

"Sleep on it, Lyn. I'll be back." He opened the door, stepped out and paused. "Perhaps!" he said, closing it firmly.

♦ ♦ ♦ ♦ ♦

Mindelo was watching for Tony Kintai outside Lyn's cottage. He was concealed in the shrubbery. He knew that Cora was waiting for him on the patio of her cottage, but the chance to see Tony Kintai in the flesh was more important.

He held his breath and shrank back into the cover of the bushes as the door to Lyn's cottage opened. He had never seen Tony Kintai but knew about his fame from *The Standard*. He was a champion of the people and a confidante of the president. He was a feared and respected *moran* warrior who had done great deeds among the Masai. It was said that he had powers.

Mindelo found it hard to believe all he had heard about Tony Kintai when he saw him on the footpath. In his fawn slacks and white shirt, he looked like other Kenyan notables.

He was tall and his face showed wisdom, and it was true he swaggered with the arrogance of a leader. But why was such a man with Lyn Preston? He parted the screen of leaves to see clearer. Tony Kintai was walking along the path slowly and appeared to be preoccupied.

Suddenly, Kintai stopped, stared into the bushes and dived through them, seizing Mindelo by his shirt collar. He was Masai again and his face leered within inches of his own.

Mindelo trembled, stricken with fear, unable even to attempt an explanation.

"You scamp!" Kintai spoke in Swahili. "What are you doing?"

While the hand at his throat held him immobile against a tree, Tony Kintai's other hand padded swiftly over his body. "Your only weapon is a pen, boy," he said, removing the gold Parker roll ball from his pocket. "Did you steal this, or can you use it?"

"No, sir, yes sir!" Mindelo answered in English, the tongue that came to him most naturally when confronted by authority. "It's mine, from a grateful guest. I am clerk to Mr. Royce of Fantasy Tours."

"Indeed?" Kintai's hard eyes softened by degrees. "Why are you spying on me?"

"I was watching you, yes..." he stammered. "I've heard so much about you. I didn't believe..."

Kintai released him. "You are of immense curiosity. That's good. But Masai say that a big gourd with a hole cannot be filled."

"Yes, sir." Mindelo lowered his eyes respectfully.

"Since you are curious about me, boy, then you shall have the honor of doing something for me.

"Yes, sir. Anything!"

"I'll ignore that pledge." Kintai's eyes bored into his skull. "You seem to have your wits about you. Now tell me, these women who come on tours, I know what they come for. Miss Preston is one such. Has she been serviced yet?"

"Not while she has been with our group. I don't know about the night in Nairobi."

"And you don't know about me, right?"

Mindelo lowered his eyes again.

"Fine. I want you to watch that American female. Inform me if she has anyone, understand?"

"Yes." The sweat trickled down his chest, soaking through his undershirt to his uniform. Even his pubic hairs tickled with fear.

A blow slashed him across his cheek and felled him to the ground. He covered his head with his hands but the next blow, a kick from Kintai's brogues, landed in his crotch.

He bit his tongue to stop the disgrace of crying out loud. He didn't want the Masai to think him a coward.

"That's for spying on me." Tony said softly. "Next time..."

He left the threat unspoken.

CHAPTER 30

Maggie studied Njonjo's stout neck from her seat at the back of the rented car. He was driving along the main highway out of Mombasa watching the road with heavy concentration. His neck was not unattractive she decided. She was watching it because she had lost interest in the patchy scenery and had no wish to see the festering poverty of the hamlets through which they were motoring.

Joe's neck was thick, like a plump German sausage, and there was a ridge of flesh that rested on his collar. His hair was close cropped. In a red-necked German the effect would have been most unattractive. For her, his skin, the jet of a Nubian slave, transformed his gross size into an Adonis in black velvet. She loved it.

Since he had burst into her cottage in his bull-like way, Maggie had become enchanted with him. He was ignorant and unworldly, but no less desirable for that. He was good at what he did. His vanity was easily gratified and he did what he was told. If he didn't, she scolded him and he was instantly contrite.

He was quite the most demanding man in bed she had ever known. God, Maggie conceded in her reverie, had been good to her again.

She saw Joe glance at her in the car's rear-view mirror. He grinned. It gave his round, simple face some character. He was probably trying to assess her mood.

"You all right?" he asked. "Joe drive well?"

"Yes, dear. Just keep you eyes on the road." She waved nonchalantly at the ramshackle huts and naked children playing at the roadside. "I've no wish to drop in on them by accident." She giggled.

Joe had drawn her out, even helped her to retrieve a sense of humor. He had done more than that. He had got her traipsing through the Kenya countryside like a missionary, when she could have been safe in the synthetic ambience of the hotel.

"You go my father's village."

"That's right, Joe, just keep on driving. Is it far?"

He shook his head.

"I hope not!" Her voice was harsh and she clenched her fists. She wanted a drink and she hadn't had her afternoon siesta. She was really making this journey to spite the others, since none of them would come with her. Cora was making the most of having Mindelo care for her, Lyn hadn't stirred from her cabin and Susan said she wanted a day on the beach. It was most annoying.

"Few miles more. I go often."

"You don't live in your father's village?" She had a grim feeling that the afternoon was going to be hard to bear.

"Yes." Joe grinned again. "Too far from beach!"

Maggie sighed and sank further into the upholstery. At times, his lack of conversation was infuriating. She closed her eyes. The heat was making her perspire.

She was thankful she was not wearing her wig and the tailored costumes of her conventional existence in Bel Air. It was a pleasure to let herself go in the loose Afro gowns and brightly colored bandannas she had bought in the hotel's boutique. The exaggerated casualness of those clothes suited her. She had bought them on a whim, after Joe had worked his spell on her.

The heat and the gentle rolling of the car lulled her into drowsiness. Joe was foremost in her mind, even as she drifted off to sleep. She relished the feel of his strong hands when he held her. She had taught him how to kiss, and she loved to have his large lips devour hers and his tongue force its way into her mouth.

The car bumped along a trail and shattered her fantasy. "Where are we?" she mumbled, pulling herself up to peer out of the window.

"Close." Joe was scanning the trail for obstacles.

She sniffed and wound up the window to prevent branches poking out her eyes when they snapped against the side of the car. Thick vegetation surrounded the trail, making her realize she was deep in the jungle. What, she wondered with a sense of panic, would happen if she had a seizure? She had not given the doctors' warnings a thought until now.

"Drive slower, you bastard!" she said. "You're shaking me to death."

"Sorry!" Joe braked and turned to look at her. His warm brown eyes were tinged with worry. "You is all right? We close to home."

You might be, she thought. *Home was never like this!* She regarded his wide nose and sensuous lips with interest; his concern was so obviously genuine. She leaned back in the seat and fanned herself with her hand. "I hope there'll be something decent to drink when we get there."

She saw Joe bite his lip and then put the car gently back into gear. He started to drive again with such excruciating care, she wished she hadn't spoken. Eventually the trail deteriorated into little more than a path through the grass and shrubs. He backed the car into the bush and stopped the engine. He wound up his window.

She sniffed again, this time with suspicion. "What are you doing? Why have we stopped?"

"We walk now."

"Walk?" She eyed him dourly from the depths of the car's seat. "I can't walk!"

"It not far." He reached under the driving seat and produced a *panga*, flourishing the long bladed knife at her. It glistened in the afternoon sunlight. "I have this."

"So I see." She blanched. "And what is that for?"

"To cut the bush." He eased his bulky frame out of the car and chopped at the grass to show her what he could do. He lifted his head proudly.

"Come," he said when the grass around the car was cleared. He opened the door with one hand, his cutlass raised in the other.

Maggie felt a touch of apprehension. She reached for her purse and willed herself to get out of the car. She looked around, but there was no one in sight.

She was appalled as she realized how little she knew about Joe. She couldn't even remember his African name. It didn't matter when she was in the hotel. In the midst of jungle and miles from anywhere, her self-assurance was a bit shaken.

He held her arm, his fingers closing around it with a grip that bruised her flesh. He urged her forward on the narrow path. She stayed silent, wondering what would happen next.

"Follow me," he said, releasing her arm and slashing at the grass in front of them. The path was not overgrown but he seemed to regard every blade of grass as a threat to be attacked vigorously.

She forgot her apprehension in the flurry of his slashing blows, and concentrated instead on his magnificent physique. His shirt was soaked with sweat and it clung to him, revealing the contours of his wide, hard chest and trim waist. His arm muscles bulged with each swing of the panga.

He stopped and gazed at her in a manner she found most disturbing. He seemed about to seize her and take her forcibly in the grass.

"We here," he said, pointing at a clearing ahead of them, where the roofs of huts poked through the trees.

"Damn!" she said when she saw children watching shyly from the perimeter of the clearing. For a moment, she thought she was going to experience something new. She put her hand out to grasp his arm while Joe shouted joyfully in Swahili at the kids.

♦ ♦ ♦ ♦ ♦

The visit was a success. Maggie was on her best behavior and as charming as any Boston matron could be, perched on a small wooden chair in the middle of a dusty African village. She drank coconut water, from the shell, leaving unspoken her qualms about its possible effect on her stomach. She patted naked, sore-ridden children, but stopped short of bouncing them on her knee.

She complimented Joe on the pole-and-daga hut he had built himself. However, she declined to enter its dark interior in case the squalor would somehow contaminate her. She met Joe's mother with her shorn gray hair and naked breasts flopping over the *kanga* about her waist.

She smiled until her jaws ached and nodded her head until it throbbed. She was doing it for Joe who seemed so proud, but after half an hour of being agreeable, she could stand it no longer.

"Joe, we must go!" She wanted the rest room.

"My father brings you gift."

"I want to go!" She kept her voice soft so its tone would not upset the women gathered around her, giggling at her Tiffany earrings.

"Mrs. Biddle-Mac, you do my father great honor by accepting gift."

She squeezed her thighs together uncomfortably. "I'm not feeling up to this." She gestured vaguely about her, unusually disturbed by the poverty. "I don't want his gift. What is it, anyway?"

Joe preened himself. "His most prize possession. A whip he make himself from the hide of cattle." He snapped his fingers and the old man shuffled forward.

Maggie watched him, almost feeling pity for the old chap. His flesh had withered until he was not much more than a bundle of fragile bone wrapped in a dry, brown skin. A blue *kikoi*, his only clothing, was fastened around his waist.

He held out a whip, which she was forced to accept. The man began an interminable speech in Swahili until Maggie stood up, cutting him off in mid-sentence.

"I've got to go, Joe, now!"

He nodded and spoke rapidly to his father. The old man's toothless mouth gaped open, and he clutched at her hand before she could move away. He hung on, giving her a handshake with his thumb linked around her hand and his free hand gripping the inside of her elbow. He released her and began to sway and chatter with high excitement.

"What ever did you tell him?" she asked as she edged away from the group, nodding and smiling although all she could think of was her urgent need to reach a rest room.

"I say you big horse owner in America and you say the whip the best ever see and you wish him long life and many more sons like me." Joe hesitated. "I also say you send him a horse."

"I'll send him anything so long as we can get out of here."

Joe looked hurt but she couldn't care about that. She nodded again at the people in the compound and used the handle of the whip to prod the children out of her way. She clung to Joe and stumbled anxiously beside him back to the car.

"Just drive to a safe spot, Joe." Her voice was brittle and strained. She wondered how much longer she could hold on.

The car bumped along the trail and she could feel her face growing redder and hotter every minute. Joe sensed her discomfort and quickly pulled the car off the trail as soon as they were beyond the village. He parked in a glade; it was growing gloomy with approaching dusk.

"Thank god!" She pushed open the door and clambered out. "Don't look. I've got to go!"

"Me too," he drawled. "Take you time. No one see us here."

She scrambled through the vegetation away from the car. The bushes sprang closed behind her. She glanced back. Joe was out of sight.

It was eerie in the dying light with the sounds of night insects whistling around her. She stopped, looked around, then hitched up her gown and pulled down her knickers. She wondered if there were any animals around but her need was too great to worry. She squatted down and was soon sighing with relief. *If the doctors could see me now,* she thought with a chuckle, *they'd think I've gone mad. Perhaps I have.*

A slight movement caught her eye. She turned her head idly in its direction, wondering if Joe was peeping at her. A branch of a tree was dangling down near her head, swaying gently. She put her hand up to brush it away and was dismayed to see it move.

She dried with fear. It was a snake. Its green head swayed from side to side and its bright eyes watched her angrily. With her dress up and her knickers at her thighs, she couldn't move. The snake's tongue darted out of its mouth and slid back again. She tried to wriggle away. The snake coiled itself, about to strike. She toppled forward and sprawled in the undergrowth.

Joe's *panga* whistled through the air. It caught the snake between its eyes, slicing its head neatly in two. It fell from the tree onto the ground beside Maggie, writhing in its death throes. Joe rushed over, kicked it aside and scooped up Maggie in his arms. He ran with her back to the car.

"Maggie, my Maggie!" he crooned, laying her gently on the back seat. "You all right?"

She shook her head, touching her neck. Slowly she pulled herself to a sitting position and looked around. "You might have chopped off my head with that thing."

"Yes," Joe agreed readily. "But I kill *nyoka*. Snake dead."

"I nearly dead too!" She looked around the clearing. He was right, no one could see them.

"Hah! You want rest, here, before we go?" he sounded strained and she saw his eyes were narrowing.

She was still in shock but her throat tightened at the tone of Joe's voice. She recognized his need. She reached for the whip his father had given her and grasped its polished handle. It was the only defense she had.

He had saved her life and now she felt exposed and vulnerable with him standing over her. She was concerned about what he might do. She was the one who had to be in control, not him. She raised the whip and pushed the handle into the hard muscles of his stomach.

"Take me to the hotel, Joe," she said firmly. "Now!"

He shrugged, closed the car door and returned to his seat. He started the engine. She smiled grimly as he reversed the car back to the trail and they drove out of the jungle into the night.

CHAPTER 31

Susan woke late. She had a headache from the thunderous noise of the hotel's disco, which she had visited the previous evening. While she showered, dressed, and nibbled at her breakfast, she thought about Lyn.

She was not used to being treated with the kind of animosity that Lyn had shown toward her. It was worrying her, and she resolved to find out the reason for it.

Instead of phoning her she walked across to Lyn's cottage. The sun was blazing down and her energetic determination was in contrast to the languor of the day. She was drenched with perspiration by the time she reached the cottage even though it was only a few yards away. She stepped in to the shade of the porch and knocked on Lyn's door.

There was no sound from inside. She saw the curtains at the parlor window were closed. She was puzzled. Lyn hadn't been at dinner the night before so she surely wouldn't still be asleep. Perhaps she had taken a sleeping pill? Or worse, was she on drugs? That might be the reason for her irrational behavior.

Anxiously, Susan knocked again on the door. "Lyn! It's me. Are you all right?" She bowed her head and listened carefully at the door. Suddenly it was flung open and she almost lost her balance.

Lyn glared at her. Her hair was disheveled and she looked as though she had been crying.

"What do you want?"

Her tone was so hostile, it made Susan flinch, but she was determined not to be put off. "I think we should talk. May I come in."

"Suit yourself!" Lyn scowled and withdrew into the room.

The parlor was in darkness and Susan had difficulty seeing after the bright glare outside. She paused to let her eyes adjust to the gloom. Lyn had walked through to the bedroom and was standing by the window overlooking the patio. A shaft of sunlight spilled into the room as she pulled the heavy curtain aside.

Susan glanced around. The dressing table lay on its side

with its mirror smashed. Pictures had been torn down from the walls, chairs were upside down and the bedclothes strewn over the floor. She was dismayed. "What happened?"

Lyn laughed dryly. "Don't look so shocked! Haven't you ever heard about celebrities smashing up their hotel rooms? I thought I'd give it a try."

"You did all this? Deliberately?"

"Yes." She sounded defiant.

"Why?"

Lyn shrugged her shoulders. "Exercise?"

Susan sat down on the ruins of the bed, feeling overwhelmed by the mess. "You've spoiled a lovely room. What will the staff say?"

"The staff! Is that all you're worried about? They'll put it on my bill. The station will pay." Lyn started to hunt in the debris.

"What are you looking for?" She was still trying to take it all in, knowing that something crazy was happening to Lyn.

"Cigarettes!" She found one and lit it with a shaking hand. She avoided meeting Susan's eyes.

"Tell me why you did this. It wasn't for exercise."

"You're very bright this morning." Lyn's voice was edged with sarcasm. "Do rock stars know why they smash up hotel suites?"

"I always thought they were on drugs."

"Perhaps you're right. Who knows?"

Susan frowned. "Are you on drugs? Is that why you have been behaving so badly towards me. I felt so wretched because of it."

Lyn drew deeply on her cigarette, ignoring the questions. A moment of calm seemed to descend on her. "Tony was here," she said with a faint smile of pride.

"He did this?"

"I did. Last night. The bastard told me he would come back, but he didn't. I was so angry, I got smashed and I smashed up the room." She shrugged.

"That's silly. Just because he couldn't make it."

"Couldn't make it! The guy fooled me again, again!" She raised her voice with anger at herself. "He took advantage of my weakness for him. He fooled me into believing he had some feeling for me."

"Did you...?" Susan wasn't sure how to phrase the question.

"Sure, Sue, we fucked, we really did. Then he said he would come back. What sort of man is he? I think he's put some kind of Masai hex on me. I've never felt so strongly about a guy, he's made me weak." She stubbed out the cigarette and sighed crossly.

"He could still come back."

"I'm not an optimist like you. I'm just another white broad he's notched up on his spear."

Susan sat quietly considering the matter. "Lyn," she began softly. "If he doesn't come back, can you really blame him? You wanted him to make love to you, just so you could say you'd had a Masai. You wanted to notch him up yourself."

There was silence between them. Lyn was standing by the window, a broken piece of the mirror in her hand. She raised it to her eyes and gazed into it. The energy seemed to drain away from her. She let the mirror slip from her fingers and it smashed on the floor.

"You're right. That was my original idea. Now I realize this is serious. For me anyway."

"Are you sure?"

"Yes!" Lyn pulled her shoulders back and surveyed the bedroom as though seeing the damage for the first time. "I must find him!"

"Why bother?" Susan reached over and put her hand on her arm to calm her. "Better to let him go. Forget him."

"Not me, honey! I promised that dude I'd marry him if he comes to States. And look what he's done to me." She waved her hand around the room. "Turned me into some kind of fucking psycho."

"So what will you do if you find him? It will only be worse if he doesn't want to see you."

"He'll see me. I love the bastard." She walked into the parlor and sat down on the couch, putting her head in her hands.

Susan followed. "Is there anything I can do?"

"Get me a vodka!"

"Do you think you ought to?"

"Why not?"

"Oh, all right." She found the vodka bottle and poured a meager measure into a tumbler, adding ice and orange juice. She sat down beside Lyn and handed her the glass.

"Sometimes I think you're from some Soul Saving ashram, Sue. Yeah, how does that sound, Sue Ross saves souls."

"I don't understand."

"Of course you don't. Niceness is your thing, that's all." Lyn emptied the glass in one gulp. "I'm checking out of the hotel. There's a flight to Nairobi this afternoon."

"Are you going home?"

"Listen, will you. I'm going to find Tony Kintai. I want him, I must see him, I must talk to him."

Susan shook her head in confusion. It was Lyn's problem and she didn't know how she could help. She wondered if Lyn was heading for a nervous breakdown.

"Look at this." Lyn stood up and walked to the curtains, pulling them open. Both of them blinked as the sun streamed in. She took a newspaper from the floor. It was folded open at an inside page. She thrust it at Susan.

There was a blurred picture of two men in suits shaking hands. The caption identified one as President Arap Moi', the other as Dr. Tony Kintai. It said that Dr. Kintai had delivered a petition to the President on behalf of the Masai nation and that he would be speaking at a rally in Nairobi on Thursday.

"Tomorrow is Thursday."

"You're going to the rally?" Susan stared at her in dismay. "Why don't you wait? Perhaps he couldn't come back because he had to go to Nairobi. Perhaps on Friday he'll be here."

"Why should I wait? I don't wait for any man. I want him, I'm going to get him."

Susan frowned again, keeping her thoughts to herself. After all, there was no reason why she should interfere. It was Lyn's decision. "Well," she said, standing up. "Do take care of yourself."

"Yeah, have a nice day! By the way," Lyn said with a cruel glint in her eye, "If I see Samson Odongo shall I give him your love? You're still thinking about him."

"My cottage is full of flowers that he sent, and yet I've never met him." Susan walked to the door. "I'm not like you, I don't mind waiting. I've been waiting all my life. When the right man does come along, the wait will have been worthwhile."

"I should have your patience!"

Susan closed the door on the devastation of the room and heaved a sigh. She couldn't be held responsible for what Lyn did. It was a relief, though, to know that the animosity wasn't her fault. She blinked as the sun hit her and looked around. Someone was squatting on his haunches in the shade of a flamboyant tree opposite the cottage.

"Mindelo!" Susan called as she saw him. She was surprised when he didn't respond with his usual cheerful grin. "Is something wrong?"

He shook his head, keeping his eyes on the ground. "Nothing wrong, miss," he mumbled.

It was so obvious that he was feeling troubled, Susan hunkered down beside him. "What's happened? You can tell me." He shook his head to indicate it was of no importance.

"Sometimes it helps to tell other people your problems," she said softly. "You've no idea how I've often wished for someone to share things with. The bad as well as the good things."

He looked at her shyly. "I couldn't tell you, Miss Susan."

"You could try." She patted his shoulder. "You know, it's a sign that you're a man when you feel so concerned about something."

"Is it?" He raised his face, his careworn features brightening slightly.

"Tell me."

He swallowed. "It's Cora. I really like her. I blame myself for what happened to her at the game park. You see, I upset her. I think that's why she went out that night. I nearly did something...something I'm ashamed of." He shut his mouth firmly and his eyes avoided hers.

"There, now you've told me it's not so bad." She patted his shoulder again. "Cora's all right, isn't she?" He nodded.

"Don't you think she is ashamed too?"

"I hadn't thought of that."

"I bet she is. She seems to like you. Maybe it was all a misunderstanding. Is she cross with you?"

"No. I sit with her outside her room and she tells me about the States and things. It's just that, well..." He pulled his ear. "I thought she might be like some of the other women who come here, you know. Now I know she isn't."

"Since you didn't do this thing you're ashamed of, why be ashamed now? You should be proud."

"She might think I don't like her."

"I bet she doesn't, Mindelo. She'd be unhappy if she knew you were feeling like this. Forget it, for her sake. Be your usual happy self and she'll be happy too." She stood up. "I'm going back to my cottage to change. The sea looks so inviting. Coming?"

"To your cottage?" He frowned.

"No, man! To the beach. Let's have an ice-cream there." She was pleased when his brow lightened and a smile quivered on his lips.

He stood up and brushed himself down. "Sometimes I don't understand myself, Miss Susan."

"Everyone's like that, Mindelo. We all have doubts about ourselves from time to time. It's natural, I guess. Anytime you want a friend to talk to, come to me." She began to walk along the path, Mindelo at her side.

"Really?"

"Try me." They reached the cottage and she hurried to open it as she heard the telephone ringing inside.

"Will you chose me when you want a friend, Miss Susan?" Mindelo said, his impish smile back in place.

She nodded and opened the door. It closed in his face as she rushed across the room to answer the telephone.

"Susan!" Maggie's hoarse voice echoed over the line. I want to see you. Can you come now?"

She thought of Mindelo waiting for her outside to go to the beach for the ice-cream. She didn't want to let him down. "I'm going out for a while, Maggie. Can I come afterward?"

"You sound strange, Susan. Have I interrupted something?" She gave a throaty giggle.

"Of course not. I'm so hot though. I must have a swim."

As she replaced the receiver, she was sure she heard a man's voice in the background saying something to Maggie, but it was none of her business.

She changed quickly into her swimming costume. She was too shy to wear a bikini. She wrapped herself in a pink towel robe and fastened her hair back in a ponytail. She needed to spend some time in the sun, so she could return home with a real African tan.

She opened the door expecting to find Mindelo waiting for her. He had gone. It was her fault, he probably thought she wasn't coming. She strolled along the path, looking out for him. The beach was packed; a whole regiment of sun worshippers lying side by side on the glistening sand. Pale women coated in coconut oil were slowly basting from a tender pink to a raging brown.

Mindelo was nowhere in sight, even by the ice-cream stand, so she changed her mind and walked instead back up the path to Maggie's cottage. She would go swimming later.

The cottage was surrounded by shrubs, which blossomed with sweet smelling yellow flowers. They had a heady perfume she rather liked. She looked up, expecting to see Maggie on her veranda, but she wasn't there. She called her name and when there was no response, she tapped gently on the door.

There was a sound of activity inside and then the door was pulled open. Instead of Maggie, it was her driver, Joe, who greeted her. He held open the door for her to enter, but didn't say anything. She was surprised to see that Maggie was lying on the couch, gasping for breath.

"I'm sorry," she said, wondering what she had interrupted.

Joe walked to the bathroom and returned with a tumbler of water and two red capsules. He held them out in the palm of his massive hand. Maggie's frail fingers closed around the pills and she raised them to her mouth, forcing them between her lips. Joe held the glass of water for her and she pushed herself up and sipped messily at it.

As he breathlessness subsided, Susan looked from her to Joe, kneeling beside her. "Have you done this before, Joe?"

"When she like this, I give the pills. Then she OK."

"See what a nurse I've got!" Maggie said scornfully, showing she had recovered. She tried to raise herself to a sitting position and Joe immediately stood up to help her.

"Shall I get a doctor?"

"I've seen enough doctors. Tell this large lump to stop mauling me. I'm all right! Get out!"

"Perhaps you should wait outside for a while," said Susan, smiling so Joe wouldn't be offended.

"I love she good." Joe regarded Maggie sternly as he sauntered to the door.

"Maggie, what's this all about?" She took Maggie's hand in hers and sat beside her on the couch.

"Nothing!" Maggie glared at her and then seemed to realize that she ought to be nice. "Be fine in a minute."

"Are you sure?"

"For heaven's sake, dear! I didn't ask you here to mope over me." There was a pause while she caught her breath.

"Susan," she said with a little gasp after each phrase. "The desk over there. An envelope. Your name...on it."

Susan released her hand and looked on the desk. There were several letters including one addressed to her. "I've found it."

"Good. keep it safe." Maggie rose from the couch, breathing more evenly. "Inside is a letter to my lawyer. In case anything happens...to me." She smiled vaguely. "Now, dear, you can go. And tell that hunk to come back in here and give me my massage."

CHAPTER 32

Susan settled down to have a holiday and joined the beach brigade. Every day she lay in the sun and, being dark-haired, tanned easily. Between sessions broiling on the beach, she dipped in the sea or the pool. Vacation lethargy enveloped her and she was content.

She rarely saw the others. Maggie spent her time with Joe who watched over her zealously. Cora kept to herself, and Mindelo seemed to be concentrating on his duties. As for Lyn, she had gone off to Nairobi in her quest for Tony Kintai. It didn't bother Susan at all and she liked the effortless routine after the hectic start to the vacation.

One evening, she was sitting on the patio of her cottage, gazing at the patterns of palm trees silhouetted in the moonlight, when the telephone rang. She wondered about answering it. In the solitude of her cottage, a telephone call seemed a major intrusion.

"You took your time," a voice said when she raised the receiver.

"Lyn?" she asked hesitantly.

"That's right! What were you doing? Running away from Samson Odongo?"

"No," she answered slowly. She had thought of him a lot but still hadn't even spoken to him. She brushed her hair back irritably. "Where are you?"

"Nairobi. New Stanley Hotel."

"I've been worried about you." It was a white lie, but polite.

"Of course, that's your nature."

"Did you find Tony?" she asked, curious about what Lyn was doing.

"Yes, I did. He's here now."

"With you?"

"Don't sound so surprised."

"I thought you wanted to..." Her voice dried.

"To bite his balls off? Not now. We're going to get married."

"No!"

"Well, he's not actually agreed yet. It's the only way I can get him to the States without hassles." There was a protesting voice in the background, followed by the sound of a slap and a masculine shout of mock pain.

"I heard that," said Susan with a laugh.

"It's Kintai. He's lying in my bed without his clothes on. His Masai mode. Such a vulnerable state to be in when I'm around." She chuckled. "How are things with you?"

"I'm getting a beautiful tan."

"No romance?"

"I didn't come here for that."

"Kintai says watch out for Odongo. He reckons when he is ready, he will strike like a snake. He's a sweet bastard who could easily fool someone like you. When he's had you, he'll throw you aside."

"How silly. He's lost interest in me already."

"Don't even think that. According to Tony Kintai, the man has you on his list."

She shrugged. "So you and Tony have made up then?"

"Sure. He's a busy guy. I understand that. He's a great one too. Doing a lot for his people." She giggled. "And for me too." There was a shriek of laughter. "No, Tony, don't do that!" There was a pause. "Sue, are you still there?"

"Yes."

"This guy's given me back laughter. I'll never be the same on TV again. I gotta go!" The phone slammed down.

Susan grimaced. She raised her eyes and gazed across the patio at the richness of the night sky and its sparkling stars. There was a silvery glow over the trees, and the hotel lights in the garden, shining red, green and yellow, enhanced the magical effect.

She decided to walk on the beach; she wanted to think. The days lying in the sun had calmed her nerves and dulled her thoughts. She wanted to consider what urges drove Lyn to pursue a wild genius like Tony Kintai, and what caused Maggie to hound the wretched Joe. She dreaded to think that one day she might be like them herself.

Spotlights placed high in the palm trees fringing the beach illuminated it brightly. She did not intend to walk outside the arc of light into the lurking darkness beyond.

She checked to see that the security guard was watching her. She felt safe because of his presence and walked without a qualm to the sea's edge.

The tide was high. She listened to the suck and sigh of the waves as the ocean rollers broke on the distant reef and surged up the beach. There was the constant muted roar and throb of perpetual movement. She watched for several minutes until she was caught in the vortex of sound whirling around her. She smiled, then slowly raised her hands to her temples and screamed.

The cry was more like a whimper in the blast of the sea's noise. She forced air out of her lungs to prolong the scream, squeezing the sides of her head and swaying. She didn't care who could see her; she was venting the tension pent up within her since her arrival.

The scream left her and vanished, not a sound was carried up the beach to the guard. He just saw a tourist swaying at the sea's edge in solitary worship of the night.

She flopped down exhausted on the sand above the advancing wash of water. She made a decision. No longer would she live the life expected of her by others. Lyn didn't, Maggie didn't, and not even Cora did.

She was going to do exactly what her heart and mind told her were right and not worry about other people. She was determined she would not finish up a sour and dissatisfied old maid.

"Yippee!" she cried to the sea, rolling over and over in the sand, letting it crease her dress, muss her hair and scratch her legs. The guard watched patiently; he had seen tourists affected by the sun before. She was in no danger.

She stopped wallowing in the sand when she saw her antics would take her out of the light. She pulled herself to her feet, brushed herself down, and walked back along the sea's edge to where her sandals lay.

As she bent down for them she became aware that something was wrong. She blinked and stood up. It made no difference. Her sandals and the entire beach had disappeared.

All that remained was the slurp and chug of the sea, the softness of the sand on her bare feet, and an impenetrable blackness. She spun around.

It was dark in front and behind and above, although diadems of stars hung overhead. Where the hotel was, there remained a glowing haze of colors, dissected by shadowy palm trees. On the beach, the lights were out.

She didn't panic; she kneeled to feel around in the sand for her sandals. Her hand contacted something solid and unyielding. It wasn't a stone; it had a softness, almost a warmth. She gripped it firmly and ran her fingers around it. It was a shoe and it was on someone's foot.

"Who's there?" she said, trying to keep her voice from quavering. She peered up into the darkness and saw the shape of a man towering over her. She rose quietly.

"What do you want?" She stepped backward softly, calculating how long it would take her to run to the palm tree where the guard should be standing.

"I'll call the guard," she said, her voice cracking.

"Don't be frightened." The man's voice was like a command..

She gasped, and the man heard her.

He drawled lazily. "You need not waste your energy shouting for the guard. He's probably checking why his lights have gone out. Relax. What were you looking for, by the way?" His voice was a husky baritone; soft and gentle with a cultured accent. He sounded in perfect control.

"My sandals." Susan's heart thumped so loudly she expected the man to hear it above the roar of the sea.

"I have them," the man said after a pause. "Shall we sit down until the lights come on?

"No!"

"Very well. Since we can't see each other, what do you suggest? A walk along the beach?"

Susan bit her lip. "If you have my sandals, please give them to me, I want to go back to my room."

"Of course you do."

She was intrigued by the man's voice. She had recovered from the initial shock and he didn't sound like he was going to molest her. Then suddenly she felt the man's hand on her foot. "What are you going?" She hobbled to keep her balance.

"Helping you to put on your sandal. Please place your

hand on my shoulders so you won't fall down."

"I can put them on myself."

"I'm sure you can. Just do as I say, please."

Her skin tingled at the touch of the man's fingers on her ankle. She raised her foot and leaned forward, clasping his shoulder for support. He slipped on the sandal with gentle care and then began to touch her other foot.

She held her breath, unable to understand the emotions flooding through her at the touch of this stranger's fingers. She released his shoulder as soon as the other sandal was on and she could stand properly.

She mumbled: "thank you," feeling the blood rushing to her face and setting it aglow. She stepped back uncertainly, longing to dash to the safety of her cottage so she could consider this new feeling stirring within her.

"It is my pleasure," the man said softly. "My pleasure."

The whistling of the night insects in the trees and the music from the dance combo drifted in the breeze. Susan took in the clean, bold scent of the man. It was distinctive and alluring. She trembled.

"You are a very beautiful woman."

"That's nonsense!" she said, believing that if she kept the man talking, she would be safe. "You can't see me in the dark."

"I have touched your feet. I am twice honored."

"I want to go to the hotel now."

The man's hand wound around her arm and his finger and thumb gripped her above her elbow. The dulcet tone of his voice contradicted the steel-like talons that held her. His face loomed close to hers. His breath was sweet as it wafted over her. "That's not what you really want."

"It is!" Her heart fluttered.

"Are you sure? Is it because you can't see me?" He pulled her closer to him and caught her free hand in his, lifting it to his chest. "I am strong. Feel my body. It can be yours."

She pulled her hand away. "I don't know what you're talking about. Please let me go." Tears welled up and her voice shook.

The man sounded puzzled. "Don't you want to screw? I thought all women came to this hotel for the same thing:

sun, sand, sea, and sex."

She raised her free hand and struck him across his cheek. "I didn't!" she cried, wrenching her arm from the man's grasp.

"I'm sorry," he said softly, taking the force out of her anger. "And pleased."

"Pleased?" She was about to run to the safety of the lights at the hotel but the stranger's muffled remorse held her. "What do you mean?"

"Because I know now that your instincts are not those of a spoilt trollop. Think how quickly your friends Lyn and Maggie would have accepted the offer of a large and anonymous cock."

"Don't speak to me like that!" She drew away from him, her skin still tingling, despite her anger.

The man's voice was soft and anguished. "Forgive me, Susan. You surprise me every minute. I was wrongly informed. I assumed...well...you were in the company of Lyn Preston who has no such modesty."

"Just who are you?" Her heart was beating loudly and she was filled with an overwhelming sensation of being caught up in some strange destiny.

The man folded her into an embrace she had no will to resist. Her cheek rested lightly on his chest. He did not attempt to kiss her, only to hold her securely while he stroked her hair.

"Will you forgive me for frightening you? I wanted to know what sort of a woman Susan Ross really is."

He shouted something in Swahili to the guard, and within seconds the lights came back on, flooding the beach with brilliance.

Susan blinked and drew herself away from him. She shuddered. "You're Samson Odongo! I knew it!" She started to cry. "They warned me about you. Oh dear, I think they were right."

◆ ◆ ◆ ◆ ◆

Susan replaced the phone after giving her breakfast order to room service, and lay back in the king-size bed. She had slept later, and better, than usual. Today she would avoid the beach. She planned to sit on the patio and read...and think. The days spent in the heat like a chicken on a spit had melted her brain. How else could she explain her reaction to Samson Odongo?

He had escorted her back to the cottage the night before. At the door, he took her hand and shook it warmly, his large brown eyes pleading for forgiveness. She had shut the door in his face. She wanted to consider him in solitude.

She knew she was naïve but found it hard to believe a word he had told her. When he realized his mistake in thinking she was an easy lay, he had merely changed his tactics.

She hugged herself. She was astonished that a man like him should be interested in her. There were lots of women on the beach; he could have anyone he wanted. The thought worried her. Because she had turned him down and hurt his pride, maybe he wouldn't be interested in her any more. She sighed: *another failure.*

There was a knock at the cottage door. She was surprised. Time had passed quicker than she realized. She had intended to shower and dress before the room service waiter brought her breakfast. Now it was too late so she decided to stay in bed instead of getting up to let him in. If he was the usual waiter, he was a nice guy, polite and self-effacing. She wouldn't be the first guest he had seen in bed.

She pulled the sheet up to her neck before calling out for him to enter. She heard the sound of the outside door being opened with the pass key, then the rattle of the breakfast tray as the waiter walked through the parlor to the bedroom. He tapped lightly on the door.

"Come in," she called again.

The door opened slowly. She didn't want to appear as though she was being suggestive, so she yawned and kept her eyes closed. She hoped the waiter wouldn't be offended. She heard the tinkle of cutlery as he cleared a space on the bedside table.

"Thank you," she said, without opening her eyes, hoping the waiter would leave quickly.

"Is there anything else you would like, miss?"

The waiter's voice triggered a thrill of emotion that shot through her like a bullet. She sat up, clutching the sheet before it slipped below her breasts. "You!"

Samson Odongo stood beside the bed, his eyebrow raised. "Do you take milk in your coffee?"

"What are you doing here?"

Samson handed the cup brimming with hot coffee across the bed so she was forced to take it. "Do you require sugar?" He proffered the silver sugar bowl.

"You make a lousy waiter, Mr. Odongo!" she managed to say as she overcame her surprise. "Take this coffee before I spill it over the bed." She returned the cup, pulled the sheet up to her neck, and settled back on her pillows to watch him.

The room was dark with the curtains closed, but the outline of Samson's profile was enough to set her heart beating with excitement. She wondered why she was affected so forcibly every time she looked at him.

"What are you doing in my bedroom?" She was delighted and quite unable to hide her high spirits.

"Bringing your breakfast, of course."

"You must be short staffed if you have to do that!"

"Do you think I need more training?" His laugh was as soft as silk. "Shall I open the curtains?"

"A little. I want to see you." She curled her toes.

"That's fine. I want to see you." The light fell across his face as he drew the curtain aside.

She saw his forehead was high, the tight curls of his hair combed back. It gave him the wise look that she had noticed when she saw him at Fisi Lodge. His eyebrows were thick, their hair merging with the ebony hue of his skin. Under implacable eyes, his nose hugged his profile and his lips were fill and sensuous above an ambitious chin. His face was as lean as his frame.

"I should scream," she said.

"Like last night?"

"You were watching me when I did that?"

"That's what drew me to you. Your anguish."

"Not anguish. I was letting out air. It relieves tension."

"You were tense, on holiday?"

"Personality problems."

"Ah yes, I think I may have those too." He sat on the edge of the bed. "Have you forgiven me for last night?"

"Did you really think I would want a stranger to make love to me?" She blushed.

"It was a test. I told you that last night."

"I don't believe you, Mr. Odongo. You're wealthy and influential and rather nice looking. You could have any woman you choose."

"You flatter me, Mrs. Ross. Of those attributes you list, which do you consider the most important: money, power or looks?"

"None of them are important to me, Mr. Odongo," she said softly.

"Then what is?"

"I don't know." She reached for the coffee. "Sincerity, compassion. The intangibles that make an attractive personality."

"Do I have those qualities?" He looked bemused.

"How do I know? Apart from when you waylaid me last night, I know nothing about you." She sipped at the coffee, letting its strength burn out her excitement. Instead, it had the opposite effect and she found herself warming to Samson Odongo more than she intended.

"Then you must get to know me better." He rose and paced across the room. "It has been years since I had a vacation. I shall take one now and join you on yours."

"Why?"

He stopped pacing. "To prove how I feel about you." He stared into her eyes.

She felt her resolve weakening and her hand shook as she lowered the coffee cup. It clattered against the saucer. "Oh dear!" she said, avoiding his eyes as she placed the cup on the tray. "I was trying to be cool and poised and now you've set me trembling like a silly child."

"I do have that effect sometimes." He grinned ruefully. "You wouldn't know it, but you do the same to me." He swallowed and took a step back toward the bed.

"No," she said, pulling the sheet closer to her chin. "I'd like you to go now. I must have breakfast."

"I'll come for you in an hour."

"Where are we going?"

"I want to show you my country. I want you to get to know me..." He paused, his eyes searching hers again. "I want you to learn to trust me."

She didn't answer; she couldn't.

He smiled broadly, nodded farewell, and walked from the room.

She was stricken with apprehension. Samson Odongo had made a mistake; there had been a misunderstanding. He would soon find out she wasn't the sophisticated, experienced wealthy woman he thought she was because she had come on this tour. Then he would surely lose interest in her.

She lay back on the pillow and tried to sort out what was happening. Of course, she wanted Samson to pursue her and to need her. It was thrilling, but there had to be a disappointment in the end. Everyone warned her.

She made up her mind to forestall the heartbreak that was bound to come. She was going to be polite and reasonable while doing nothing to encourage him. If she kept her heart frigid, she felt that when the inevitable parting came, she would be safe from being hurt.

CHAPTER 33

Samson Odongo was rich and successful. He owned a country lodge near Mount Kenya, penthouses atop his own apartment blocks in Nairobi and Mombasa, the Mpingo Beach Hotel and several other desirable, and not so desirable, properties.

When his father had died, he energetically parlayed the dismal holdings he inherited into the foundation of the Odongo Corporation. Bright young lawyers, backed by eager bankers tended the business, which, by reason of his shrewdness and efficiency, expanded profitably year by year.

Samson's prime delight was making money. He had the golden touch. His father had bought real estate in unfashionable places at cheap prices, and incredibly all became choice properties. However, it was Samson's touch that made them so. He had confidence and vision to build beach hotels before the tourist boom, and to construct apartment blocks and office complexes before they were in demand.

The thrill of business preoccupied and hardened him and he never yearned for the approbation of his countrymen. When he needed friendship, he relied on his henchmen. When he needed a woman, he bought one. Sex was a cold, physical act to be paid for like any business transaction.

Recently, he had begun to take an interest in the white women who flocked to his hotels. Local women were a liability; a foreigner was no risk to his peace of mind. It amused him to avail himself of white women who had lovers and husbands waiting for them. They were so easy, such women; they did not even have the dignity of whores.

Susan Ross looked like being a little more difficult.

So what! he thought as he lay on the beach beside her and watched while she packed the picnic things. It was amusing. He would take her when he was ready and discard her at the end of her vacation. He would win her with ease: a smile, a whisper, and a caress. White women were cheap. He toyed with her now because it pleased him; it was a break from business.

They were on their third outing together and he had tried nothing. He knew she must be wondering why he was so correct toward her. She was surely bursting with desire for him to take her. That was the secret: to let a woman contrive her own seduction.

He watched her curiously. She was a neat person, he liked that. She stirred him with her cotton dress clinging to her slim, boyish figure. She would make an excellent lay, he thought. She had the wistful smile of an unfulfilled passionate creature waiting to be roused.

They were on the beach by the ruins of the Jumba La Mtwana mosque. A notice on the huge, gnarled trees under which he sat, said: "Jumba Ruins. Entry is not free. Please go to the ticket office."

They were the only people on the beach to read it. The tide was out, laying bear the pink and white powdery sand and rocky outcrops. It was a soft, hot moment in time.

He reached out his hand and touched her shoulder. "I enjoy myself in your company," he said. "Business is far away. You know how to make a man relax. See how you've packed up so effortlessly."

"A wife's training, Samson."

"Ah yes." She had told him about her loveless marriage and the divorce. It was of no interest to him, despite her thinking that it would be. She was sitting with her back to him.

He moved closer and slowly began to massage her shoulders. She wriggled a slight protest but made no move to prevent him. He enlarged the circular motion of his hand until he was caressing the whole of her back. Soon she would surely turn so he could stroke her breasts. They would make love.

"It's hot," she said, standing up and moving hastily beyond his reach. "We should be going."

"What for?" He swallowed his annoyance. "Let's stay here. These ruins are deserted. We have the place to ourselves..."

She hesitated. "I know...I enjoyed the picnic. You are very kind. I'd like to go to the hotel now."

"Do you always stop in the middle of something you enjoy?"

"No." She brushed crumbs off her dress. Through the flimsy fabric, he saw her slender legs outlined against the sun. She seemed to be taunting him. *Very well!*

"Lie with me here, Susan. Let's enjoy the afternoon even more."

She tossed her head and laughed. With carefree strides she began to run along the path up to the ruins. "Bring the picnic things," she called, tantalizing him. "I'm going to the car."

He frowned. Why did she think she could treat him like a servant? He rose to his feet slowly, trying to keep his temper under control. He picked up the basket and followed her up the path.

Jumba La Mtwana was a national monument, the ruins of a 14th century slave trading settlement. It had been cleared and opened to the public in 1972. It covered several acres with ruins of four mosques, a cemetery and three houses. The path was cool, shaded by the boughs of venerable trees.

Each time he rounded a corner of the ruins, he expected to see her ahead of him, laughing and beckoning. Wasn't that the way these white women behaved? How they loved to joke.

Susan was no where to be seen. He strode on, puzzled. When he reached the car she was sitting in the front seat with her purse open, tidying her hair in a small mirror. He knew that the moment he had been expecting had passed.

Why? What made this woman believe she was different from the others he had taken?

She was looking at him with large, guileless eyes. "I'm sorry, Samson, let's not spoil everything."

He raised his eyebrows, got into the car and patted her hand gently. "Susan, don't worry, I understand." He didn't but it was what women liked to hear.

"You don't mind?" She squeezed his hand.

"Of course not." He reversed the car out of the deserted park, his mind troubled. There *was* something different about this one. He wanted to curse her for wasting his time, yet she intrigued him. It was almost as though she really was someone special.

Charles Royce was taking stock. He was sitting at a low table in the hotel's open-sided lounge, which linked the reception lobby with the outside terrace restaurant.

He liked sitting there because he could observe the activity in the lobby as well as the diners in the restaurant. If he craned his neck to the right, he could see the garishly lit swimming pool. To his left were the flower gardens and the path winding through them to the VIP cottages.

He looked up as the steward replaced his drink with a fresh pink gin. He smiled at him and the boy grinned back. He had eager eyes, a bright face and a neat, slim body. He winked and the boy's grin broadened as he sashayed away from the table. He stroked his moustache thoughtfully and returned to the matter on his mind.

It was a telex from Harrison Muldoon. He pulled it out of his pocket to study it again and frowned. He could picture the promoter of Fantasy Tours sitting comfortably in his air-conditioned office in North Hollywood, while he, Charles Royce, had to cope with his troublesome clients. He read it slowly:

REQUEST URGENTEST FULL REPORT ACTIVITIES FANTASY GUESTS STOP BUTCH PRIVATE EYE GRILLED ME ABOUT SUSAN ROSS BACKGROUND THIS MORNING STOP LYN PRESTON'S TV STATION REPORTS UNABLE CONTACT HER AT HOTEL STOP WHAT HELLS ONGOING QUERY

He replaced the telex in his pocket, sighed wearily and reached for his drink. He sipped it slowly, letting the gin mellow him.

Why was Muldoon panicking, he wondered. It would be typical of his luck if the most troublesome of the four women turned out to be the one he would least expect to upset the equilibrium: Susan Ross.

From where he sat, he could see Susan. She looked sensational, even to his jaundiced eye. Her floor length dress was classical in design and its off-the-shoulder style highlighted the beauty of her features.

He had not considered her attractive until now. He supposed she had done something to her hair, but she carried herself better too. It was easy for him to guess the reason for the change. The reason was having dinner with her, his thigh pressed against hers: Samson Odongo.

Charles Royce was puzzled by that development. Odongo's usual technique was to operate anonymously on the beach at night, picking up a guest after dinner and leaving her before dawn. It was unlike him to spend so much time landing a catch.

It made him wonder if it could have been Odongo who had hired the private investigator to check on Susan's habits in Los Angeles. It was his style.

He drained his drink, clinking the ice in his glass while he pondered the possible consequences of Muldoon's frantic telex.

The odious Preston woman had indeed left the hotel. According to Mindelo, Tony Kintai had been seeing her. He was a legend, a campaigner for Masai rights. It was bewildering to think that he would have anything to do with someone as caustic and calculating as Lyn Preston. Why should her studio worry, she could surely take care of herself.

The steward was hovering by his shoulder. He raised his eyes in surprise. There was a pink gin on his tray.

"I didn't order that," he said, touched by the boy's smile.

"I bring it, bwana. If you don't want, I take it back."

"Fine. That's good." He pursed his lips and took the glass. "I haven't seen you before. Are you new here?"

"Yes, please, sir."

"What's your name?"

"Enoch, sir."

"I'll remember you, Enoch. You're showing initiative, that's what will get you ahead."

"Yes, bwana." The boy looked uncomfortable. "Please, sir, Mr. Mindelo, he say he come late, sir. He say he in disco."

"Humph!" Royce gripped his glass in anger. "He said that, did he? The little bastard's taking too many liberties." He lapsed into thought as the steward moved away.

He was worried by the changes he could sense in Mindelo's behaviour. Was it his fault or Mindelo's? If he had kept him as a houseboy and not encouraged him to improve himself, this wouldn't be happening.

Imagine! Mindelo sending a message that he is in the disco. He would never have dared do that a few weeks ago. *He's probably with that stupid American bint, Cora,* he thought with a sigh of despair.

He reached for his drink and sipped it blindly, letting the gin wash over the depression beginning to gnaw at him. He clutched at a small blessing: at least Cora had recovered from that foolish incident in the game park. And Njonjo had turned up to take care of Maggie.

There was something odd about that too, he realized. Mindelo had claimed that Njonjo was out of order. Well, he suited Maggie, whatever was wrong with him. He couldn't actually picture even Njonjo in bed with Maggie but she was enraptured with him.

He felt reasonably satisfied by the way things were going. He would reply to Muldoon's telex in the morning and tell him that everything was top hole.

◆ ◆ ◆ ◆ ◆

Cora looked over the shoulder of the boy she was dancing with and saw Mindelo glowering at her from the edge of the dance floor. That annoyed her. She had come to the disco to escape from him.

"Paul," she said to the boy. "Hold me closer."

"Sure, baby," the tennis pro replied.

Cora had chosen the darkest corner of the beach disco, appropriately called The Cave, because she didn't want the other hotel guests to see her. She hadn't expected Mindelo would find her there. She glanced at him again and saw he was waving at her, trying to attract her attention. She clung closer to Paul.

"That's it, baby," he murmured into her ear, pressing himself against her.

She had accepted Paul's invitation to the disco because she was bored. For a week, Mindelo had been fretting over her. Her behavior at Fisi Lodge made her feel foolish and she resented him as the cause of it. All she could do now was to count the days before she could get back to Scobie and the guys in the ghetto. They were her soul brothers.

"Hey, what are you doing?" Cora eased back, alarmed at the intensity of Paul's grasp. His lips had brushed against her cheek.

"Cora," he said softly in her ear. "I love to dance with you like this, cheek to cheek. It's the only time you let me be close to you."

"Shoot!" Cora pushed him away. "What's come over you, Paul?" She continued dancing by herself, rotating her forearms in front of her breasts in time to the music, to prevent him approaching closer. "You're very passionate tonight. Save that for the tennis courts," she warned him as he moved into her space.

"I'm sorry." He looked abashed as he swayed away. "I thought you liked me"

"I do, Paul." She moved closer. "Though not if you try to force yourself on me."

"I was only dancing." The record stopped and Paul stood still, cracking his knuckles.

Cora saw Mindelo beckoning to her. He looked unhappy. "Come on, Paul," she laughed brightly and caught the tennis pro's hand in hers. "I'm not staying here if you're going to do your exercises." She tugged him away from the alcove toward the exit. "Let's go for a walk."

"A walk!" He sounded excited. "Do you trust me?"

"I don't, but I'll take a chance."

"I'm not somebody to fool around with, Cora."

"Neither am I, Paul."

"I am a man!"

"Shoot! I hadn't noticed." She tossed her head and strode up the path away from the disco.

Paul walked rapidly behind her. "You're making fun of me. I'm serious."

She stopped and waited for him to come to her side. She looked into his wild eyes and sighed. "You're a good looking dude, Paul," she said, raising her hand and touching his cheek with her forefinger. "I think you're really cool, I really do."

She dropped her hand and was surprised when Paul caught it and squeezed it passionately.

She shook her head. "No, leave it." Her mouth tightened

when he didn't let go. "What are you doing, Paul?"

"I told you not to fool with me."

She tried to free her hand but he moved closer so that her palm was lodged against his chest.

"Feel my heart beating. That's what you do to me, Cora. The blood races through my body when I'm near you. I almost lose control."

"Cool it, Paul!" She jerked her hand out of his grasp. "Forget that scene." She walked away, increasing the speed of her steps as he came after her.

"Are you rejecting me, Cora?"

"Shoot!" She spun around and glared at him. "Why do you have to ruin every bloody thing?" She felt her guts shrinking. "I wanted a walk, not a work out. I'm going to bed."

"Cora..."

"I said cool it!"

He stepped back and grinned. "Okay, Cora," he said softly. "We'll do it your way." He spun around and disappeared into the darkness.

She watched the space where he had been standing. She shuddered. There was something odd about his smile. She felt vaguely threatened by it.

She swallowed nervously and hurried along the path to her cottage. She was at the door when she heard the sound. A figure emerged from the hedge. She opened her mouth to cry out for the guard.

"Cora!" a small voice said, softly pleading.

She stared in dismay, the scream dying on her lips. "What do you want?"

Mindelo shifted uneasily. "Did I frighten you?"

"Yes." She was cross. "Are you spying on me?"

"It's difficult for me, Cora."

"Like hell it is! How do you think I feel." She wondered how she had ever been attracted to him. He was standing in front of her like a sick dog, not like Paul Katana who at least had the physique of a man, even if he did come on too strong.

"Cora...!"

"Can't you think of any other bloody thing to say? Why are

you following me?"

"I want to tell you something."

She sighed. The more she looked at Mindelo, the worse she felt. She was angry with herself, and angry with him for being the cause of it.

"Tell me then. I'm tired, I want to go to bed." She inserted the key in her door to emphasize her intention.

"That man you were with in the disco tonight."

She looked at him sharply. "Are you going to warn me about Paul Katana?" She laughed in his face. "I know what he is. He's the only man who's a man around here."

"He's shameless, Cora. He's the worst possible kind of person."

She groaned. "Mindelo, I don't want to hear about him. I know. You understand?"

"He's dangerous, Cora."

"And you're a bloody bore!" She pushed open the door to the cottage and rushed in, slamming it behind her. She sighed and threw herself down on the couch, covering her eyes with her hands. "What am I supposed to do? She cried aloud.

She lay on the couch for several minutes, listening to the chirp of the night insects and the faint sound of music drifting up from the disco. She looked at her alarm clock. It was still early, too early to go to bed.

Damn Mindelo, she thought. He had spoiled her evening. Paul would think she was a prude. She hadn't even let him kiss her.

She got up angrily from the couch and walked over to the front door. She opened it and peered out. The music was louder outside, bolstered by the breeze from the ocean. She shut the door behind her and stepped across the path to the garden. She leaned against the trunk of a huge tree to listen to the music and gaze at the stars. Perhaps she would find some salve for her restlessness in the heavens.

It was peaceful there. She slid slowly down the trunk and made herself comfortable in the grass, tilting her head so that it rested against the tree. The bright lights of the path hardly penetrated to where she lay and the thick clusters of bushes added to the darkness. At least, she thought, there were no hyenas to worry about.

She closed her eyes. She wondered if she had been too hard on Mindelo. He had always been so kind to her. Yet she had noticed that wild look that had entered his eyes when she slammed the door on him. He had reminded her then, suddenly, of Paul.

She twisted, stretching her body and feeling the hardness of the ground underneath her. She slid her hand under her blouse and idly stroked her breasts. She loved the feeling that flowed through her when she did that. She wished Mindelo had taken her that crazy evening at Fisi Lodge. On safari, it would have been so romantic and memorable.

She was aware of someone beside her before she felt his hand on her thigh. Strangely, she wasn't alarmed. She assumed it was Mindelo so she kept her eyes closed and didn't move.

She was feeling lonely and perhaps she had been hoping he would find her. She knew how to handle him, so she kept still when his hand slid up the inside of her leg, drawing her skirt to her waist.

She wondered why he didn't speak. All she could hear was the heavy rushing of his breath. If he was going to behave like an animal, she decided, then she would too. She lay back, determined not to look at him. She would stop him as soon as he went too far. It would be her revenge! She froze herself into indifference.

A finger stabbed into her. She gasped in pain at this unexpected development.

"Stop that!" she cried, alarmed at the strength she could feel pitted against her. She opened her eyes, shaking her head from side to side, trying to roll over. She didn't like this.

An arm banged across her breasts, pinioning her to the ground. She struggled but the weight of the arm and the body lying on her, prevented her moving. She realized, too late, that the boy had gone beyond reason and really intended to have her.

She winced as another finger jabbed inside her. She cried for him to stop and was appalled when a hand clamped roughly over her mouth, stifling her. She arched her body to throw him off; it was useless. She hadn't realized he was so strong.

She tried to keep her legs locked together but he spread her easily with his knee. He poked his fingers further. She was dry with shock, dismayed that he had changed into a raging brute intent on devouring her.

She strained to breathe. A rough hardness pushed then thrust, unyielding, deep inside her. Pain slashed through her like a razor-sharp panga ripping into her guts. It was a wound, which swelled, raking her body with raw agony.

She was too shocked to cry. She was whipped into silence by the brutal lunging and the savage splitting of her body apart. There was no relief. The pain increased as her assailant grew larger, driving himself into her, again and again.

♦ ♦ ♦ ♦ ♦

There was a stir in the well-regulated routine of the restaurant. Charles Royce noticed it spreading through the room like ripples in water when a stone is dropped in. One waiter spoke to another who trotted over to the next station and repeated the process. He picked up the vibrations and wondered what was wrong.

He glanced across the room and saw the black-suited captain whisper into Samson Odongo's ear.

Odongo leaned across the table, held Susan's hand and spoke to her rapidly. He watched Susan's reaction, she faltered, fear creeping into her timid eyes. She stood up, put her hand onto Odongo's chest to steady herself, and then they both hurried from the restaurant.

He glanced at the bar. The stewards were grouped with their heads together. He snapped his fingers. The boy called Enoch detached himself from the others.

"What's the matter, Enoch?"

"Nothing, sir."

"Don't lie, boy. Something is up."

"I don't know, sir. They say a girl been found in the garden. She bleeding bad, sir. She raped."

He drained his gin and placed it on the table, trying to keep calm. "Which girl?" He guessed the answer.

"The one Mindelo went to see in the disco."

He sighed. "Where's Mindelo now?"

"He gone, sir. He take off."

CHAPTER 34

The doctor closed his bag. "She'll be able to talk in the morning." He was a man of few words, chosen for his job as the hotel doctor for his discretion as much as for his ability.

Charles Royce, who had been standing at the cottage window staring out at the unforgiving night, turned around wearily. "The authorities...?"

"Mr. Royce, I treat my patients. She's your client. That's nothing to do with me."

"I'm most grateful." He moved away from the window, reaching into his hip pocket.

The doctor watched him coldly. "It is what I am paid to do. By Mr. Odongo." He picked up his bag and walked purposefully away from Royce toward the door. He paused before opening it.

"The girl was a virgin. She is in deep shock. She should not be disturbed. There are bruises but no lasting injuries. Her mental state..." The doctor shook his head gravely. "I don't know... She should return to her home and the love of her parents as soon as she can."

"I'll arrange it." Royce opened the door. He was unnerved by the doctor's refusal to take a bribe. It had been a nerve-wracking experience.

The two security guards who were standing outside the door where the ones who had found Cora and carried her to her cottage. Royce knew them both. They were reliable. He peeled off some notes and passed them to the guards who palmed them quickly, a contrast to the doctor's reaction.

"You didn't see anyone running away from the girl, did you?"

The guards watched him silently.

"No one you would recognize again?"

"Oh no, sir."

"Fine. Keep watch here, boys. The doctor's sending a nurse to stay with the girl. She'll be all right." He stuffed his wallet back into his pocket and hurried down the path to the car park. He was worried.

Cora had been babbling incoherently before the doctor

calmed her with a sedative. Royce alone recognized the name she had said over and over: Mindelo.

Mindelo! Rage streaked through his brain. How could his boy have done such a thing?

He reached his jeep in the lot and jumped in. He gunned the engine into life and shot off into the night. He drove fast, his headlights bright, handling the vehicle by instinct. He slowed only when he reached the labyrinth of streets in the old part of Mombasa. He parked the jeep a few blocks away from the alley to his apartment. Two boys moved out of the shadows and blocked his path.

He brushed them aside. "Not tonight," he snapped in Swahili.

The apartment was in darkness. "Mindelo!" he shouted, pushing open the door. He stumbled across the clutter of the living room and switched on the standard lamp. "Hell! Where is the boy?" he said aloud.

"Here, bwana," Mindelo said from behind him. He was closing the door.

"Mindelo!" Despite his anger, he was relieved. "I thought Odongo's goons had got you."

"Why, bwana? I was asleep in the back of the jeep. You drove plenty fast tonight." Mindelo glided across the room to the liquor cabinet.

"What the devil are you doing?"

"Pink gin or whisky, sir?" Mindelo smiled with the confidence of the innocent.

"Whisky!"

He snatched the full glass from Mindelo's hand and began to pace the floor. "Damn you, boy. Do you know what you've done? That girl's mother is bound to sue. She's American. They love litigation."

He gulped down the drink and took the bottle from Mindelo's hand. He filled his glass again. "Why the hell did you have to rape her?"

"Rape?" The color drained from Mindelo's face. "Who was raped?"

"Don't gawp at me like that, boy. You know who I mean."

"I don't, sir. Truly I don't."

Royce scowled. "Don't play innocent with me. I'm in this

too. Cora was raped in the gardens tonight, as if you didn't bloody well know."

"Cora?" Mindelo seemed stunned. He stared at him. "Say it's a joke, bwana."

"Boy!" Royce glared at him. "If you think it's a joke, you should see her. Don't fool with me, Mindelo. I haven't got the patience for it."

"Is she hurt? I must go to her."

"You can't go anywhere." Royce gulped the whisky. "Everyone thinks you did it."

"Me? Not me, sir, oh no!" He looked ashen. "I saw Cora and warned her about Katana. You know, the tennis pro. Then I went to sleep in the back of the jeep, as usual, to wait for you."

"Katana?" Royce shook his head. "Are you trying to pin it on him?"

"It wasn't me, sir. Ask Cora."

"She was calling your name." He stared long and hard at Mindelo. The boy lowered his eyes, but didn't blink.

"We can't ask her until morning. The doctor's put her under sedation. Why did she call your name?"

Mindelo frowned. "I didn't do it, bwana. I was her friend, perhaps that's why."

"You never had sex with her?" Royce felt his guts twist as he waited for the answer.

"No, sir. I swear to you, sir. She wanted, yes, at Fisi Lodge. It was not right, sir."

"Hah!" Royce drank his whisky and flung the empty glass at Mindelo. It smashed against the wall by his head. He stood his ground without flinching.

"She wanted it, did she?" Royce lurched toward him and pushed him in his chest.

"You're lying. She was a virgin, the doctor said. She didn't want you! You forced yourself on her!"

"Bwana!" Mindelo pleaded. "It's not like that - " He stumbled as Royce slapped him across his cheek with the back of his forearm.

"You bastard! After all I've done for you."

"Not my fault, sir." Mindelo said frantically. "I didn't touch. I left she in her room!"

Royce growled drunkenly. "I told you not to have...anything...to do with those women, I warned you!" As he lurched toward Mindelo planning to strike him, he suddenly felt exhausted, drained of energy, destroyed. He grasped the boy's shoulder and pulled him toward him.

"I'm sorry this happened, Mindelo. I love you, do you hear!" He sobbed, his tears moist on Mindelo's neck.

◆ ◆ ◆ ◆ ◆

Susan leaned on Samson's arm, her head resting lightly on his shoulder as they walked through the gardens. Now the night was dark, the sky at its blackest beyond the ribbons of light illuminating the trees and shrubs.

Their evening together had begun romantically. She wore the exquisite gown Samson had bought her as a surprise that afternoon. With her hair glowing from the attention of the hotel hairdresser and her face highlighted with the make up she had bought in Mombasa, she looked radiant. The dinner by candle light beside the pool seemed to set the tone for a long, lingering evening together. The rape of Cora put an end to that.

"Who could have done such a dreadful thing?" Susan voiced her thoughts aloud, slipping her arm around Samson's waist. She loved to touch his body and hold him close. Especially tonight. What had happened to Cora might have happened to her.

"Cold?" Samson tightened his grip around her shoulders.

"Frightened. I was remembering how I met you. On the beach."

"That was a cruel joke of mine. I didn't know you. I thought..." His deep voice was sad.

"I know what you thought. I suppose that's what the man who raped Cora thought too. Every white woman seems like an easy lay here."

"You don't."

She pulled away. "What does that mean?"

"Nothing, Susan. My joke. I'm ashamed." He reached for her and she stood still, letting his arm settle around her waist.

"Samson, she whispered. "I like you very much, you know that. I enjoy your company. It's just that I don't want to be hurt."

"I won't hurt you, Susan." He lowered his head to within inches of her nose. Her eyes were moist, sparkling in the glow from a lantern hanging in the flamboyant tree close to her head. He kissed her gently.

When she felt his lips touching hers, there was an answering quiver within her. She turned aside hastily, brushing the kiss away. "Not now, Samson."

He scowled briefly, but she defused his anger with her timid smile. "Why not, Susan?" he hugged her tenderly.

"I don't mean hurt like Cora was tonight. It's deeper than that. You want me as a vacation affair, don't you? I'm sorry, I'm not what you think I am. I wouldn't be able to say goodbye." Strangely, she drew strength from his body pressing close to hers.

"I understand," he said slowly, his eyes probing her face. He put his hand behind her neck and ruffled her hair.

She gazed at him, wondering if he knew the effect that his touch was having on her.

"I know all about you, Susan." His voice was gentle. "One of my contacts in Los Angeles told me."

She drew away from his hand, overwhelmed with sadness. "Then you know I'm not wealthy like Maggie, or important like Lyn. I'm nobody." She paused. "You don't have to waste your time on me any more."

"Susan!" He opened his arms like a long lost brother. "Come here, let me hold you! Why are you fighting it?"

She stepped backward, scrambling away from his embrace. "You're cross that I'm not the wealthy catch you expected."

"What do you take me for, Susan? You're the one who doesn't understand. Why should I care if you have money or not? It's you I'm interested in."

"But only until I leave at the end of the holiday."

He beckoned her without speaking and she stepped forward despite her misgivings. He embraced her firmly. She rested her head against his chest, thrilling to the touch of his fingers stroking the soft hair at the base of her neck.

Slowly, she felt him withdrawing from her. His fingers crept around to her face and softly caressed her cheek. He held her chin lightly between his fingers and thumb, tilting back her head so her eyes met his.

She quivered as he lowered his mouth on hers. "No." She placed her fingers gently on his lips. "In a few days I'll be gone."

"Then let's not waste any more moments like this." He released her and they continued along the path to her cottage in silence.

"I can't help it," she said suddenly.

"Can't help what?"

She blushed, unaware that she had spoken aloud. "I was thinking. The way I am, that's all."

"I wouldn't have you any other way." He slipped his arm around her waist and tightened his grip until she was almost lifted off the ground.

She laughed. "Now you are hurting me!"

He relaxed his grip and smiled in a way that made her realize it was already too late. She was going to miss him when she left. She was indeed going to be hurt.

CHAPTER 35

Mount Suswa, which Tony said the Masai called *Ol Donyo Onyoke*, Red Mountain, could be seen where it rose in the vast distance from the Rift Valley floor. To the north, Mount Longonot reared broader and more massive.

The view of the Rift Valley was superb yet Lyn scarcely took any notice of it as she followed the zigzags of the highway to the valley floor.

She was alone in the rented car, and felt it. She recalled one of the sayings Tony had breathed into her ear as they lay together in her suite at the New Stanley Hotel. "I can't distinguish between loneliness and danger," he had said.

She thought he was joking but now she sensed the truth in the remark. She was alone, and it was the same as being frightened.

Fear was a new sensation for her, and she didn't like it. It was compelling her to behave irrationally, making her forget the restraints and practicalities of years of hard-won professional liberty. She was supposed to be a crack journalist, not a crackpot.

She smiled grimly as she kept the small car growling on the highway at top speed. A trio of giraffes thrust their heads disdainfully over the scraggly trees of the plain and watched her car speed past.

Her fear came from the suspicion that she had lost Tony. He had left her alone in the hotel the previous night. After the few days they had shared together, Lyn was attune to his moods. She accepted how much he prized his independence but she sensed a stronger force was keeping him from her.

Every evening while she had been in Nairobi, Tony escorted her to the Thorn Tree Café where she sat with Rena Odongo and her token fiancé, Larry.

Lyn loved those evenings. The eddy and flow of people in the café fascinated her. There was always activity around their table and she was proud to be with Tony. People treated him with respect and sought his views. The only problem for Lyn was the bond between Rena and Tony that excluded her.

When she taxed Tony about his relationship with Rena, he got angry and accused her of prying. She saw Rena as a threat to her plan to marry him and take him to the States.

Events had come to a head the previous evening. Instead of taking her downstairs to the café as usual, Tony had held her in his arms and given her a long, lingering kiss.

"I have to go," he said.

"What?" She pulled away and studied his face.

"I have some business to attend to."

"Where?"

He shook his head without speaking.

"Why are you so goddam mysterious?"

He was offended. His expression told her she had pushed him too far. "In my homeland," he said, pausing to let his words sink in, "we say there is a rat in the calabash."

Her eyes blazed at the challenge. "Am I supposed to be the rat?"

He shrugged his shoulders with a Latin eloquence. "If you choose to think so. There is something hidden which you can't see."

He swung around and walked out of the room and down the corridor with a gentle spring in his heel. She suppressed her urge to shout after him. She could only wait for him to return.

From her window above Kimathi Street, she kept watch on the people and the traffic below. Eventually she caught a glimpse of Tony, with Rena riding pillion, weaving though the traffic on his Suzuki motorbike. That night, she slept fitfully, awaiting his tap on the door. At breakfast she accepted the obvious: he had gone.

She was drawn to the Rift Valley by intuition. When he said 'In my homeland' the night before, his eyes had shone with meaning. She was convinced that he had returned to the Masai Reserve. And she was frightened.

Her fear made her careless. She drove through Narok and past the gas station without checking her tank. She realized it only after she passed through the Game Sanctuary gate. But she didn't worry and continued across the Loita Plains.

She was in such a hurry, she was blind to the proud majesty of the animals grazing on both sides of the trail. It was a rough ride and she drove as though possessed. With luck she would have enough gas to reach Fisi Lodge. She was certain she would find Tony there.

Lyn's luck, which so often came to her aid when she was on a story, ran out. The car bounced and rattled; it was caked with dirt and a mist of brown dust settled over her like a powdery sun tan as it rolled to a halt.

She tried to start it again but the tired vehicle wouldn't respond. The gas tank was empty.

She put on the handbrake and cursed. As she was getting out of the car, she noticed a gang of elephants tearing down trees fifty yards ahead. She sat back and closed the door quietly. She would have to wait there until another vehicle came along. She cursed again.

The heat in the car made her drowsy. She longed to sit in the shade under the trees a few yards from the track and feel the breeze in her hair. She was thirsty. She peered ahead and saw in the distance, beyond the elephants, the mud mounds of a Masai settlement. She sighed, and settled down to doze until help came.

The car door burst open. She opened her eyes in terror. A Masai warrior was leering at her. He reached into the car, grabbed her wrist, and yanked her out. He was tall and ugly and regarded her with an arrogance that was familiar.

She gasped as the fetid odor of his body hit her nostrils. "Rinko!" she exclaimed, covering her mouth to stop choking.

The Masai peered at her through eyes that were narrow slits, like scars carved into his already scarred face. His skin gleamed and he stood as proud and as indifferent as a giraffe.

"Don't you recognize me? I'm Kintai's friend." She took a step forward, gesticulating. "Have you seen him? He came here last night, I'm sure."

Rinko's face was impassive. Other tribesmen had surrounded the car. They began to talk excitedly at the mention of Kintai's name.

She thought they were impressed. Rinko jabbed the shaft of his spear in the ground and nodded his head. The ornaments hanging from his ears jangled. Suddenly her arms were seized from behind.

She shrieked. "What are you doing? I'm a friend!" She struggled but it was hopeless. Her wrists were bound behind her back and she was prodded with spears to make her walk off the track into the scrub. "You can't do this!" she said in vain. "I'll report you to the authorities. Where are you taking me?"

She was answered by the group's arrival at a mound overgrown with grass. They pushed her behind it. There was another Masai crouching there, a woman with her head shaved and her body wrapped in a checkered cloth. Her face was angular and her eyes hard.

Rinko spoke rapidly and a flicker of interest showed in the woman's face before she moved away. Lyn felt a blow on her back and she staggered forward. Another blow felled her to the ground.

She was dismayed by her helplessness. No one knew where she was. Hidden behind the mound, she couldn't be seen from the track even if a passing vehicle bothered to stop at the sight of her car. She wriggled into a sitting position, anger replacing the initial shock of her capture.

"Rinko!" The note of command in her voice attracted his attention and he stared at her haughtily. "I am going to marry Tony Kintai, do you understand that? I am going to be Kintai's wife. You wouldn't harm his wife, would you?"

Rinko squinted blankly at her. She remembered what Tony had said about Rinko and his gang preying on unsuspecting whites. Perhaps if she offered him money, he would let her go.

"Money," she said, less sure of herself. "I have money. Kintai's money." She nodded her head at her hip pocket, hoping Rinko would understand. He just stared.

The Masai standing behind her spoke rapidly. He mentioned Kintai's name and repeated 'wife' and 'money' in English.

Lyn twisted and smiled at him, grateful at finding an ally. He took no notice of her. Whatever he had said caused a great stir and they all started talking at once. Even the woman moved back to the circle and, scratching her head all the time she was speaking, added her contribution.

Rinko puffed out his chest as though he had made a decision. He spoke slowly with authority. The others crouched on their haunches and watched him with respect. They looked at Lyn, looked at Rinko, and seemed to come to an agreement.

Thank god! she thought. *They're going to free me.*

Rinko walked over and crouched on the grass beside her. His thick lips parted in a grin that showed his yellowed, broken teeth. She sank back as the smell of his breath wafted over her. His hand clawed at the top of her jeans. She was puzzled.

"The money's in my pocket," she said. "Untie me. I'll get it."

It made no difference. A pair of strong hands gripped her shoulders and bent her backward. Another Masai knelt beside her. With horror, she realized that they were trying to remove her clothes.

She lashed out with her legs and her knee struck Rinko's cheek. He fell back in surprise, snarling. Two men grabbed her ankles and pinioned her to the ground. There was a flash of a knife blade as it caught the sun and her jeans were cut open. She lay exposed and humiliated in front of them.

The eyes of the four Masai towering over her showed no interest in her nakedness. Rinko spoke to the woman. She waved a bunch of nettles in his face. He grinned.

"Kintai!" Lyn said frantically, struggling to throw off the man holding her shoulders to the ground with his knees. "Wife!"

The man seemed to understand and repeated the words to Rinko. His eyes glinted evilly. "Yes," he said between clenched teeth. "Wife. Yes."

"Then let me go," she pleaded. "Let me go!"

Rinko pushed the Masai woman forward. The two men holding Lyn's legs pulled them apart. Her heart sank as she wondered in despair if she was going to be raped.

The woman hunkered down between her open legs. She was muttering, her voice rising in what seemed to be a ritualistic incantation. She glanced at Lyn as though she expected her to chant in unison with her. Rinko picked his nose.

Without warning, the woman's hand darted between Lyn's thighs. The two men straddling her made it impossible for her to move. The woman's fingers plunged into her and she shrieked loudly at the unexpected pain.

The woman lowered her head between her legs, and her fingers probed. She began to massage her, causing Lyn to squirm in a combination of ecstasy and terror. The woman grinned, squeezed and held her hard.

Lyn screamed, rolling her head from side to side in useless protest. Reaching back in her mind she recalled what Kintai had told her the day he rescued her from Rinko. "A Masai can't marry a woman who hasn't been circumcised," he had said.

The woman picked up the bunch of stinging nettles and brushed them against her flesh. The nettles stung painfully and she screamed again. The woman's voice rose and she sang loudly, shaking the bells on her wrists. The men swayed in time to the woman's dirge.

Lyn bit her tongue, swallowing her screams until she was crying from the back of her throat like a wounded animal. She lost count of time. She thought only of Tony Kintai, clinging to the vision of his noble face and strong proud body while the woman defiled her.

The stinging nettles made her numb and swollen. She was blinded by pain and dulled by the heat and hypnotic chanting.

The woman reached a peak in her singing and sliced at her with a small, curved knife. The numbness from the nettles dulled the pain but Lyn felt the cut as though her heart had been torn out. She swooned.

CHAPTER 36

Susan sat on the patio and stared at the sunset. She was sick with despair. For the whole day she had been thinking of Samson. The previous night, when he kissed her, she had melted in his embrace, totally confused.

He had seen the panic in her eyes. He had withdrawn slowly, made no demand, and left her at the door to her cottage.

She had slept badly. It was the thought of what had happened to Cora, mingled with her doubt about Samson, that kept her awake. At least her doubt was resolved. Samson had gone out of her life.

When he didn't telephone her in the morning as he usually did, she had tried to contact him. Eventually she got hold of a supercilious woman who claimed to be his secretary.

"No, Mr. Odongo was not available. No, he was not in Mombasa. No, he hadn't left a message for her. No, she needn't phone again. No, she did not know if Mr. Odongo would call her."

She was close to tear as she thought about it. Samson had dumped her. She had been warned; she hadn't realized it would hurt so much. The secretary's bored tones sounded like she was used to handling rejected women who phoned for her boss. Susan bit her lip to stop herself crying.

"Darn!" she said aloud, startling the birds who were strutting around the patio. Why had she let herself fall for him? Now she hated him, and she hated herself.

She must have been mad to think she could keep him by denying what he wanted. It wasn't such a big deal. *Why didn't I give in to him last night?* she thought. At least she would have the memory. Now she had nothing.

Tears blurred her eyes. The sun slipped from the horizon and the dusk darkened rapidly. In a few days she would be home. That added to her despair. She didn't want to go back to her dull life, and yet she had no alternative.

Someone coughed politely at her side. She looked up in alarm. "You startled me!" She caught her breath and tried to smile.

"I'm sorry." Mindelo sounded as sad as she felt. He was twisting his hands awkwardly as he stood at the patio edge.

"I'm pleased to see you, Mindelo," she said, trying to put him at ease. And she meant it. He was so uncomplicated and genuine.

"I haven't seen you for a while." The lights around the garden paths were being switched on. She stood up and pushed open the sliding door and walked into the parlor. She turned.

"Come in," she said, beckoning him through the open doorway. "I'd like your company."

He seemed relieved, wiping his shoes carefully on the mat before stepping into the parlor.

"Sit down."

"I'd rather stand."

"Just as you like." She sat on the couch, straightening her skirt so it covered her knees. "How is Cora? I wanted to see her but the nurse wouldn't let me."

Mindelo shrugged his shoulders but he didn't answer.

"Have they found who did it?"

Mindelo sighed. "It was Paul Katana, the tennis pro. Cora identified him."

"Paul!" She shifted uneasily, and quickly concealed the memory of the incident with him so that Mindelo didn't notice.

"I warned Cora," Mindelo said, slicing the air angrily with his hand. "She wouldn't listen to me. Now she's gone and I didn't see her to say goodbye."

"Gone?"

"Mr. Royce has taken her to the airport. She's flying back to the States tonight. Mr. Royce wouldn't let me see her before she left." Mindelo scowled. "I liked her, Miss Susan, I really did."

"I know." Her reply was automatic. "What happened to Paul?"

"I don't know. It will be hushed up, of course. Mr. Odongo will take care of that. I was the one who was punished." He sat down gingerly on the edge of the couch.

"You?" Susan wanted to hold him and comfort him but she sensed he might be startled by such a display of affection so she let him talk.

"Mr. Royce thought I did it. I told him I didn't but he didn't believe me. I always thought he trusted me. Even though he knows now that I didn't do it, he has this mistrust. I don't think he'll let me be free, ever."

Susan felt his anguish as her own and put her arm around his shoulder. "You poor thing," she murmured. "I know how you feel."

He raised his head and looked into her eyes. "Are you crying?"

She tried to smile. "It's silly of me."

He faced her and touched her shoulder. "You don't have to cry for me, Miss Susan.

"I'm not really." She sniffed, wiping her eyes with her fingers. "I'll get over it."

"Get over what?"

She sighed. "I've had a bad time, too, Mindelo. I'm a bit like you, I've lost someone's trust as well. I think."

"You mean Mr. Odongo?"

She brightened. "Have you seen him today?"

He shook his head. "Mr. Odongo is a very busy man."

"That's what everyone says." She hugged him, trying to draw strength from his presence. "Everyone warned me about him. I suppose I believed them. I didn't want to give myself to him and then get hurt, you see. Now he has left me anyway."

"And you feel hurt?"

"Yes." She dabbed at her eyes. "Then this news about Cora, and Paul, and you, and Mr. Royce not believing in you any more. It's also so pointless. It makes me depressed."

"Don't cry, please." Mindelo patted her shoulder gently. She shook, fumbling in her skirt pocket for a handkerchief. Mindelo pulled a tissue from the box on the table. He leaned over and wiped her cheeks.

She sniffed, tried to smile, and the tears dried. She peered at his soft, kind face wreathed in anxiety. "You must think I'm foolish."

He shook his head, his eyes crinkling with compassion. "I'm unhappy too, remember."

"We're quite a pair."

There was silence. She stared at him, feeling her heart race at his closeness. She saw the fine arch of his eyebrows, the compassion of his eyes, his delicate nose and the pulsing of his lips. She raised her hand to touch his chest.

He bit his lip hesitantly.

She saw his doubt and smiled to reassure him. Slowly she slid her hand down from his chest.

His fingers closed over it. Timidly, he moved closer until his lips brushed against her cheek. She moved to meet him. He gave her a gentle kiss on her lips and she waited.

The cottage was in darkness; outside the lights in the gardens threw shadows as the leaves of palm trees rustled in the breeze. The soft caress of the sea thrusting up the beach drifted into the silence between them.

She rose from the couch and, clasping his hand in hers, walked slowly to the bedroom.

◆ ◆ ◆ ◆ ◆

Maggie sat with her head held high in the back of the automobile. She had bought Joe a chauffeur's peaked cap and a dove-gray safari suit as a uniform. It exaggerated the size of his body, showing every ripple of his muscles when he moved.

He wore it proudly. She had forbidden him to slouch when he was at the wheel and demanded that he looked smart at all times.

She enjoyed being driven by him. She found she wanted to be on the move all the time, instead of staying inside her cottage. She had taken several trips with Joe and now this one was the longest. In the back seat of the car peering at people toiling along the roads with burdens on their heads, Maggie felt like a queen. Joe - with his superb physique - treated her like one. It was a satisfactory arrangement.

A picnic hamper made to her instructions was in the trunk. There was champagne in the icebox and some slices of pink roast beef and Blue Highland cheese to eat. Joe had a container of a flour-and-dried-fish concoction.

Her plan for the day was to be driven the hundred kilometers north along the coast to Malindi. She had set out early at Joe's recommendation so she could view the ruins of the old Arab city of Gedi on the way.

She felt restless. She had slept little in the night because of pain. She had brought enough painkillers and other medicaments to last the entire trip. Was it her imagination, she wondered as she gazed out of the window, or were her medicines losing their effectiveness? Nothing seemed to help any more.

She smiled grimly to herself. She had no regrets. The pain of the past few weeks was nothing compared with the fulfillment and happiness of previous years. Then she was whole and healthy, not under the sentence of death meted out by caring doctors who showed no care when they sent in their bills.

She glanced at Joe. She was pleased she had found him before it was too late. Africa had been good to her. The relationship distracted her from reality. Yet now, as his proud profile dissolved in the moistness filling her eyes, she sensed it was time. She sighed, knowing that she could no longer stave off the inevitable.

She felt she was falling. She blinked, struggling with her thoughts, catching at memories to steady herself. *At last!* She saw her first husband, Boris. He was reaching out to save her, but his handsome face was thrust aside by Arno. Then Raul intruded.

"Damn you!" she cried, gurgling for air.

"Yes, miss." Joe said politely as he glanced at the back seat. He realized he couldn't see Maggie. He braked, bringing the car to a halt, and got out quickly. He pulled open the back door and stared.

"Mrs. Biddle-Mac!" There was panic in his voice when he saw she had slipped off the seat and was lying on the floor of the car, her face a bright puce.

"What...are you...doing?" Maggie was puzzled at how difficult she found it to speak.

"You sick again, miss? Why you lying on the floor like that?" He sounded gruff.

"Floor...?" She was panting, fighting to breathe. She heaved, terrified by the sight of the giant shadow looming over her. She tried to cry for help but all she could utter was a strangled sob. She knew the man was going to rob her. Where was Raul? He was never around when she needed him!

The man was rifling her purse. She made another effort to stop him, raising her arm weakly. "You...!"

"Yes, miss." Joe found the pills and shook two out of the phial. "Take these!" he kneeled down beside her and held them to her mouth, cradling her in his arms

Her head lolled forward and her lips opened. Instead of swallowing the pills she belched, and a tickle of vomit spilled into his palm.

"Mrs. Biddle-Mac!" he begged. "The pills! Please!" He tilted back her head and shook her shoulders. His hand brushed against her bandanna and it fell off. She was completely bald, her head shriveled like a pale, sickly pomegranate.

She was staring at him. The faces of Boris, Arno and Raul swam in front of her eyes, blurring together into the visage peering at her. She opened her mouth to scream but not even a whimper passed her lips. The pain ripped through her chest, robbing her lungs of air, closing her eyes to sight and her ears to sound.

She cursed silently at the face pressed close to hers.

"Mrs. Biddle-Mac!" Joe cried. "Don't die on Njonjo! I love you, missus. Don't go, don't go!"

A tear crept down his cheek as the last wordless curse rattled from her throat and she fell limp in his strong, caring hands.

CHAPTER 37

Susan was amazed at the amount of clothes she had accumulated. She folded them neatly on top of her bed in prepa-
ration for packing. Samson had bought her so much; every
day there had been a new dress, shoes, and jewelry. She
touched her cheek thoughtfully. She could always send it
back.

She had resolved that morning to leave the hotel. She had
no idea where she would go. The holiday wasn't over but she
was convinced that Samson had left her. There had been no
word from him for days. She wanted to get away from the
hotel as it reminded her so much of him.

She sighed when she caught sight of her faded jeans and
sensible frocks; the clothes she wore before Samson came
into her life. She would not send the new dresses back; she
loved them and the change they represented in her life. She
would keep them to remind her of how she had discovered
a new side to herself.

She wanted to weep again. It was no good. Tears wouldn't
bring him back. She picked up her old bag and began to
pack the new clothes in it. Perhaps she should send her old
clothes to him instead, with a note. It would say one word:
Sorry.

She smiled bitterly. It had taken a teenage boy to make
her see herself as she was. Mindelo was loving and kind but
no, she thought, *never again!* She must leave now before she
was sucked into the mold they were all cast in. She no longer wanted to be needed; she wanted to be free.

She forced the last pair of shoes into her bag and zipped
it up. There was a knock at the door. It would be the bellboy
for the bag. She brushed back her hair and walked toward
the door. She opened it sadly, taking one last look around
the cottage. Time to go. She stood back to let the boy enter.

"Susan!" The man seized her in his arms. She pulled away
from his chest and squealed, bright with shock. "You look
like you've seen a ghost."

"Samson!" she spluttered as tears of joy that began to
stream down her cheeks. "I thought you'd gone. I thought

you'd left me."

He brushed the idea aside with a wave of his hand, releasing her so she stood in the center of the room, catching her breath. "I was busy, what with that girl's rape and Maggie's death. Things to do." His eye fell on her traveling bag.

"I was packing. To leave."

"Good. I'm glad you're ready. That's why I came for you."

"You knew?"

"Oh, yes. Have you got everything?" He walked around the room opening cupboards and drawers.

She gaped at him. The pleasure she had felt when he entered the room was dying. "You're not asking me why?"

"I know." He held up an envelope. "What's this?" His brusqueness distracted her. "It was in the drawer of the writing desk."

"That's Maggie's letter." Susan was confused. "I should have thought of that before. She gave it to me last week."

Samson tore open the envelope.

"Samson! That's not for you."

He looked at her with his eyebrows raised. "Everything concerns me, Susan. Everything." He pulled a second envelope from the first and read the address on it. "It's for a firm of lawyers. In New York."

"Are you going to open it?" She was confounded by the harshness of his manner.

He grinned and pulled a chair up to the desk. He took a pencil from the desk drawer and slid it under the sealed flap of the envelope. He laid the envelope on the desk and carefully rolled the pencil under the flap, unsticking it neatly without tearing it.

"No one needs to know," he said, winking at her. "Unless you tell them." He opened the envelope and extracted the letter carefully. "Well, well, well."

"What does it say?"

"It doesn't concern you, Susan."

"Yes, it does. You shouldn't have opened it but now that you have, I have a right to know what it says."

He smiled as though she had won a victory. "It's a letter to her executors, about her will."

"She knew she was going to die?"

"She had an idea. Muldoon has telexed me some information on her. She had cancer."

"Poor Maggie. She must have been in terrible pain."

"She should have stayed at home."

"No, Samson. She wanted to enjoy herself to the end. I suppose it was the pain that made her so grumpy. Oh dear!" She sat down and buried her head in her hands.

"What's wrong?"

"I'm sorry I wasn't nicer to her."

"Don't worry about that, Susan. Maggie had Njonjo to care for her. She liked him." He waved the paper at her. "She's left instructions that he's to have a hundred thousand dollars from her estate."

She looked at him in disbelief. "Let me see!" She took the letter from his fingers and read it quickly. "Samson, that's wonderful!" She stood up and threw her arms around his neck, kissing him repeatedly.

He held her off. "I'll see this gets to the lawyers. Njonjo will need some advice." He lifted her bag and walked out of the cottage, leaving her to follow him.

♦ ♦ ♦ ♦ ♦

Larry Leacock was waiting at Nairobi airport when they landed in Samson Odongo's private plane. He shook hands with Samson and drew him ahead, ignoring Susan and leaving her to walk along behind them.

She heard Larry talk in a low, agitated voice and once he glanced back at her and made a comment that was obviously about her. She was bewildered, and annoyed.

On the flight, Samson had told her what had happened to Lyn. He had assumed that she wanted to leave the hotel because she had heard that Lyn was in hospital.

She didn't tell him the real reason. After that, they hardly spoke on the flight and Samson gradually drew within himself as the plane got closer to Nairobi.

She walked up to Samson and Larry still talking and ignoring her as they stood by the limousine. She spoke crossly. "Do I get in the car or do I stand here until you've finished your conference?"

Samson smiled an apology and snapped his fingers at Larry to open the door for her.

She got in, pleased by the look of astonishment on Larry's face. It seemed he had never heard a woman address his boss like that before. Samson slid in beside her and Larry drove the limousine off the tarmac.

"Forgive me for neglecting you, Susan. Larry was briefing me on Lyn."

"How is she?"

Samson shrugged. "She's in hospital and has the best doctors in Kenya attending her. I've arranged that."

"You're very kind." She squeezed his hand. The limousine slipped out of the airport and headed along the highway to Nairobi.

"I'm not," he said, withdrawing his hand and frowning. "It's expediency. If I help Tony Kintai he owes me. He'll be less inclined to, how do you say, upset the band wagon."

"I think you mean apple cart. Why should he do that?"

"He and I are on different sides. He wants to change things, I support the president."

"I thought he was a friend of the president."

"That's what the president thinks too."

Susan felt out of her depth. "What has Tony Kintai got to do with Lyn being in hospital?"

"I didn't tell you on the plane because you would be more worried." He put his arm around her shoulders and she let him move closer.

She spotted Larry scowling in the rear-view mirror.

"Lyn didn't have an accident as I told you. Some rogue Masai, Kintai's followers, attacked her. They're in jail now."

"How awful!"

"They cut her up, Susan."

"On her face? Poor Lyn, she won't be able to do television again."

"Not her face, Susan. Here!" He placed his hand firmly between her legs.

She slapped his face immediately but couldn't stop the feeling that vibrated through her at his touch. She opened her mouth to protest but Samson leaned over and kissed her. She closed her eyes, blocking out Larry's angry stare in the mirror.

Samson's hand found her again and he stroked her gently. His tongue forced its way into her mouth. She wriggled furiously out of his embrace. He withdrew with a sigh.

"Susan," he said quietly. "Why are we fighting each other? I'll come tonight. To the hotel."

She saw stars sparking around his head when she opened her eyes. She adored him, despite his occasional brutishness. She yearned in her heart for him to make love to her. *Forever!* Not for one night, leaving only the memory and loneliness for the rest of her life, but forever.

"No!" she whispered gently, touching his cheek with her finger. She was trembling. "I'm sorry. I can't."

Larry changed gears with an angry flourish and the limousine hurtled into the Nairobi traffic.

◆ ◆ ◆ ◆ ◆

Lyn was sitting up in the hospital bed with a wry expression on her face. She was in a private room. Tony and Samson were speaking outside in the corridor.

"How horrible!" Susan said in a voice hushed with shock after she had listened to Lyn explaining the details of what had happened.

Lyn raised the sheet. "Do you want to see?"

Susan blushed. "It's just too horrible."

"Not really. It's the custom here. Usually when a girl gets circumcised it's part of an elaborate ceremony. With the dancing and the liquor and the frenzy of the moment, it probably doesn't hurt that much."

"How can you be so calm about it?"

"I wasn't calm at first, but now I'm rather proud. The doctors have fixed me up so I'm none the worse for it. Thank god there's no infection. I don't know if it will improve my sex life, but it's great material. Think of the publicity for my program when this gets out."

"What does Tony say?"

"What can the guy say? He's got no excuse for not marrying me now, has he?" Lyn puffed a cloud of smoke from her cigarette into Susan's face.

"Are you really going to marry him?"

"Who knows? He's so goddam worried about me. That's nice. I'll decide tomorrow."

"We fly home tomorrow. This is our last night."

"Exactly." Lyn was gazing at her as though she was the one who was sick. "How are you making out with Odongo?"

Susan paled. "I want to ask you about him. I like him, Lyn, I really do. In fact, I believe I love him." She paused.

"Go on." Lyn sounded sympathetic. "What's the problem?"

"I suppose you wouldn't see it as a problem, Lyn. I'm going to miss him terribly. It's been so exciting. It's just that, well, he wants me to sleep with him tonight."

"For god's sake, honey, pull yourself together! You're going to lose him tomorrow. Do it tonight, otherwise you'll regret it for the rest of your life."

Susan hung her head, shame creeping into her cheeks. "You make it sound so...so sordid, as though it's nothing important."

"It isn't. Sue. It's animal. Look, these cats aren't the average WASP, are they? It's a basic instinct that drives them. There's no love involved. So be an animal too. Grab it while you can, honey." She stubbed out her cigarette in the bedpan.

Susan shook her head. "I told him no."

"Sue, you don't want to listen! You believe Odongo has intelligence and charm. So what?" She lit another cigarette. "Just don't expect love from him and then you won't get hurt."

Susan considered Lyn's words. "I think you're wrong." She stood up. "There's more to our relationship than sex. There has to be. I love Samson and I believe he is fond of me.

"When I get back to California I want to remember the beauty of the time we shared together. I don't want that memory dirtied by knowing I'm just another woman he's bedded."

Lyn blew out smoke and laughed mockingly. "Get out, Sue. You're making my circumcision hurt."

◆ ◆ ◆ ◆ ◆

Susan left the hospital room, fighting back tears. Samson and Tony were nowhere to be seen, so she walked along the corridor to the exit. Larry Leacock was waiting inside the limousine. He made no effort to get out as she opened the back door.

"Where's Mr.. Odongo?" She settled into the back seat and blew her nose.

"Sam's gone. Business. He said to take you to the hotel."

She flushed at Larry's rudeness. His attitude toward her was reflected in the arrogant way he drove the vehicle into the traffic.

She clutched the strap hanging by the door. "I'm sorry," she said. "I didn't mean to keep you waiting."

Larry scowled. "You've done more than that, Mrs. Ross."

"What do you mean?"

"What are you trying to do with Sam?"

"I'm not trying to do anything."

"Then get out of Kenya. Fast."

She was baffled. "I'm going home tomorrow."

"Right!" Larry's knuckles were white as he clenched the steering wheel.

"You sound jealous." She was so surprised at the thought, the words slipped out before she could control her tongue. She was more surprised when Larry grinned and didn't reply. The tension passed.

"Why?" she asked tenderly.

"You wouldn't understand, Mrs. Ross. I've known Sam for ten years. He's a genius. His devoted his life to building his firm and his country. He's got no time for women beyond a brief fling. That's why he likes tourists, they come and go. But you...he's never acted this way with a woman before."

"I see." She steeled herself. "Why shouldn't he have time for women?"

"He doesn't need them! I'm his friend. I give him the support he needs."

"You love him, don't you, Larry?"

"Yes."

"Why are you telling me this?" She leaned forward.

Larry's tenseness had gone. He seemed pleased to have

ROYSTON ELLIS

someone to talk to.

"So that you know why you must leave. Sam and I, we're partners. He can do great things for Kenya with me beside him. I'm white, but I'm Kenyan too.

"Maybe he thinks he needs you, but he doesn't. I know him. When you get on that plane tomorrow, he'll go back to Mpingo Beach and look for another broad."

Larry turned his head and looked directly at her. "One who gives him what he wants, when he wants it."

CHAPTER 38

It was Sunday morning. British Airways flight 060 was scheduled to depart Nairobi at 1120 via Zurich for London, with a flight to Los Angeles the following day. Susan longed to be on the plane; she had never felt more miserable. All the memories she had packed so carefully in her mind like clothes in a suitcase, were in disarray. Their value had been destroyed.

After Larry had left her in the vestibule of the New Stanley Hotel the previous afternoon, her one desire was to see Samson. She waited anxiously for him, rehearsing what she would tell him; how she would love him that night. He didn't come. She had told him No, and he believed it.

Now, as she waited to go to the airport, she realized that Larry had been his messenger. *Get out of Kenya fast.* The thought shattered her memories.

Samson was so heartless he couldn't even tell her himself. What was the point of being a prude, not an easy lay like other tourists. All she had left to show for being so prim and proper was bitterness.

She looked at her watch. In a few minutes she would be on her way to meet Lyn at the airport. The phone rang. She stared at it. Was it Samson? Her heart swelled with delight. She would forgive him if he would hold her in his arms again. She picked up the receiver.

"Good morning, Mrs. Ross. There's a gentleman here to see you."

"Send him up!"

"Very good, Mrs. Ross."

She replaced the phone in a daze. Samson had come! He respected her, that's why he had stayed away on her last night. Hurriedly she smoothed down her hair, frowning in the mirror at her reddened eyes.

The knock on the door was so timid, she listened again to see if she had been mistaken. The gentle tapping was repeated. *How contrite he is,* she thought happily. She walked slowly over to the door and opened it, a smile on her face.

"Jambo!"

Her smile collapsed. "Mindelo! What are you doing here?"

"I came to see you." He tugged nervously at his ear. He was wearing his uniform safari suit. His hair was freshly combed but his face, normally bright and cheerful, had a luster of uncertainty hovering over it. He looked at her shyly.

"Oh, well...come in."

She realized that it was her fault she was disappointed, not Mindelo's. She just wasn't sure if she wanted to see him now. She had felt sorry for him, and he for her, but that was finished. Really, it shouldn't have happened at all.

She let him enter the room and sat down. He sat in a chair opposite her.

"Have you had breakfast?" she asked to break the awkward silence.

"Yes, Miss Susan. Thank you."

"I'll order coffee." She picked up the phone and gave Room Service her instructions, using the time to think. She turned to Mindelo. "I have to leave for the airport soon. I don't have much time."

"That's why I hurried from the station. I caught the sleeper from Mombasa. I guessed you'd be staying here."

"Really?" She frowned, tapping her fingers on the top of the table. "It was nice of you to come."

"I came to ask you a favor. I hope you don't mind."

She was confused. The room service waiter delivered the coffee, set up the tray on the center table, and left them together. She poured coffee for Mindelo and handed him the cup. She took a deep breath.

"What's happened has happened, Mindelo." She prayed that he wasn't going to ask her for money. It would make it worse.

"I've left Mr.. Royce."

"Oh?" She looked at her watch.

"Mr. Royce... used to sodomize me, miss."

She gulped, almost choking over the coffee. She set the cup down clumsily on the table and it clattered against the saucer. She gaped at him, unable to speak.

"You made everything all right for me, that night. That's

why I came here. To thank you. And to ask you a favor."

"I don't know how..."

"You know Mr. Odongo. He's a great man. One day he could be our President. Tell him about Mr. Royce. He'll have him punished. He knows men who could do that."

"Mindelo! You don't mean that." Was he telling her that Samson was really a gangster; that he would hire men to beat up Mr. Royce?

"No." Mindelo looked wise. "Perhaps I don't." He sighed.

"It's past, I'm free now." He waved his hand to brush away the idea. "I really came to tell you I've got a real job. Here in Nairobi, with the American Express travel agency. I'll be a tour guide and get commissions as well as my salary. I'll be able to save for a house, get married..." He looked at her shyly as if he were afraid of saying something to upset her.

Susan sat back and looked at him. There was silence. She could feel his troubled eyes watching her, as though he needed her approval, a release from her too.

She smiled faintly. "You've done the right thing, Mindelo. Good luck. I wish I knew where Mr. Odongo is so I could tell him. But I'm glad you've got a new job. You'll be all right." She stood up.

"I must go to the airport now."

Mindelo stood up too, watching her curiously. He tugged at his ear again in confusion. "I shouldn't have come. I'm sorry."

"Where are you going?"

"To look for somewhere to stay."

"Here." She reached for her purse. "Take this. It's all I have left now." She held out a hundred-dollar bill.

He recoiled from her outstretched hand. "No, miss. I don't want money."

She swallowed with embarrassment and hurriedly folded the bill into her palm. "Will you come to the airport with me? To say goodbye."

◆ ◆ ◆ ◆ ◆

Lyn sat frigidly in the taxi taking her from the hospital to the airport. Rena Odongo was in the back seat beside her and Tony sat in front with the driver. She had expected Tony to come alone to collect her from the hospital. She couldn't talk to him in front of Rena. He seemed embarrassed, as though he was eager for her to leave. She understood.

Rena helped her out of the taxi while Tony paid the driver. She was still very sore but she walked unaided, letting Tony carry her bag. The Kintai influence extended to the check-in counter and she was processed rapidly. She felt weak as she turned to say farewell.

Tony seized her tightly in a hug. She couldn't move even if she wanted to. He shook her gently, his eyes anchoring hers. "Lyn," he begged, his voice soft.

"Listen to me before it's too late. You wouldn't speak to me in the hospital so it will have to be now with all this crowd around us."

"I've nothing to say to you, Tony. I'm going. I've caused you enough trouble."

"Lyn, you still don't understand, do you?"

"You left me that night, Tony. I saw you on the motorbike with Rena. She's the one for you, Tony. I was wrong to think that I could ever possess you."

"Is that why you went back to Fisi Lodge?"

"Yes, I thought I'd find you there."

He shook his head, but kept his arms around her. "Yes, I was with Rena. It was for the cause, Lyn. I don't love her. There was a meeting, a secret one. We have to be careful in Kenya. Rena is fighting for her people too. She can do it better with me than with her brother, Samson. Believe me, that's the way it is." He grinned ruefully.

Lyn grimaced. Tony's eyes were so close and sincere, she just knew he was telling the truth.

"Tony Kintai," she said as tears welled in her eyes. "You're a shameless motherfucker."

"And you love me?"

"Yes!"

He shook her. "I can't come to the States, Lyn. You must know that really. My place is here, in Kenya, with my people. Who knows, one day I might even be president. Stay with me, Lyn. Stay here with me."

She gazed at Tony long and carefully. She was trembling

under the pressure of his hands on her arms. Beyond him, she saw Rena waiting. Anxious passengers queued for their flights and uniformed customs officers inspected travelers' currency forms. Above the forecourt, the delicate blue of the sky was patchy with wispy clouds.

She removed herself slowly from his grip, bending down to pick up her shoulder bag. "Stay?" She shook her head. "I have my career too, Tony." She smiled wryly. "I guess it was fun while it lasted."

"I guess it was."

They both laughed at his unconscious imitation of her accent. It created a new vibration between them, which somehow made everything seem all right.

"I'll be back," she said, "I've got a TV documentary to make. We'll do it together." She glanced again over his shoulder where Rena waited. "For the cause?"

He opened his arms and she let him hold her again, understanding then that she was a carrying a part of him with her. Just as she was leaving part of her behind.

♦ ♦ ♦ ♦ ♦

Susan walked to the end of the gleaming corridor with its exact displays of duty free watches and calculators. In her hand she held a printed invitation. She read it gloomily:

"British Airways cordially invites M/s Susan Ross to the Executive Lounge, Nairobi Airport, especially provided for your comfort. British Airways. We'll take more care of you. Bring this invitation with you."

More care! she thought. That's what she needed. She handed over the card to an efficient ground hostess who took her handbag, her coat and showed her to a seat. She refused coffee. It hadn't been long since she had shared coffee with Mindelo. Already memories were settling in.

She tried to look poised and assured, dreading that some hearty traveling salesman might talk to her. Shyly she glanced at her fellow passengers.

There was an elderly couple, an African engrossed in a file, and two women, perhaps mother and daughter. The door opened and a man with red hair and the aggressive manner of someone out for a good time entered the lounge. She lowered her head anxiously as the hostess ushered him to a seat far away from hers.

She wanted time to let her sorrow mature. Her faint hope that Samson might be at the airport to see her leave had been dashed. Mindelo had escorted her to the departure gate, shaken hands gravely, and left. She was leaving Kenya sadder and wiser.

The lounge door opened and Lyn entered. Susan was appalled by her appearance, She stood up hastily to help her to the seat beside her. "You look so ill. You should have asked for a wheel chair."

"What kind of greeting is that, Sue? Don't fuss! I'm not dying."

"Didn't Tony come to see you off?"

"You bet he did. Get me a vodka, will you?"

Susan walked to the self-service bar and fixed Lyn's drink. The red haired man was watching her. She ignored him purposefully and took the drink back to Lyn.

"I guess we're two old maids, Sue. Odongo didn't show?"

She nodded without speaking.

"Never mind." Lyn brightened as the vodka restored the color to her cheeks. "We'll drink that jumbo jet dry of champagne and then we'll hit London town. I'll get you a refined English fuck to take your mind of these animals."

"Excuse me, are you Mrs. Ross?"

Susan was startled. A security guard stood over her. "Yes," she said cautiously.

"Will you come with me, please."

"Why?" Lyn banged her glass down on the table. "She hasn't done anything. What's the problem?"

"Her currency form. There's a query about it."

"Don't go, Sue. He can't make you."

"Yes, Lyn. I'm sure it's all right. I won't be long." She picked up her handbag and coat and followed the guard out of the lounge.

"Did I make a mistake?" she asked anxiously. "I used the form whenever I changed money." She remembered how Mr. Royce had cautioned all of them to be careful about the currency regulations. The guard said nothing and she began to fret.

A man in a dark business suit was waiting for her. He wore sunglasses, a white shirt and a black tie. He blocked the corridor. "Mrs. Ross? Come this way, please."

The security guard left her and the swarthy man opened a door leading off the corridor into a narrow passageway. It didn't seem right.

"Where are you taking me?" She began to break out in a sweat of apprehension. She clutched her bag so she wouldn't tremble. "Please. Where are you taking me? I haven't done anything! My plane is leaving soon. I don't want to miss it."

The man's face was grim and unsmiling. He opened a door at the end of the passageway. She blinked in the bright sunlight. "Step outside, please." The man held the door open and nodded to another man wearing blue overalls.

"Follow me," the other man said indifferently.

She looked around. She was on the tarmac outside the terminal building. The sun was beating down making steam rise from puddles on the runway. In the distance was the British Airways 747 she should be boarding. The man leading her indicated a small plane a few yards ahead. He stood back.

"There must be some mistake..."

"The plane is waiting for you. Your luggage is on board."

She looked at the small private plane and gasped. A man leaned out, a sweet smile spreading across his ebony features. "Samson!"

"Hurry, Susan. We've got clearance to take off immediately."

"Samson!" She ran the last few yards and reached up for his hands. He helped her climb on board. "Samson!" She was nearly in tears.

"We're flying to Mount Kenya Safari Lodge." He guided her into the window seat and fastened her seat belt. Someone shut the door of the plane. The pilot started the engines.

"I can't let you leave me, Susan. I need you. I want you to be my wife."

She felt his powerful arms draw her to him, holding her firmly. His mouth closed over hers in a kiss, which lingered until they were airborne.

THE END

32886429R00180

Made in the USA
Lexington, KY
06 June 2014